THE GOLD OF CAPE GIRARDEAU

THE GOLD OF CAPE GIRARDEAU

Morley Swingle

Southeast Missouri State University Press • 2002

First published in the United States of America, 2002
Copyright 2002 by Southeast Missouri State University Press
Cape Girardeau, MO 63701
All rights reserved.

ISBN: 0-9724304-0-7, softcover
ISBN: 0-9724304-1-5, hardcover

Cover art: watercolor by Jake Wells
Author photo & artwork photo by Steve Robertson
Book & cover design by Susan Swartwout
Printed by Concord Printing Services, Cape Girardeau, MO

Quotation from *O.J. The Last Word* by Gerry L. Spence used with permission of the author.

To Alberta
who gave me life
and a love of books,
And to Candy
who fills my life
with joy and happiness

"They who lived in history only seemed to walk the earth again."
Henry Wadsworth Longfellow
"The Belfry of Bruges," 1842

"Cape Girardeau is situated on a hillside, and makes a handsome appearance… Uncle Mumford said that Cape Girardeau was the Athens of Missouri and he directed my attention to what he called the strong and pervasive religious look of the town, but I could not see that it looked more religious than the other hill towns with the same slope and built of the same kind of bricks."
Mark Twain
Life On the Mississippi, 1896

"Cape Gi rar deau (jə-'rär-"dO), a city in SE Missouri, on the Mississippi River. 33, 361."
The Random House Dictionary of the English Language
2nd edition, 1987

"Before a settlement was established on the Mississippi within the limits of the present county of Cape Girardeau, this stretch of the river was designated on the old maps as 'Cap [sic] Girardot,' and so known to the voyageurs passing up and down the river . . . How this locality received the name of 'Cape Girardot' cannot now be definitely known. It is conjectured . . . that the name is derived from that of an ensign of the French troops named 'Girardot,' who as early as 1704 was stationed at Kaskaskia. The supposition is that a person named 'Girardot' removed from Kaskaskia to the west side of the river and took up his residence in the charming woodlands extending to the water's edge on the promontory above the present town, trading and trafficking there with the Indians, and that thus the name was bestowed on this river promontory by the early voyageurs. No authentic information is now available as to this point."
Louis Houck
A History of Missouri, 1908

Contents

PART I

Treasure Trove

"I now had a license to practice law, but no one had called me to practice on him."

Clarence Darrow
The Story of My Life, 1932

"These were the men who had never had to say to themselves, 'It's my fault. If I had been a better lawyer, better prepared, if I had had a quicker wit, if I hadn't been so afraid, if I had been a *real* lawyer instead of this piteous, beaten bastard who made a bad final argument, maybe he wouldn't have to die.'"

Gerry Spence
O.J. The Last Word, 1997

"'Treasure-trove' is a name given by the early common law to any gold or silver in coin, plate, or bullion found concealed in the earth, or in a house or other private place, but not lying on the ground; the owner of the discovered treasure being unknown."

William Penn Whitehouse
Associate Justice, Maine Supreme
Court, writing in *Weeks v. Hackett*,
104 Me. 264, 71 A. 858 (1908)

Chapter 1

"Tell the jury what you found, Mr. Armstrong."

"Buried treasure."

"Where?"

"In my basement, about five feet down."

"How much is it worth?"

"Over eleven million dollars."

Allison Culbertson's guts churned with fear, and the young lawyer hoped it didn't show. This was her first jury trial. She represented Steve Armstrong, whose fifteen minutes of fame was finding a chest of gold buried in his basement. He was about to be grilled by Dwight Pemberton, the best trial lawyer in Missouri, down from St. Louis representing Claxton Flint, a wealthy businessman who had sued Armstrong, claiming the gold was rightfully his.

The trial was being held in the Common Pleas Courthouse in Cape Girardeau, Missouri, the site of thousands of legal battles waged over the decades since its erection in 1854. A red brick building with towering white columns and cupola, it crowned an imposing hill overlooking the Mississippi River, high enough to avoid the greatest floods, but close enough for the smell of river water to whip at the faces of those who stood at the top of the long courthouse steps on windy days.

Inside the courtroom, Allison brushed a strand of hair from her face. Her fingertips were icy.

She felt like a fraud. The day Steve Armstrong had come to her law office after finding the chest of gold buried in his basement had been one of the happiest days of her life, one of those landmark moments always remembered— the first big case.

It was simple in the beginning: legal research, just like law school. She delved into arcane aspects of property law, then explained to Steve Armstrong that buried gold or silver is called treasure trove. Different laws applied to it than to other lost or hidden property. Under the law of treasure trove, the finder of buried gold is entitled to keep it against anyone but the true owner or the owner's descendants. The gold was his unless someone else could prove otherwise.

She'd filed the public notices required by Missouri statutes. The notices triggered a television interview and several newspaper articles. It was exciting, interesting, and easy work—until Dwight Pemberton filed the lawsuit on behalf of Claxton Flint.

She had acted cool and confident when Steve Armstrong rushed to her office after being served with the petition in *Flint v. Armstrong*. After all, she'd made good grades in law school, passed the bar exam first try, and had a law license hanging on her wall proving she was a lawyer.

She was anything but cool inside, however, when she noticed Dwight Pemberton's name at the bottom of the legal document. Pemberton, as in *Pemberton On Trial Technique*, the textbook used in her trial practice class.

"Would you describe the treasure in a little more detail?" Dwight Pemberton asked Armstrong. Pemberton, mid-fifties, black hair turned silver at the temples, barrel-chested in an immaculate charcoal suit, prowled the floor in front of the jury box, stroking his distinctive deeply-dimpled square jaw as he focused on Steve Armstrong.

"Well," began Steve, "there were 15,845 gold coins in the chest. Lots of ten dollar pieces, called Eagles. Some five-dollar Half Eagles. Some Quarter Eagles. A few Liberty Head □ Gold Dollars. All minted from 1854 to 1858. Face value of the coins is $44,856, but a coin dealer appraised them at $11,450,000."

Looking at Steve, his lean frame crammed into the small witness box, it struck Allison Culbertson how much he resembled a clean-shaven Abraham Lincoln: rangy, tall and lean, with a long face, high forehead, generous mouth, and sunken eyes. He was an assistant baseball coach and P.E. teacher at Central High School. Some of his students were scattered among the unusually large crowd of spectators watching the trial from the rows of wooden benches at the back of the courtroom.

Steve Armstrong was the first witness to testify, called as a hostile witness by the man suing him.

Pemberton toyed absently with the end of his gold-flecked maroon tie, then said, "Describe for the jury exactly how you happened to find the treasure in your basement."

"My house, it's over 200 years old. I was remodeling, digging out the dirt floor of the basement, making a laundry room. I found the chest buried about five feet deep."

I'm a fraud, Allison thought again. Dwight Pemberton not only wrote the book on trial technique, he'd also been a guest lecturer for her trial practice class in law school, just fourteen short months ago, because her professor had wanted them to hear the wit and wisdom of "the state's most celebrated litigator." At the time of his speech, he'd won eighty consecutive jury trials, authored twenty scholarly articles in addition to his book, and was a member of the Inner Circle of Advocates as a result of several million-dollar verdicts. His speech had been excellent, peppered with examples from magnificent trial lawyers like Clarence Darrow and Abraham Lincoln. She'd taken extensive notes and had slipped up to the podium afterward to ask several questions.

What was she doing alone in a courtroom against him, she asked herself. She possessed only a fraction of his knowledge or trial skills. The answer, she hated to admit, was ego.

"What did you do when you found it?" Pemberton continued.

"My spade hit something hard. At first I thought it was a hunk of rock. Before long, I realized it was a metal chest. I dug faster and faster, finally digging a trench all the way around it, but it was too heavy to pick up, and locked. Took my spade and pounded the lock until it opened."

Allison had heard the story before, in her office that first day, at depositions later on, and again in her office as they prepared for trial; but the jury had never heard Steve describe finding the buried treasure. Several leaned forward on the padded swivel seats.

"When I opened the chest, I couldn't believe the sight—a sea of gold."

Dwight Pemberton crossed the open floor of the courtroom. "Your Honor," he said. "Would you ask the bailiffs to carry in Plaintiff's Exhibit 1?"

Circuit Judge Samuel N. Sterns, his wrinkled tan face topped by longish Ivory Soap white hair, nodded to his bailiffs. "Get it."

The courtroom was silent as everyone waited for the bailiffs. The delay added to the drama, undoubtedly part of Pemberton's orchestration.

The large courtroom was the most impressive chamber of the courthouse. Six tall windows, each seven feet in height, covered the wall facing the Mississippi River. Anyone who looked out, including jurors, could gaze upon the bold river stretching lazily from the Cape Girardeau riverfront to the Illinois shore, extending endlessly north and south.

At one end of the fifty-foot courtroom, the judge sat high on his light oak bench, adorned in black robe, seal of the State of Missouri ornamenting the paneled wall above his head, Missouri flag to his left, and United States flag to his right. Beneath the judge, slightly to his left, a court clerk perched with stacks of files and books, ever ready to provide the judge with anything needed during the trial. Nearby, the pretty young court reporter straddled a stenograph machine, fingers now paused, but ready at a moment's notice to resume recording every word for posterity.

Ego, Allison rebuked herself. She had always *needed* to be the best. Valedictorian in high school, but also cheerleading Captain. Honors College as an undergraduate at the University of Missouri, but also one of Mizzou's Golden Girl dancers, and the lead part of Maria her junior year in *The Sound of Music*. Law school had been the first time she hadn't been number one at something, but she'd done reasonably well, finishing high enough scholastically to make Law Review.

But her competitive spirit had propelled her too far too fast this time. She was no match for Dwight Pemberton. Nevertheless, she'd refused the settlement offer and never once considered requesting additional trial counsel. She had wanted to beat the best all by herself. *Ego*. Well, here she was. Not only would Dwight Pemberton run rings around her professionally in court, it was also entirely possible that Steve Armstrong, her client, a nice guy who trusted her to protect his golden find from dollar-sign vultures, would end up with nothing.

Unconsciously, her gaze landed on Claxton Flint. He sat at the table adjacent to hers, book-ended by two young attorneys from Pemberton's 100-man St. Louis law firm, silent blue suits shuffling papers for the great litigator. Claxton Flint, sixty-something, notoriously wealthy, was a bull of a man, red faced, bushy eyebrowed, pockmarked, heavy jowled, with a full head of salt-and-pepper hair shellacked like Ronald Reagan's. Thrice-divorced, he was currently married to a woman Allison's age, three years younger than Steve Armstrong's twenty-nine. He lived life in grand style, in a large mansion just outside the city limits, complete with tennis courts, swimming pool, private plane, expensive cars, country-club membership, and St. Louis Rams season tickets.

Claxton Flint was glaring at Steve Armstrong. There was no mistaking the dislike registered upon his face.

The twelve oaken pews at the back of the courtroom were filled with spectators. Among them was Cory Blaze, the flamboyant local television reporter, flanked by several newspaper and radio people, including the rumpled-looking columnist from the *St. Louis Post Dispatch* who tended to cover sensational or odd trials.

The crowd murmured as the doors to the courtroom opened and the bailiffs and four deputies pulled the chest into the courtroom. It rode in upon a sturdy platform with wheels. Dwight Pemberton directed them to an area on the brown carpet just in front of the jury.

"Step forward, Mr. Armstrong," he said, "and identify Plaintiff's Exhibit 1."

Steve Armstrong bumped his knees as he clambered out of the small witness box and approached the chest. "That's the chest I found in my basement."

It was a rusty metal strong box with brass corners, four feet long, two and a half feet wide, three feet tall. The lid was closed.

"Were any markings on it when you found it?"

"Yes, sir. Little metal plate right here on top of the lid, somewhat tarnished, but I cleaned it up so you could read the two words, all in capital letters— GIRARDEAU ROSE."

Pemberton frowned.

"Those words mean anything to you?"

"No."

"Would you open the chest, please?"

"Sure."

Even though she'd seen it before, Allison felt a jolt of excitement as the light from the courtroom windows and chandeliers danced across the mass of tiny gold coins in the chest, making them sparkle brilliantly, as if each were thrilled once again to feel the warmth of sunlight.

"Are these the coins you found?"

"Yes."

"You may return to your seat."

Dwight Pemberton reached into the chest, touched the coins, caressed them with his fingers, stirred them, and finally grasped a handful, holding them up. Tiny gold dollars smaller than dimes trickled through his fingers and dropped with soft clinking noises back onto the pile.

Steve Armstrong was settling into his chair as Pemberton resumed the questioning. "Now, you've already testified that this chest was locked when you found it?"

"Right."

Pemberton pointed to the dented metal around the lock of the chest.

"These scratches and marks, how did they get there?"

"I hit it with a shovel to get it open."

"So, you didn't have a key?"

"No."

"Did the lock itself open or did the metal around it crack?"

"The metal cracked."

"So, you broke the chest open."

"Yes."

"You've seen it opened with a key, though, haven't you?"

"Yes."

"Claxton Flint's key opened it, right?"

"Well, I wasn't sure whose key it was at the time I saw it opened at the deposition."

"Did you think the key had dropped out of thin air?"

The question was argumentative. Allison could object. But did she want to? Before she made up her mind, Pemberton had moved on.

"You realize now, don't you, that the key you saw open the chest was Claxton Flint's?"

"He says it is."

"Fine," said the lawyer. "Let's describe for the jury the other things you found buried in your basement."

Allison, who had been considering what questions, if any, she should ask when Pemberton finished, noticed that Steve's Adam's apple was bobbing like a ping-pong ball in a lottery-ball air tube. The jurors might find it unattractive.

"A human skeleton," Steve said slowly, "was buried next to the chest, perpendicular to it, skull about three feet from the chest."

Dwight Pemberton, standing behind Claxton Flint, patted the shoulder of the older man comfortingly.

"Would you describe the finding of the skeleton in a bit more detail, please?"

"Well, I'd already dug the trench around the chest, already found the gold. An hour or so later I noticed something white stuck in the wall of the trench. At first I thought it was a rock, but then I decided it might be bone. That got me digging again. It turned out to be a skull. I went fast after that. Ended up finding a disarticulated human skeleton."

"What do you mean, disarticulated?"

"Not fastened together anymore. Bones lying loose in the dirt, no skin or anything."

"Tell me, when you found the skeleton, you called the County Coroner, didn't you?"

"Well, no."

"You didn't? Well, then did you call the Sheriff?"

"No."

"The Cape Girardeau Police Department?"

"No."

Pemberton pointed a finger at Steve Armstrong, an expression of incredulity on his face. "Are you telling this jury that you found the body of a murder victim and you failed to notify the police?"

Allison stood up. "I object, your honor. First, it's argumentative. Second, my client had no legal duty to call the police about the skeleton. The 1987 Missouri 'Unmarked Human Burial Site' statute specifies that whenever human skeletal remains are disturbed or removed during construction, the state historic preservation officer is the appropriate person to contact. My client did that. This other line of questioning is irrelevant."

Judge Sterns ran the fingers of his right hand through the thick white hair at his temple. "Sustained. Move along, Mr. Pemberton."

Allison sat down, pleased, realizing she'd been holding her breath.

Pemberton sauntered slowly to the exhibit table and picked up a clear plastic baggie containing several brass buttons. He moved toward Steve Armstrong.

"You found some other items with the skeleton, didn't you?"

"Yes."

"What were they?"

"A belt buckle and some buttons." Steve identified the buttons Pemberton handed to him. "These are the buttons I found. They have eagles on the front."

"This next exhibit," Pemberton continued. "Identify it."

"The belt buckle I found with the skeleton. Says U.S. on the front."

Dwight Pemberton dropped his voice so low it was almost a whisper. "The belt buckle has a name on the back, doesn't it?"

"Yes, it does."

"The same name was on the back when you found it, right?"

"Yes."

"Would you read for the jury the name engraved on the back of the belt buckle, please?"

"Horace J. Claxton."

Dwight Pemberton, nodding, crossed the room to the exhibit table, picked up a cardboard box, recrossed the room, and placed it on the floor in front of Steve. Pemberton reached into the box, fumbled around for a moment, then pulled out a human skull, its empty eye sockets turned toward the jury, a round hole slightly smaller than a dime between its eyes, with a similar hole at the rear top of its head.

"This box," Pemberton said, "is marked Plaintiff's Exhibit 8. These are the bones you found in your basement, correct?"

"Right."

"You found this skull?"

"Yes."

"It had the hole between its eyes at the time you found it, didn't it?"

"Yes."

"Plus the hole in the top of its head?"

"Yes."

"And the belt buckle with the name Horace J. Claxton was just about waist level of the skeleton, wasn't it?"

"Yes."

"And Horace J. Claxton was the great-grandfather of my client, Claxton Flint, wasn't he?"

"That's what you say."

"No further questions, Your Honor." Dwight Pemberton gingerly placed the skull back into the box and returned to his seat at Claxton Flint's table.

"Any questions, Miss Culbertson?" asked the judge.

The jurors looked at Allison expectantly. She would have the opportunity to call Steve as her own witness after Pemberton rested his case. She decided to save her questions for then.

"Not at this time, Your Honor."

Steve Armstrong untangled himself from the witness box and walked self-consciously back to the counsel table next to her. She wanted to say something reassuring to him, but the jurors were watching and Judge Sterns seemed somewhat impatient.

"Call your next witness, Mr. Pemberton."

"Dr. Phillip A. Sanford, forensic pathologist."

Thoughts of comforting Steve Armstrong evaporated, replaced by prickly chills shooting down her back. Allison had never cross-examined a doctor, much less one of Sanford's reputation. Trying to cross-examine any expert was always a difficult assignment, since the expert always knew far more about his field than the lawyer. She'd spent hours preparing questions calculated to score points against Dr. Sanford. She had them written out on the yellow legal pad she pulled from her briefcase as the doctor strode to the witness box. Those questions didn't seem quite as clever on the notepad here in the courtroom as they had appeared in the safety of her office.

She folded her arms across her chest as the expert witness settled himself into the witness chair.

Chapter 2

Allison Culbertson was under no disillusions as to why Steve Armstrong had picked her to be his lawyer—dumb luck and her appearance in a leotard. The luck was that they attended the same Monday morning aerobics class. She was quite likely the only lawyer he knew personally. The leotard, twelve years of dance lessons, and her stint as a Golden Girl had prepared her well for her place in the front row of Aerobics 101. She looked good in a leotard, no question. But how did this jury see her? Twenty-six years old, blonde hair cut stylishly short, off-the-rack conservative Brooks Brothers charcoal gray, wool suit hiding the curves. She did her best to look professional. But would the women jurors find her threatening? Did the males assume her a bimbo until she proved otherwise?

Dr. Phillip A. Sanford, forensic pathologist from St. Louis, was telling the jury his name. She'd met him when she took his deposition, but she'd forgotten how young he looked. Late thirties, preppy face topped with blow-dried hair, he was not the sort of person one expected to find cutting up dead bodies.

Dwight Pemberton, standing so close to the jury box that he was almost in it, nodded toward the jurors as he asked his next question. "Dr. Sanford, would you describe your medical background and experience in pathology for the jury, please?"

Allison rose to her feet, hoping to steal some of the momentum from Pemberton. If she stipulated to the expert's qualifications, there would be no need for him to impress the jury with his long list of accomplishments.

"We'll stipulate to Dr. Sanford's qualifications as an expert in the field of pathology, Your Honor."

Pemberton smiled graciously.

"I appreciate counsel's comments, Judge, but I would prefer to reject the stipulation and allow the jury to hear the doctor's qualifications. It's important for them to understand how extremely well-qualified he is, although I'm pleased Miss Culbertson admits it."

The judge shrugged. "Very well, Mr. Pemberton. Proceed."

Allison, outmaneuvered, sank into her seat as the pathologist recited his training. It took quite awhile, with his multiple undergraduate degrees, his Ivy League medical degree, his numerous board certifications, his years of experience at the Medical Examiner's Office, his scholarly publications, his adjunct professorship at St. Louis University Medical School, and his 2,000 autopsies, over 500 of which, incidentally, involved gunshot wounds to the head.

Allison glanced at the jury. They seemed spellbound by Sanford, especially the four women in the front row.

Pemberton carried the skeletal remains across the room and carefully placed the box on the witness stand in front of the pathologist. The skull rested on top of the other bones. "Dr. Sanford, have you had occasion to examine the bones in the box marked Plaintiff's Exhibit 8?"

"I have."

"Tell the jury your findings and conclusions, please."

"The bones are those of an adult male, approximately 40 years old at the time of death. He would have been rather tall, slightly over six feet in height." The pathologist, obviously at ease handling skeletons, reached into the box and removed the skull. Due to its age, its jawbone was no longer attached, but the upper teeth displayed a half grin. "The bones are in reasonably good condition. I'd say they were buried in fairly dry earth, protected from the elements."

Pemberton interrupted. "Would it be consistent with your findings if other evidence proved the body had been buried in a basement under a house?"

"Yes, it would."

"Any opinion how long this skeleton was in the ground?"

"I was assisted in that determination by Dr. Song Kim, a physical anthropologist. Would it be permissible to relate his findings?"

"Certainly," Pemberton said, turning to Allison. "Unless you have an objection?"

Dr. Sanford's testimony about Dr. Kim's findings was arguably hearsay. But the findings were accurate. If she objected, they could simply read Dr. Kim's deposition into the record or fly him down from St. Louis to testify later. She would come across as trying to hide evidence from the jury.

"No objection."

"Very well," continued Dr. Sanford. "The time of death of a skeleton can be established fairly accurately when you have bones in reasonably good condition. Dr. Kim subjected them to four chemical tests: a test for nitrogen content, a thin-layer chromatography to determine the level of amino-acid content, a benzidine-peroxide test, and an ultraviolet fluorescence test." Dr. Sanford glanced for a moment at his notes. "Results indicate that this man probably died around 1863, give or take five years. We're virtually certain he died between 1858 and 1868." Dr. Sanford held up the skull for the jury. The grayish bone gleamed in the sunlight from the windows. "The skeleton was, for the most part, unremarkable. The only abnormality I found involved the skull. As you can see, it has a hole 1.25 centimeters in diameter in its frontal bone, just above and between the two superciliary ridges."

Pemberton frowned slightly. "In layman's language, doctor, where's the hole?"

"Forehead, right between the eyes, just above the eyebrow line." The pathologist rotated the skull in his hands. "Another hole of similar size is in the top rear portion of the skull, in the parietal bone, near the vertex."

Pemberton moved forward smoothly like a big cat.

"Do you have an opinion, doctor, to a reasonable degree of medical certainty, as to the cause of those holes?"

"Gunshot wound. The hole in the forehead is the entrance wound, the one in the rear the exit."

"How can you tell?"

"Well, the skull is essentially two flat bones with a space in the middle. Gunshot wounds in bone are funnel-shaped. You can tell the entrance wound from the exit wound. The entrance wound, in this case the one in the forehead, has a smaller hole on the exterior of the bone than on the interior. It's what we call beveling. The exit wound is the reverse—the smaller hole is on the inside, the larger on the outside. In this case we know the man was shot from the front, the bullet traveled backward and slightly upward before exiting from the top of his head. The tiny linear fractures in the frontal and parietal bones indicate the force of the projectile. Definitely a gunshot."

"So, Dr. Sanford, is it your opinion that this skeleton, once a living, breathing human being, suffered at some time in 1858 to 1868 a massive and fatal gunshot wound to the head?"

"That is my opinion."

Pemberton stood silently for several seconds, then slowly turned to face Allison.

"Counsel, you may cross-examine."

Allison stood up so quickly her wheeled chair creaked loudly and rolled backward several inches across the carpet. She glanced at her legal pad. The questions she'd written in longhand to ask Dr. Sanford looked silly and petty. "You were hired by Mr. Pemberton's client to examine the skull, weren't you? They paid you to come testify, didn't they? You weren't present when this skeleton, whoever he was, was shot, were you? You didn't find a bullet, did you?"

When a witness hasn't hurt you, or you can't hurt him, it's best to ask no questions in cross-examination. She'd written down that maxim when Dwight Pemberton had lectured her trial practice class.

"No questions, Your Honor," she said.

She hoped she was foregoing cross-examination for the right reasons. She assured herself it was because Sanford had not hurt her case, because his testimony was unassailable, because she didn't want to come across to the jury as being nit-picky and petty when there was nothing to be gained.

Yet, she admitted, it had been much easier to ask no questions than to try to cross-examine the expert witness. Had she declined the opportunity simply because of the fear that was making her toes feel like ice cubes?

She didn't know the answer.

During the noon recess, Allison Culbertson and Steve Armstrong walked the block from the courthouse to her office, a second-story suite over an antique store on Main Street. She was talking as they climbed the steps. "By eating lunch at my office, we'll be able to get some work done. Rita makes first-rate sandwiches, too."

When they entered the office waiting room, the elderly secretary, hair puffed in an old-fashioned bouffant style, rushed them to a portable television set perched on a bookcase between a dignified bust of Blackstone, the eminent sixteenth-century legal scholar, and a plastic statuette of a bespectacled, fat-nosed wigged judge, bearing the inscription: SUE THE JACKASSES!

"You're just in time. KFVS-TV is about to run a big story about the trial. Announced it right before the commercial."

"That's nice, Rita," said Allison, "but I don't have time to listen to Cory Blaze. We've got work to do."

The hurt expression on Rita's face made Allison pause.

"Well, how long could it take to watch it?" Allison shrugged. Rita, long-retired from one of the bought-out banks, was an excellent secretary, an attentive, nurturing woman, just the sort of person Allison needed in her life.

They stood in front of the television, sandwiches in hand, watching the handsome face of Cory Blaze fill the screen. He stood at the base of the long steps in front of the Common Pleas Courthouse, the breeze standing his short-cropped blond hair on end.

In today's top story, a sensational trial began this morning that will decide who gets to keep a buried treasure found in Cape Girardeau earlier this year. The jury trial pits Steve Armstrong, local physical education teacher, against Claxton Flint, millionaire developer.

The trial may also shed light on what some people are saying is an unsolved murder in Cape's history. A pathologist testified this morning that a skeleton buried next to the gold had suffered a gunshot wound to the head.

Steve Armstrong found the gold and the skeleton buried in the basement of his house last June. The gold was in a chest bearing the mysterious label "Girardeau Rose." He also found a belt buckle with the skeleton. The belt buckle was inscribed with the name "Horace J. Claxton."

Shortly after Armstrong found the gold, businessman Claxton Flint came forward and claimed it. In opening statements this morning, his lawyer said he will prove that Horace J. Claxton was Flint's great-grandfather, and that Flint has a key in his possession that opens the chest, as well as an old letter written by Horace J. Claxton describing the burial of the gold.

Courtroom observers say this case will turn into a battle of expert witnesses, since both sides plan to call handwriting analysis experts. Armstrong's expert says the Claxton letter is a forgery. Flint's expert says it's genuine.

KFVS-TV was on the scene back in June when Steve Armstrong first found the gold. This was his reaction at the time:

The old clip showed Cory Blaze in short sleeves, interviewing Steve in front of his house on Lorimier Street. It was shot the same day the gold was found. Steve, hair sweat-plastered to his forehead, wore faded blue jeans caked with dirt and a white T-shirt streaked with dirty fingerprints. A red bandanna dangled from a front pants pocket.

"Tell me, Mr. Armstrong, how much gold did you actually find?"

"I'm . . . I'm not really sure. A whole chest full!"

"Where'd you find it?"

"In my basement. Got a dirt floor down there."

"Was the chest locked?"

"Yes, but there wasn't any key, so I knocked it open with a shovel."

"Tell us about the skeleton, Steve."

"Well, it was buried next to the gold."

"I understand it had some identification. Tell us about that."

"I'm not sure what you mean by identification. There was a belt buckle buried with it. Had a name on it."

"What name?"

"Horace J. Claxton."

"Your lawyer filed some papers with the Circuit Court this afternoon. Tell us, Steve. What's the next step? Is the gold yours to keep?"

"Well, we filed those notices. I've been told the gold's mine unless someone else proves it's his."

The television picture flashed back to a live shot of Cory Blaze standing in front of the Courthouse.

Since finding the gold, Steve Armstrong's life has changed tremendously. We interviewed him back in August, after his home had been burglarized a second time.

The picture switched to Steve standing in gym shorts and T-shirt in his living room next to the fireplace. A camera shot panned the room, showing overturned tables and chairs, desk drawers flung about the room, the floor littered with pencils, pens, papers, clothing, pieces of glass, and broken knick-knacks.

Cory Blaze, dapper in sports coat and tie, was holding a microphone to Steve's face.

"This is the second time I've been burglarized since I found the gold. The first time was the night after I found it, after you guys ran the story on TV. Now, today, while I was at my lawyer's office, someone broke in and ransacked my home. I wish you'd tell these people that the gold isn't in my house. It's at a bank. I've got nothing here worth stealing, and I'm getting tired of cleaning up the messes they leave."

The picture switched to Cory Blaze on the courthouse steps.

Steve Armstrong says he's had to get an unlisted telephone number because of the crank calls he's received since finding the gold.

Lawyers for both sides say the law of treasure trove applies in today's trial. That means Steve Armstrong will keep the gold unless Claxton Flint proves it belonged to his ancestors.

There you have it, folks. One of the most fascinating trials in Cape Girardeau history began today. Buried treasure in the city of Cape Girardeau. Steve Armstrong, who found it, is hoping the old saying, "finders keepers," applies to him.

I'm Cory Blaze. In Cape Girardeau. We'll bring you the story as it continues to unfold.

Allison ushered Steve from the waiting room into her private office, tossing the half-eaten ham sandwich into the trash can as she plopped onto her leather desk chair, dabbing her lips with a handkerchief.

"I never should have done that interview after the burglary," Steve said. "Did you see the tears in my eyes? At least they weren't running down my face. I wish they'd stop playing that clip."

Allison let her gaze wander to the window overlooking the Mississippi River. One reason she leased the upstairs office was the view. The Mississippi was visible from the window that ran the length of the room. Bookcases covered the opposite side, filled with tan, red, and gold volumes of the *Southwestern Reporter*, and brown and gold *Vernon's Annotated Missouri Statutes*.

The wall behind her desk was splashed with framed certificates and plaques, mostly from law school. At one end of the wall was a photograph of Abraham Lincoln with the quotation so well known and dearly loved by attorneys: "A lawyer's time and advice are his only stock in trade."

Allison hadn't realized until Dwight Pemberton's lecture that Abraham Lincoln had been a practicing trial lawyer for twenty-three years, recognized as the best "jury lawyer" of his day, trying literally thousands of cases, and arguing 243 cases to the Illinois Supreme Court and two before the United States Supreme Court.

At the other end of the wall was her framed print of Degas' *La Classe de Danse*, featuring ballerinas in tutus listening with varying degrees of inattention to their instructor, an elderly man in ballet shoes.

Usually, the beige and brown tones of her office, the panoramic view of the river, and the solid comfort of the lawbooks combined to give her a sense of strength, of calm, and pleasure. Now, as she glimpsed the muddy river stretching north and south beyond her line of sight, she felt nothing but the heaving and flopping of her stomach.

"If you pull that handkerchief any harder," Steve Armstrong was saying, "you'll rip it."

Allison jumped and blushed.

She poked the wrinkled handkerchief into a jacket pocket.

"You seem awfully nervous for a lawyer who's winning a trial. We *are* winning, right?"

She smoothed her dark skirt across her thighs. "I don't know. Maybe."

"Maybe!"

She sighed. "You never know what a jury will do."

"Oh, great! What happened to that big talk about looking forward to trying a case against the great Dwight Pemberton? You don't seem too confident now. Maybe we should settle. How much did they offer?"

"One hundred thousand dollars as a finder's fee for locating Claxton Flint's family fortune. It's a pittance compared to eleven million dollars, Steve."

"It'd be better than nothing. I'm starting to wonder. After all, you haven't even asked a question of a witness yet."

"Trust me, I know what I'm doing." She hoped it was true. "I advise you not to settle. They've revoked the offer, anyway. Dwight Pemberton says it's all or nothing now."

She considered how stupid she would look if she lost the case and Steve got nothing when he could have had one hundred thousand dollars. It was not a pleasant thought.

She held up the abstract of title to Steve's house, a two-inch stack of legal-sized papers with a manila cover.

"We've got your testimony about finding the gold, the abstract showing you're the owner of the property and that neither Claxton Flint nor his ancestor Horace Claxton ever owned it, plus our expert witness who says Claxton's letter is a forgery."

She sighed and leaned back in her chair. The troubled look on Steve Armstrong's face bothered her, matching too closely her own submerged feelings.

"Pemberton, on the other hand, has that letter from Horace Claxton saying he buried the gold, plus his expert claiming it's authentic. Most of all, he's got that darn key. If the jury finds against you, it's going to be because Claxton Flint has produced the key that opens the chest."

Steve rolled his eyes. "If the glove don't fit, you must acquit."

She grimaced. The O. J. Simpson trial was a grim reminder that the jury system did not always work.

"Something like that. Pemberton's probably spent countless hours thinking of things that rhyme with key."

"Maybe the gold really does belong to Claxton Flint," he muttered. "Maybe his great-grandfather did leave him the key. Maybe I'm wrong not letting him have it and just taking the finder's fee. Maybe you should see if they'd renew the offer."

Allison Culbertson felt a bolt of hope. If they'd settle out of court, the trial would be over. She wouldn't have lost. She wouldn't be knocked all over the courtroom by Dwight Pemberton, coming up empty-handed for her client.

She was tempted, very tempted, but finally shook her head adamantly.

"Don't settle, Steve. I truly believe the letter is a forgery. I don't know how Claxton Flint got the key. I have my suspicions, but can't prove them."

"You think he stole it out of my house, don't you?"

"Yes. In one of the burglaries."

"I don't see how," Steve said. "The first burglary was two punk kids breaking in the same night the story ran on the ten o'clock news, thinking they'd get the gold to buy drugs. Flint isn't stupid enough to hire dumb guys like that to work for him."

"You're probably right."

"The second one happened while he was right here with us at your office, our first meeting with him. He couldn't possibly have done it."

"Well, we can speculate all we want," Allison said. "Speculation and what we can prove in court are two very different things."

Allison glanced at her watch. In twenty minutes the trial would resume. She felt a wave of nausea.

Chapter 3

Allison Culbertson and Steve Armstrong worked their way through the crowd in the hallway, heading back to the courtroom. Allison turned sharply when someone grabbed her arm.

Cory Blaze, expression apologetic, quickly withdrew his hand. "Miss Culbertson, could I tape a quick interview with you?"

"Not now. The trial's about to resume."

"Just a couple short questions?"

"No."

"How about dinner, then?"

She scowled. He reminded her of Brad Pitt, cleaned up. His eyes were pretty.

"Maybe some other time."

She and Steve hurried into the courtroom.

Allison sat motionless at the counsel table, watching Dwight Pemberton whisper to the two younger lawyers assisting him. His next witness would probably be either Claxton Flint or the handwriting expert. Both were key witnesses. Her cross-examination of each would be critical. She had reviewed over and over the questions she planned to ask them, her written outline branching in all directions, like tree limbs, taking different routes depending upon the answers given.

When Dwight Pemberton had taught her trial practice class, he had emphasized the importance of a good cross-examination, quoting the famous words of Professor John Henry Wigmore: *Cross-examination is the greatest legal en-*

gine ever invented for the discovery of truth. The difficulty with cross-examination, Allison reminded herself, is that the lawyer is asking questions of a
hostile witness, trying to get the witness to admit or disclose something that the
witness would not reveal. Pemberton had called it the hardest aspect of trial
lawyering to do well.

"Next witness," Dwight Pemberton announced. "Claxton Flint."

The crowd murmured. Allison squirmed. She wasn't sure that cross-examination would be such a great legal engine with her hands at the controls.
She could feel the ham sandwich rising in her esophagus.

After Flint was seated and sworn, he turned directly to the jurors, large
eyebrows climbing high on his forehead, appearance friendly and open.

Well-rehearsed, thought Allison.

Dwight Pemberton sauntered to the farthest end of the twenty-one foot jury
box and stood behind it. Flint kept facing the jury as he looked at his lawyer.

Allison remembered Pemberton's lecture to her law school class: *When
you want the sincerity of your witness to impress them, stand at the far end of
the jury box, if the courtroom permits, so the witness can look directly at the
jurors as he answers your questions.*

"Sir, would you state your name, please?"

"Horace Claxton Flint." The witness nodded almost imperceptibly at the
significance of his own name. *Claxton.*

"Where do you live, sir?"

"Cape Girardeau. Just outside the city limits, actually."

"How long have you lived in Cape Girardeau?"

"All my life. Sixty-one years, to be exact."

"Are you married?"

"I am, to Christina Flint, the most wonderful woman in the world."

"Do you belong to a church?"

Allison Culbertson found herself standing up. She heard herself talking.
"Objection. Irrelevant."

"Sustained."

Surprised, and feeling a bit better, Allison sat down.

Pemberton retrieved a large brown Bible from his counsel table, then handed
it to Flint.

"I'm showing you Plaintiff's Exhibit 9. What is it?"

"My family Bible."

"How long has it been in your family?"

"Since way before my time. Been around all my life, long as I can remember."

"Who has possession of it now?"

"I do."

Allison glanced at the jurors. They were watching Flint closely. Two of the
older women seemed smitten by him. Allison clenched her teeth.

"Where'd you get the Bible and when?" asked Pemberton.

"Got it from my dear mother when she passed away. I was fifteen."

"Does it contain any handwritten notations in it?"

"Certainly does."

"What are they?"

Flint carefully opened the old book and turned yellowed pages slowly. "For one thing," he said, "it has records of the births and deaths in my family, going way back."

"Does it have a record of your birth?"

"Sure does."

"What does it say?"

"Horace Claxton Flint, born to David P. Flint and Betty Claxton Flint."

"Does it contain information about the birth of your mother?"

"Born in 1910 to Joseph Claxton, my grandfather, and his wife Beatrice."

"What about Joseph Claxton's birth?"

"Born 1859 to Horace J. Claxton and Eula Claxton. They were apparently the original owners of the Bible, because the notations stop there."

"Does the Bible contain any reference to the death of Horace J. Claxton?"

"An inscription. Here it is."

Claxton Flint squinted as he read from the Bible.

"Horace J. Claxton. War hero. Killed in 1863, Battle of Cape Girardeau. Body never recovered."

"Do you know who wrote those words?"

"Not hardly. Wasn't around when they were written."

"Does your family Bible contain any other writings?"

"You mean the letter from Horace J. Claxton?"

"That's right."

"Yes. The letter from Horace J. Claxton is on the first blank page of the Bible. All my life I've wondered if that gold was really buried somewhere."

"What does the letter say? Read it for the jury, please."

Allison rose again. She knew from the pretrial conference that the judge would rule against her, but the objection had to be made to protect the record on appeal. "I renew the objection made earlier, Your Honor. The notations are hearsay, not sufficiently proven to constitute an ancient document. They should not be admitted into evidence."

"Overruled."

Dwight Pemberton smiled triumphantly.

"You may answer the question, Mr. Flint. Please read your great-grandfather's note to the jury."

Claxton Flint cleared his throat, spread the Bible wide open on the rail of the witness box, leaned forward, and read aloud, his voice quivering with emotion. "On this twenty-third day of April 1863, fully aware that the Confederate army under General Marmaduke is approaching Cape Girardeau, I set my hand to this holy paper in the hope of benefiting my family should I perish in the defense of my city. I have placed the family gold, every bit of it, in our GIRARDEAU ROSE chest. The key to the chest I leave with this Bible for my loving family, God bless you all. I shall bury the chest under the home of our good friend J. He won't mind. My family knows who J. is. May God protect us all and guide us through this conflagration. Horace J. Claxton.'" Tears ran down Claxton Flint's cheeks as he finished reading the words from the Bible.

After a long pause, Pemberton resumed his questioning, handing Flint a small key. "Mr. Flint, please identify Plaintiff's Exhibit 10 for me."

"That's the key. Always been with this Bible."

Pemberton backed away from the witness, facing the jury as he asked his next question.

"Mr. Flint, would you please show us whether that key opens the lock on the chest?"

"Sure."

In spite of her dismay at the rapt attention the jurors were giving the demonstration, Allison couldn't help but admire Pemberton's smooth technique. The jurors were engrossed.

Claxton Flint left the witness chair and walked confidently to the chest in front of the jury. He inserted the key into the closed lock and turned it gently. The lock clicked open. Flint raised the lid, once again revealing the gold to the jury. "There," he said. "Easy."

"Your witness," said Dwight Pemberton to Allison, an air of satisfaction upon his face.

Allison rose, her cross-examination notes in hand. Legs wobbly, she leaned against the counsel table for a moment, an image of training wheels on a bicycle flashing through her mind. "You may return to the witness chair, Mr. Flint," she said, hoping her voice did not betray the terror she felt.

"Certainly, Miss Culbertson. Be glad to."

He sat down, folding his arms across his ample stomach, pausing a moment to straighten his silk tie.

Allison dared to move a step away from the table. "This chest of gold was not found on property you owned, was it?"

"No. If it had, we wouldn't be here *now*, would we?"

She glanced up from her notes, but let his tone slide by unchallenged. "In fact," she continued, "you've never owned that particular piece of property on Lorimier Street, have you?"

"No, ma'am."

Claxton Flint turned and smiled pleasantly at the jurors. *This isn't so bad*, his expression said.

"Isn't it true that not *one* of your ancestors ever owned that property?"

"To my knowledge that is correct, Miss Culbertson."

"You admit, don't you, that Steve Armstrong owns the house where the gold was found?"

"Yes, ma'am, I'll grant you that. Doesn't change the fact it was my great-grandfather's gold, though." Flint smiled again, a patient grandfather teasing a favorite youngster.

Allison seethed inside.

"Your Honor," she protested to the judge. "Will you instruct the witness to keep his answers responsive to the questions?"

Judge Sterns peered over narrow glasses perched on the end of his nose. When he spoke his voice contained no more enthusiasm than a pager at an airport terminal. "The witness is instructed to keep his answers responsive to the questions."

"By all means, Judge Sterns," said Flint, glancing slyly at the jurors.

Allison advanced toward Flint, stopping about five feet from him. "Mr. Flint, you own a Lincoln Continental about one year old, don't you?"

"Objection," said Pemberton, rising to his feet. "That's irrelevant to the case before the jury today."

"Your Honor," Allison argued, "our position is that Claxton Flint forged the entries in the Bible. This line of questioning is intended to show his financial troubles and motive."

"Objection overruled," said the judge.

"Go ahead, answer the question," Allison said.

Flint's eyes narrowed slightly. "Yes, I own a Lincoln. So does the judge." Several people in the audience tittered.

"Your Honor. . . ," Allison began.

Judge Sterns, showing considerably more interest, interrupted her. "Objection sustained. Keep your answers responsive to the questions, Mr. Flint."

"Yes, sir," he said, humbly.

"The Lincoln's mortgaged, isn't it?" continued Allison.

"That's right."

"You also own a Mercedes?"

"I do."

"It's also mortgaged, is it not?"

"Sure is."

"You own a Cessna airplane, don't you?"

"Yes."

"Mortgaged, too, right?"

"Right."

"You own a twenty-room mansion outside Cape Girardeau, don't you?"

"It has twenty rooms, but I don't know if I'd call it a mansion, Miss Culbertson."

"Whatever you call it, a bank carries a mortgage of half a million dollars on it, correct?"

"If you say so."

"I'm not asking for my say-so, Mr. Flint. I'm asking for the truth. There's a half-million mortgage on your home, isn't there?"

"Sounds right."

"You don't own a bit of property that's not heavily mortgaged, do you, Mr. Flint?"

"I'm sure I do, Miss Culbertson."

"Name something."

"My family Bible, for one thing, and thank God I have it, under the circumstances." He made a comical face, pantomiming great relief. Most spectators and several jurors laughed. Flint winked at the jury. Cory Blaze, the television reporter, scribbled in his notepad.

Allison felt a blush crawling up her neck. She'd let him get the best of her. She'd never anticipated *that* answer when she'd laboriously outlined her questioning. "Let's talk about the family Bible a second," she said, eager to regain control. "You claim it's been around as long as you remember?"

"That's what I said."

"And the key has always been with the Bible?"

"Always."

"There are no marks, rust spots, nor indentations on the pages of the Bible indicating the key was kept inside it, are there?"

"I didn't say it was kept *inside* the Bible, Miss Culbertson. It usually sat on the shelf next to it."

"You're saying that for one hundred years the key has lain loose next to the Bible and has not been lost?"

"Apparently not, thank goodness," he said, glancing at the jury.

Allison grabbed the Bible and walked to the witness box. She opened it and pointed to the page containing the letter. "This page allegedly written by Horace Claxton, where would a person buy the type of ink used to write this?"

"I wouldn't have the faintest idea. I wasn't around one hundred years ago."

"I know you weren't, Mr. Flint, and neither was this writing!"

"Objection!" shouted Dwight Pemberton, leaping up. "Counsel is commenting on the evidence and making argument, rather than asking questions."

"Sustained. Save it for closing argument, Miss Culbertson."

Allison glared at Claxton Flint. "Let me be more specific, Mr. Flint. Where did you get the ink you used to write this page?"

"Objection. It's argumentative," interrupted Pemberton.

"It may be, but I'm going to overrule the objection. Answer the question, Mr. Flint."

"I most certainly did *not* write this page, Miss Culbertson, and I highly object to the tone of your voice and your insulting insinuations."

"Isn't it a fact, Mr. Flint, that this page was not written in this Bible until after Steve Armstrong was on television in June?"

"That is *not* a fact."

"Speaking of Steve Armstrong's being on television, you saw him on the news the day he found the gold, didn't you?"

"I believe I did."

"You believe you did. Aren't you sure?"

"I believe I did. The clip's run so many times I'm not sure when I first saw it." Flint was no longer smiling. Allison was glad the jury was getting to see the cold look in his eyes.

"As a matter of fact, you heard the name Horace J. Claxton mentioned as the name on the belt buckle, didn't you? You heard that on television, right?"

"At some point, yes."

"That was the name of your great-grandfather, wasn't it?"

"Yes."

"Your ears really perked up when you heard that name on television, didn't they?"

"I recognized the name, yes."

"Now, I suppose when you heard the name Horace J. Claxton mentioned, and heard that a chest of gold bearing the name GIRARDEAU ROSE had been found, you remembered this notation in your Bible, didn't you?"

"Certainly."

"It came immediately to mind."

"Immediately."

"And I suppose you picked up the telephone and called Steve Armstrong right then to let him know about that note in your Bible and about that key, didn't you?"

"No."

"You didn't? You had in your possession your family Bible indicating that the gold was yours, and you didn't go tell Steve Armstrong?"

"Not right off."

"It's a fact, isn't it, that you never mentioned the existence of this Bible to Steve Armstrong until *six weeks* after the gold was found? *After* you'd filed suit against him?"

"I didn't have the obligation to tell him anything, Miss Culbertson."

"The fact of the matter is that you *didn't* have the key at the time the gold was found, did you?"

"Yes, I did."

"The truth is that you or someone working for you *took* the key from somewhere in Steve Armstrong's house, isn't that right?"

"Preposterous!"

"The truth is, you heard about the gold on television and someone forged that page in your Bible, isn't it?"

"Preposterous again, Miss Culbertson."

"You and your lawyers met with Steve Armstrong and me at my office on June 27th, didn't you?"

"That's right."

"You claimed then the gold was yours, didn't you?"

"I did."

"But you didn't say a word then about having the key and the Bible, did you?"

"No. Sometimes it's best to hold your trump card."

"Matter of fact, you didn't tell anyone about the key and the Bible until much later, did you?"

"I told my son Malcolm all about it the night Steve Armstrong was on television. He'll confirm that for you."

"But you and Malcolm didn't tell a soul, did you?"

"No. Guess we never told anyone until after I met with you, after you made it abundantly clear that Armstrong wouldn't give me the gold. What of it? I didn't have the duty to tell anyone."

"Mr. Flint, your wife never even knew this Bible existed, did she?"

"Not until all this came up, no. We've only been married a year. The family Bible is sort of a morbid thing, what with all those deaths and such. Nobody in the family died this past year. Guess I never got around to talking to her about it until after this thing about the gold came up."

"Doesn't it strike you as extraordinary, Mr. Flint, that even your own wife didn't know about the existence of your family Bible?"

"I'm an extraordinary guy."

Allison tossed her legal pad onto the table, moving toward him empty-handed. "Tell me, Mr. Flint, what was Horace J. Claxton's occupation?"

"No idea."

Allison plucked a gold coin from the chest. "There are over fifteen thousand gold coins in this chest, are there not, Mr. Flint?"

"I believe that's correct."

"The face value of the coins would have exceeded 44,000 dollars back in 1860, right?"

"Could be."

"That was a lot of money in 1860. Where do you suppose Horace J. Claxton got all that money, *if* you are correct it was his?"

"I couldn't tell you. All I know is he's a war hero, killed in the Civil War."

"Did he own a lot of real estate?"

"Don't know."

"Are you aware, Mr. Flint, that the land records of Cape Girardeau County show that Horace J. Claxton never owned a single piece of real estate in Cape Girardeau?"

"Objection," interjected Dwight Pemberton. "That question states facts not in evidence. It's also hearsay."

"The witness may respond to his knowledge of the facts," said the judge. "Answer the question if you know, Mr. Flint."

"I don't know," said Flint. "Don't see the significance, anyway."

"Have you ever been inside Steve Armstrong's house on Lorimier Street?"

"No."

"Has your son?"

"Not to my knowledge."

"Have any of your employees?"

"No."

"Where was your son when you and your lawyers met with Steve Armstrong at my office on June 27th?"

"No idea."

"Where did Horace Claxton live during the Civil War?"

"On the battlefields, I presume."

"What about his family. Where did they live?"

"I haven't the faintest."

"Mr. Flint, you admit that Steve Armstrong is the person who found the gold?"

"Sure."

"You didn't find it yourself?"

"No."

Allison Culbertson turned to the judge. "No further questions, Your Honor."

The moment Judge Sterns called a recess, Allison rushed for the downstairs women's room. Nervousness, fright, relief, and anxiety all combined to make her insides roil. She'd known she was going to be sick the moment Claxton Flint made the jurors laugh while she was cross-examining him. Perry Mason would have made Flint crack; she made him crack jokes.

Stomach heaving, she saw with horror that Cory Blaze and his cameraman were set up for a live report from the first floor hallway between the stairway and the women's room. Blinding lights from the television camera assaulted her face as he called out to her, microphone waving and camera rolling as he beseeched her for an interview. She envisioned shots of herself, vomiting in the corridor, played on the evening news. Choking out a "No Comment," she ducked through the closest doorway, the entrance to a small witness waiting room. Sickness looming, she slammed the door behind her, escaping the television camera, searching frantically for the nearest trash can.

It was already taken.

Malcolm Flint, a scarecrow in an expensive suit, knelt on the carpeted floor, next to a large green metal waste can, his thumbs hooked on the rim, leaning deep inside the can. His tie, too, dangled inside it.

His head jerked from the depths of the can after she slammed the door, his eyes red and brimming with tears. His hair stuck out in several directions. Spent cigarette butts were strewn on the carpet around him, and the room was filled with a cloud of Marlboro smoke. Malcolm Flint was Claxton Flint's only son. He'd played high-school baseball with Steve Armstrong, the only player besides Steve to win all-conference honors. Steve had told her that they'd never been close, that Malcolm never wanted anyone to forget that his family was among the richest in town.

"Do you need help?" she asked.

His mouth was ajar, eyes wild. "No!" he choked out, stumbling to his feet and brushing past her toward the door. He paused, hand on the door knob. "I always liked Steve, even if he never liked me." He left the room, slamming the door behind him.

Grateful for his speedy exit, she pushed the button to lock the door and lurched urgently to the abandoned trash can, just in time.

Please God, she thought afterward, kneeling on the carpet, Brooks Brothers skirt hiked up her thighs, her damp face raised upward, *let justice be done today. If the gold truly belongs to Claxton Flint, so be it. But if not, please give me the strength to do an adequate job for my client. Don't let an injustice occur because of me.*

Minutes later she was back in the courtroom, seated next to Steve Armstrong. The jury was still enclosed in the soundproof jury room. The judge was chatting on the telephone from the bench, leaning back, enjoying his conversation. Claxton Flint was laughing and joking with his three lawyers, glancing occasionally toward the judge.

Steve was whispering something about making another attempt to settle the case. She was trying to listen. She kept wondering, though, whether she'd succeeded in rinsing the odor of vomit off her face and chin. Could Steve smell it? Her gaze landed on the exhibit table, where the skull rested next to the cardboard box containing the other faded bones. Its hollow eye sockets and upper row of teeth seemed to defy and mock her. Those empty sockets had once contained seeing eyes. The hollow skull had once enclosed a thinking brain. Yet now emptiness was its most overpowering feature.

You will never know the truth about me, she almost heard the skull challenge. *Understand well how quickly and thoroughly those who depart this world are forgotten.*

She focused her attention upon the chest of gold resting on its dolly, the GIRARDEAU ROSE label gleaming. Once-living fingers had hidden the gold in the chest. Blistered hands and an aching back had buried it. Vibrant hopes and dreams of recovering it had somehow gone awry.

If only inanimate objects could talk, she thought. *What a story these courtroom exhibits could tell!*

PART II

Son of a Riverboat Gambler

"Mississippi steamboating was born about 1812; at the end of thirty years it had grown to mighty proportions; and in less than thirty years more it was dead! A strangely short life for so majestic a creature."

Mark Twain
Life On The Mississippi, 1896

"The decade preceding the civil war is often referred to as the golden age of steamboating in the Mississippi Valley. . . . In terms of the amount and quality of steamboat service, of the speed and splendor, of the packets running in the leading trades, and of the prestige attached to careers on the river, these were indeed the bright steamboat years. But fundamentally the decade of the fifties, for the steamboat interest as a whole, was marked by depression and misfortune and by the beginning of the trend which within a few years was to relegate steamboats to a minor role in the economic role of the West. The increasing diversion of traffic to the railroads, the shifting routes and changing direction of internal commerce and, stimulated by these conditions, the growing severity of competition among steamboatmen themselves were the basic factors in this decline. There were, in addition, heavy losses from steamboat disasters, particularly in the early fifties, which increased public distrust of steamboats and resulted in the annoyances, ultimately beneficial, of government regulation."

Louis C. Hunter
Steamboats On the Western Rivers, 1949

"[I]t was the steamboat which made Cape Girardeau prosperous."

Robert Sidney Douglass
History of Southeast Missouri, 1912

Chapter 4

October 1851
Cape Girardeau, Missouri

Sixteen-year-old John Carmichael heard the bedroom door creak open but he pretended to be asleep. He lay still under his quilt, chilly predawn air nipping at the back of his neck. He heard his father enter the room, and he waited for Austin Carmichael's deep voice to wake him. Keeping his eyes closed, he hoped his father would just let him sleep.

His father was watching him. He could tell. After a few moments, his father turned and moved back toward the door. As it closed, John opened his eyes and glimpsed the back of the black woolen frock coat and tall silk top hat.

He pressed his face into the pillow and tried not to listen as Austin Carmichael's boots clopped down the hardwood steps outside the door. He attempted to go back to sleep, but a nagging thought kept tugging at his mind. *Why was his father wearing the hat?* It wasn't the hat itself that was unusual. The combination of towering top hat and black frock coat was everyday dress for Austin Carmichael and many other men of his era. But wearing the hat this time of morning indicated that he was going somewhere. Where was he going this early? And without his son?

Moments later, rubbing sleep from his eyes, John crawled from the bed, stumbled into his dungarees and a white shirt, and shuffled downstairs, just in time to hear the jingle of a carriage wheeling away from the front of the house.

Lindy was perched upon the seat of the bay window next to the door, peering through the windowpanes.

Her real name was Rosalind, but she'd ordered him to call her Lindy when they'd met the day before. Her father, Patrick O'Malley, was a steamboat captain on the Mississippi River. He and John's father, a former riverboat gambler, had long been best friends. They hadn't seen each other for years, though, until John and his father had arrived in Cape Girardeau by stagecoach the day before.

Lindy wore a white flannel nightgown. She was fifteen, her body just blooming. Her big brown eyes were wet with tears, her dark hair a mass of tangles.

"Papa's gone with your father!" she blurted. "Your father's going to fight a duel!"

"A duel?" Dread kicked John in the stomach.

"I heard them talking," she continued. "Their voices woke me. Your father was playing poker on one of the riverboats last night and won lots of money. Someone called him a cheater. Now they're going to fight a duel on Cypress Island."

John yanked open the door and stared down the empty street. "Where *is* Cypress Island?"

"In the middle of the Mississippi River, just across from Cape Girardeau, near the Illinois side of the river. You can't get there except by boat. Papa's taking your father over on the *Lucky Molly*."

"I've got to get down to the levee fast," John said, "before the *Lucky Molly* leaves. I've got to stop them."

"Don't go down there! Wait here with me. If your father wanted you with him, he'd have taken you, don't you think?"

John remembered the way he had feigned sleep when his father looked in on him only minutes before. If anything happened to him. . . .

Feet barely touching the ground, he hurried through the doorway and sprinted down the dirt street toward the riverfront. Panting, he reached Water Street and dashed across the cobblestone levee next to the river. He stopped abruptly, staring toward the Mississippi. The *Lucky Molly* had pulled out already. Patrick O'Malley's white and red steamboat, barely visible in the twilight, churned toward the Illinois side of the river like a gigantic floating castle.

"Father!" he yelled. "Austin Carmichael!"

No one on the boat could hear him over the cannonade of the steamboat's two engines. John looked around frantically. Three other steamboats were docked at the Cape Girardeau levee, parallel to each other, noses almost touching the worn bricks. He ran to the first, a small sidewheeler called the *Lady Belle*. "Sir!" he called to a man bent over some rope at the bow of the steamboat, only eight feet from shore. "Please take me across the river! My father's going to fight a duel on Cypress Island!"

In the darkness, John couldn't see the man's face clearly, but he heard the voice plain enough. "Son, if your pa's dumb enough to fight a duel, he deserves what happens to him. Least he was smart enough not to take you. Now get along with you."

John tried each of the other two boats, with similar results.

He scanned the river in despair. The hazy form of the *Lucky Molly* moved steadily toward the Illinois side.

"John!" He heard Lindy's voice before he saw her. She rode a brown pony, galloping down Themis Street toward the riverfront, her white nightgown flapping in the wind. "Come on, John! I know a place where we'll have a good view of Cypress Island!"

The pony snorted nervously as John clasped her proffered hand and swung onto its bare back behind her. Her heels jabbed the pony's sides as it hurtled down the empty dirt road toward the north end of town. He slipped to the left on the back of the bouncing pony, almost falling. He wrapped his arms tightly around Lindy's slim waist. Struggling to keep his balance, he scooted against her, the insides of his thighs pressed against her nightgown.

"We've got to stop my father," he spoke into her ear.

Brick buildings flashed by, hoofbeats of the galloping pony echoing off red facades. Soon the buildings were gone, replaced by an anfractuous dirt trail winding through dense woods. Tree limbs jabbed them. They ducked low against the pony's back. The trail became a steep incline, the pony slowing as it neared the crest, its barrel chest heaving. Above the dark tree tops, the purple sky began to assume a reddish glow in the east.

"Here we are," she gasped. The pony brought them out of the woods and onto a grassy plateau high above the Mississippi River. "This is Cape Rock."

They slid from the back of the sweating pony and hurried across a massive promontory of rock that extended into and over the river, like the towering foot of a huge giant, creating a natural cove in its shadow.

"That's Cypress Island." She pointed across the river. In the deep pink glow of approaching dawn, Cypress Island was nothing more than a huge sand bar sprouting trees in its middle. The river, reflecting the sunrise, shimmered like floating rose petals around the long island.

The *Lucky Molly* was tied at the edge of the island, dark clouds of smoke billowing from her two tall chimneys. Several men congregated at her bow, looking toward the island's beach. Fifty yards from the white steamboat, five men stood on the sand talking. One was Austin Carmichael.

"Father!" John yelled. His voice sounded small as it dissipated over the huge expanse of the river.

"They can't hear you from here."

"Who are those other people?"

"Too far away. I can't recognize any of them except my papa and your father."

Most of the men wore dark frock coats and top hats. One exception was Captain Patrick O'Malley, clad in his captain's uniform: dark blue coat and pants, brass buttons, white chevrons on the arms. One man wore a dark wide-brimmed hat. He seemed to be doing most of the talking. Austin Carmichael and Patrick O'Malley stood to the left of the man in the wide-brimmed hat; two other men were on his right. John's father's shoulders were squared, his arms crossed over his chest. It was a pose he often assumed when angry. He no longer wore the top hat. From this distance his black hair perfectly matched his dark coat. As the men talked, daylight broke fully. The red tint on the sand and water gradually faded away.

The man in the wide-brimmed hat held out a box somewhat larger than a cigar box. Patrick O'Malley and another man each removed something from it. O'Malley pointed the object toward the sky, inspecting it.

"Oh, no," whispered John. "Dueling pistols!"

The man in the wide-brimmed hat stepped away from the others. He drew a line on the sand with a stick. He paced off forty feet and drew another line. He gestured and talked to the other four men as he walked back to them. John's throat constricted as if large thumbs pressed upon his Adam's apple. He fought to squeeze air into his lungs as he watched his father stride confidently to a place at one of the lines. Austin Carmichael gripped a pistol in his right hand.

Another man held the other pistol for Austin Carmichael's antagonist, who wore a large white straw hat and was slowly removing a dark overcoat. Once the overcoat was off, the duelist's white suit, white vest, and white shirt glistened in the early morning sun. A bow tie made a splash of red under his chin.

"Tyler Fitch," said Lindy. "I recognize his clothes. He always wears a white suit and red bow tie. He owns the *Andrew Jackson*, the steamboat that's Papa's biggest competitor. He's only twenty-six, but he's already one of the richest men in Cape Girardeau. He's fought duels before. Lots of them. Everybody knows, even though you're not supposed to. They go to Cypress Island because dueling's against the law in Missouri."

John held his breath as Tyler Fitch removed his suit coat and carefully rolled up the sleeves of his white shirt.

"I can't watch," choked John, unable to tear his gaze from the two men on the beach. His father, standing erect and motionless in black frock coat, gun in hand, barrel pointing straight down, stood on the line in the sand to the left of the beach. Tyler Fitch, white shirt and vest gleaming, took a position on the right, flexing his shoulders.

The man in the wide-brimmed hat raised his right hand and seemed to be counting. John's fingernails dug into the palms of his hands and drew blood as the man brought his arm down in a sweeping motion. John watched in horror as each man raised his pistol and fired. Both dropped to the ground as if kicked by invisible mules. The staccato pops of the shots drifted up to John as he watched the witnesses scramble to the fallen men.

Patrick O'Malley knelt next to Austin Carmichael. John's father lay flat on his back. O'Malley tried to hold down legs that were kicking gouges in the sand in a wild dance of death.

"No!" screamed John, moving toward the edge of the rock promontory.

"Don't!" cried Lindy, grabbing him by the arm. "This is a cliff. The drop's too steep. There's nothing you can do."

He jerked his arm from her grasp and started again for the edge. She lunged for his leg, caught it, and wrapped herself around his calf. He crashed to the ground. Her nightgown tore from her shoulders, completely exposing her young breasts. Undaunted, she pressed tightly to his leg, her naked skin mashed against his dungarees.

"There's nothing you can do for him, John. If he's alive, Papa will get him to a doctor. If you try to go down to the river from here, you'll kill yourself." Her voice filtered through his curtain of grief. He rolled onto his back and covered his face with his hands, sobbing uncontrollably.

She released her hold on his leg and quickly pulled her torn nightgown back over her shoulders, covering her nakedness. She crawled closer to him and cradled his blond head in her arms, pressing his face against her soft chest, his wet cheeks rubbing soft flannel. He shuddered, torrents of tears and gasps wracking his body.

Finally, he was able to wind down the pounding engine of his grief. Pulling his head from her arms, he rose slowly to his feet and stared again at the scene below. On the beach of Cypress Island, Tyler Fitch, aided by his second, staggered to his feet. He held a hand over his left ear. Blood ran down his hand and arm, covering the side of his white clothing. With an arm over his companion's shoulders, Fitch stumbled to the steamboat.

Crew and deck hands from the *Lucky Molly* wrapped the body of Austin Carmichael in a tarp and carried it to the boat. Patrick O'Malley followed them, cap in hand.

"If only I hadn't pretended to be asleep," whispered John, struck with an awful realization. "I didn't even get to tell Father good-bye!"

Two hours after seeing his father shot to death, John Carmichael sat on the wooden floor of the small second-story bedroom of the O'Malley house, room key clutched in his hand. After returning to the house with Lindy, he'd locked himself in the room, and then slumped against the wall near the door. Through his blur of pain he heard Lindy knocking at the door every few minutes, calling his name. He ignored her. He was finished crying. Now he merely stared at the cold, dead fireplace.

A sharp rapping on the door caught his attention. He heard the voice of Maude O'Malley, twin sister of Patrick O'Malley, Lindy's spinster aunt. "Open this door," she demanded. "Captain O'Malley is coming up the street right now. He'll want to talk to you. He won't like it that you've locked the door, young man. Please unlock it, and let us see that you're all right."

He stared at the key in his hand but said nothing. He didn't want to open the door, didn't want to see anyone right now, didn't want anyone to see him, either. He wished he were back in Virginia, with his friends at school. He wished his mother hadn't died of cholera two years before. He wished his father hadn't sold the dry goods business after his mother's death. He wished they'd never come out here to Cape Girardeau, Missouri, for his father to resume riding the river with Captain Patrick O'Malley. Uncle Pat. An uncle related to his father only by friendship, not blood. An uncle John had never met until yesterday.

He sat motionless, stunned with grief. The elderly woman's coaxing ceased. Minutes dragged by, weighted by the hurt of death. Suddenly a loud pounding on the door shook him into the present. "Open up, lad," boomed the voice of Patrick O'Malley.

John watched disinterestedly as the doorknob turned and the door rattled noisily against its lock.

"John Carmichael, I want to talk to you *now*, and God gave me less patience than He granted most men. Open the door. *Now!*"

He glanced at the key in his hand and tried to remember locking the door. Instead, he remembered his father leaving earlier that morning, his last glimpse of him before the duel.

A terrific crash made John throw his arms over his face. The door next to him burst into splintered pieces as Patrick O'Malley kicked his way into the room. John gaped at the towering bulk of Captain Patrick O'Malley. The big man's green eyes flashed under bushy eyebrows. His left hand bore no fingers. The sight of the shiny scarred flesh was unsettling.

"Nobody locks me out of a room in my own house, boy! I don't give a blasted ball of fire how miserable you are!"

John stiffened against the wall. The key dropped to the floor.

O'Malley removed his cap and knelt next to him. His face was flushed under a ruddy tan, bordered by curly hair, brownish red on top, mostly white on sideburns and temples. His moustache was completely white. His eyes glimmered with surprising kindness as he reached out a massive hairy forearm and placed a hand on John's knee.

"Son, I know what you're going through. Rosalind told me you saw the duel. I'm sorry about your father. Sorry you had to see it. You need to be a man about it, though. Your father would want that."

John's eyes filled with tears. "A man? Like you? You just stood there and watched him get shot! I saw you!"

O'Malley recoiled, but then leaned toward John, so close John could see the reddish whiskers interspersed in the white sideburns. "John Carmichael, your father was the best friend I ever had, a good man, an honorable man. We rode many a riverboat together. Out of respect for him I'm going to have this talk with you. Might be the last time we talk. Up to you about that." O'Malley's brow creased into a frown. "True, boy, I did nothing to stop the duel, nothing you could see, anyway. Those are the rules of dueling, the unwritten code. I was his second, there to make sure the duel was fought fairly, to be his friend and companion. I did those things. It was a fair fight. Each man had an equal chance."

O'Malley gestured in helplessness. "I tried to stop it long before we ever got to the island, lad. Tried to talk both of them out of it. They wouldn't compromise, though. Fitch thought your pa had cheated him, and your pa was powerfully angry to be accused of cheating, especially in the loud and belligerent tone Fitch used."

"My father wouldn't cheat."

"I know he wouldn't. Your father was a riverboat gambler on my boats long before you were born. Never knew him to cheat. Most do, but some, rare ones like your father, are professional cardplayers who rely on skill to win."

"I'm going to kill that Fitch," John vowed softly.

"I understand your feelings," said O'Malley gently, "but I hate to hear you say that. Fitch has a short temper and a sharp tongue, but he isn't a bad man, least I don't think he is. I honestly believe he thought your father *was* cheating him. Two men used fighting words too quickly. Your father was just as much to blame for what happened as Fitch."

"My father didn't cheat."

"True. But the duel happened, nonetheless. Your father's dead. Fitch has an ear shot off. And the money."

John looked up dully.

O'Malley nodded.

"Your father and Fitch agreed that fate would tell whether your father had been cheating. Whoever got hurt the worst was wrong. Winner take all. It's crazy to say a pistol ball, an ignorant piece of lead, is going to decide who's telling the truth and who isn't, but that's what they did."

"Then I'm not only an orphan, I don't have any money, either?"

O'Malley nodded, absently massaging his scarred left hand with the good fingers of his right.

"John, I'm here to finish raising you for your father. I owe that and more to him for the great friendship we enjoyed. Soon as he's properly buried, I want you to come onto my steamboat as Second Clerk. Unless you've got other plans."

John was prepared to refuse, but the ice of his hostility melted in the warmth of the big man's eyes.

"What does a Second Clerk do?"

"Little of everything. You'll try it, then?"

John pictured his father lying on the sand and fought down another urge to cry.

"I guess so."

O'Malley put his good hand reassuringly on John's thin shoulder.

"Things will work out for you, lad."

John swallowed hard, frightened by another realization.

"I can't even swim, Mr. O'Malley. I've got no business working on a steamboat."

"Call me Uncle Pat."

O'Malley stood up, tugged at the sleeve of his navy blue captain's coat, and winked at John.

"You'll learn to swim. You'll learn a load about life on the river. I promise you that."

Chapter 5

The next morning, John and the O'Malley family walked together on the macadamized streets of Cape Girardeau toward the riverfront. He was to board the *Lucky Molly* with O'Malley. Earlier that morning he'd read O'Malley's advertisement in the *Western Eagle*, Cape Girardeau's weekly newspaper:

```
                    FOR NEW ORLEANS
    The fine steamer, LUCKY MOLLY, Patrick O'Malley, Mas-
ter, will be at Cape Girardeau on her downward trip to New
Orleans on Sunday, the 19th, at 7:00 P.M., positively, and
will leave regularly every third Saturday until further
notice.
         For freight or passage apply on board.
                  PATRICK O'MALLEY
              CAPE GIRARDEAU, MISSOURI
```

O'Malley ran similar advertisements in rivertown newspapers all along the Mississippi. The steamboat was scheduled to leave Cape at nine o'clock for a day-and-a-half jaunt up the river to St. Louis, where it would load freight and passengers for the long trip down the river to New Orleans.

As they walked toward the levee, John was careful not to glance toward the hill at the northern end of town, where Austin Carmichael was buried in the green expanse of Lorimier Cemetery overlooking the Mississippi. The short funeral had been yesterday afternoon, only seven hours after the duel.

"I know it hurts, John, I really do." Lindy was walking next to him. Her gingham dress was a collection of ruffles. A small silver cross dangled on a chain around her neck.

"Do you, Lindy? I don't think so." His voice sounded meaner than he'd intended.

Some of the pity left her eyes. "Least you had both parents until you were almost grown up. My mother was killed when I was eight, you know."

He glanced at her with surprise. "I didn't know. I'm sorry."

"Mother was killed in a steamboat explosion. Odd thing," she said without smiling, "she wasn't even *on* the steamboat when she died. She was walking on Water Street next to the river when the boilers exploded. Big piece of boiler cut her head off."

"It's a peculiar method you're employing to make John feel better, my little Rose," said O'Malley. "I doubt telling him of your dear mother's tragic death is making him feel any happier about his own loss. Misery doesn't love that sort of company."

"Sorry, Papa, but it's true. He's lucky he had both parents as long as he did."

"Rosalind," said her Aunt Maude. "If you're going to bother John by talking to him, at least choose a different subject."

"I'm sorry if I said something wrong," Lindy said to John. She brightened. "Did you go to school back in Virginia?"

John's chin rose almost imperceptibly. "Of course. I finished grammar school, in fact. Would've started college this month at the University of Virginia had we stayed there. I'd already been accepted."

"College?" she said. "At sixteen!"

"Many people start college at sixteen. I liked school. I did well. That's one reason I didn't want to move out here to the middle of nowhere. Now I guess I'll never go to college."

"Maybe you'll still go, although I don't think you need to. You're plenty smart already. Personally, I'll be glad when I get *out* of school. Won't be long, you know."

John grunted and shifted his suitcase to his other arm. His right arm was tiring.

"Heavy?" she asked. "Shall I carry it for a while?"

Heat simmered in his cheeks. "No, I've got it. Thank you." He looked her in the eye, trying to decide whether she meant to insult him by offering to carry the bag. The friendly expression on her pretty face convinced him she had no way of knowing he'd always been sensitive about his scrawniness.

As they approached the waterfront, the street became more crowded. Merchants hurried from stores to steamboats, overseeing the loading and unloading of cargo. Clerks stood near the boat ramps jotting notations about freight and passengers, collecting and dispersing money. Cotton and corn were loaded onto southbound steamboats for passage to New Orleans, while steamboats arriving from the gulf port unloaded foreign luxuries, staple goods, tools, nutmeg, gunnysacks, rivets, linseed oil, scales, buggy wheels, sugar, dried herring, coffee, cocoa, lemons, hardware, tinware, and earthenware. Carriages and people on horseback threaded slowly through the crowd of pedestrians. Attire varied from merchants and city folk in frock coats and dresses to frontiersmen in buckskins to farmers in plaid shirts, faded trousers, and shapeless dirty hats. Steamboats belched dark clouds of smoke, engines chugging loudly, filling the air with vibrating sound.

"Look at the *Lucky Molly*, John. Isn't she a beauty? Just like her namesake." O'Malley pointed at his steamboat.

"She's named after my mother," Lindy whispered.

The *Lucky Molly* was tied up between a half dozen other steamboats. She was second in size only to a big steamboat with the name *Andrew Jackson* painted on large circular paddle wheel housings on each side of the vessel.

The *Lucky Molly*, like the other riverboats, was almost entirely white. Two large smoke stacks rose in the front center portion of the boat, twelve feet apart, parallel to each other as one faced the steamboat. The chimneys were black, the lettering and trim red. The steamboat was a dazzling mass of fancy latticework, fretwork, and jigsaw gingerbread patterns.

John glanced at the other boats docked at the levee. He stopped abruptly and stared at a man in a white suit and red bow tie sauntering up the loading stage of the *Andrew Jackson*, a large white bandage wrapped around his head.

"Tyler Fitch," Lindy confirmed. "That's his steamboat, the *Andrew Jackson*."

Tyler Fitch glanced over a moment later and his eyes met John's. They stared at each other. Sudden recognition of the son's resemblance to the father flashed in Fitch's eyes, and he quickly looked away.

"I see Carnahan's got the *Molly's* engines fired up already," grunted O'Malley with satisfaction as he surveyed the dark smoke and sparks billowing from the stacks of his steamboat. "Good thing, too. It's almost nine o'clock."

"This is when we say good-bye to the womenfolk," announced O'Malley, turning to face Lindy. "Good-bye, darling," he said to his daughter. "Take good care of this grumpy old aunt of yours."

Maude regarded her brother with affection. "I'll have you know, Patrick, that I'm not a bit grumpy when you're out of the house."

"Aye, sister, and I'm sure it's because you hit the bottle vigorously when I'm not there to behold your teetotaler act."

Maude snorted with mock indignation.

"My sister," explained O'Malley, "is one of the founding members of the local chapter of the Daughters of Temperance, a women's group dedicated to harassing drunkards and banishing the use of alcohol across the country." The big man winked. "I love her anyway."

Maude O'Malley tipped her bonneted head and permitted her twin to peck her face with his lips.

"I'll miss you, Papa," said Lindy, standing on the tips of her toes and kissing the ruddy skin between his sideburns and moustache.

"And I'll miss my little Rose," he said, engulfing her slim body in a hug.

Maude O'Malley approached John and hugged him stiffly.

"Take care of yourself, young John Carmichael. Don't let Captain O'Malley and his crew corrupt your innocence in the big cities of St. Louis and New Orleans." She reached out and touched his chin. "God be with you."

Lindy drew close to him and kissed him hastily. "I'll think about you every night before I go to bed, John. Keep in mind that someone is thinking of you."

"Come on, lad, time's a-wasting," muttered O'Malley, clapping him roughly on the shoulder.

As they neared the gangplank leading to the *Lucky Molly*, O'Malley yelled, "Artemus Primm! Come meet your new Second Clerk!"

A dapper midget who had been standing on a crate near the *Lucky Molly*, scribbling notations into a logbook, hopped down and hurried to join them. He wore a black suit with a gold-colored brocade silk vest.

"John, this is my Clerk, Artemus Primm."

Artemus Primm grinned and extended a short arm. His head was as round as a white onion, and just as bald on top, with thin wisps of black hair on the sides and back. Off the crate, he stood no higher than John's belt buckle.

"Pleased to have you on board," Primm chirped. "Can always use more help."

They shook hands.

"As clerk," O'Malley continued, "Artemus is in charge of the day-to-day business transactions of the steamboat. Keeps records of what freight and passengers we pick up and deliver. Collects money. Gives receipts. He also buys our provisions and makes sure we've got adequate food and firewood. Handles the payroll, too. Because of your fancy education, John, you should be a big help to him. As Second Clerk, you'll be his assistant."

"Yes, sir," John said.

"I look forward to getting to know you better," said Artemus Primm with a slight bow, "but right now I need to make sure we've unloaded everything destined for Clark & Greer Dry Goods. We were missing a box of shovels, last time I checked."

"Right. Get on with it," O'Malley said. "Plenty of time for visiting later."

As Artemus Primm hurried off to look for shovels, John followed O'Malley up the plank and onto the steamboat, where O'Malley gave him a quick tour of the 225-foot-long boat. It had four levels.

The main deck, thirty-five feet wide, was the lowest level. It housed the firewood and most of the freight, evenly distributed in boxes, barrels, hogsheads, and sacks. Deck hands and passengers who paid only deck passage rode on this level, sitting amid the freight and firewood.

Huge paddle wheels adorned each side of the steamboat, one-third forward from the back of the boat. They measured fifteen feet across and thirty feet in diameter. They were encased in white wooden circular boxes called paddle wheel housings, the name *Lucky Molly* painted just above a red shamrock on each.

While on the main deck, O'Malley escorted John into the engine room, shouting to be heard over deafening noise. O'Malley introduced him to the engineer, Pete Carnahan.

Carnahan, glistening with sweat, was just under six feet tall, with a wiry muscular build, dark hair, and stubble on his face that bespoke only occasional familiarity with a razor.

"Pleased to meet you," the engineer nodded. "I'd shake your hand, but mine are a might dirty." He held up his hands as proof of his statement. They were black with filth.

After the tour of the lower deck, O'Malley guided him to the next level, the boiler deck. A huge indoor cabin area filled most of the space on this level. A narrow walkway surrounded the cabin, allowing passengers to stroll from bow to stern without going inside.

The main area of the cabin was one long room about fifteen feet wide and 200 feet long, with twelve-foot arched ceilings, elegant crimson carpeting, ornate chandeliers, and a glistening white baby-grand piano. Rows of cabin doors lined each side of the long narrow room. A women's lounge filled with card tables was located at its far end.

"I've never seen anything so fancy."

"Steamboat Gothic," boasted O'Malley with pride. "Just as splendiferous as anything back East or in Europe. And designed right here on the western rivers."

After a quick tour of the hurricane deck, with its captain's cabin and small rooms for other officers, they climbed one last flight of stairs to the pilothouse, where O'Malley introduced him to Abner Conrad, the pilot on duty.

John extended his hand to the older man, but awkwardly withdrew it when he saw Conrad had only one arm, leaving no right hand to shake.

Conrad laughed good-naturedly. "It's all right, son. It's the thought that counts."

Abner Conrad sported a full beard and a slightly paunched stomach. His hair and beard were mostly gray.

"I'd be nowhere without the pilots," said O'Malley. "We always carry two paid pilots on board every trip. Each works a twelve-hour shift. We keep running night and day. We'll always let any pilot needing a ride travel with us for free. You can never have too many pilots in the pilothouse. They've got maps of the river in their heads. They know every sunken wreck and rock. Know where the channel cuts from one side to the other. Know where the shoals are close to the surface of the water. If they don't do their job, we're sunk, literally. Hell, I pay 'em each more than I draw as salary myself. Abner here makes $500 a month. Why, that's more than the Vice-President of the United States makes. An arm and a leg, that's what I pay 'em."

"Poor choice of words, Captain," grinned Abner Conrad, flopping his stump. "But I appreciate the sentiments."

Minutes later, back on deck level, they watched the deck hands carry the last of the cargo up the ramp and onto the steamboat.

"How many deck hands are there?"

"Roustabouts? Depends. Usually carry about fifteen on this boat. Sometimes as many as thirty. It varies between stops. Unlike the pilots, the clerk, the kitchen help, and the mate, they aren't hired for a full season. They're hired by the trip. Some just want to get from one place to another and are willing to work for their passage. Most are full-time riverboat men, though, working their way up and down the river. I pay them twenty-five dollars a month when they work for me."

He pointed to four deck hands carrying a large crate up the wooden plank. "Some captains use slaves for that sort of work. Not me. First place, Maude has damned near convinced me slavery isn't right. Second, if you ever travel north of St. Louis on the Mississippi or north of Louisville on the Ohio, slaves tend to escape into the free states. Then you've got to reimburse their owners for losing them."

John watched as the four men neared the top of the plank. One, a slender young man with a thatch of yellow hair, slipped.

His end of the crate struck heavily against the edge of the boat. A huge man shot out of nowhere, brandishing a large cudgel at the deck hand.

"Peterson, you worthless fool! Break that crate and I'll break your teeth!"

The big man struck the deck hand across the back with the cudgel. The blond fell to his knees.

"He hit him!" John said in surprise.

"Not hard," said O'Malley, his voice tinged with concern. "That big fellow's the mate, Horace Claxton. A captain has to let his mate use discretion in handling deck hands. Roustabouts are a rough lot, frontiersmen and flatboatmen, plenty mean and tough. The mate's got to be as tough as they are, got to earn their respect. It's a fine line between generating respect and inflicting cruelty. Claxton's got a difficult job, but he's good at it. Reminds me greatly of Mike Fink."

"I've heard of Mike Fink," John said, "Did you know him?"

"Knew him well. I'll tell you about him some day."

They watched Claxton pull the fallen deck hand to his feet.

Claxton's arms were nearly as thick as John's waist. The big mate was over six feet tall and weighed at least 240 pounds. Approximately 30 years old, with extremely short brown hair, he wore soiled white pants and a white shirt with its sleeves torn out. Large sweat stains covered the shirt from armpit to belt.

Claxton's snarl faded into an expression of servility when he saw O'Malley approaching.

"Oh, hello, Captain. Didn't know you was here, yet."

"Do we have a problem here, Claxton?"

"No, sir. No problem at all." Claxton nudged the deck hand standing next to him. "Is there, Peterson?"

Peterson's eyes narrowed as he returned the gaze.

"No. Everything's fine."

O'Malley dropped the subject and strode to the front of the steamboat. He turned to face the crew. Deck hands stopped working and moved toward the captain. Abner Conrad peered down from the pilothouse.

"Fellows," bellowed O'Malley, "before we pull out I want to introduce you to the newest officer on board. This is my nephew, John Carmichael. His father was one of my closest friends, best cardplayer ever to float the Mississippi. Many of you saw him fight the duel with Fitch yesterday, may his soul rest in peace."

O'Malley placed his hand on John's slender shoulder. Most of the small crowd smiled pleasantly at him. Horace Claxton glared with undisguised fury.

"John's going to be our Second Clerk. He'll work directly under Artemus Primm. I also want him to spend time with you deck hands for a while to see what your job's like, then in the engine room for a spell. Introduce yourselves to him when you get a chance. Make him feel at home. Don't show him special treatment just because he's kin to me. Make the lad earn his way and do a man's share of the work." O'Malley gestured toward the pilothouse, 30 feet above. "Pull out!"

Lindy and Aunt Maude waved at them from the shore. O'Malley swept off his captain's cap and executed a deep bow to his daughter. She pulled a handkerchief and waved it rapidly. Over the loud pounding of the steam engine, John thought he heard his name included in her good-bye.

The *Lucky Molly*, paddle wheels churning water on both sides of the boat, pulled away from the levee and started upriver against the powerful current of the Mississippi.

O'Malley, shouting to be heard over the roar of the engines, pointed to the deck hands tossing more firewood into the gaping mouths of the two furnaces at the front of the steamboat.

"The design of a steamboat is a wondrous thing. Fire is built up in the furnaces at the front of the boat, then the draft from the forward motion of the boat sucks the heat, smoke, and fire back through the pipes, under the boiler, heating the water and making the steam to power the engines. The smoke is then carried up the stacks, going out the tops of those magnificent chimneys.

The stacks on the *Lucky Molly* stand fifty feet above water level. Amazing, isn't it? Taller stacks help pull hot air up the chimneys faster, you see."

O'Malley gestured toward the banks of the Mississippi.

"Some day people will build bridges across this grand old river, and it's going to make it mighty inconvenient for steamboats with fifty-foot chimneys. Don't know what we'll do then. Right now, though, there's not a bridge across the Mississippi anywhere. Hope it stays that way forever."

John enjoyed the sensation of the boat's movement and liked the feel of the moist river breeze upon his face. "How fast are we going?"

"We generally go ten to fourteen miles per hour upriver and sixteen miles an hour downriver. Depends on the weather, the flood stage, the number of snags we encounter, the weight of the load, and plenty of other things."

The captain pointed at a huge cliff of gray rock.

"There's Cape Rock, the landmark that gave Cape Girardeau its name. A fur trader named Girardot built a trading post up there years ago."

O'Malley squinted into the bright sunshine. "Jean Girardot was one of the original French soldiers sent in 1708 to Kaskaskia, just north of here, to help restore order after a mess of rowdy *coureurs de bois* created trouble by inciting forays to capture Indians to sell into slavery to the British. Girardot eventually resigned and built a trading post on Cape Rock. The way it extends into the river, it creates a natural cove at its base, the perfect place for landing canoes. Also, it's easy to find and describe. As a landmark it can't be missed."

O'Malley frowned. "No one knows what happened to Girardot. He traded with the Indians for several years, occasionally paddling to Kaskaskia to sell his furs. A one-year expedition in the wilderness for fur trade in those days could bring a profit of 1,000 percent. I guess we'll never know for certain whether he got killed or simply packed up his profits and headed home to France. Whatever became of him, he left his name upon this unforgettable hunk of rock."

John stared at the massive rock promontory and recalled watching his father die in the duel. *Unforgettable* was right.

"Steamboats are the greatest invention known to man," O'Malley continued. "They're bringing civilization to the world."

"I didn't realize they're so loud." John put his hands to his ears, watching orange sparks fly from the chimneys amid great clouds of black smoke. "Are those sparks supposed to be there?"

"They're inevitable," said O'Malley. "Steamboat engines aren't efficient. We lose lots of good heat and fire up those chutes, no doubt about it. Wood's so cheap, though, it doesn't really matter. We pay only $1.75 a cord." O'Malley clapped John on the back, "So tell me, young man. How do you like your first steamboat ride?"

John touched the rail in front of him, experiencing the motion and power of the boat under his feet. He liked it more than he'd expected.

"It's tolerable."

John scanned the immense white body of the steamboat and took a deep breath of humid river air. It was a pleasant feeling, riding at the bow of a steamboat.

He noticed Horace Claxton staring at them from the deck below. The sight of his glowering face reduced John's sense of pleasure considerably.

Chapter 6

In the fading twilight of early evening, John Carmichael tried to count the other steamboats ornamenting the St. Louis landing as the *Lucky Molly* chugged along the mile-long levee, looking for a place to tie up. He lost count at 50.

"I've never seen so many boats in my life," he marveled.

"St. Louis is a booming city," said O'Malley. "Just 40 years ago, Cape Girardeau, Ste. Genevieve, and St. Louis were all towns of about 2,000 people, Ste. Genevieve the largest of the three. Now St. Louis dwarfs the others. From 1840 to 1850, St. Louis' population increased from 16,000 to 77,000, mostly because of its location near the joining of the Missouri and Mississippi Rivers. People pause here on their way westward and end up staying. They're calling St. Louis the 'Gateway to the West'."

John was impressed by the view of St. Louis from the river. The vast majority of buildings were made of brick or stone, almost all three or four stories tall. Several spires and cupolas reached even higher into the skyline.

"Tie up over there," O'Malley yelled over the din of the engines. He pointed to a wooden post on the wharf between two other steamboats.

Abner Conrad guided the bow of the *Lucky Molly* to the post. Deckhands leaped ashore and lashed the boat securely to the wharf.

O'Malley, John, and Artemus Primm followed them.

The St. Louis landing buzzed with excitement. Steamboats were tied up side by side in a row several hundred yards long. The center section of the levee was paved with stones, but most of its surface consisted of packed dirt trampled by hundreds of feet. Scores of drays, wagons, and carriages crowded the streets.

Thousands of boxes, crates, and barrels blanketed the landing. Hundreds of people covered the riverfront hastily tending to business as evening approached.

"I want us loaded for New Orleans by midafternoon tomorrow," O'Malley told his clerk.

"Yes, sir," answered Artemus Primm.

Out of the corner of his eye, John glimpsed Horace Claxton approaching. The big mate was carrying a piece of firewood in his right hand, holding it like a club.

"Captain," said Claxton in a raspy voice. "You want the boxes of wine from Cape unloaded?"

"Definitely. Stack them near the buildings, and put a tarp over them. That way we'll be ready to take new cargo immediately." O'Malley prodded John's thin arm, "John, why don't you help the deck hands unload? Put some muscle on that skinny frame of yours." O'Malley then turned to Artemus Primm. "Come on, Artemus. We need to find merchants with goods to send to New Orleans."

As the big captain and the tiny clerk departed, O'Malley called over his shoulder, "Claxton, don't be too rough on John."

"Don't worry about the boy, Captain. I'll take care of him." Horace Claxton looked directly at John, bushy eyebrows lowering over hawk-like blue eyes. "Yes, sir. I'll take care of you real good, Johnny-boy."

Eyes narrowing, Claxton slowly raised his club, touching it to John's chin. "Riverboat work's hard, boy. Dangerous, too. Things can fall on you. You can slip off the boat and drown in the river. There's people who'll knife you just for the fun of it. Fires and explosions. Snags in the riverbed waiting to tear the hull right out of your boat. People who'll knock you down, just to see you crawl." Claxton moved closer. A heavy odor of rotten teeth clung to his breath.

"Me, I don't think you're cut out to be a riverboat man. Too frail a creature. Don't believe you'll survive. Captain's making a big mistake taking you on our *Lucky Molly*."

He abruptly removed the club from John's chin. "Get your carcass back on the boat and start earning your pay. Help Peterson with them boxes."

John hurried up the ramp to the stern of the boat, where Peterson was lifting one of the wooden crates of wine. The muscles in the tall man's arms rippled as he lugged the box toward the ramp.

"Need some help with that?" John asked.

Peterson smiled.

"Nah. These boxes ain't heavy. Only takes one man to carry the small ones." Peterson nodded toward the stack of boxes.

"Help yourself."

John bent over and picked up one of the wooden crates. The bottles clinked together inside. He gasped in surprise at its heavy weight.

Grunting, he hoisted the box to waist level and staggered toward the gang-plank, amazed at how heavy four dozen bottles of wine could be.

"Get your hindquarters moving, Johnny-boy," yelled Claxton, who stood near the gangplank. "You're slowing up the real men."

John glanced over his shoulder. Sure enough, several deck hands crowded behind him, each carrying two crates of wine.

When he reached the plank leading to the steamboat, he paused. It was five feet wide. It had seemed plenty wide when he walked it empty-handed, but it now looked uncomfortably narrow for navigating while carrying a heavy crate of wine bottles. The sucking noises made by the flowing muddy water of the Mississippi underneath didn't help matters.

"Get moving!" Claxton bellowed, kicking the seat of John's pants.

The blow propelled him down the ramp. He partly danced and partly slid down the slick wood, tripping when his feet touched the cobblestones. He fell forward, hearing bottles breaking inside the wooden box, and feeling splinters embedding themselves in his hands.

"Oaf!" Claxton yelled, yanking him up by his collar and spinning him around. "You just *bought* some broken bottles of wine!"

"It's not my fault. You kicked me."

Claxton slapped John's face hard with his huge open hand. John's head rocked back sharply, the taste of salty blood in his mouth. Then Claxton's massive face was nose to nose with his own. "Don't you *ever* back-talk me again. Do we understand each other?"

Fear sunk icy tendrils into John's gut as the mate raised his meaty hand again. "Yes, sir," John whispered.

"Now pick up that box and take it over next to the pile on the levee. I'll have the buyer open it and see how many bottles are broken. Artemus Primm'll take the breakage out of your pay." Claxton glowered with impatience. "Move it, boy!"

John hoisted the crate and did as he was told. Trip after trip, box after box, he carried wine boxes to the stack on the levee. By hurrying, he could keep up with the other deck hands. Mostly, he worked next to Peterson, who labored smoothly and methodically, humming to himself as he lifted and carried.

After thirty minutes, John's back was aching, his arms were dead, his hands clamored for the removal of the splinters, and his ears were ringing. He couldn't keep from flicking his tongue over the ragged flesh on the inside of his cheek, where Claxton's blow had caused his teeth to cut soft tissue.

The last ray of sunlight evaporated from the sky as they worked. The levee around the *Lucky Molly* was soon lit by torchlight; the sweat of the deck hands glistened in the flickering light. At one point, Artemus Primm returned briefly and spoke with Horace Claxton, pointing to a stack of furs. John tried unsuccessfully to catch Primm's eye before the clerk returned to town. John eagerly anticipated O'Malley's return. He'd had his fill of working for Claxton.

After the wine was unloaded, Claxton ordered the deck hands to carry the bales of fur pelts onto the *Lucky Molly*. They were large and awkward, each weighing fifty to seventy pounds. After several trips, John's arms were quivering. He began worrying that he would drop one.

As he was lifting a tightly roped bale, Peterson tapped his shoulder. "Ace, you're wore out. Why don't you rest a spell and let me and the others tote some loads without you? You're white as a ghost."

Claxton was approaching.

"No, I'd better keep going," muttered John.

"What's the matter here?"

"Nothing," said John.

"The boy's had enough for his first day, sir," said Peterson. "Look at his arms just hanging at his sides. He's dog tired."

Claxton wagged a finger in the deck hand's face. "Don't tell me how to work my men. You should've stayed on your pa's farm in Illinois. You don't know beans about steamboating. I've half a mind to knock your teeth out of your face so I don't have to listen to you jabber."

Peterson's face flushed. His hand moved to a knife worn in a sheath on his belt.

"Pull that knife and it'll be the last thing you ever do," Claxton said, eyes glittering.

Peterson returned the stare for thirty seconds, but then dropped his hand.

Claxton spat and glared at the half dozen deck hands nearby.

"So, Johnny-boy," he said, moving closer. "Peterson, farm hick turned boat master, thinks I should look at your arms. Let's see 'em."

Claxton roughly grabbed John's left arm and rolled up the sleeve of his shirt.

"Why, by thunder, his arms *are* different," exclaimed Claxton, examining John's bicep. "He's got women's arms, fellows!" Several deck hands snickered. Peterson's face was expressionless. John felt his neck and face reddening.

"Yes, sir," Claxton said, kneading John's slender arm. "This ain't a man we got helping us today. It's a filly." Claxton gestured toward some bales of furs piled nearby. "Have a seat. Let the men do the rest of the work. You just take a rest."

"No, sir. I can keep going."

"I said rest!" Claxton grabbed him by the shoulders and shoved him onto a bale of furs.

Tears of humiliation burned his eyes, but he stayed where he landed, watching silently as the deck hands loaded the rest of the furs. Many laughed as they worked. He suspected he was the butt of more than one joke. The muscles in his back were tightening. His blistered hands stung. He knew he'd be sore for days from the unaccustomed heavy lifting.

Claxton sauntered toward him. John stood.

"I didn't tell you to get up, did I, Johnny-boy?"

"No." John sat back down.

The big mate stood directly over him, yanking him to his feet. "Didn't hear you say 'sir'."

"No, sir," said John, averting his eyes.

"Johnny-boy," spit Claxton, leaning closer. "I'll bet you're just itching to tell Captain O'Malley what mean old Horace J. Claxton did to you today in front of all the deck hands."

John felt his face coloring. In addition to Claxton's other endearing traits, he was apparently a mind reader. Seemingly from nowhere, Claxton produced a slender knife and pressed it inches from John's pounding heart.

"I carry this little jewel in my boot. Not that I need it. I can break a man's neck with my bare hands." Claxton's blue eyes gleamed with pleasure. "If you ever complain about me to Captain O'Malley, I'll get you. I'll hunt you down and cut you up like a holiday turkey. That's a promise!" Abruptly, the knife disappeared into Claxton's boot, and the big mate swaggered up the ramp to the steamboat.

John was still sitting on the bale of furs an hour later when Artemus Primm and Captain O'Malley returned to the *Lucky Molly*. Claxton and the deck hands had finished loading the steamboat and had charged off to find rowdy enjoyment in the saloons and brothels of St. Louis, leaving two crew members to watch the boat.

"Well, John," boomed O'Malley's cheerful voice. "How did your first stint as a deck hand go?"

"Could have been worse." John remembered the sharp point of Claxton's knife.

"Good. I want you to keep loading and unloading the boat with the deck hands for the next few months. Got to build up those muscles of yours."

John's stomach sunk.

"This is our room," announced Artemus Primm as they entered a small cabin on the hurricane deck. Eight feet square, its sparse furniture consisted of two narrow beds separated by two tiny wooden dressers and a desk. Using a wooden match, Artemus Primm lit the candles in the sconces on the wall, illuminating the room with a flickering yellow light. "We officers don't live in luxury, but it's comfortable enough."

John removed his pocket-sized *Gulliver's Travels* from his breast pocket and tossed it onto the desk.

"What's that?" Artemus Primm asked.

"Swift's *Gulliver's Travels*. I started reading it when my father and I left Virginia."

Primm picked up the book and examined it. "Well, I don't much care for fiction, but the size of the book suits me."

John wanted to smile, but couldn't.

"Do you read much?" Primm asked.

"I have practically nothing but books in my suitcase," John answered. "Dickens, Shakespeare, Scott, DeFoe, Cooper, Fielding. I recently finished Cervantes' *Don Quixote*. That took awhile."

"Well, you're undoubtedly the only person on this boat who's read Cervantes. Personally, I prefer history to fiction. Have you read Brackenridge or the *Journals of Lewis and Clark?*"

"No."

"You might start with this one," Primm suggested, lifting a large book from his bottom dresser drawer. "The *Journals of Lewis and Clark*. I guarantee you'll like it. They even mention Cape Girardeau."

"Thanks." John placed the book next to him as he lay down on his bed. His back and arms throbbed. He thought of the humiliation he'd suffered at the hands of Horace Claxton, and he felt his cheeks reddening. He glanced at Artemus Primm, who sat cross-legged on his bed, thumbing through a large stack of newspapers he'd carried into the room with him.

Primm saw him staring. "I always pick up several newspapers at every stop," Primm explained. "After I read them, I drop them off at newspaper offices elsewhere along the river. These frontier editors just delight in plagiarizing each other."

John didn't respond.

"Where do the deck hands sleep?" John eventually asked, thinking suddenly of Peterson.

"Down on the deck, on and around the cargo."

Primm lowered the newspaper.

"They eat down there, too. You won't see them at our supper table in the dining saloon. After we officers and first-class passengers eat our magnificent meals off snowy white tablecloths and glistening silverware, the leftovers are slopped into three big tubs and carried down to the lower deck. One is filled with leftover meat. Another with bread and cake. The third gets all the pudding and custard. Do you remember hearing the shout, 'Grub pile!'?"

John nodded.

"That was the summons for the deck hands and stokers to come get their meal, which, by the way, probably tastes every bit as good as ours even though they eat it with their fingers."

John was silent as he examined the various blisters and scratches on his hands.

Artemus Primm studied him. "Something bothering you, John?"

"No," he lied, remembering the way Claxton had embarrassed him. Would Austin Carmichael have quivered fearfully in front of Horace Claxton? John knew better. His father was undiluted courage from the top of his handsome head to the toe of his polished boot. He bitterly wished he were still alive. Why did he have to die? Why did he have to leave him so alone? He felt tears arriving unsummoned and desperately tried to fight them off.

"Did Claxton give you trouble today?"

He heard the question but didn't answer. He stared at the wall of the cabin through a blur of wetness. He was determined not to cry. He'd promised himself after his father's death that he would never cry again.

"Yeah, I imagine he did," continued Artemus Primm, answering his own question. "Claxton acted like a jackass, probably." Artemus Primm rolled off his bed and busied himself putting things away. "Horace Claxton is a malicious bully," Primm muttered. "He enjoys hurting other people. Back when I was brand new on the boat, just a Second Clerk . . . "

Primm paused. John was uncertain for a moment whether the little clerk would continue.

" . . . I made the mistake of going into a saloon in New Orleans where Claxton was carousing while we were off duty. He convinced everyone how much fun it would be to have a midget tossing contest." Primm's lower lip quivered. "Well, you can imagine the humiliating night I endured, not to mention the bruises."

John frowned, "I don't understand why O'Malley doesn't fire Claxton. Why does he keep him around?"

Primm plucked a red handkerchief from a drawer and waved it. "It goes back to O'Malley's younger days. Before steamboats, you had the 'Golden Age of Flatboating' on the Western rivers from about 1795 to 1820. In those days the Mississippi and Ohio rivers were alive with boats of all kinds transporting brawny pioneers to the frontier. Mike Fink was the epitome of the roistering and rowdy keelboat captain, and O'Malley was part of his crew. Fact is, O'Malley wore the red scarf for a couple of years."

"The red scarf?"

"That's right. Keelboatmen had to be strong and powerful. Boats were often dismantled for the wood after they made it downriver, but at times the crew had to pull boats upriver by brute strength. To a man, they loved a good fight. At night they'd tie up on shore and engage in wrestling matches. The best fighter on each boat earned the privilege of wearing the red scarf. When different boats would stop together, the man wearing the red scarf would fight his counterpart on the other boat."

"Sounds like a good way to get hurt."

"Exactly. But that explains why O'Malley admires the tough streak in

Claxton. O'Malley's respect for Claxton's fearlessness blinds him to the pure meanness of the man."

"Someone should tell him. Did you ever report him for the, uh, midget-tossing contest?"

"Not me. My job's managing the facts and figures of this boat, not interfering with the discipline of the deck hands or the judgment of the mate. You should do what I do, John. Steer clear of Horace Claxton as much as possible. The man's no good."

"I can take care of myself." John's voice sounded unpersuasive, even to his own ears.

Artemus Primm shook his round head. "O'Malley was practically raised by Mike Fink. He worshipped him. Claxton reminds O'Malley of Fink. Difference is, Fink had a good side. Claxton's totally mean. There'll be trouble with Claxton, mark my words."

Horace Claxton paused in front of the door to the Pink Lady. The Pink Lady was one of the nest of brothels clustered behind the boarding houses known as "Battle Row" at the north end of the mile-long levee in St. Louis. He'd never been to this particular establishment, but he'd heard it was not as dingy as most. As he stood on the steps in front of the brothel, he thought again of John Carmichael. It just wasn't fair that the sixteen year old boy was getting special treatment from Captain O'Malley just because the whelp's low-life-gambler father had been a friend. Claxton entwined his massive fingers and popped the knuckles of his large hands. It wasn't fair.

Claxton had been with O'Malley longer than any of the others. He'd been his mate ever since O'Malley's wife was killed when the pretty little daughter, Rosalind, was only eight years old. First on the *City of Cape* and then on the *Lucky Molly*, Claxton had been O'Malley's trusted mate. Seven long years he'd worked his tail off for O'Malley, lying awake at nights dreaming of the time he'd marry Rosalind and become O'Malley's son-in-law. Then, heir to the throne, he'd become a steamboat captain himself some day.

He hadn't liked the way John Carmichael had suddenly wormed his way into O'Malley's life, nor the way O'Malley's daughter had been chattering with the boy. Feeling bile rising in his stomach, Horace Claxton spat on the wooden porch and decided to ponder the John Carmichael problem later. He opened the door and entered the brothel.

The next thirty minutes brought unexpected humiliation to Horace Claxton. He found himself unable to banish thoughts of John Carmichael from his mind. Remembering the way the boy had weaseled himself into O'Malley's life made Claxton's blood boil. Such thoughts proved unconducive to successful fornication, thus bringing his trip to the brothel to an inglorious conclusion.

Chapter 7

The *Lucky Molly* was making good time to New Orleans. John was in the engine room, where oppressive heat and humidity made beads of sweat speckle his forehead. The pounding of the *Lucky Molly's* engines assaulted his ears. The vibrating floor rattled his teeth. "You don't have the most comfortable seat on the boat," he told Pete Carnahan, shouting to be heard over the cacophony of thrusting metal rods.

The wiry engineer wiped his chin stubble with a large white handkerchief. "Naw. Being an engineer ain't the most glamorous job in the world. You might end up wishing Captain O'Malley hadn't assigned you to work with me today." Carnahan grinned and pointed upward. "Other officers get more glory. Pilots and captains are the most visible, but even the mates and clerks have little boys at landings dreaming of having their jobs." The engineer pointed at his chest. "Engineers? We work our tails off in sweltering hell holes and nobody ever hears of us unless a boiler explodes. Then they say we screwed up. And when the boiler explodes, who's standing right next to it? Engineer, that's who. His name will top the casualty list every time."

"Why do it, then, if you don't like it?"

"Hell's fire, boy! Didn't say I didn't like it. I plumb enjoy tending a steamboat engine. A steamboat's nothing more than a magnificent engine plopped onto a raft, with thousands of dollars worth of fancy trim added to it. The steamboat engine is the most powerful invention man ever created, and I'm proud to run it!"

A bell rang loudly in the engine room.

"What's that?"

"Pilot's signaling me to put her in reverse. Must be making a sharp turn. Stand back."

The muscular engineer lifted a large metal lever and raised it two feet, sliding it into a new position. Grunting, he stepped back and wiped his brow. John felt the steamboat turning.

"What did you just do?"

"That lever's the cam-rod. Anytime the pilot wants one of the paddle wheels put in reverse, he signals the engineer on that particular side of the boat. We do it by hand. The cam-rod weighs about fifty pounds. Not too bad when you just do it once in a while, but sometimes on tricky parts of the river, them bells will be ringing like flies on dung."

The bell rang again.

"Time to put her back in forward. Go ahead, John. Do it."

John gripped the lever firmly and moved it to the lower position.

"Nicely done, boy. You're learning fast. Now, the main job down here is to keep an eye and an ear on the boilers. The deck hands keep filling the furnaces up front with wood as long as we tell them to. The fire and heat come back through these pipes under the boilers and warm the water. The bottom of these boilers is filled with tons of water. Top filled with steam. Steam's what powers the engines."

"Main thing," added Carnahan, wiping his brow, "is to be sure there's still plenty of water in the bottom of the boilers so the steam pressure don't get so high the boilers explode."

"How do you do that?"

"Mainly by ear. Listen to the sound of the boiler now. That's how it should sound. Keep it like that."

Carnahan pointed to several small plugs midway up the cylindrical sides of the boilers. "Those are called the gauge or try cocks. Made out of a softer metal. Two to three inches below the normal water line. If the water evaporates so it's below these rascals they'll melt because the steam is hotter than the water. It's an emergency measure. They'll melt and let the steam out, hopefully preventing an explosion. But watch 'em, John. If you're standing next to one of those devils when it melts out, you'll get yourself boiled alive." Carnahan pointed to a valve at the top of the boiler. "That poppet valve up top's the best kind of safety valve. If the pressure builds up too high in the boiler, the top of the valve will start popping up, letting off pressure." Carnahan grinned. "Sometimes in races, John, an engineer will put a weight on top of that valve so it can't open. Pressure builds up to terrific force. You go a lot faster, too, unless you blow up."

Carnahan took off his shirt, revealing a hairy chest with wiry hardened muscles. A shiny maroon scar covered his left shoulder. "Feel free to take your shirt off, son. Gets powerful hot in here."

John removed his shirt. His own chest was hairless except for a few tiny wisps of fuzz over his breastbone. Both men glistened with sweat. Carnahan saw him glance at the scar. "Happened once when I was standing too close to escaping steam. Hurt like hell, too. Better believe it."

The engineer dipped his handkerchief into the water bucket and wiped his face with the wet cloth. "Yep, Captain O'Malley's one fine steamboatman, most honest man on the river. He'll pick up a farmer's crop, give him a receipt, take it to New Orleans, sell it, and bring the money back to the farmer in a couple weeks. His word's good as gold."

"What did you do before you were an engineer on a steamboat?"

"Me?" he said, pondering the question. Carnahan leaned back on the bench and crossed his legs. "I was a soldier. Fought in Mexico. Don't miss them days none, though." Carnahan regarded John thoughtfully. "Tell you what, son. Probably ain't none of my business, but this here riverboat veteran would like to give you a piece of friendly advice." He reached under the bench and pulled out a bottle of whiskey. "I noticed the way Claxton's been treating you. Just plain bullying. Keep being polite to him, though. He's a mean man, plenty tough. Used to give me some guff, couple years ago, until I cut a button off his shirt with a knife. Ain't bothered me since." He offered the bottle. "Want a swig?"

"No, thanks."

Carnahan tilted his head back and took a gulp. He replaced the cap and slid the bottle under the bench with a clink. "No, John. You don't want to mess with Claxton. He's too much bigger than you. Meaner, too. Seen him beat deck hands unconscious. Couple disappeared completely. Wouldn't surprise me none to hear he tossed 'em overboard."

"The bad thing," John admitted, "is that Captain O'Malley wants me to keep helping the deck hands load and unload during the next few months. I'll be around Claxton every day."

"Hell, toting cargo's the best thing could happen to you. Nothing will build up a man quicker. I was you, I'd be lifting and carrying more crates, boxes, and barrels than anyone else. Once you've gotten stronger and appear to be a tough customer yourself, Claxton'll probably leave you be."

Five days after leaving St. Louis, the *Lucky Molly* arrived at the Gravier Street Wharf in New Orleans in late afternoon. New Orleans in 1851 was a city of over 116,000 free people, plus an additional 20,000 slaves. A swarming amalgamation of Americans, Spanish, Irish, French, Germans, English, and Italians, New Orleans seethed with life. With extensive western railroads still half a decade away, most manufactured goods brought to Americans who lived along the Mississippi and westward were shipped from the East Coast to New Orleans, then brought up the river. Conversely, tons upon tons of cotton, furs, and other raw materials were carried by riverboat down the Mississippi to New Orleans, where they were shipped to the rest of the world. New Orleans in the

1850s boasted a prominence in commerce never equaled by the city before or since.

As the deck hands roped the *Lucky Molly* to the landing, John stared with awe at the pageantry around him. More than 200 steamboats were docked at the New Orleans wharf, several miles long. The "Steamboat Dock" was the area of the levee between Toulouse and Julia streets. The paddle-wheelers tied up not only side by side, but in some places row upon row. Interspersed with the steamboats, there were ocean ships, flatboats, small schooners, sloops, skiffs, pirogues, and barges. People of all shapes and sizes thronged the landing like bees on a hive. The noise level from the pounding steamboat engines and shouting voices was so loud, John felt he could touch the sound with his fingers.

"Looks like the *Bostona* has a fine load of cotton," said Artemus Primm, who stood on a hogshead next to John at the top of the gangplank. "Must have 2,000 bales." The deck level of the *Bostona* was covered with cotton bales stacked fifteen feet high.

O'Malley stood on a nearby street, shaking hands with a tall bearded man who also wore a captain's uniform.

"Who's that fellow talking to Captain O'Malley?" asked John.

"John W. Cannon," Primm answered. "He's one of the best steamboat captains on the river. That's his steamboat, the *Louisiana*, tied up on the other side of the *Bostona*. And that's the *Storm* on the other side of the *Louisiana*."

Each of the three impressive steamboats docked near the *Lucky Molly* was a flurry of activity. The *Louisiana* was finishing loading, and the *Storm* and the *Bostona* were in the midst of unloading.

"Come on, John. Let's go meet him."

O'Malley's face brightened as they approached.

"Captain Cannon," he said, "do you remember Austin Carmichael?"

"Certainly. Only honest gambler I ever met."

"This is his son, John Carmichael. John, this is John W. Cannon, finest steamboat captain on the river, one of the best pilots, too."

"Pleased to meet you, sir."

Cannon's physical presence was intimidating. The man was no bigger than O'Malley, but seemed to be. His strong face was framed by a thick beard. His wide nose, tan face, and bright eyes produced a tough weathered look.

"How's your father, boy?" asked Captain Cannon.

A rekindled hurt seared John's heart, yet at the same time he was surprised by the realization that he had not thought of his father all day.

"He was killed in a duel, sir."

Cannon's eyes softened. "Sorry to hear that. He was a good man."

"How's John working out helping you with the books, Artemus?" asked O'Malley, resting his mutilated hand on John's shoulder.

"His mind's amazing, Captain. He can calculate numbers faster than anyone I've ever seen. Must be all that Shakespeare he's read."

O'Malley patted John on the back, then turned his attention to Captain Cannon. "Where are you and the *Louisiana* off to today?"

"St. Louis," answered Cannon. "Leaving in a couple of minutes. Got a full load of cargo and more than 200 passengers."

O'Malley smiled. "The *Lucky Molly* will be leaving tomorrow morning. You'll have a twelve-hour head start, but I figure we'll pass you somewhere around Memphis. If your passengers are in a hurry, they can switch over to my boat."

Cannon guffawed. "That rat trap? Not likely, Patrick. You need to get yourself a real boat and quit floating 'round on that glorified wharfboat."

"The *Lucky Molly's* a fine boat," John interjected defensively, worried about Patrick O'Malley's pride.

O'Malley, however, was grinning. "Thanks, John. That's loyal of you." He winked at Cannon. "Mark my words, Cannon. I'll have a steamboat someday that even you will covet."

John noticed Horace Claxton supervising a group of deck hands removing cotton bales from the *Lucky Molly*. He took a deep breath, "May I be excused Captain O'Malley? I need to help carry."

O'Malley raised his eyebrows. "You've been helping Artemus with the bookwork this afternoon, John. You don't have to do legwork today."

"I want to, sir."

O'Malley shrugged, "Very well, lad. Go to it."

When John joined the deck hands carrying cotton bales, Claxton scowled at him, but assigned him a spot behind Peterson.

Each man carried at least one eighty-pound cotton bale, walking single-file down the ramp to the wharf. Most slung the bales over their shoulders. Some carried one over each shoulder. John lugged his single bale in front of him, twine digging into his fingers. After several trips, his hands were bleeding, but he kept pace with the other deck hands.

After John's third trip down the plank, a sudden roaring blast of noise and heat knocked him to the cobblestone levee. The deafening concussion rocked the ground and shook houses for many square blocks.

John scrambled to his feet and stared with horror at the source of the explosion—Cannon's steamboat *Louisiana*. Seconds earlier it had been abuzz with life and activity. Now it was an inferno of fire and smoke. Every boiler on Cannon's splendid steamboat had exploded, hurling metal, wood, and mangled body parts onto the wharf, onto the tops of steamboats and buildings, and into the river. The earsplitting force of the blast drove the demolished remains of the *Louisiana* into the channel dozens of yards from the shore. The upper works completely disintegrated. The majestic chimneys simply vanished. The boat's carcass was burning in the river, and screams of victims filled the air.

The *Lucky Molly* had not suffered severe structural damage, but disfigured human bodies and hunks of wood and metal littered the decks of the Cape

Girardeau steamboat. Human bodies were strewn upon streets and buildings as far as 200 yards from the water.

The *Storm* and the *Bostona*, the two steamboats moored on each side of the *Louisiana*, were not as fortunate as O'Malley's boat. The chimneys of both were shattered, the upper works destroyed. The *Storm* had been knocked away from its moorings and was floating aimlessly in the channel.

John's skin crawled as he heard an inhuman scream behind him. Spinning, he saw a mule, sliced and gutted by a ragged shard of boiler, lying tangled in its dray harness, braying pitifully as its blood steamed amid the cool air. Its master, still seated on the dray behind the mule, reins dangling from limp fingers, was headless, his slumped torso gushing blood.

John fell to his knees and retched.

Peterson ran toward the *Lucky Molly*.

"Drop the yawl!" O'Malley's strong voice called from the deck of the *Lucky Molly*.

John staggered to his feet. O'Malley and Artemus Primm were at the stern of the *Lucky Molly*, lowering the yawl into the river. John stumbled toward the *Lucky Molly*, stepping carefully to avoid severed body parts. He froze when he felt something clutch his leg. A naked man sprawled at John's feet, fingers digging into John's calf. The man's dark hair was wet and plastered to his head. Face and neck scalded bright red from searing steam, his eyes were clinched shut, mouth open, breath rattling in his throat. He gripped John's calf with terrible intensity, fingernails breaking John's skin through the pants leg.

John gasped involuntarily and pulled backward, dragging the stricken man along the cobblestones, leaving oozing pieces of flesh stuck to the stones. John glimpsed bone under the flayed skin of the man's shoulder. He closed his eyes and felt himself falling onto the street and into blackness, where he lay quietly for several seconds, fading in and out of consciousness. The death grip on his leg relaxed, and John opened his eyes. The man was dead. He jerked his leg from the lifeless fingers. Stumbling to his feet, he ran for the *Lucky Molly*, carefully avoiding the bodies of the dead and dying.

The people of New Orleans thronged to the Gravier Street Wharf, yelling and screaming. The cries of the living mingled with those of the dying as survivors searched frantically for friends and relatives.

John reached the ramp of the *Lucky Molly* and hurried onto the steamboat. A hole in the side of the pilot house marked the spot where a human body had blown through the thin wooden wall like a huge cannonball. Bare feet hung motionlessly from the gaping hole. Deck hands on the *Lucky Molly* were doing what little they could to ease the suffering of the few living souls who had landed on the decks of O'Malley's boat. Most were beyond help.

"Oh, Lord," gasped Peterson.

John spun toward the sound of the familiar voice. Peterson was kneeling next to a victim. He'd tried to remove the man's shirt, but hunks of skin had come off with it. Peterson held the cloth and flesh in his hands, tears in his eyes.

John rushed to the stern of the *Lucky Molly*, but arrived too late to go with O'Malley and Primm, who were already rowing the yawl out into the river, trying to save victims still alive.

"Help!" The cry came from the muddy water to John's left. A man flailed helplessly in the Mississippi twenty yards from the stern of the *Lucky Molly*. His head bobbed out of the water and then under, then out again. His white arm stretched toward John, fingers clawing at the air.

"I can't swim!" John shouted, voice cracking. He loathed the helplessness in his own voice. John's eyes scanned the deck of the *Lucky Molly* and fastened upon the stacks of cotton bales not yet unloaded. He grabbed the closest bale and heaved it toward the man. It landed in the water near him. The man thrashed frantically, finally catching a corner. The current carried him away from the *Lucky Molly*, but John saw with relief the man's firm grip on the floating cotton.

Inspired by his success, he began throwing other cotton bales into the river. Time froze in place as he gripped bale after bale, dragging them to the edge of the boat and hurling them as far into the river as he could manage. The river accepted each offering with a slight gulp, demanding more and more ransom for human life. He worked mindlessly, brain numbed by terror and fatigue. Then he was jarred into attentiveness by the harsh voice of Horace Claxton behind him.

"What the blue flaming hell are you doing?"

John stopped, the twine of a cotton bale gripped in his bloody fingers. Claxton stood nearby, glaring at him. O'Malley's yawl was out of sight, evidently on the other side of the sinking *Louisiana*. On the wharf, everything was a mass of confusion, people running, crying, kneeling, and screaming. They were alone at the stern of the boat.

"Maybe you didn't hear me, boy. I asked what the thunder you think you're doing!"

John stepped back as Claxton neared him. "Throwing cotton bales into the water to help the people who can't swim. I'd go out to help them, but I can't swim." He nodded toward the man on the cotton bale hundreds of yards downstream. "Already saved one life, I think."

"Fine and dandy. One problem, though. This ain't your cotton you're tossing overboard." Claxton pointed at the bale in John's hands. "Put that down right now."

"Don't be ridiculous! People are dying. It doesn't matter who owns the cotton."

"Put it down *now*," Claxton repeated, moving menacingly toward him.

John turned quickly and heaved the cotton bale into the river. It landed with a splash. Claxton gripped him by the shoulders. The raspy voice hissed in his ear, "Sorry to hear you can't swim."

Suddenly John was airborne over the muddy waters of the Mississippi River. The last thing he saw before hitting the water was a ruthless smile on Claxton's face.

Under brown water, John's eyes bugged open, cold water pouring into his clothing and wet material gripping his skin and pulling him down, down, down into the blackness below. He'd never been in water over his head. Testicles tightening, terror exhorting him to scream out, he instinctively held his breath, rolling slowly with the current, sounds above him muffled, as the powerful river carried him away from the *Lucky Molly*, sucking him southward, hurrying him relentlessly to the stillness of death.

He forced himself to think, allowing his body to relax and glide with the flow of the current for several long agonizing seconds. Beneath him was cold blackness, icy death. Above, light filtered through muddy water, a dark rectangle floating in the center of the light. A cotton bale!

He thrashed his arms and kicked his legs. With surprise and hope, he rose toward the bale. His fingers gripped wet cotton and he pulled himself upward, tearing into the bale like a cat on a burlap bag as he fought out from underneath it and pulled at its side until his head emerged from the water. Gasping and choking, he sucked deep breaths of air, fingers clutching deep into soggy cotton. John pressed the side of his face against the cotton bale and held on tightly. Later, he was only vaguely aware of men in a yawl helping him to shore. Once on the wharf, he lay in a haze on the cobblestones, fighting for air and shivering uncontrollably.

A week later the *Lucky Molly* was heading upriver, nearing Cape Girardeau on a stretch of river between Cairo and St. Louis called "The Graveyard." The winding section of the river had earned its name because of its accumulation of dozens of sunken boat skeletons. John was in the pilothouse with Captain O'Malley and Abner Conrad, watching and listening as the experienced pilot guided the steamboat through the obstacle course of wrecked dreams.

"See that, John?" Conrad said, pointing with the stump of his right arm toward an object the size of a dog's head protruding from muddy water twenty yards away. "That's a snag, son. A steamboat's worst enemy. Three-fifths of all steamboat disasters are caused by hitting snags."

The word "disaster" summoned memories of the *Louisiana*. John couldn't forget its fiery destruction. The latest count estimated more than 150 people killed.

"What exactly is a snag? A tree growing underwater?"

"You're half right," said the pilot, firing a wet glob into his spittoon. "The Mississippi River eats its bank away. Year by year the river widens in places, its channel changing. The banks actually crumble and fall into the river, acres at a time. Trees along the bank are gradually pulled into the river, too. That's how a snag is born." Abner Conrad turned the wheel of the *Lucky Molly*, gliding the steamboat several feet toward the object in the water. John could see the dark tip of soaked wood protruding from the river. "These trees ain't just twigs, John. Some of 'em are 50 to 70 feet long, weighing as much as 75 tons." Conrad pointed to the snag they were passing. "That one right there's probably 70 feet long."

"If the channel is constantly changing, how do you possibly remember it?"

"Learning the river is a constant process of memorizing the names, shapes and locations of innumerable reefs, shoals, islands, points, and bends. It's never-ending study, John. Never-ending study." Conrad pulled on a rope to sound a bell in the engine room. Within moments the *Lucky Molly* came to a full stop in the middle of the river. "Can you tell how deep this water is, John?"

John looked at the flowing brown surface of the water, "No."

"Well, at this point I can't either. Sometimes we've got to do what I'm fixing to do right now. Our boat rides eight feet deep in the water. If we venture into water more shallow than that, we'll run aground or tear a hole in her bottom. This channel looks like it might have shifted since the last time I came through." He squinted as he peered at the murky fast-moving water, "Watch our leadsman at the bow of the boat. He's dropping a rope with a leaden weight, checking the depth. He'll tell us if it's safe to go forward."

The leadsman pulled up his rope and called back to the pilothouse. "Mark twain!"

"What's that mean?" John asked.

"Twain means two. In other words, the water is two fathoms deep. A fathom is six feet. So the water directly ahead is twelve feet deep. Plenty safe for any steamboat. We pilots are always glad to hear those two pretty little words."

Minutes later the *Lucky Molly* safely crossed through "The Graveyard" without further scares.

Later in the day, O'Malley's steamboat rounded a sharp bend a mile below Cape Girardeau. A large crowd was gathering on the levee, drawn to the riverfront by the terrific noise of the steamboat engines, and by the roustabouts on the wharf who delighted in being the first to sight the approaching smoke and greet it with the call, "S-t-e-a-mboat a-coming!"

From the hurricane deck, John saw Lindy waving at him, her face radiant with a smile. Something deep inside him glowed with satisfaction.

After the *Lucky Molly* tied up near Tyler Fitch's boat, the *Andrew Jackson*, John hurried down the gangplank, one of the first to reach the levee. She was waiting for him, hopping with excitement. She grabbed one of his hands and held it in both of her own.

"I've been thinking of you every night, just like I promised. Been mentioning you in my prayers." She smiled and lowered her eyes. "Have you been thinking of me?"

Surprised by the question, he answered it in his head. Although he'd forgotten about her during the long hard workdays on the boat, he'd often remembered those brown eyes while lying in his bunk at night. "I've thought of you, yes."

"Good," she said with finality. She pointed a finger and waved it at him teasingly. "You steamboatmen can't go off on the river and forget all about your women."

He blushed at her choice of words.

Her gaze darted over his shoulder and fastened upon her father descending the ramp. "Papa!" she cried, running to him.

"My little Rose!" O'Malley answered, sweeping off his cap and opening his arms like wings, embracing her in an affectionate hug, his own reddish hair contrasting with her dark curls.

John smiled as he listened to Lindy gush about how much she missed her father. O'Malley grinned widely, large teeth flashing white under his ivory mustache. Lindy's blue dress accented her tiny waistline. John found himself looking at her figure, his eyes lingering an extra second on the cloth covering the swell of her breasts. The one time he'd seen them, he recalled, he hadn't been inclined to look. But now? Embarrassed, he looked away.

His gaze rested unexpectedly on Horace Claxton, who stood near the ramp of the *Lucky Molly*. Claxton was also leering at Lindy's body, his fat pink tongue flicking over his lips as he eyed her.

"Papa," Lindy was saying earnestly, "Aunt Maude and I were just last night discussing the possibility that I might have a coming-out party. Esther Giboney had one last week when she turned sixteen. I want one, too. I'll be turning sixteen next spring, you know. Please, Papa? We could have such a grand party on the steamboat!"

Maude O'Malley, in an austere dress, stood in the background behind Lindy. As O'Malley listened to his daughter he kissed his twin sister fondly on a downy cheek. "Your daughter's conversation with me about a coming-out party," Maude said, "was largely one-sided. I told her it would be completely up to you."

"I'm sure little Rose talked enough for both of you," laughed the Captain, green eyes sparkling.

"Please, Papa?"

"We'll see," he said, mussing her hair.

A hammering noise caught their attention.

"What the blue blazes is Fitch doing?" O'Malley said as he peered toward Fitch's boat shop and office. The *Andrew Jackson* was moored on the river in front of Fitch's store. Fitch was erecting a large sign between two tall posts where he docked his steamboat. It was white, with bold red lettering: *FASTEST STEAMBOAT OF CAPE GIRARDEAU*.

"Hell's bells!" muttered O'Malley.

"Is that legal?" asked John. "How can he do that?"

"Few months ago, Fitch tried to pass me just north of Memphis, and we had a little race to Cape. At the end he put lard in his fires and barely won. Declared his boat the fastest and said he'd put up a sign. By golly, he's doing it." O'Malley shook his head. "You'd think he beat me by sixty days instead of sixty seconds."

Fitch hopped down from the crate and made his way toward them.

"Wonderful," O'Malley said. "Here he comes."

"Papa, your boat's just as good as his. Don't let him upset you."

Fitch, white suit and red bow tie immaculate, shook hands with O'Malley. "Nice to see you, Captain O'Malley."

John's eyes were drawn as if by magnetic force to Fitch's left ear. The lower half was completely gone. The part remaining was rimmed by thick dark scabs.

"How do you like my sign?" Fitch asked.

"Very well-painted," said O'Malley. "When I beat you in our next race, do I get it?"

"By all means! But don't go digging your post holes just yet. Been to Cincinnati recently. Just completed arrangements to have another steamboat built, even bigger and faster. I'll call her the *Andrew Jackson II*. If you can't beat the boat I've got now, you'll never touch the *Andrew Jackson II*."

"Maybe I'll start carrying lard as fuel." O'Malley smiled slightly.

Tyler Fitch was unperturbed. "Some captains find an occasional bit of lard helps a racing boat go faster," Fitch said. "Some captains weigh down safety valves to give their boat a last minute surge of steam. Wouldn't know about those things, myself, being my boat's so fast no tricks are necessary." Tyler Fitch turned to John and nodded politely. "You must be John Carmichael."

"I am."

Fitch bowed slightly from the waist. "I want you to know how deeply sorry I am for what happened to your father. In fact, I've been carrying something for you ever since I found out your father left an orphan."

Fitch reached into the pocket of his white jacket and produced a leather wallet. "This wallet contains several thousand dollars, the money your father and I were quarreling over. I want you to have it."

John's hands stayed at his sides. "I don't want the money. I want my father back. Can't give me that, can you?"

Fitch lowered his eyes. "No, I can't. Wish I could. I'm truly sorry." He still held out the wallet. "Take the money."

"No."

O'Malley reached for it. "I'll take it, John, and hold it in trust for you. It was, after all, your father's money."

"No!" John said sharply, pulling O'Malley's hand away from the wallet. "I won't *ever* take money from this murderer."

Fitch stared at him silently for several long moments, then shrugged. "Murderer? If you weren't so young. . . . Oh, well. If you change your mind, come see me." Fitch faced O'Malley again. "Captain, I'm afraid you've been negligent."

O'Malley drew up to full height. "In what way, Fitch?"

"I've been lingering here waiting for an introduction," Fitch said, his eyes sweeping up and down Lindy's figure, "and you've not allowed me to make the acquaintance of that lovely creature on your arm."

Lindy smiled at the compliment, eyes glittering.

O'Malley glanced at his daughter with surprise. The big captain seemed to see his child as a woman for the first time.

"This lovely creature, as you describe her, is my daughter, Rosalind O'Malley."

"Pleasure to meet you, Miss O'Malley," Fitch said, bowing gracefully. "Hope I'm fortunate enough to see you again."

"Cape's not a big town," she said, coloring. "I'm sure we'll run into each other now and then."

"I eagerly look forward to it." He made polite farewells and returned to his steamboat.

"Look at the crowd of passengers on his boat," muttered O'Malley. "Whatever else you want to say about him, Tyler Fitch is quite a businessman."

John glanced at Lindy. She was watching Tyler Fitch with interest, her fingers thoughtfully playing with the silver cross on her neck.

The *Lucky Molly* was tied up for the night at Cape Girardeau, and John accepted an invitation to spend the evening at Captain O'Malley's home. After a mouth-watering dinner of smoked ham, corn dodgers, peach cobbler, and buttermilk, Lindy entertained John, Aunt Maude, and Patrick O'Malley by playing the piano in the parlor. John was amazed and impressed by the beautiful sounds Lindy coaxed from the piano. From classics like Bach and Mozart to newer pieces by Chopin and Foster, her fingers flew over the keyboard with confidence and musicality. As she played, her trim body swayed with the music. She seemed to be summoning notes from the instrument by sheer willpower. The sound enveloped her, making her a part of that sound and it a part of her. John found himself gazing at her soft cheeks, her long neck, and her slim waist. When she finished playing, he was surprised to discover that an entire hour had passed.

The impromptu recital done, Captain O'Malley and Aunt Maude soon resurrected a heated discussion over the pros and cons of alcohol temperance. They removed themselves to the kitchen to dish up seconds of peach cobbler.

John, sitting on a chair near the piano bench, found himself so attracted to Lindy and so impressed by her that he was irreparably tongue-tied.

"Well, how did I do?" she finally asked.

"Beautiful," he said. "It was beautiful. You are beautiful."

Several moments passed as she sat expectantly on the bench and he sat stiffly on the chair, trying to think of something else to say. Eventually, Lindy rose from the piano bench and glided to him. Bending primly, she kissed him on the lips. His heart pounded in his chest as he tasted her mouth and felt her lips caressing his. She gently pulled away, her face full of happiness.

"I had the idea you wanted to kiss me," she said.

"I guess you were right."

Rising to his feet, he moved to her and kissed her again. Their kiss was long and sweet and wonderful. It lasted until the rattling of dishes in the hallway warned of the impending arrival of the peach cobbler.

Chapter 8

On a weekend in late November, O'Malley let Lindy accompany the *Lucky Molly* on a roundtrip from Cape Girardeau to Hannibal. "So what if I miss a couple of days of school," Lindy said to John. "You're so smart, I learn more from you than from that silly old school teacher."

John felt himself blushing. Lindy always made him feel good about himself. They sat alone on two wooden chairs on the hurricane deck as the *Lucky Molly* churned upriver toward Hannibal, 130 miles north of St. Louis. Normally John spent his off-duty hours reading or haunting the pilothouse trying to "learn the river" from Abner Conrad. With Lindy on board, though, most of his time off was spent with her. They had already read *Romeo and Juliet* together out of his dog-eared copy of the complete works of Shakespeare. Now they were dividing up the parts of *A Midsummer Night's Dream*.

"In fact," Lindy continued. "Papa says you're the smartest fellow he's ever met. He says he's never seen anyone learn all of the aspects of the steamboat business so quickly. He says you already know the inventory system better than Artemus Primm and that Abner Conrad brags that once he tells you something about a particular point on the river, you never forget it."

John glowed inside, but said nothing.

"I believe you've read more books than anyone I've ever met," Lindy added. "Have you ever thought of writing one?"

"Often," admitted John. He hesitated before adding, "My biggest dream has always been to publish a book and see my name in print as its author."

"Well, why don't you?"

"It's not quite that simple. It's not enough to be a good writer, to be able to string words together well. You need to have something important to say. To write well you need to have lived, to have experienced life. I'm only sixteen, after all."

"You'll be seventeen soon," she observed. "I suppose you'll be wanting to leave the *Lucky Molly* as soon as you've saved up enough money to go back East to college. Harvard or Yale or wherever you were planning to go."

"The University of Virginia," he corrected. "Founded by Thomas Jefferson, no less."

"Oh, pardon me! How could I have forgotten!"

He chuckled. "Actually, I have no intentions of going back East to college, much as I'd enjoy never seeing Horace Claxton's ugly face again."

"You don't?"

"No. Somehow during the past several weeks I've quit missing Virginia and the prospect of college. I guess this muddy river water has seeped into my veins. I love working with your father. I enjoy helping Artemus Primm with the business affairs of the steamboat. I am fascinated by Abner Conrad and his stories about piloting. I get a kick out of helping Pete Carnahan in the engine room. Believe it or not, I even enjoy loading and unloading the *Lucky Molly*, in spite of Claxton's continuing efforts to make my life miserable."

The *Lucky Molly* slowed to a stop on the Mississippi, holding its place in the water until the comforting call of the leadsman rose toward the pilothouse. "Mark twain!"

"Well, what about writing a book? When are you going to be old enough to get started? Mozart wrote his first piece of music when he was five. You won't be able to use the youth excuse forever!"

He laughed. "I guess I just don't feel I have anything special to say yet. I'm starting to lean away from fiction and toward history at this point. Artemus Primm has got me reading Brackenridge and Flint and Schoolcraft. What I'd like most now is to research and learn as much history as possible and then publish a history book."

"That's ambitious," she said. "But I have no doubt you'll succeed." The sun glistened off her brown hair, which was pulled back into a bun.

"What are *your* ambitions, Lindy?"

Her eyes twinkled. "Well, I simply won't rest until I'm able to play the difficult parts of Chopin's Nocturne in E Flat Major without tripping over my fingers." They both laughed. She put her hand on his. "I also plan to be married before too awfully long to a man who would be a good husband, who would love me and cherish me—perhaps an author or historian—and have lots of children."

John tried not to grin. "That's ambitious," he said. "But I have no doubt you'll succeed."

When the *Lucky Molly* reached Hannibal, John joined the deck hands unloading cargo. He noticed with pleasure that he could easily lift and carry boxes and crates that had seemed so heavy six weeks earlier. John had gained more than twenty pounds, all muscle. His shoulders were broader and his legs thicker. His arms were firmly muscled, twice the size as before. His blond hair was sun-bleached nearly white, his skin deeply tanned.

The Hannibal of 1851 had a population of 3,000. The mile-wide Mississippi was bounded by the towering Holliday's Hill on the north and by the steep bluff of Lover's Leap below. The wideness of the river and the dense forest on the Illinois shore opposite the town gave the river the deceptive appearance of a still and peaceful sea. The town boasted several three-story brick mercantile buildings, looming over little frame shops wedged between. The businesses included two hotels, three saloons, four general stores, two schools, two churches, two slaughterhouses, three sawmills, two planing mills, three blacksmith shops, a tannery, a hemp factory, a distillery, and a cigar factory. The slim, white steeple of the Presbyterian Church on North Fourth Street utilized a bell retrieved from the wreck of the steamboat *Chester*.

Amid the hustle and bustle of the unloading steamboat, Captain O'Malley and Lindy disappeared into one of the general stores. Artemus Primm was standing on a barrel making notations in his ledger book and giving directions regarding the placement of freight. Horace Claxton stood at the foot of the gangplank, supervising the roustabouts and deck hands doing the carrying.

As John descended the gangplank, a heavy box of tinware in his hands, he scanned the storefronts of Hannibal, trying to catch a glimpse of Lindy. At the bottom of the plank John's foot stubbed into something immoveable and he lurched sideways. As he fell, his momentum slammed him against the barrel on which Artemus Primm stood. The barrel toppled to its side, and the midget, arms waving and papers flying, was pitched headfirst to the hard cobblestone levee.

John quickly scrambled to Primm and knelt next to the *Lucky Molly's* clerk. "Artemus, I'm so sorry! Are you all right?"

Primm sat up slowly, gingerly touching a small cut on his bald pate. "The jury is still out on that question."

John was suddenly yanked to his feet by his shirt collar. Claxton's face was inches from his own. "I don't allow midget-tossing on this boat, Carmichael!" Claxton bellowed. "I saw you toss that midget! You need to show him respect. Even if he is something less than a full man."

John bristled. "I didn't knock him down on purpose. I tripped."

"Don't give me that. I saw you calculating where you wanted to bump that barrel as you were carting that box down the plank."

"Don't be ridiculous, Claxton. Artemus is my friend. My roommate."

Primm rose uncertainly to his feet, dabbing his head with a handkerchief. A crowd was starting to gather. "Leave him be, Claxton. I'm satisfied he didn't do it on purpose."

Claxton sneered at John. "You think you're really something, don't you, Carmichael? All of the special treatment the Captain gives you! Well, you just wait. Your time is coming." Claxton nodded at Artemus Primm. "One other thing. If anybody's going to do any midget-tossing around here, it's gonna be me."

Artemus Primm's face blanched, but he said nothing. Chuckling, Claxton turned and swaggered up the gangplank.

"Honestly, Artemus, it was a mistake," John said. "I tripped."

"I know, John. I know."

Primm's eyes followed Claxton's departing figure. "Oaf!" he hissed.

Later in the day, as the *Lucky Molly* steamed downriver, John was approached by one of the passengers in the grand saloon of the steamboat. "Excuse me, but may I have a word in private with you?" The passenger was a clean-shaven young man about John's age, sparely built, with narrow sloping shoulders and a head somewhat too large for his small-boned body. Although he was dressed in a shabby suit, there was something striking about his unruly shock of curly auburn hair, thick eyebrows, and piercing blue-gray eyes.

"The name's Sam Clemens," the passenger continued in an unusually slow drawl. "No impressive title yet. We haven't met, but my powers of observation being somewhat keen, I suspect I have witnessed something that might be of interest to you." Although the face was deadly serious, the blue-gray eyes were twinkling.

Extending his hand, John introduced himself, then led the mysterious stranger to a private place on the hurricane deck, where they stood next to the rail on the Missouri side of the boat. Clemens seemed to be in no hurry to divulge his information. He spent several minutes retrieving a cigar from a pocket and lighting it.

"Care for one?" He offered a large cigar to John. "They're 'Garth's Damndest.' Made right there in Hannibal. What they lack in quality they make up for in inexpensiveness."

"No thanks. I don't smoke."

Clemens raised the huge eyebrows.

"Don't you! I've been smoking since I was nine. Secretly the first two years, and brazenly since my father died when I was eleven." He took a deep pull from the cigar and let his eyes close halfway before exhaling. "I made a solemn vow to my mother when I took leave of her this morning that I will not throw a card nor drink a drop of liquor while I'm away from Hannibal these next few months. Thankfully, she sees nothing wrong with my smoking, long as I keep my hands off her tobacco."

John smiled. "You said you had something that might interest me."

"You haven't found my conversation interesting so far?"

"I didn't say that."

"I know you didn't. You are obviously enthralled." Clemens flicked cigar ashes over the railing where they stood. "Before I tell you what I witnessed that will be of particular interest to you, may I ask you a question or two?"

"Sure," said John.

Clemens fixed his blue-gray eyes upon him. "How is it that you seem to have free run of this steamboat? I've seen you participating in everything from carrying cargo with the roustabouts to hobnobbing in the pilothouse with the pilot himself. I was raised next to the river, and I know the hierarchy on a steamboat. How is it you are able to dabble in so many facets of the trade?"

John, normally taciturn with strangers, for some reason felt no qualms in answering the question. "My father was best friends with Captain O'Malley. When he died earlier this year I came on board as Second Clerk. I guess I'm really an apprentice in all aspects of steamboating. The Captain has sort of taken me under his wing." John felt pride as he said the words. Especially when he noticed the appreciation, approaching envy, in Clemens' eyes.

"I am acutely jealous of you," Clemens drawled. "Every boy in Hannibal would trade places with you in a second. We all grow up wanting to be pirates or circus performers or riverboat pilots. We outgrow the former two but never the latter."

John felt drawn to the young man. "Would you like me to check with Captain O'Malley to see if we need another clerk?"

Clemens tapped his cigar on the railing. "Give me a year or two to decide. I'm on my way now to St. Louis to live with my sister and find work as a printer. I should have no trouble finding work. I've been paddling my own canoe as a printer since I was fourteen. I first worked for Joe Ament at the *Courier*, receiving the princely sum of free room and board and two suits of clothing per year. More recently I've been working for my brother Orion at his newspaper, the *Hannibal Journal*. Perhaps you've read it?"

"No," admitted John.

"Well, then. Perhaps that lack of circulation explains why my brother has not been able to pay my wages for several months."

"Are you a printer or a writer?"

"Both. I lay out the cleanest print in the West, if I say so myself, which I do. But I also write pieces to fill the space when needed. Fact is, I was published nationally for the first time this past month. The experience has given me the confidence to leave the nest, so to speak. After I save some money in St. Louis, I'm heading for New York."

Interest whetted, John asked, "You said you were published nationally. How did you go about doing that?"

Clemens took another puff of his cigar. "Well, I wrote two little stories about Hannibal, Missouri, and stuck them in the mail to publishers. 'The Dandy Frightening the Squatter' was published in *The Carpet-Bag* in Boston. My little piece 'Hannibal, Missouri' was published in the *American Courier* in Philadelphia. I was sixteen when they were published. Of course, I'm an older and more mature seventeen now." Clemens snorted self-mockingly. "Well, you seem to bring out the braggart in me. The point is, I'm going to give the newspaper business a shot. If it doesn't work, I may be seeking you out for a job on the river. Piloting should be a safe line of work for me. I'm the best swimmer in Hannibal. In the process of learning to swim I nearly drowned nine times, three times in the Mississippi and six times in Bear Creek. My mother says people who are born to be hanged are safe in the water."

"I envy you," said John. "I've never met anyone who was published at sixteen."

Clemens grinned. "Nor have I ever met a deck hand who reads Poe. Yes, I saw the book fall out of your pocket when you knocked the midget over. Fact is, I share the habit of carrying a book in my pocket at all times."

He pulled a pocket-sized edition of Longfellow poems from his breast-pocket, adding, "I read somewhat larger-sized editions, too. Thanks to my brother concocting the idea of reprinting a chapter from a novel in each edition of his paper, I've read scores of books as I've set them in print. Just finished Dickens' *Bleak House* last week."

John was still wincing from the comment about Artemus Primm. "You saw me knock poor Artemus off his barrel."

"I was in the audience, yes. Front row seat. Saw the entire operation from an unobstructed vantage point." He took another draw from his cigar. "That, my friend, is what I wanted to talk with you about."

"It was an accident," John said quickly. "Artemus is my friend."

Clemens' bushy eyebrows charged each other as he frowned.

"It was no accident. That big mate tripped you intentionally. I saw the whole disgusting spectacle."

"Claxton! I should have known."

"I take it he doesn't care much for you or the short fellow," Clemens drawled.

"He hates me. From the moment I came on board, he's done everything possible to torment me."

"It's not only you," Clemens said. "I've watched the way he treats the other deck hands. It's obvious he's nothing but a vile, ignorant, malicious, snarling, fault-finding, mote-magnifying tyrant."

John chuckled. "You read my thoughts."

Clemens removed the cigar from his lips and gestured with it as he spoke. "Although my official career has thus far been limited to the printing field, I have also become somewhat accomplished in the disreputable practice of practical joking. It occurs to me that if you are willing to play the part of accomplice, we could pull a good one over on that big mongrel of a mate."

John recalled the advice of Artemus Primm, so studiously followed, of avoiding, rather than provoking, Horace Claxton. "I don't know . . ."

"Bosh!" exclaimed Clemens. "Look right here at this passage from Longfellow!" He flipped open the book to a well-worn page and read aloud.

> In the world's great field of battle,
> In the bivouac of life,
> Be not like dumb, driven cattle—
> Be a hero in the strife.

Clemens snapped the book shut and eyed John. "For my campaign I will need a large wooden board, some paint, a big box, a table, a tablecloth, and an item or two from the boat's kitchen. Are you with me? Be you bovine or hero?"

John threw up his hands. "I'm enlisted. Tell me what to do."

The passengers in the grand saloon of the Lucky Molly watched with interest as the young man with the wild-looking auburn hair painted lettering on the big sign he had erected over the large covered box.

BONAPARTE CROSSING THE RHINE
A REMARKABLE & UNFORGETTABLE
HISTORICAL EXHIBITION
5 CENTS PER HEAD

Before the paint was even dry, people bored with searching the tree-lined shores for entertainment, crowded forward with coins in their hands.

"No, no," Sam Clemens said, waving them back with his hands. "This performance is aimed principally for the mate of this boat, if he can be lured up here to the grand saloon. The rest of you shall see the trouble free of charge, if you merely follow my instructions."

"What are we to do?" asked Lindy, who had joined the crowd near the sign.

"If Horace Claxton asks whether any of you have yet peered into the box, simply say you have done so, but refuse to reveal to him what you saw. Tell him, though, that you saw the varmint and it was remarkable."

"Well, I've got my five cents. Let's see it!" one man yelled.

"Patience," Clemens drawled. "Please, let's wait for the mate. John, do you think you can fetch him?"

"I'll try," John said, feeling suddenly less enthusiastic about the prank.

"I'll come with you," Lindy insisted.

They found Claxton chatting with the leadsman at the front of the Lucky Molly.

"All right, here we go," John whispered to Lindy. "You know what to do?"

She nodded.

"Wasn't it remarkable?" John said loudly, when they were within earshot of Claxton.

Lindy practically hopped with excitement. "I've *never* seen anything so unforgettable! It was well worth the five cents!"

They stopped at the front rail of the steamboat, four feet from Claxton.

"It was simply remarkable," John repeated.

"We are so *fortunate* the exhibit is right here on our steamboat," Lindy gushed.

"What are you talking about?" Claxton interrupted, stepping toward them.

"The historical exhibit in the grand saloon: Bonaparte Crossing the Rhine," John said. "A passenger brought it on board and is charging five cents per view. It's really something."

Claxton's eyes narrowed. "What's so special about it? What is it?"

John shook his head. "I don't think you'd want to see this exhibit, Claxton. You have to know something of European history to appreciate the humor of it. I really don't think you'd like it at all."

Claxton bristled. "You jackass! I know who Napoleon is! You think I'm stupid? You and your fancy education! I'll get as much out of this exhibit as anybody else!"

"You won't like it, Claxton," John warned. "I'm sure of it."

"Get out of my way!" Claxton brushed past them and hurried to the upper deck. John followed him, weak with a dizzying combination of stifled laughter and nervous apprehension.

Claxton burst into the grand saloon and immediately spotted the crowd gathered around Sam Clemens and his historical exhibit. As Claxton worked his way through the crowd surrounding the exhibition the words "remarkable" and "unforgettable" seemed to emanate from every conversation.

At last Claxton was face to face with Sam Clemens, the purveyor of the show. "All right, Mister. I want to see your high-falootin' exhibit," Claxton snarled. "How much is it?"

"Well, let's see," Clemens drawled, turning to study the sign he had painted. "I believe the sign says five cents. Do you carry that much on you?"

Claxton pulled the coins from his pocket and handed them to the curly-haired young man.

"Be quick about it! I want to see it now."

Clemens stuffed Claxton's money deep into his own pocket.

"You want to see the historical exhibit, Bonaparte Crossing the Rhine?"

"No, I want to see a burlesque show!" Claxton mocked the slow drawl of Clemens. "Of course I want to see Bonaparte Crossing the Rhine! Why else would I be standing here!"

"Well, then," smiled Clemens, his eyes sparkling, "you shall see it, and I hope to impress upon your mind this valuable piece of history and illustrate it in so plain a manner that even the dullest among you will readily comprehend it."

Clemens carefully spread a white tablecloth over a small table, then opened the box a crack and plunged his arm inside it.

"Come on, man, I don't have all day!" urged Claxton.

"Patience, sir," said Clemens, as he withdrew something small from the box. "Learning cannot always occur in a split-second." Sam Clemens held up a bone from a chicken leg. It was approximately four inches long. "Behold," he announced, "the bone."

He snapped it in two, then held up the pieces. "Behold, ladies and gentle-men—the bone apart."

The saloon shook with laughter. Claxton's face reddened and his fists clenched. "Is that all there is to it?" he growled.

"Oh, no," assured Clemens, "that is merely the first part of the exhibition." He took from the box a piece of pork rind and placed it on the table. "Now, ladies and gentlemen, draw near and give me your undivided attention for a moment, because this is the most interesting part of the exhibition."

He moved the two broken pieces of bone back and forth over the pork rind.

"I give you, my esteemed audience," Clemens said solemnly, "this remark-able and unforgettable and very apt illustration of that noted event in history: Bonaparte Crossing the Rhine."

Everyone in the large room, except Claxton, shrieked with laughter. The knuckles of Claxton's shivering, meaty fists were turning white, but the num-ber of potential witnesses effectively thwarted the mayhem and dismember-ment he was so obviously contemplating.

"This was a swindle!" he hissed.

"No, sir. This was entertainment," Clemens smiled. "Much more amusing than midget-tossing. And it cost you a mere five cents."

Claxton stormed out of the salon amid howls of merriment.

Clemens found John's gaze and winked. "He should have read my brother's newspaper. He would have found my account of this very ruse in the January 16th issue and been forewarned."

Chapter 9

Two weeks later, the *Lucky Molly* was heading south on the Mississippi two miles north of New Madrid, Missouri. John stood with Patrick O'Malley on the front of the hurricane deck. They were alone, hands on the wooden railing. A cold spell had driven most of the cabin passengers, who had paid twenty-five dollars for passage from St. Louis to New Orleans, into the warmth and splendor of the saloon, leaving the cold to the deck hands and deck passengers, who huddled around cooking stoves scattered over the main deck.

"I felt bad leaving Rosalind behind," O'Malley said, his words transfixed by the cold air into clouds of white that disappeared instantly. "But I want her to finish her schooling on time. Besides, a Mississippi riverboat's no place for a lady."

"That's not necessarily true. Some of the finest ladies in Missouri are riding in your passenger cabin right now."

"Guess I mean a woman has no place on the *crew* of a steamboat."

"Lots of captains take their families on their boats with them, Uncle Pat." Although he never referred to the Captain as "Uncle" around others, he had grown comfortable using the word when they were alone.

"I've thought about taking Lindy and Maude with me on the river," said O'Malley, "but Maude is scared to death of steamboats, and I wouldn't want to bring Lindy without a chaperone of some sort."

"Lindy told me you usually tie up the *Lucky Molly* in the Tennessee River and spend the winter months with her and Aunt Maude in Cape Girardeau."

"Not this year," O'Malley said. "I want to work the lower Mississippi and make enough money to build that new steamboat."

"Lindy's disappointed you wouldn't let her come."

"From that hang-dog look on your face, it seems to me she wasn't the only one disappointed."

John knew he was blushing.

"That's all right, lad. You've a right to miss her. She's a true friend to you. Cares about you." O'Malley winked. His face then sobered. "I just wish she hadn't been so mad when I forced her to stay the winter in Cape. First time she's ever refused to come to the levee to see me off. Hate to leave on such a sour note." O'Malley squared his broad shoulders and faced the river breeze. He changed the subject abruptly. "After this trip, I just might have enough money to buy the steamboat of my dreams. Picked the builder already, in Louisville. Just a matter of gathering or borrowing the money. Been talking to Jason Farley, Vice President of the Missouri Bank in Jackson. He might find a way to get me the cash."

"How much will it cost?"

"Close to 150,000 dollars."

John whistled. "That's a lot of money, Uncle Pat."

"She'll be a lot of boat." O'Malley placed his fingerless left hand on the railing in front of him. "The *Lucky Molly* might look nice to you, John, but she's not the steamboat she used to be. Fraying carpet, smoke stains, chipped gilt, dirt and manure from thousands of muddy feet, gouges from knives and spurs—fresh paint can't hide it all. You should've seen her a few years ago, bright and pretty like her namesake. Ah, Molly Blanchard, what wonderful years we had!" O'Malley looked toward the sky, eyes shining.

"What was your wife like, Uncle Pat?"

"Molly was just like Lindy. Bubbling with life. Slender. Curly hair. Always laughing. I'll never love another woman. I'm one of those one-man-dogs you hear about, I guess. A big part of me died with her."

They stood silently for several seconds, each lost in his own thoughts.

"I met her," O'Malley continued, "right before the New Madrid Earthquake. I was serving with a group of men Louis Lorimier put together to rid the river of a band of pirates on Crow's Nest Island."

"Who's Louis Lorimier?"

"Who's Louis Lorimier! Why he's the founder of Cape Girardeau! True, Girardot set up the trading post that gave Cape its name, but Girardot didn't stick around permanently. Lorimier is the one who created Cape Girardeau in 1793 after the Spanish Governor-General Carondelet made him Commandant and gave him title to thirty thousand acres of land to keep or sell as he saw fit."

"Thirty thousand acres! He must have been rich!"

"Not only rich, but powerful. He served with the Spanish government as Commandant until 1804, when the entire Louisiana Territory was transferred to France and then to the United States by the Louisiana Purchase. In 1805, Territorial Governor William Henry Harrison appointed him judge of the Court of General QuarterSessions of the Peace. He stepped down as judge, though, when the Federal government tried to claim that the title to his land wasn't valid since it came from Spain rather than the United States. He eventually won that fight, too, but it took years." O'Malley examined the scars on his fingerless left hand. "I met Molly Blanchard at Lorimier's house. It was called 'The Red House.' It was a big wooden two-story house that sat on a hill well back from the river, surrounded by a grassy field, with a fine view of both the town and the Mississippi. It was a mecca for important people traveling the river. Lewis and Clark stopped there at both the beginning and end of their famous expedition in 1804 and 1806. Davy Crockett and Daniel Boone visited Lorimier there." O'Malley chuckled. "Yes, sir, John. If there were any justice in the world our hometown would be called Lorimont instead of Cape Girardeau. Lorimier himself pushed for the name but it just didn't catch on with the locals."

"Tell me about those pirates you were talking about, Uncle Pat."

O'Malley's eyes stared unblinkingly into the past. "It was December 1811. Steamboats weren't invented yet. Keelboats and flatboats carried furs from the Western frontier downriver. River piracy was at its height. The areas along the river were sparsely populated. Boats coming downriver were sure to be loaded with valuable furs. You had river pirates like Samuel Mason, John Murrell and the Harpe brothers who would swarm out on lighter boats, pirogues and skiffs and try to kill you and steal your cargo. Fighting to protect your boat was a way of life." O'Malley's eyes shone with anger at vivid memories. "One day Lorimier got word from a survivor that a gang of pirates on Crow's Nest Island had ransacked his boat."

"Crow's Nest Island?"

"It was a beautiful little spot about 55 miles south of Fort Nogales, where Vicksburg is today." O'Malley grinned. "Mike Fink and his crew, of which I was one, signed on with Lorimier. We headed south to take on those pirates."

"What happened when you got there?"

"Well, the pirates had erected a big sign. It said, 'Liquor Vault and House For Entertainment—Open to the Public.' They'd built a shabby old wooden house with a long porch, and kept three female members of the band preening on that veranda, laughing and chattering, as bait to lure flatboat crews to stop. We were wise to the plot, though, because of that survivor.

"We fought those pirates for two days. I lost my fingers during that fight. The thing ended suddenly, though, when the New Madrid Earthquake struck and wiped out the whole blamed island, pirates and all."

"What a story!" John said, thinking how much Sam Clemens would have loved to hear it, and wondering how his friend's printing career was going in St. Louis.

"Story! It's true!" said O'Malley. "Though I must admit, my memory isn't what it used to be. Like that Clemens fellow said, 'When I was younger, I could remember anything, whether it happened or not.'" O'Malley slipped his maimed hand into the pocket of his coat. "Anyway, when we got back to Cape Girardeau, Lorimier convinced me to leave Mike Fink's crew and stay in Cape. The whole town had been shook up by the earthquake, and got hit two more times during the next three months. I helped rebuild it, though. Afterward he staked me enough to get my own keelboat. That's how I got from being just another deck hand to being the owner of my own business." O'Malley winked. "I met Molly Blanchard the very day Lorimier and I left Cape to go to Crow's Nest Island. Couldn't forget her. Guess it was love at first sight. Don't suppose you know anything about that."

John smiled self-consciously. "Whatever happened to Louis Lorimier and Mike Fink?"

"Fink died the way he lived—recklessly. Winter of 1822 to 1823 he was working at a remote trading post at the mouth of the Yellowstone River. Thought he'd show off his marksmanship by shooting a tin cup off a young man's head. He'd done the same flapdoodle plenty of times before, but he'd been drinking. He missed the cup and shot this fellow named Carpenter right smack in the forehead. Carpenter's friends thought he did it on purpose. One of them killed Fink a few days later."

"That's not right," John said. "If that boy was stupid enough to put the cup on his head, he deserved what happened to him."

The corner of O'Malley's mouth twitched with the makings of a smile. "Lindy's got a tin cup you need to see sometime, John. I'm ashamed to say I let Fink shoot it off my head one night. Young people do stupid things. It's a wonder we live past the tomfoolery of our teen years. As for Louis Lorimier, he died in 1812 after a lengthy illness. In his will he canceled my debt to him. From then on I owned my keelboat free and clear."

"That was nice of him."

"Nice hardly covers it," said O'Malley. "Every man has two or three mentors in his life who really help him grow up as a man. Mike Fink and Louis Lorimier were mine. I'll never forget either one."

They were silent as New Madrid came into view. The town nestled in the crook of a horseshoe bend twenty-five miles in length, commanding a view six miles upriver and ten miles downstream. Founded in 1789, it was a booming river town before being devastated by earthquakes in 1811 and 1812. Only the brave and the reckless remained afterward. Although gradually rebuilt after the destruction, eventually boasting a population of more than 5,000 by 1850, the growth process of the river town had been irreparably stunted by nature's malicious whim.

"They say the Mississippi River ran backward during the New Madrid Earthquake," said John. "Must have been awful for people on the river."

"That's a fact," O'Malley said.

"Where were you exactly during the quake, Uncle Pat? Why didn't you go down with Crow's Nest Island and the pirates?"

"I was perched in a tall tree across from the island. I had a bird's eye view. I saw the Mississippi suck it right down like the river Styx pouring into the Devil's Cauldron."

At that moment, Artemus Primm rushed toward them, his usually calm face agitated. "Captain, you'd better get to your cabin."

"What the blazes are you talking about?"

"I'd rather not say. You'd better go see for yourself!"

They charged into the captain's quarters and stopped abruptly. Lindy sat cross-legged on O'Malley's bunk, grinning at them.

"What are you doing here?" O'Malley thundered, his face growing dark. He whipped off his cap and threw it to the floor.

Lindy bounced off the bunk and faced him. "I'm a stowaway."

"By God, there's no ice on the river yet! I can still turn around and take you back to Cape Girardeau, young lady!"

Tears formed in Lindy's eyes. "Papa, please let me come with you! I want to, more than anything. I'll work. I'll study. I'll do anything you say."

O'Malley put his fists to his temples. After a few long seconds he shook his head. "A stowaway," he repeated, chuckling. "John and I were just saying how much we missed you."

Her eyes flashed with pleasure. "Is that so, John?"

He said nothing, but knew his involuntary smile proclaimed a clear answer.

"What about your Aunt Maude?" asked O'Malley.

"I left her a note. I told her I was with you and that I'd be back in the spring. She'll be fine. She's got all her friends in the Daughters of Temperance to keep her busy. I even talked to Doc Wilson before I left. He said he'd look in on her once in a while."

O'Malley rolled his eyes. "My little Rose, how like your mother you are."

The next two months passed quickly for John Carmichael. The *Lucky Molly* flourished in the lower Louisiana trade, picking up cotton and passengers from the upper parts of Louisiana and taking them to New Orleans, then making the return trip upriver loaded with passengers and cargo including hats, coffee, New Orleans molasses, brown sugar, salt mackerel, brooms, shovels, axes, hoes, rakes, shot, gunpowder, printed calico, needles, scissors, and spools of thread. The river was crowded with steamboats; the competition, keen. The *Lucky Molly*, a good boat with a fine captain, more than held her own, making as much as 3,000 dollars profit on a three-day trip.

The weather on the lower Mississippi in January and February was mild and pleasant. John and the deck hands often worked with shirts off, letting the winter sun warm their skin.

His seventeenth birthday passed in January. He received three birthday presents. Lindy and her father gave him an archaeology book, Pete Carnahan gave him a set of dumbbells, and Abner Conrad gave him the most recent pilot's map of the Lower Mississippi. Carnahan had made the dumbbells himself, out of machine parts. He let John store them in the engine room, and encouraged him to visit the bowels of the steamboat each evening, where John would hoist them over and over, bare-chested amid the heat and steam. John spent hours and hours working with them, watching with pleasure as his muscles gradually hardened like the metal of the boilers themselves.

John had grown again. At six feet tall, weighing 175 pounds, he could lift and haul with the strongest of the deck hands, who all enjoyed working with him. The pilots liked having him in the pilot house. Abner Conrad had unofficially adopted him as a cub pilot. The only person he didn't get along with was Horace Claxton, whom he avoided as much as possible. There had never been any retaliation for his role in the Bonaparte Crossing the Rhine prank. He hoped Claxton remembered that John had, after all, warned him that he would not find it amusing .

John had never been happier in his life.

What made him happiest was seeing Lindy every day. He often dined with her and her father at the Captain's table in the luxurious passenger's saloon. He and she took walks around the boiler deck at least once a day. They spent a great deal of time discussing books.

Shortly after stowing-away on her father's steamboat, Lindy decided that the *Lucky Molly* needed a library. She passed the word at every steamboat stop and soon people were selling her books, sometimes several at a time. She often visited New Orleans booksellers, spending as much money as O'Malley would allow. Before long the *Lucky Molly's* library was filled with titles by Cooper, Dickens, Swift, Goldsmith, Longfellow, Poe, Shakespeare, Carlyle, Macaulay, Prescott, and Fielding. It was visited frequently by O'Malley's passengers.

John and Lindy shared several kisses on peaceful nights under the stars as the *Lucky Molly* steamed up and down the lower Mississippi, during moments when the full moon would loom over the trees on the shoreline, casting its bright glow over a glittering river of watery silver, the hoot of an owl sometimes drifting eerily across the water from the dark shoreline.

One warm February afternoon, in a river cove south of Baton Rouge, O'Malley ordered the yawl lowered while the *Lucky Molly* was being loaded with firewood. He called John to join him. "Promised you four months ago you'd learn to swim," bellowed O'Malley, standing in the yawl. "Today's the day. Shuck your shirt and boots."

"I'm going to learn to swim *here*? In the Mississippi River?"

"Exactly right. Climb in."

John obeyed, reluctantly, recalling the comment of Sam Clemens that men born to be hanged are safe in the water. John had never felt destined to hang. A crowd of passengers gathered at the stern of the *Lucky Molly* and watched with interest as O'Malley rowed out into the cove, thirty yards from his steamboat.

"There's practically no current in this cove," said O'Malley as he rowed. "Less than one mile an hour. You won't have to worry about being sucked under."

John nodded silently, letting his hand trail in the brown water. It was cold. Unpleasantly cold. "I'm not so worried about being sucked under. I'm more concerned about sinking. I can't swim a lick."

"We're changing that right now." O'Malley reached his chosen spot and stopped rowing. The yawl bobbed calmly on the muddy water. "I taught your father how to swim, you know."

"Really? This same way?"

"Sort of. I threw him off my steamboat into the deepest channel of the Mississippi while my boat was going full speed."

"No!"

"Yep. Once your dad got out of that burlap sack he did all right, too." O'Malley howled with laughter. "Just kidding, John."

John glanced at the muddy water. If he disappeared under its brown surface, O'Malley wouldn't be able to see him to save him.

Wiping a mirthful tear from the corner of his eye, O'Malley tossed a length of rope to John. "Here, son. Tie this around yourself. Circle it under your armpits and run a piece between your legs and over a shoulder, front to back. I'll tie the other end to the yawl. That way, if you drown, I'll find your carcass." O'Malley helped him with the knots. "Well, guess you're ready for your first lesson."

Suddenly, with a flick of his large forearm, O'Malley knocked John out of the boat. Laughter of *Lucky Molly* passengers rang in his ears as he landed on his back in the water. He sank into the cold depths, eyes bugging, staring toward the surface, seeing only bright brown above. Something very much alive slithered against his bare foot. He flailed his arms and legs wildly. Moments later, his head bobbed out of the water.

"Something touched my foot!" he yelled, inhaling a mouthful of river water. He began choking. His head went under again. He was jerked rapidly through the water like a hooked catfish. Within moments he was clinging to the side of the wooden yawl, gasping and shuddering. O'Malley loomed in the yawl above him, holding the wet coil of rope in his hands.

"First rule, John, and one of the most important—don't talk while you're under water."

John finished coughing, and sucked in several breaths of air.

"Second rule—any fool can dogpaddle. Watch."

O'Malley lay down on the bottom of the yawl and kicked his feet vigorously.

"See my feet and arms, lad? That's what you need to do."

The steamboat passengers whooped with laughter.

John cautiously let go of the edge of the yawl and followed O'Malley's example. To his surprise, his head stayed above water.

"That's it. You've got it. A born dog!"

Flushed with excitement, John paddled in large circles near the yawl, wet hair plastered to his head. The crowd on the *Lucky Molly* applauded loudly. He faced the steamboat, picking Lindy out of the crowd. She stood at the stern of the boat. Paddling with both feet and one hand, he waved at her. Smiling, she waved back.

Minutes later, as O'Malley leaned over to help him climb into the yawl, John was struck by an irresistible impulse. He clasped O'Malley's wrist and yanked hard. All 200 plus pounds of steamboat captain sailed over him and struck the water with a terrific splash. The spectators on the *Lucky Molly* roared.

"Why you little whippersnapper!" sputtered O'Malley when he surfaced.

After two powerful and graceful strokes, O'Malley was next to him, dunking his head, but then tousled his hair to show he was not really angry. Dripping wet, they returned to the *Lucky Molly*.

Shortly after he boarded the steamboat, while he was drying his chest with a towel, Lindy approached him, stopping in front of him with her hands on her hips. "My, my, I see one skinny roustabout has certainly filled out nicely."

John smiled self-consciously. Clad only in wet pants, he stood on one foot, drying the other with his shirt.

Lindy looked at him coyly. "I'll be sixteen tomorrow."

"Oh?" he said, drying his hair.

"My mother was sixteen when she married Papa," she added, before turning and hurrying away. She paused to look over her shoulder to gauge his reaction. "I'll see you at supper if you're lucky, John Carmichael."

Feeling a glow in his chest, he watched her scamper up the steps to the boiler deck, sunlight shining off dark curls. He was still smiling to himself when Horace Claxton walked by and knocked him into the white wall of the steamboat with a thrust of his big shoulder. "Watch where you're going, Carmichael!"

"Sorry. Didn't see you."

Claxton moved his stubbly chin near John's face. His breath smelled like dead fish. "Listen, boy. Just because you learned to swim don't mean you're a match for me."

"I don't pretend to be a match for you. At least now, next time you throw me overboard, I'll be able to swim."

Claxton shoved him roughly against the wall. "Don't count on it. Dead men can't swim." Claxton spat on John's bare feet and abruptly stalked away.

Late the next night the *Lucky Molly* was moored at the steamboat wharf in New Orleans. O'Malley's boat rested among other riverboats docked between Toulouse and St. Louis streets. Mile after mile of levee was packed deep with steamboats, barges, flatboats, and every other variety of river craft. Even at nighttime, steamboats were still arriving and departing, the noise of their engines combining with the shouting and singing of the roustabouts to create the symphony of sound that defined the New Orleans levee. Most of the *Lucky Molly's* crew were on shore, carousing at rowdy dance halls like the Globe, Stadt Amsterdam, Homeward Bound, and Orleans Ball Room. Others had disappeared into the numerous houses of prostitution clustered like sores in the red-light districts on "Sanctity Row." The passengers dispersed into the immense city, many of the wealthy staying at the huge St. Charles and St. Louis hotels.

John remained on the boat. He lay on his bunk in his small cabin, reading by flickering yellow candlelight. He was poring over an account of Hernando de Soto's exploits along the Mississippi River. A knock on his door gave him a start. He moved to his cabin door and opened it cautiously. Lindy brushed past him and quickly closed the door. John, wearing only his pants, glanced at the closed door nervously. "We shouldn't be alone in my cabin," he said.

"Balderdash!"

She removed the shawl from her head and ran her fingers through her dark curls, fluffing her hair casually, letting the dark waves fall softly onto her shoulders. She wore a pale green dress, tight at the waist, its billowy, unhooped, floor-length skirt accenting her perfect figure. Her collar modestly covered her neck, but the pastel material rounded over her feminine curves as it made its journey from chin to floor. Her petticoats made a rustling noise, and the sound excited him.

"I was lying on my bed, unable to sleep, bored to tears, wishing I could be talking to my best friend—you," she said, dark eyes lowering as she looked at him. "I finally said to myself it is utter foolishness not to be able to come talk to you when I want to talk to you. No matter if the sun happens to be down. I decided to get dressed and come see if you had a candle burning."

"It must be close to midnight!"

"Half past," she corrected, moving to the edge of his bunk, where she seated herself gracefully.

"Lindy," he said, looking again at the closed door. "Your father is awful strict about unmarried men and women being in the same cabin on his boat. He's thrown couples off in the middle of nowhere when it turned out they weren't married but only traveling together. What if he finds me alone in my cabin with his only daughter?"

"I can control my Papa."

"That's a comforting thought," he said, "but very possibly incorrect."

"John Carmichael, do you know what *your* problem is?" she said, looking him directly in the eye. "You are too, too, *too* serious."

He glanced again at the cabin door and sat stiffly on Artemus Primm's bunk, directly across from her.

"There, you see?"

"See what?"

"You did what a serious fellow will do when alone with his girl in a cabin. You looked at the door, scared to death someone would come in, and you sat on the bed across from her, instead of next to her, which is what she would have preferred."

He leaned forward and whispered urgently. "Lindy, in case you've forgotten, Artemus Primm sleeps in this cabin, too. If he comes back and finds you here alone with me, I could wind up *off* the boat, friend of the family or not!"

"Now, you *see*," she chided. "That's the way a serious person would think."

"Well, be serious."

"Very well," she said, casually picking up the de Soto book. "I know something you don't."

"What's that?"

"Papa sent Artemus Primm to spend the night on a plantation outside New Orleans to try to get the rich old owner to give us some extra business."

"Spending the night?"

"That's right," she said, running her fingers delicately over the cover of the book. "What is this you're reading now?"

"It's a history of Hernando de Soto, the Spanish explorer who discovered the Mississippi River. After serving under Pizarro in the conquest of Peru, and finding all of that Inca gold, de Soto and a group of Spaniards came to Florida and then traveled up the Mississippi in 1541 hoping to find gold in North America as well. The whole trip was a disaster, a virtually endless fight with the Indians."

"If the Indians were already there, I don't see how anyone can say de Soto discovered the Mississippi River," Lindy said.

"Well, that's true. The Indians had been living along the river for hundreds of years. In fact, archaeologists think the Indians were not simply nomadic savages who merely hunted and fished for food, pitching their wigwams wherever game was plentiful. It seems likely that at least four centuries before de Soto arrived they had built a huge trading network, the center of which was an extraordinary city of perhaps 30,000 inhabitants in the area where a gigantic mound still stands at Cahokia, just across the river from St. Louis. Now we call them the Mound Builders, but they undoubtedly did more than stack dirt."

"Did de Soto ever find his gold?" Lindy asked.

"No."

"Well, then, he was probably glad to get out of here and back to Spain."

"Oh, he didn't make it back," said John. "The Spaniards were vastly outnumbered by the Indians and lasted as long as they did only because of their superior armor and weapons and horses. Also, they had convinced the Indians that de Soto was a God. After he died of a fever, that ruse became a bit harder to pull off. They buried him in their horses' pen and tried to convince the Indians that he had temporarily left to visit the God in the sky. But when the Spaniards saw the Indians eyeing the corral suspiciously they dug up de Soto's body in the middle of the night and sunk him in the Mississippi. Then they melted down their armor and used the metal to make nails and build rafts. They escaped the Indians by floating down the Mississippi. Some of them eventually made it back to Spain."

"My!" said Lindy. "Bits of Hernando de Soto could be floating underneath us right now!" Lindy examined the book closely. "It's amazing to me how quickly those who are gone are forgotten. Not just individuals, but whole civilizations."

"That's what makes me want to be an historian," John said. "To stop some of the forgetting."

"History sometimes seems so boring, though," she said. "Just a collection of dry old facts and figures."

John found himself staring at her face, softly shadowed in the flickering candlelight. "Sometimes," John admitted, "but not always. In this de Soto book, for example, it quotes one of the survivors as saying an Indian Chief named Capaha insisted upon giving two of his wives, Mochila and Maconoche, to de Soto as gifts. This presented something of a problem since de Soto already had a wife named Isabella waiting for him back home."

Lindy's eyes twinkled. "What did Mr. de Soto do?"

"He accepted the gift. I mean, you can't go around hurting the feelings of generous Indians."

"What were the sleeping arrangements? Does your history book tell you that?"

"No. Those dry old facts weren't recorded for posterity."

"Pity," Lindy said. "I guess we'll never know. See, history would be a lot more interesting if they'd tell you more about the really good parts."

"Probably," he said, chest pounding. They were totally alone and likely to remain that way the whole night. If he were smart, he told himself, he'd make her leave immediately. Or he'd leave. Or he'd at least quit watching the way the cloth of her dress strained tightly against her young body.

"John, do you remember when I held you in my arms on Cape Rock after your father was killed?"

"Of course. How could I forget?"

She looked up at him, her face pure and honest. "That's when I knew I wanted to marry you some day."

Tenderness rushed over him like steam heat in an engine room. "We're too young to talk of marriage."

"Are we? I turned sixteen today. My mother was married at sixteen. My grandmother was married at sixteen. I want to marry and have a house full of children. I need to get started. That's my dream. What's yours?"

"I've told you many times, Lindy. I want to be a famous historian. I want to write books that stir readers' souls and make them feel the past like they've never felt it before." He stood up and paced the small cabin. "I also want to help your father get his dream, help him earn the money to build the fastest and most beautiful steamboat on the Mississippi River."

She took his hands and pulled him toward her. "I want all those things, too. I truly do. But for now can't you be a bit less serious than usual?"

They fell softly back onto his bed, wrapped in each others' arms. His mouth covered hers, and he was surprised and tremendously aroused when her tiny tongue began toying with his. Their kiss was long; her breath, sugary and moist.

He moved his mouth gently from her lips and slowly brushed his own lips over her chin and down her neck. She tossed her head back, stretching her long satiny throat. He kissed her dozens and dozens of times.

Chapter 10

Spring brought an end to the ice in the Upper Mississippi, and the *Lucky Molly* resumed its regular St. Louis to New Orleans roundtrips. By dint of his aptitude, skills, and intelligence, John Carmichael was playing an even more important role in the day-to-day functioning of O'Malley's steamboat. Lindy had been returned to the O'Malley home in Cape Girardeau, where she resumed her schooling and piano lessons.

One late afternoon in April, Lindy stood with Aunt Maude in front of the St. Charles Hotel at the corner of Themis and Main streets in Cape Girardeau. The awnings of the hotel's verandas flapped gaily in the spring breeze, and the sun glistened brightly off the white cupola that covered the red brick building.

"I'm not taking you to another store this afternoon," Maude said firmly.

"Oh, please!" urged Lindy. "There's *got* to be a ready-made dress just perfect for my coming-out party. Let's try Clark & Greer Dry Goods."

As they started across the street, an elegant two-horse coach pulled to a stop nearby. Tyler Fitch emerged, white suit shimmering in the bright sun.

"Coach at your service, ladies."

The scabs were gone from his ear. The ugly dueling wound had evolved into a peculiar ear simply missing its lower half.

"Thank you, Mr. Fitch," said Maude O'Malley hastily, pulling her shawl more tightly around her shoulders, "but we are quite capable of walking."

"Why walk, ladies? It would be my pleasure to share my coach with you."

"I doubt Captain O'Malley would want us to ride in *your* coach," said Maude O'Malley.

Lindy saw a flash of apparently genuine hurt pass through Fitch's brown eyes.

"Nonsense, Aunt Maude. Papa admires Mr. Fitch. I've heard him say so himself. We'll ride in your carriage, sir."

Fitch held Lindy's hand and helped her into the coach. He was John's size, and handsome, but the similarities ended there. His hair was dark brown, John's blond. His eyes were brown; John's, blue. Although clean shaven, his face was darkly shadowed and could have benefited from an evening razor. John could often go three days without shaving.

She nestled into the seat next to Maude while Fitch engaged in a short conversation outside the coach with the driver.

"Wait until your father hears about this," Maude whispered.

"He won't care." As she spoke, she thought of John, of his gentle voice, his caresses. *John* might care, she realized with mixed feelings. Smoothing her skirt nervously, she considered the matter carefully. John had never asked her to marry him, despite her numerous hints. Perhaps if her riding in Fitch's coach bothered him sufficiently, thoughts of matrimony would bloom in his scholarly head. Besides, she cared nothing for Tyler Fitch. It would be silly for John to get upset about a little ride in a coach. A slight smile played across her lips. She would be certain to tell John about the coach ride as soon as possible—enthusiastically.

"This is ridiculous," continued Maude O'Malley. "We're just going down the block, after all."

The coach shifted slightly toward the open door as Tyler Fitch climbed gracefully inside. He slid onto the leather seat across from the two women. "What's your pleasure?" he asked, his eyes questioning Lindy.

"We're going to Clark & Greer's Dry Goods," answered Maude O'Malley, "right down the block."

"We're *eventually* going to Clark & Greer's Dry Goods," Lindy corrected. "But as long as we get to the store before they close, we have time to take a little ride in the meantime."

Fitch grinned happily. "A ride it is!" He leaned out and gave the driver brief directions. As the coach took off noisily, Lindy surveyed its interior. Its polished leather seats were clean and comfortable.

"Your coach is beautiful, Mr. Fitch."

"Nothing compared to your beauty," he said, laughter wrinkles surrounding his brown eyes.

Lindy smiled as she thanked him for the compliment. He was a very interesting man, she decided.

The coachman took them on a leisurely drive over the dirt streets of Cape Girardeau, past the brightly painted sign in front of Temperance Hall, announcing the weekly meetings of the Daughters of Temperance; past several steamboats, including the *Andrew Jackson*, tied up on the levee; past St. Vincent's College, the Washington Female Seminary, and the Eclectic Institute; and past

Sturdivant & Company's Steam Mill and St. Vincent Marble Works Company. They rode almost a mile out Old Jackson Road, toward the town of Jackson, then turned around and came back into Cape Girardeau.

"Look!" said Lindy, as they passed a large house at the end of Water Street, allegedly a bordello owned by a prostitute named Samantha Peabody. "There's a lady in a fancy blue hat coming out the front door. Maybe it's Samantha Peabody herself!"

Fitch cocked his head and looked out the window. "Yep," he said. "That's her. Want to meet her?"

Maude O'Malley gasped. "Really, Mr. Fitch! We certainly do not!"

"I would!" said Lindy.

"Your father will hear about this!" Maude warned in a harsh whisper.

Lindy was excited by the prospect of meeting the infamous Samantha Peabody. She climbed from the carriage quickly when it stopped. For years she'd heard the notorious name whispered by riverboatmen working for her father.

Samantha Peabody's brown eyes were friendly as she greeted Lindy. It was rather disappointing. She was nothing like Lindy had imagined. She had high cheekbones and deep color, suggesting Indian blood in her ancestry. Although it was difficult to tell her age, she was probably in her thirties. She wore no make up. Her dark hair was pulled underneath a yellow silk bonnet, tied under her chin. Her dress was yellow taffeta adorned with black lace, and she wore black gloves.

"Pleased to make your acquaintance, Miss O'Malley. Never met your father, but I've heard lots of good things about him."

As they exchanged small talk, Lindy concluded that the rumors about Samantha Peabody's occupation must have been incorrect. From the banter between Fitch and Peabody, it was obvious they knew each other well. Surely a man of his stature wouldn't be seen in public with her otherwise.

"Where are you off to?" Fitch asked Samantha Peabody.

"One of the girls has a problem," she answered in a soft voice, tinged with concern. "I'm going to the apothecary to pick up a few things."

"What sort of problem?" asked Lindy. "Maybe we have something that could help."

"Honey, I appreciate your concern, but my friend wouldn't want you to get involved, if you know what I mean." Samantha Peabody shared a conspiratorial wink with her.

Lindy had no idea what she meant by either her words or the wink, but didn't want to expose her ignorance by saying so.

"Where's your carriage?" asked Tyler Fitch.

"My horse foaled this morning. Thought I'd give the old girl a day off and use my own hoofs to get to the store. Jiminey! I've got more pregnancies in my house than I can handle."

Lindy gasped with surprise. Finally she understood the nature of the friend's problem. "We just saw Doc Wilson on Main Street," she said.

"Sweetie, my friend doesn't want her baby *delivered*. She wants it removed, the sooner the better."

Lindy's mouth dropped open and then shut. She glanced over her shoulder to check whether her aunt had overheard the conversation. Maude wasn't within earshot. Thank goodness.

"I'd offer you a ride," said Tyler Fitch apologetically, "but my coach is already full."

"Oh, that's not true," Lindy said. "There's room for another."

Tyler Fitch and Samantha Peabody regarded her with surprise.

"It wouldn't be too much trouble, then, Tyler?" Samantha Peabody purred, obviously pleased she would not be walking.

"I suppose not," said Fitch.

When the three of them climbed into the coach, Maude O'Malley's eyes widened. She shot an icy glance at Lindy when the others weren't looking. Tyler Fitch sat next to Samantha Peabody as they rode back to Main Street. Lindy noticed that the woman left several inches of empty seat next to the window, and sat with the yellow taffeta of her dress lightly touching his leg. They rode in silence for a minute or two, the coach jostling now and then when hitting a bump in the road. Lindy occasionally broke the silence with some chatter about her father's steamboat business.

"You're a sweet girl," Samantha Peabody announced, breaking the silence.

"Thank you. It's been exciting to meet you, after all I've heard." Realizing the implications of her words, Lindy blushed profusely.

Samantha Peabody laughed merrily. "I like you, girl. You've got spunk to invite someone like me to ride with you in a coach, you know that?"

Maude O'Malley coughed, covering her mouth with her handkerchief, nearly gagging.

"As long as you don't drink alcohol, my aunt and I will tolerate you," Lindy said, glancing teasingly at Maude.

"Speak for yourself," said Maude O'Malley, squaring her narrow shoulders and removing her handkerchief from her mouth. "On second thought," she added, looking at Lindy severely, "it would be best if you don't."

The coach pulled up in front of the nearest drug store. Maude leaned back, to avoid being seen through the window, and pressed her slender arm across Lindy's shoulder, forcing her to do the same.

Samantha Peabody noticed and frowned. "It's been a pleasure meeting you, Rosalind, but it wasn't much of a thrill meeting you, Maude O'Malley. You are ill-mannered, to say the least."

"I *can be* ill-mannered, and you *are* a harlot, madam. The difference is that I'll be polite tomorrow." Maude O'Malley yanked opened the door on the other side of the coach and stepped out unassisted. "Come on, Lindy. This ride is over."

"Thanks for the ride, Mr. Fitch," Lindy said as Maude O'Malley pulled her toward the other side of the street.

He tipped his white straw hat, an amused sparkle in his handsome dark eyes.

Three days later, John was on the Cape Girardeau riverfront, carrying boxes from the deck of the *Lucky Molly* to the worn cobblestone surface of the levee. He easily carried a box under each arm. Not so many months before, even one would have been too heavy. As he put down the latest load, he saw Lindy coming toward him, smiling happily.

"Got something for you," she announced, handing him an envelope. It was an invitation to her coming-out party, to be held on the *Lucky Molly* at the levee in three weeks.

"So, you're finally getting your party."

"Yes, I'm having it, and you'd better be there. I intend to dance with you until my feet fall off."

He glanced at his own feet, clad in dirty boots. He'd never danced in his life. How in the world could he learn in three weeks? Who could teach him? He shifted uncomfortably.

"I almost didn't get to have my party," she continued. "Aunt Maude told Papa to cancel it because I went for a ride in a coach with Tyler Fitch and Samantha Peabody."

John quit contemplating his inability to dance. "Tyler Fitch!"

"Well, yes," she said, pretending to glance through the many invitations she held in her hands. "Aunt Maude was with me, of course. I wasn't *alone* with him."

"How could you ride in the same carriage with the man who killed my father!"

She glanced up from the invitations, surprised and secretly pleased by the anger in his voice. "It wasn't anything. Really it wasn't."

Lindy looked at his muscular shoulders. She wanted to touch them, to caress his arms and kiss his reddening neck, to tell him truthfully that she loved him with all her heart and soul, and that she fully intended to marry him before her seventeenth birthday. She stifled the impulse, deciding it more strategic to pursue her plan of fanning the flames of jealousy.

"How did you happen to be riding with him?" John asked.

She told the details, subtly emphasizing the compliments Fitch had lavished upon her.

"Lindy, I don't mind your riding with Samantha Peabody half as much as the fact you let Tyler Fitch escort you around town. That white-suited snake killed my father. He's your own father's biggest competitor. I wish you wouldn't have gone with him."

"I do believe you're jealous."

"Maybe so. Maybe I'm also shocked and disappointed that *you*, of all people, would socialize with the man who stole my father from me."

She saw muscular cords tighten in his neck. "Well, it's done," she said defensively. She was a bit flustered. He was much more upset than she'd planned. She decided to quit stoking the fire. "I'm sorry. Let's forget it, shall we?"

John looked at her beautiful face. Her brown eyes gazed at him with open affection. The irritation left him like hissing steam from a boiler's safety valve.

"Forgotten," he said quietly, but not quite truthfully.

John Carmichael brooded for days over his inability to dance. Lindy expected him to dance with her at her party. He didn't know the first thing about dancing. It worried him greatly.

The solution to his problem came unexpectedly one evening when the *Lucky Molly* was docked for the night at the levee in St. Louis. The passengers and most of the crew had left the boat. John was in his room reading, to the backgroud accompaniment of the lapping of the waves upon the sides of the boat, punctuated by loud spirituals sung by a group of roustabouts gathered around a cooking fire on the cobblestone levee. Normally able to read amid any conditions, John was finding the singing extremely distracting. It was something of a relief when the deck hand doing nightwatchman duties knocked on his door.

"Someone out here's asking for you."

John put down his history book and followed the deck hand to the gang plank. Sam Clemens was leaning against a stack of cotton bales, smoking a cigar and tapping his foot to the rousing rythem of the roustabouts' roistering. "Howdy, John," he smiled.

"What brings you here?" John asked, pumping the extended hand. "Finally decided to sign up as a cub pilot?"

Clemens swept a hand through his unruly shock of dark auburn hair. "Not yet, sir. Haven't given up on the newspaper business. I've been working as a printer for the *St. Louis Evening News*, a daily. I've finally saved up enough to head for New York. Plan to leave this week. I was strolling along the levee just now and saw the *Lucky Molly*. Figured I might catch you holed up with a book."

"Well, come on in," John said, "although I don't know if we'll be able to hear each other talk over the racket *they're* making." He nodded toward the roustabouts.

"Oh, they don't bother me," Clemens said. "Reminds me of what my mother told me when I complained about our young slave Sandy's singing, whistling, yelling, whooping, and laughing all day long while he waited on the table and helped with the house and yard chores." Clemens continued his story as the two of them ascended the gangplank. "I went raging to my mother one day complaining that Sandy's noisemaking was maddening, devastating and unendurable. I insisted that she put a stop to the clamor." Clemens took a puff from his cigar, his eyes bright in the moonlight. "Tears came to my mother's eyes, and she said, 'Think, he is sold away from his mother; she is in Maryland, a thousand miles from here, and he will never see her again, poor thing. When he is singing it is a sign he is not remembering and that comforts me. It would break my heart if Sandy should stop singing.'"Clemens shrugged. "Powerful argument, espcially when made by one's mother. I've always liked music, but since that moment I've been especially fond of listening to slaves or roustabouts sing."

John had been heading for his cabin, but stopped. "You say you like music? Do you play any instruments?"

"Sure," said Clemens. "I excel on the piano, the guitar, and the banjo."

"By chance," said John, "do you dance?"

"I do," answered Clemens, warily, "but I am particular in my preference for girls as partners for that endeavor."

"I'm sure I would be, too, if I could," said John. "The problem is I can't, and I must, within two weeks!"

"Hang it! What are you talking about?"

"Lindy is having a party in two weeks and expects me to dance with her. I can't dance a lick!"

"Well, providence has brought your angel, my friend. Lead me to the ballroom."

Once in the grand saloon, they lit several of the lamps near the piano. Clemens removed his broadcloth coat, folded it, and placed it upon the piano bench.

"First," he announced, "you must learn a quadrille."

He showed John where to stand.

"A quadrille is very simple and easy. All you have to do is stand up in the middle of the floor, being careful to get your lady on your right and yourself on your lady's left-hand side. Then you are all right, you know."

Standing to John's left, he showed him the pose to assume, then hummed a few bars of an unidentifiable tune.

"When you hear a blast of music you lay your hand on your stomach and bow to the lady of your choice. Then you turn around and bow to the fiddlers." He demonstrated. "Then the first order is, 'First couple fore and aft' or words to that effect. This is very easy. You have only to march across the house, keeping out of the way of advancing couples, who very seldom know what they are going to do. When you get over, if you find your partner there, swing her; if you don't, hunt her up, for it is very handy to have a partner."

John laughed as Clemens pantomimed searching for his lost partner.

"The next order is, 'Ladies charge.' This is an exceedingly difficult figure and requires great presence of mind. At this point order and regularity cease.

The dancers get excited. The musicians become insane. Turmoil and confusion ensue!" In spite of his words, Clemens demonstrated the dance steps with precision and skill. To his delight, John found that he could mimic the movements.

"Well, I'll be dog-darned," Clemens said, finally, grinning at John. "You're dancing!"

The lessons lasted over two hours, with Clemens teaching John everything he knew about dancing, from quadrilles to reels to waltzes. When the lessons ended, Clemens plopped onto the piano bench and broke into a mournful and practically never-ending song about an old horse named Methusalem who was sold in Jerusalem many a long year ago. His tenor voice was clear and his fingers competent upon the keys.

Clemens was sweating by the time he pounded out his last verse: "I had an old horse, and he died in the wilderness, died in the wilderness, died in the wilderness, I had an old horse, and he died in the wilderness, many a long year ago." As he played the last chord, the roustabouts on the levee burst into applause and cheers. "Well," he drawled, "I didn't realize we had ourselves an audience." He wiped the sweat from his brow. "Whew. I don't usually work this hard. There may be lazier men than I, and there may be men more tired than I—but they're dead men."

John Carmichael and Sam Clemens spent the rest of the night trading stories in the pilothouse of the *Lucky Molly*. They were kindred souls. Each was the most well-read young man the other had ever met. Both dreamed of being great writers. Both dreamed of being steamboatmen. Both aspired to be rich and famous. Both had their whole lives ahead of them. When the pink fingers of sunrise reached across the sky and tickled the tops of the trees covering the Illinois side of the river, Clemens stood and clapped John on the shoulder. "I'd best get going," he said. "I'll look you up when I get back from New York."

"I'll be watching for your by-line," John said. "Or will you be writing under a *nom de plume*?"

"Who knows? When I was writing for the Hannibal *Journal* I used the pen name 'W. Epaminondas Adrastus Blabb' for a while. I need to come up with something a bit more catchy, though."

"Definitely," John nodded. "That's much too ordinary. You simply can't go anywhere without running into a W. Epaminondas Adrastus Blabb. They're all over the place."

"I'll let you know when I think of a good one," promised Samuel Langhorne Clemens.

Chapter 11

"How do I look?" John asked Artemus Primm. It was the night of Lindy's coming-out party. The officers and much of the crew of the *Lucky Molly* had spent the afternoon whipping the steamboat into first-rate shape for the dance. O'Malley had invited all of the prominent families of Cape Girardeau. Hundreds of potential customers would be on the steamboat for the first time. He wanted the *Lucky Molly* to make a grand impression. The party was set to start in fifteen minutes. John could hear the orchestra warming up.

"You look just fine," pronounced Artemus Primm, standing on a chair in front of the mirror on the wall as he carefully knotted his own black string tie.

John thought of Lindy with eager anticipation. O'Malley had bought him a suit in New Orleans. The coat's style was known as the "Prince Albert," a dapper black frock coat. The trousers were the latest fashion. He was itching to try out the dance steps Clemens had taught him. Lindy was going to be pleasantly surprised.

A sharp knock sounded on the door.

"Carmichael, you in there?"

John crossed the floor of the small cabin and opened the door. Horace Claxton stood in the doorway, his large body filling the door frame.

"Pete Carnahan needs you in the engine room. He's been cleaning mud from the boilers all afternoon. There's something caught inside one of them. Someone with small hands needs to help. Carnahan says you're the one."

John studied Claxton doubtfully. If Carnahan needed his help, why hadn't he sent for him sooner?

Claxton sneered impatiently. "Don't worry none, Johnny-boy. Carnahan said it won't take no more than ten minutes. You'll still get to your party."

John frowned. If he went to help Pete Carnahan he'd almost certainly be late to the dance. Lindy would be looking for him. He was tempted to tell Claxton to find someone else to do it. But, on the other hand, if Carnahan needed him . . .

"All right," John said. "I'll help out."

"I wouldn't wear them clothes if I was you," said Claxton, looking with contempt at John's new suit. "The inside of a muddy boiler will ruin a pretty little outfit like that real quick."

John changed into clean work clothes and contemplated the timetable of his evening. If he got down to the engine room quickly and fixed the problem in ten minutes, he'd be able to get to the party on time.

"I'll come with you," offered Artemus Primm, looking coldly at Claxton as they left the cabin. "If your hands aren't small enough, mine will be."

Although John didn't acknowledge it, he felt relieved to have an escort. Something in Claxton's expression had seemed peculiar.

When John opened the engine room door, the warm air of the guts of the steamboat enveloped him. Although the main engines were shut off, the auxiliary pump was fired up, heating the room with its escaping clouds of steam. Pete Carnahan had a boiler opened up and was leaning inside it, cleaning out the last of the mud.

"I'm here, Pete," John announced, anxious to complete his job and get back to the upper decks.

The wiry engineer stood up and stretched his back. Mud from the boiler covered his work clothes. "Awful nice of you fellows to come down here to help your old pal, but you're a mite late. I'm just finishing up."

"Sorry. Claxton didn't tell me you sent for me until just now."

"I could've *used* help," said Carnahan, resting an arm on the big boiler, "but I didn't send Claxton after you fellows. I'm done, like I said."

Exasperated, John hurried back to his cabin. Claxton's scheme revealed itself when John reached the bed where he'd left his suit. It was gone. "Claxton stole my clothes," John spoke aloud as the realization hit him.

"Well, one thing's for sure," Artemus Primm frowned. "Mine won't fit you."

Minutes later, John found Horace Claxton on the boiler deck at the stern of the *Lucky Molly*, chatting nonchalantly with Jason Farley, Vice-President of the Bank of Missouri in Jackson. Farley was the man O'Malley had consulted about getting a loan to buy another steamboat. He was a slender cotton-haired man in his fifties, immaculately dressed.

Claxton grinned as John approached. "Looking for something, Carmichael?"

"You know I am. Where'd you put my suit?"

Claxton held up a dark ball of cloth. "This what you're looking for?"

The suitcoat and pants had been knotted together.

"Very funny. May I have it back?"

Claxton held it above his head. "Come get it." John reached for the suit.

Claxton effortlessly extended his long arm out of John's reach. "Just not big enough, are you?"

Artemus Primm, who had been following, arrived near them. "Come on, Horace," said the clerk in his high-pitched voice. "Let John have his suit."

Claxton faced Artemus Primm, his eyes glittering yellow in the torchlight. "Stay out of this, Primm, or I'll twist your bald head right off your scrawny neck and throw your misshapen carcass right into the river. I haven't tossed me a midget in a long time."

The two couples near Claxton backed away, the women murmuring. Claxton faced John. "You want your fancy duds, boy, beg for them."

"Claxton," John said steadily, nodding toward the dapper banker and his wife, "I'm surprised you'd let nice people like this see what an oaf you are. You're a disgrace to the *Lucky Molly*."

Claxton spit on the deck. "Well, John, I'm sorry your friend Clemens isn't here to see my little production of John's Duds Crossing the Mississippi." With a flick of his wrist he tossed the suit over the rail.

John watched with dismay as the wadded ball of clothing sailed through the air and disappeared beneath the flowing waters of the Mississippi River.

Lindy glanced anxiously around the saloon of the *Lucky Molly*. John Carmichael was still not at the dance. She tapped her foot impatiently. The small orchestra from St. Vincent's College launched into another tune, the music filling the steamboat's huge ballroom. Tables and chairs were neatly arranged along the walls of the long steamboat saloon. The center of the big room was a dance floor filled with laughing, talking, dancing guests, all present to honor Lindy. Yet the most important guest, she fumed, was conspicuously absent. She'd already danced with her father and some of his customers, but she'd only been half interested in the dances so far. She'd been dreaming for weeks of dancing with John Carmichael, and he was still not here.

Where could he be? Her small hands knotted into tight fists. She knew he was planning to come. He'd told her so. Her father had told her, too, about John's new suit and the dancing lessons from Sam Clemens. Maybe John was sick or hurt. She touched her father's arm lightly. "Papa, may I go see if John is in his cabin? He ought to be here by now. I'm worried about him."

"Nonsense, Rosalind. This is your party. You can't leave." O'Malley leaned his large face close to hers, white whiskers tickling her cheek. "Tell you what, my little Rose. I'll go look in his cabin myself, if you'd like."

"Thank you, Papa. It's just not like John to be late."

O'Malley worked his way through the crowd toward the doorway.

As the orchestra began playing a beautiful Strauss waltz, Lindy swayed slightly from side to side. She wanted to dance with John. He was ruining her evening by his absence.

"May I have this dance, Miss O'Malley?"

The deep voice startled her. Tyler Fitch, white suit gleaming in the candle-light, stood next to her, his dark eyes shining.

"No, thank you, Mr. Fitch. I'm waiting for my father." Her eyes uncon-sciously flicked toward his wounded ear. The missing flesh and cartilage did not detract significantly from his handsome appearance.

"Miss O'Malley, I simply won't take *no* for an answer. After all, I was kind enough to take you for a ride around Cape when you were looking for a dress to wear to this very party. Surely I'm entitled to at least one dance as repayment?"

Although she remained poised and calm on the outside, she fidgeted ner-vously on the inside. John had been so angry about her riding in Fitch's car-riage. Unreasonably so. He'd be furious if she danced with Fitch. Yet, Fitch *had* been awfully nice to let her ride in his carriage. She glanced at the door-way. If she were going to dance with Fitch at all, it would be much better to do it before John arrived. "Very well," she said, holding out her hand. "One dance."

He was a graceful and elegant waltzer, guiding her effortlessly. She real-ized with a small twinge of pride that of the dozens of couples on the floor, they were the best dancers.

"Surprised I dance well?" he asked softly, the rest of the room a blur as they revolved in perpetual circles.

"No. I'm surprised by myself, actually. I was never one of Mr. Bruns' bet-ter dance students. You must bring out the best in me."

Tyler Fitch smiled. "The best in *you* is truly worth seeing. You are by far the most beautiful woman in this room."

They glided around the floor wordlessly for a few moments.

"I was surprised when I got your invitation," Fitch said.

"Why is that?"

"I wasn't born with a silver spoon in my mouth, for one thing. I started out with nothing and scratched and clawed my way to the top. I'm one of the rich-est men in town, now, but I still get snubbed by certain families when it comes to social matters."

Lindy noticed his neck growing bright red, matching the bow tie under his clean-shaven chin.

"Perhaps it's the company you keep, Mr. Fitch," she said, thinking of Samantha Peabody.

"What do you mean by that?"

"I think you know."

They continued gliding to the melody of the waltz.

"The O'Malleys weren't born with any silver spoons, either, Mr. Fitch. We'd be the last to snub you for that reason. Papa started out as a deck hand working for Mike Fink. He's built his business by hard work. He does his job honestly and tirelessly, the best he can, and lets acceptance and respect come naturally. That's what America's all about."

Tyler Fitch smiled at her. "Those are awfully wise words from such a young girl."

"This *is* my coming-out party. I'm not a child anymore."

He let his eyes boldly navigate her figure.

"That, my dear, is an understatement."

She blushed. Glancing at the crowd, she saw O'Malley standing near a door to the boiler deck. Her father's face wore lines of concern. In answer to her questioning eyes, the big captain held out the empty palms of his large hands. Obviously, he had not located John. *Where in the world could John be?* Her mind raced as her feet moved with the waltz. This was not like him at all. He was the most industrious, conscientious person she'd ever met. He'd been looking forward to the dance. Where was he?

"What's wrong?" Tyler Fitch asked.

"Nothing."

As they glided past the bow entrance to the saloon, John came through the door, walking with Jason Farley. John was tall and dashing in a dark suit, the black coat accenting his broad shoulders and the white shirt emphasizing the deep tan of his face and hands. His sun-lightened blond hair shone in the candle-light. He was smiling as he glanced around the room. He was searching for her, she knew, and her heart glowed. Wouldn't this dance ever end?

She was watching John when his eyes found her in Tyler Fitch's arms. The smile vanished from his face as if slapped off. He turned abruptly and shoved his way to the door, leaving a wake of disgruntled people behind him. A sinking sensation filled her stomach as she danced with Fitch. She *had* to follow John, she simply had to.

"I'm afraid I'm getting sick. Please excuse me." She broke away from Fitch. Hiking her long, hooped dress so it didn't drag the floor, she dodged dancing couples as she hurried to the door John had exited. She found him on the hurri-cane deck. "It wasn't nice of you to leave my party like that."

He glared at her, torchlight flashing in livid eyes. "Nice! Was it *nice* of Tyler Fitch to shoot my father to death? I saw him do it. You saw him do it. Lindy, how can you dance with that man? How can you let him touch you?"

She saw the pain in his handsome face, and she longed to caress it away. Yet, the O'Malley blood in her veins was rising to the occasion .

"I can dance with whomever I please. Besides, where have you been all night? You're an hour late to my party. I was hurt you weren't there when it started. I really was."

"So hurt you were cavorting with Tyler Fitch! First he murders my father, and now he's stealing you away from me!"

She felt a rush of exhilaration. *He did love her.*

"I was just dancing with him. It isn't like I kissed him or anything."

"You have so little regard for me that you'd humiliate me by dancing with the man who murdered my father."

"It wasn't *murder*. It was a fair duel. Papa says so. They both were at fault for dueling. It was a stupid thing for both of them to do, your father included."

He stepped back and looked at her coldly. "Oh, I see. Now you even talk like Tyler Fitch. Well, I'll tell you what. Go back to your insignificant little party and dance with him to your heart's content. You can both just waltz all the way to hell for all I care!" He left abruptly.

She stood alone under the night stars for several long minutes, listening to the orchestra music floating magically over the river, accompanied by the rhythmic beat of the waves softly kissing the side of the steamboat. Eventually she returned to the ballroom, carrying a painful emptiness in the pit of her stomach.

The next morning, at daybreak, John sat cross-legged on the roof of the pilot house of the *Lucky Molly*, the grainy surface of the roof making ridges and indentations in the skin of his palms. He'd been awake all night, unable to sleep. At some point during the starlit evening he'd decided he owed Lindy an apology. He planned to apologize before breakfast.

After a while, he heard the loud voice of Horace Claxton waking the deck hands. Within minutes, the stokers were loading wood into the furnaces. Smoke began climbing tentatively out of the twin chimneys.

In the growing morning light, O'Malley strode alone down Themis Street toward the *Lucky Molly*.

John clamored down from the steamboat roof and met O'Malley as the captain came up the gangplank.

"We aren't leaving this early, are we, Uncle Pat?"

"That we are."

"I didn't know. Are all the crew on board?"

"Should be. I announced it yesterday."

John glanced nervously up Themis Street.

"Is there time for me to say goodbye to Lindy?"

"Lad, I don't think so. I want to pull out soon as we've built enough steam. Besides, the girl's not up yet."

John glanced at the chimneys of the *Lucky Molly*. The smoke was becoming blacker.

"How long will we be gone?"

"At least ten days."

The Captain put a hand on John's shoulder.

"I don't know what kind of spat you and Rosalind had last night, but things of that sort happen. Why don't you just write her a little note? Have one of the roustabouts on the levee take it to the house. You can talk to her when we get back."

John rushed to his cabin and hastily scribbled a letter to Lindy:

May 13, 1852
Lindy,

I'm sorry for what I said to you. It was inexcusable.
I have no justification other than the fact I love you.
Please accept my apologies.

Yours,
John

He sealed it inside an envelope and gave it to a black roustabout on the levee.

Sitting at the desk in his office, Tyler Fitch folded John's note to Lindy and tore it into pieces. It had not been difficult to get it from the roustabout. After reading it, he was glad it would never reach its intended destination. Tyler Fitch fingered the scarred flesh of his left ear and considered his plans for Rosalind O'Malley. She was destined to be his wife. He didn't love her; but then he had never truly loved anyone. Marrying her would be a shrewd business move. As her husband, he'd eventually absorb O'Malley's steamboat business into his own. O'Malley was not a young man. Also, she and her aunt were an accepted part of the respected society of Cape Girardeau. Marrying her would give him access to social circles always closed to him in the past. With the lovely Rosalind O'Malley as his wife, his steamboat business would grow even faster than it had already.

He glanced again at the shredded letter. The biggest obstacle to winning Lindy was the author of this bit of drivel. John Carmichael was a mere boy, though. Tyler Fitch was 26 years old, hardened and seasoned by years of living by wits and panache. He would beat out this boy for the affections of the young lady, by one means or another. He moved to his office fireplace and lit the scraps of paper with the glowing fire from the end of his expensive cigar.

The *Lucky Molly* was docked at the New Orleans wharf. A white full moon cast its glow over the scores of steamboats. Most of O'Malley's crew had ventured onto Gallatin and Barracks streets, gravitating toward the tinkling music of the bars and bordellos of New Orleans. The *Lucky Molly* rested lightly on the water, completely unloaded, practically empty, bobbing gently with the flow of the Mississippi.

John Carmichael had stayed on board. He didn't feel like celebrating. He stood alone on the lower deck at the front of the steamboat, under the starlit sky, leaning on the railing, facing the bright lights of downtown New Orleans. It had been six days since he'd seen Lindy, six long days since he'd spoken so harshly to her. He cringed. He hoped his note had soothed her injured feelings. All he wanted in the world was to be back in Cape Girardeau, talking with Lindy O'Malley, knowing that everything was all right between them.

A creaking noise caught his attention. He turned and glanced upward toward the latticework and railings above him. A warm shower of stinking human urine and excrement splashed onto his face and shoulders. Horace Claxton stood on the boiler deck above him, an empty chamber pot in his large hands.

"Well, fancy that!" Claxton said, grinning. "Didn't see you down there. Just emptying my pot."

John wiped globs of reeking slime from his face. "I'll just bet this was an accident, Claxton."

Claxton laughed derisively. "What if it ain't? What would you do about it? You're getting bigger. Getting some muscle. But I'll kick your hindsides from here to Memphis if you give me half a reason to. You gonna give me a reason? I told you it was an accident. You calling me a liar?"

John lowered his eyes.

"Glad to see you're still yellow. Some things even a little muscle don't change."

After Claxton disappeared, John unbuttoned his shirt. The sooner he removed the urine-soaked cloth from his skin, the sooner the humiliation might leave his soul. As he undid the last button, he noticed Pete Carnahan standing in the shadows under the boiler deck, fifteen feet away. A newer and more powerful wave of embarrassment washed over John. Carnahan had seen it all.

"How long have you been here?" John asked.

"Long enough." Carnahan offered a bottle. "Have a drink. Nothing soothes the nerves like a shot of straight bourbon."

"No thanks. I don't need anything for my nerves."

"Don't you? Well, at least have a swig to take the stench out of your nostrils."

John felt his cheeks reddening in the dark. He accepted the bottle and downed a deep gulp. A fiery explosion passed through his mouth and throat.

"Good stuff, hey?" chuckled Carnahan.

"Yeah," gasped John. The fire bit anew as he took a breath of air.

Carnahan reclaimed the bottle. "I don't believe none of your books ever taught you how to deal with a bully like Horace Claxton. Captain O'Malley— who'd be the best teacher you could possibly have, all the fights he had when he wore the red scarf—ain't likely to teach you, 'cause he don't see what's going on. Artemus Primm can't teach you 'cause he don't know hisself. Looks like it's up to me, your favorite engineer." Carnahan took a long draw from his bottle. "First, you got to know you did the right thing out here just now. You took his abuse and kept your tongue. You two were alone. He would've loved the chance to fight you tonight. He had a knife on him, no doubt. You were smart to avoid a tussle. You're going to have to fight him some day, though, if you both stay on this boat. But don't *ever* fight Horace Claxton without witnesses. He'd knife you and toss your corpse into the river when no one's watchin'. You fight him, you got to do it with lots of people around to keep him honest."

A shudder shot down John's spine like a tangible streak of yellow. He was glad Pete Carnahan hadn't noticed his hands shaking.

"Secondly, you need to *prepare* for fighting Horace Claxton or someone like him. Don't just wait for it to happen. Get ready."

"How?"

Pete Carnahan picked up a piece of firewood. "See this piece of cotton-wood?"

John nodded. It was three feet long and three inches in diameter.

Carnahan held the wood in both hands straight out from his body. "Pretend this piece of wood's Horace Claxton's face. He's coming right at me. Watch this."

The engineer lowered his head and jerked the wood sharply against the top of his dark brown hair. The wood snapped, the two pieces falling to the floor at his feet.

"You broke it with your head!"

"Darn right I did. The human noggin can be one of your best weapons in a fight. A good head-butt can smear a man's nose all over his face."

Carnahan tossed John a piece of firewood. "Here. Start out with a small one."

"You want me to break it with my head?"

"Don't jabber about it. Just do it."

John didn't relish the thought of striking his head against the hard wood.

"Well, get on with it. We don't have all night."

John closed his eyes and jerked the piece of firewood toward the top of his head, wincing when it struck his forehead. Pain flashed across his brow. The wood snapped, one of its ragged ends scratching the skin just under his hairline.

Carnahan clapped him on the shoulder. "Not too bad! You smacked it with your forehead, though, cut yourself a little. You should do your butting with the top of your head. Like this."

Carnahan effortlessly snapped another piece of wood over his crown. Grinning, he gathered an armful of firewood. "Come with me to the engine room, John. We got to work on your technique."

Two weeks later, the *Lucky Molly* rounded the bend in the Mississippi south of Cape Girardeau, sounding her bell as the crew made preparations to land at the levee. John Carmichael stood on the lower deck at the front of the steam-boat, between the twin gangplanks, shading his eyes with his hand as he looked for Lindy. The levee swarmed with activity. Two other steamboats, the *White Cloud* and the *Reindeer*, were tied up at the landing. Dark clouds of smoke drifted over the river north of town announcing that yet another steamboat was coming downriver from St. Louis. Merchants, deck hands, and roustabouts scurried about the levee like ants on an ant hill, hurriedly carrying cargo on and off the boats. Finally, John spotted Lindy. She stood next to Maude O'Malley near the *White Cloud*.

As soon as the *Lucky Molly* lowered a gangplank, John rushed down it. "How are you, Lindy?" he asked as he approached the two O'Malley women.

Lindy's brown eyes were cool. "Look, Aunt Maude. There's Papa now." She brushed past John and hurried to her father.

John exchanged a surprised glance with Maude O'Malley. "I take it Lindy is still angry with me."

"So it would seem."

Patrick O'Malley wrapped a large arm over his daughter's shoulders as they strolled toward John and Maude.

"Will you be able to stay for supper, Papa?"

"No, Little Rose. We're just unloading a few things here in Cape. We'll be back on the river in less than an hour, headed for St. Louis."

O'Malley ran his fingers through her dark curls. "I'll be back in Cape Girardeau tomorrow night. Maybe even in time for supper. Say, John," O'Malley said, green eyes twinkling, "I don't necessarily need you on board for the next twenty-four hours. If you'd like, you can have some time off, stay here in Cape and visit the inhabitants."

John smiled with relief and gratitude until Lindy spoke.

"John can stay if he wants, of course, Papa, but I have other plans for the rest of today and tomorrow. I won't be able to entertain him."

"Rosalind," said Maude O'Malley. "John's family. You don't need to worry about entertaining him. You're being rude. Of course he can stay with us."

"Never mind," John said. "I'll stay with Uncle Pat on the *Lucky Molly*." He was staring at Lindy as he spoke. Her face was flushed. She had still not looked at him since he'd arrived.

Suddenly, she pointed north. "Look! The *Andrew Jackson II* is coming! Excuse me, Papa. Tyler told me yesterday he'd be bringing me a present from St. Louis."

Tyler. Her use of the given name wasn't lost on John.

She gathered her skirts above her ankles and hurried to the sign in front of Fitch's store: *FASTEST STEAMBOAT OF CAPE GIRARDEAU.*

"What in tarnation has gotten into her?" Captain O'Malley asked his sister.

"She's been seeing quite a bit of Tyler Fitch these past couple weeks. Started right after you left."

"What do you mean 'seeing'?" asked O'Malley loudly.

"Well, he took her to a slave auction, took her on some carriage rides, called on her at the house. I've been chaperoning them, of course. It's an arduous task. I can't tolerate that man." Maude O'Malley glanced uneasily at John, whose cheeks burned crimson.

"Blast it! I'll never understand women!" Patrick O'Malley shook his head. "Two weeks ago John here was all she could talk about." O'Malley patted John's shoulder. "Get that hangdog look off your face, son. Women are fickle. I'm sure she's going through a spell of some sort."

John wasn't sure if he replied audibly or not. He knew Lindy wasn't going through any sort of spell. She'd simply decided not to forgive him. She'd read his note and remained angry, maybe even laughing at his feeble effort to apologize. Well, he wouldn't grovel forever. He'd apologized. He'd done his part. Now it was her turn.

They moved toward the *Andrew Jackson II* as the 300-foot sidewheeler neared the levee. A painting of Andrew Jackson's head adorned each paddle wheel housing. The towering black twin chimneys rose much higher than the *Lucky Molly's* stacks.

"Big as she is," muttered O'Malley, his eyes studying every detail of his rival's boat, "she's still sleek. Bet she's fast."

"Oh, the *Andrew Jackson II*'s fast, Papa," said Lindy, who had returned to his side. "Tyler says she's much faster than the *Andrew Jackson*. And you know, the *Andrew Jackson* beat our boat."

O'Malley grimaced. "Don't remind me. Isn't this gaudy sign reminder enough?"

Tyler Fitch was the first person off the *Andrew Jackson II* when it finished docking. Impeccable in his white suit and red bow tie, he bounded up the cobblestones to join them. "Good afternoon, Captain O'Malley, Mr. Carmichael."

O'Malley nodded. John didn't move.

"Lindy, you look charming today," said Fitch, bowing slightly. "As promised, I've brought you something from St. Louis."

"Did you?"

"Absolutely. Candy from the finest store in the city."

He handed her a box.

"Why, thank you, Tyler." She glanced almost imperceptibly at John as she accepted the gift. Their eyes met for a fraction of a second.

"Tell me, Fitch," said Patrick O'Malley. "How does your new steamboat run?"

"Like a charm. She's fast and smooth, probably the fastest boat on the river right now, except for perhaps the *J. M. White*. I aim to shoot for a couple of the *White's* records this summer."

"What sort of time does she make from New Orleans to St. Louis?"

"Four days, twenty hours and fifteen minutes."

O'Malley stroked his beard. "Not bad. You're still a ways off the *J. M. White*'s 1844 record of three days, twenty-three hours and nine minutes."

"As I said, Captain O'Malley, I'll go for that record soon." Tyler Fitch winked at Lindy. "Just think, young lady. Once I break that record you'll be able to tell people that the fastest boat on the entire Mississippi River belongs to a friend of yours."

"That would be nice." She looked at her father and smiled fondly. "It would be even nicer, though, to be able to tell them it's owned by my very own papa."

Fitch nodded graciously. "Say, O'Malley, when *are* you getting a new boat? I keep hearing rumors you're buying a bigger and better one, but then I see you bobbing around on that same old washtub."

"I'll have a new one soon, Fitch."

"Splendid. Get something comparable to the *Andrew Jackson II*. I need some competition so I'll have a good excuse to open up the engines. In my last dozen races, my opponent wasn't even in sight after the first ten miles."

"Enjoy it while you can. When I get my new boat she'll give the *Andrew Jackson II* a race you won't be forgetting. You can bet on it."

"I just might." Tyler Fitch smiled again at Lindy. "I'm tying up in Cape Girardeau for two days. May I see you tomorrow?"

"I'd be delighted."

John glanced at her. She was facing Fitch, smiling. John's gaze moved to Fitch's crippled ear, and he found himself wishing his father's shot had gone just a few inches to the right.

As Tyler Fitch sauntered jauntily back to his majestic white steamboat, John finally caught and held Lindy's eyes with his own. His questioning gaze was met with frosty indifference.

Chapter 12

"It's a dangerous situation financially," declared Patrick O'Malley, "but I'm going to do it, anyway."

John moved a candle closer to the paperwork as he tried to decipher O'Malley's handwritten calculations. "Your new steamboat's going to cost 182,000 dollars!" John gasped.

O'Malley shifted uncomfortably in his chair. "I'll be mortgaged up to my neck, true enough, but one or two good seasons on the river and the *Girardeau Rose* will pay for herself."

Hearing the proposed name of the steamboat brought images of Lindy's face into John's mind. He hadn't seen her in five weeks. She was supposedly spending quite a bit of time with Tyler Fitch. He pushed the thoughts away and forced himself to concentrate upon O'Malley's words.

"I can round up the money, John."

"How?"

"Jason Farley at the Bank of Missouri in Jackson says the bank will loan me 20,000 dollars with the Lucky Molly as collateral. They'll loan me another 7,000 with my house and my other Cape Girardeau real estate as collateral. I've got 50,000 in cash saved up. And I've got 5,000 dollars from you, if you'll loan it to me."

"Five thousand from me? I'd loan it to you if I had it, but I don't have anywhere near 5,000 dollars."

He could see O'Malley's face reddening even in the candlelight. The big man seemed uncomfortable. "John, I've something to admit that you might not like." O'Malley raised his green eyes to meet John's. "Do you recall, lad, when Tyler Fitch offered to return to you the money he'd won from your father in the duel?"

John was silent. He realized what was coming next.

"After you turned it down, I went to Fitch and offered to hold it for you. You were too young to know what you were doing when you refused it."

John's hands turned cold. "Uncle Pat, how could you take money from him! You knew I didn't want his blood money."

"I'm sorry. I truly am. I honestly believed I did the right thing for you, though. Still do."

"You did the right thing for *yourself*, you mean. I bet you knew all along you wanted to use my money for your own steamboat."

John regretted the words as soon as he'd spoken them. O'Malley sat stiffly in his chair. They were both silent for several long seconds.

"I'm sorry, Uncle Pat. That was uncalled for. I know you were just trying to help."

"No. It probably *was* called for. To tell the honest truth, I guess I *have* known all along that some day I'd try to talk you into investing in a steamboat with me." Guilt shone in O'Malley's honest eyes. John was sorry he'd placed it there.

"Oh, well, it's done. Count me in as an investor."

O'Malley brightened. "Once I put up the $82,000, Jason Farley is going to loan me 100,000 dollars out of his own funds. The other people at his bank might not like it. Against bank policy or something. But we'll keep quiet about it. Farley will be a silent partner with us, and I'll give him a demand note. We have a gentleman's agreement that he won't demand it for at least two years. By then, we'll be ready to pay him off. The *Girardeau Rose* will average at least 5,000 in profit on each St. Louis–New Orleans trip, two trips per month, nine months per year."

"Will you keep the *Lucky Molly* running, too?"

"That I will, lad. Have a mind to make *you* her captain."

"Me! I'm only seventeen!"

"I can read a calendar. I also know that in the time you've been on this boat you've learned her inside out. You've worked as a deck hand, you've learned the engineer's trade, you've worked with the pilots, you've worked with the clerk. You know the operations of the *Lucky Molly* better than I do. You can do it."

"I don't know what to say."

"No need to say anything, yet. The *Girardeau Rose* won't be built for several months. Just start thinking how you'll handle things as captain of the *Lucky Molly*. Prepare for the challenge of a lifetime."

Several months later, in the late summer of 1852, John Carmichael stood on the levee in Louisville, preparing to assume the captaincy of the *Lucky Molly*. For the first time, he was wearing the dark blue uniform of a riverboat captain.

O'Malley had presented him with the specially tailored uniform that morning. The *Girardeau Rose* was still resting on large blocks next to the river. She hadn't been painted yet. Much of the detailed woodwork still needed to be completed. Even in her rough and naked state, though, her graceful lines were impressive.

"I'm going to stay here in Louisville, supervising the finishing touches myself," O'Malley was saying. "I'm trusting you with the *Lucky Molly*, John."

"Yes, sir. I can handle it," John said, hoping his words were true. From where they stood, John and O'Malley heard Horace Claxton yelling at a deck hand.

"If Claxton won't obey your orders," said O'Malley resolutely, "you have my permission to fire him. I know he was upset when I made you Captain. Hopefully, it won't affect his work. He's a good mate, but if he gives you trouble it's his mistake. Understand?"

A heavy burden lifted from John's shoulders.

Three days later the *Lucky Molly* was navigating the Mississippi on a stretch of muddy river between Cairo and Cape Girardeau. There were no towns in sight, no signs of civilization except an occasional woodyard punctuating the lush green wooded swampland on each side of the river. The late summer air was hot and humid. The sun shone brightly off the sand bars, almost blinding in intensity.

All in all, thought John Carmichael as he gazed out of the pilothouse windows, it was a fine day to be the captain of a steamboat. He'd experienced little trouble substituting for Patrick O'Malley as captain of the *Lucky Molly*. Abner Conrad accepted him completely. The one-armed pilot obviously appreciated the fact John didn't try to pretend he knew more about steamboating than the pilots. Likewise, Artemus Primm had been completely supportive. The clerk, totally satisfied with his position, harbored no interest whatsoever in shouldering the responsibility of captaining a boat. One relationship that had changed, to John's disappointment, was his friendship with Pete Carnahan. Although John visited the engine room every evening and still lifted the homemade dumbbells daily, Carnahan now seemed uncomfortable around him, less likely to take a swig from his bottle, less likely to offer advice or criticism.

John's thoughts were interrupted by frantic shouts.

"Captain," sputtered a red-headed deck hand who'd just scrambled up the steps from the lower deck. "Man overboard! One of the deck hands. Peterson!"

"Where is he?"

"Back behind the boat a little ways. Got up here to tell you quick as I could."

"Turn us around, Abner," John ordered, giving him the wheel.

John and the deck hand hurried down the steps to the lower level of the steamboat.

"How did Peterson fall off?"

"Ask someone else, Captain. I can't answer that."

Several deck hands, roustabouts, and stokers stood in a crowd near the railing at the stern of the steamboat, shouting and pointing. Peterson splashed and struggled 500 yards downriver from the *Lucky Molly*. His bobbing head and waving arms looked like animated snags.

"Get a rope!" John ordered.

The *Lucky Molly* circled and began racing downstream toward Peterson, who kept disappearing from view, only to reappear moments later, thrashing wildly. Horace Claxton stood near the railing of the steamboat, leaning against it nonchalantly, large forearms folded across his chest.

"Claxton, get the yawl ready to lower in case we need it!"

Claxton didn't move. John stared at him. The big mate returned the gaze.

"I told you to get the yawl ready to lower."

Horace Claxton spit over the railing.

"That ignorant Peterson ain't worth turning around for. Let him swim to shore, if he can."

A deck hand interrupted. "Too late, Captain."

John looked back where Peterson had been splashing seconds before. The water was smooth. Empty. Not even bubbles marked the watery grave. The *Lucky Molly* slowly prowled the area where Peterson had last been seen. Abner Conrad set both paddle wheels running backwards, letting the big steamboat tread water, holding its position against the powerful current as dozens of pairs of eyes searched for the fallen deck hand.

John scanned the water, carefully studying the shoreline on both sides of the wide river. He felt physically ill when he realized that as a Captain, he'd lost his first man. Peterson was gone.

"Claxton, you're the mate. You're in charge down here. What happened?"

Claxton spread his big hands, palms up. "Peterson went berserk, twitching and jerking. Some kind of seizure, I guess. Next thing you know, he flipped over the rail. Ain't that right, boys?" A dozen deck hands were gathered nearby. A few nodded. "The way I see it, *Captain Carmichael*," said Claxton, spitting out the title, "anyone who interfered would've ended up breathing Mississippi mud, just like Peterson. When a man goes crazy like that, it's best not to get involved."

"Did anyone else see this? Did anyone see Peterson go berserk and fall overboard?"

Several deck hands studied their feet. No one answered. John's exasperation increased as silent seconds passed.

"I haven't heard an answer. How did Peterson fall off this boat?"

"You got your answer," said Horace Claxton, still leaning against the railing. "He jumped off. I seen him. Guess I was the only one saw it." Claxton shrugged and looked lazily at the other deck hands.

A skinny roustabout who'd been with the *Lucky Molly* only two weeks stepped forward. "It ain't so, Captain. Peterson didn't jump. He was pushed."

Claxton jerked his head toward the roustabout. "You don't know what you're talking about! If you don't shut your mouth, I'll shut it for you. Permanently!"

"What do you mean?" asked John. "Who pushed him?"

The roustabout, color visibly draining from his face, eyed Claxton nervously. "I wasn't close enough to see who did it, Captain."

John moved toward Claxton, stopping directly in front of him. "Claxton, I don't believe you. Peterson didn't go crazy and jump off the boat. You threw him off, didn't you?"

A sneer formed on Claxton's face. "I told you what happened. You calling me a liar?"

John felt a tingling sensation in his stomach. "Yes. Furthermore, even if you're telling the truth, you didn't handle the situation properly." John met Claxton's glare and continued. "You should've immediately had the pilot turn around to go back for Peterson. You should've tried to throw him something to hold onto. You should've gotten the yawl ready to lower when I told you to. You should've done something besides standing there picking your nose."

Claxton bristled. "Look here. I run the deck. Run it damn well. Ran it years before you came along. You leave the handling of the deck hands to me. You run things on the upper decks. I'll take care of business down here. Everything will run smoothly, just like it always has."

John glanced at the faces around him. Pete Carnahan, still sweating from the heat of the engine room, stood silently near the passageway to the lower cabins. He smiled grimly. The thin smile had meaning: countless hours spent lifting weights in the engine room, dozens of grain bags ruined by punching, stacks of firewood broken over bleeding noggins, long talks of tactics in the heat of the engine room. John's palms were moist with sweat. "You misunderstand the question of rank on this boat, Claxton. I'm the captain of the *entire* boat, not just the upper decks. You're accountable to me, sir. Now, tell me what really happened to Peterson."

"I told you."

"Have you any explanation why you just stood and did nothing while Peterson was drowning?"

"If he wanted to drown hisself, that's his business."

"That's unacceptable to me. You're fired. I want you off this boat at Cape Girardeau."

"You can't fire me. Patrick O'Malley hired me. He's the only one can fire me."

"Not true. I not only can *fire* you, I can order you off this boat. I can put you ashore right now if I want to. I'm giving you the courtesy of taking you as far as Cape Girardeau before putting you off."

"You pompous little jackass! I'd like to *see* you try to throw me off this boat!"

John nodded to Abner Conrad in the pilot house. "Abner," he called. "Take us to the sand bar on the Missouri side of the river."

Minutes later, the steamboat nosed up to the sand bar, and the twin planks were lowered. Artemus Primm and two deck hands carried Claxton's belongings down the gangplank and tossed them onto the sand bar.

"This is it, Claxton. This is where you get off."

"I ain't moving."

John addressed the deck hands gathered around them. "I'm ordering each of you to help eject Horace Claxton from this boat. I'll pay an extra ten dollars wages to every man who helps."

"Wait a minute!" Claxton yelled, confronting the circle of men closing in on him. Claxton glared at John, his eyes wild with fury. He shook a large finger. "It ain't fair you've got a whole army to help you. You're captain just because you brown-nosed the boss man. You're a gutless worthless cheat like your old man. If you're a real man, throw me off this boat yourself."

John looked steadily at him. "Tell you what. You go down that plank and I'll fight you one-on-one on the sandbar."

Claxton's face broke into a grin. He popped the knuckles of his meaty hands. "My pleasure, boy. I've been waiting for this for a long time."

Claxton stormed down the gangplank and began pacing back and forth on the sandbar like a bull working itself into a frenzy.

"Boys," Pete Carnahan called out to the deck hands, "bring 50 barrels down here."

John was glad Carnahan was taking charge of the preparations. He was in no condition to worry about them. His stomach was flopping wildly as barrels were carried down the gangplank. Carnahan arranged them into a large circle on the sand bar. Both deck and cabin passengers hurried ashore and crowded around the forming circle, buzzing with excitement. Two professional gamblers were organizing bets on the fight. John had the impression the odds-makers were not giving him much of a chance. Not that he blamed them. He felt as though he were moving in a fog as he made his way to the circle of barrels. His mind cleared as he climbed over the wooden barrels and took a place in the impromptu ring. Claxton and Carnahan were the only others inside the circle. John ran his tongue over his front teeth, wondering whether he would still have them when the fight was over. For that matter, would he still be alive?

Claxton stripped to his dungarees, his chest naked and hairy. John slowly removed his dark captain's coat and tossed it to Artemus Primm. He kept on his white shirt and dark pants.

"Couple of rules in this fight," Pete Carnahan announced, looking at them both. "First of all, no weapons." Carnahan frisked Claxton, removing a knife from his boot. His search of John produced nothing. "Second rule—the fighters can't leave the ring." The circle of barrels was surrounded by the crowd of deck hands and passengers. John doubted a fleeing fighter could get through the throng. "Last rule—when one man gives up or is unconscious, fight's over. All right, gentlemen, go to it!"

Horace Claxton unleased a bone-chilling howl and sprinted for John, shoulder lowered like a battering ram. John leaped to his right as Claxton roared past, grazing John's forearm. John threw a sharp punch, missing Claxton's face but landing flush on the mate's left ear. Claxton stumbled to his knees, but was up instantly, snarling like a wolf. He lunged, arms outstretched, fingers reaching for John's neck. John ducked to the left, under the arms, and drove his fist hard into Claxton's midsection. Claxton grunted; John backpedaled quickly.

Claxton advanced warily, hatred energizing his eyes. He now raised his fists like a fighter, a pose he might have taken sooner had he anticipated having any trouble dispatching John quickly. "You bought your ticket," Claxton rasped. "Now I'm mad." He threw a haymaker at John's head. John ducked and pounded a fist into Claxton's gut. He hurriedly retreated to his left, a punch catching him on the right shoulder, jarring nerve-endings from fingertips to toes. Claxton pursued like a dog after a rabbit. Claxton threw another punch. John dodged backwards, the breeze of the miss tickling his chin. He jabbed sharply at Claxton's uncovered face. His fist smacked solidly into Claxton's nose. It mashed under his knuckles.

Roaring, Claxton blindly unleashed a barrage of punches. John dodged from side to side, twice tagging the big mate's broken nose. He jabbed at Claxton's throat, missed, then felt a tremendous punch crash into his left ribs. Pain exploded through his side as he suddenly found himself knocked to his knees on the hard sand. A booted foot kicked toward his head. He rolled to the right, the boot missing by mere inches, the force of the kick spinning Claxton to the sand.

Like a cat, John was back on his feet, charging as the bigger man rose to his knees. John drove his fist into Claxton's meaty face, again squashing the nose under throbbing knuckles. Claxton shouted a torrent of obscenities and clutched angrily at John's leg. Thick fingers fastened around his left thigh. John twisted, trying to pull away. The groping hands traveled upward, snaking between his legs, powerful pinchers groping for testicles. Desperately, John yanked backwards, dragging Claxton across the sand. As the fingers gouged at his crotch, John hammered his right fist again and again into Claxton's exposed face.

John felt a muscle in his inner thigh tear as he finally jerked free of Claxton. The mate sprawled on hands and knees in the sand, pausing, glaring at John through a mask of blood. John took a deep breath, his left ribs fiery hot with pain.

The big mate suddenly sprang forward as if catapulted. John ducked under a wild swing, but huge hairy arms encircled him, hands locking behind John's back in a powerful face-to-face bear hug. John's elbows pressed to Claxton's chest as the mate tried to crush him. Air squeezing from his lungs, John gripped Claxton's ears with his hands. Remembering night after night in the engine room, John began butting Claxton's face with his head. Again and again John smashed the top of his head into Claxton's messy face. Like a battering ram, he pummeled Claxton's already broken nose, a pink spray of blood and froth splashing over both faces.

Claxton abruptly dropped the bear hug and gouged at John's eyes with powerful fingers. John jerked his head away from Claxton's hands, but the vicelike fingers closed around his wrists. He was suddenly airborne as Claxton flung him to the left. He landed solidly on his side. He rolled to avoid a kick aimed at his head. The heel of Claxton's boot clipped his left eyebrow, opening the skin to the bone, blurring John's vision with a river of blood. He kept rolling as Claxton kept kicking. As he rolled, he clenched his hand tightly, gathering a fistful of sand. After his last roll, John bounded to his feet. Claxton was charging. He hurled sand into Claxton's face. Claxton's eyes clenched tight and he staggered blindly, groping for John. John, left eye swelling closed, shot forward and smashed his fist into Claxton's throat. Gagging, Claxton fell to his knees. John stood in front of Claxton, planted his feet solidly in the sand, and slammed his fist full strength into Claxton's throat, bristly stubble scraping skin from his knuckles. Choking, Claxton fell to his side. John kicked repeatedly at Claxton's head, suddenly exhilerated.

Through a veil of pain, he sensed Carnahan dragging him away from Claxton's squirming form, the cheering and yelling of the crowd, the hurt in almost every cell of his body, and the blood streaming down his face from the gash above his eye. Most of all, he felt the heady intoxication of having caused Claxton pain, of having beaten Claxton, of having driven him into the sand, of having won, finally and at last.

Claxton was soon sitting up, nursing his wounds like a beached whale while the roustabouts moved the barrels back onto the *Lucky Molly*.

John stood next to Pete Carnahan as the *Lucky Molly* backed from the sand bar and into the channel of the Mississippi. He thought of Peterson, whose lifeless body was somewhere underneath the flowing brown water. "I should've killed him," John whispered hoarsely, surprised by the malice in his own voice.

"I'm so proud of you I could bust!" Carnahan declared, adding a few colorful profanities to punctuate his pleasure.

"I should've killed him," John repeated, sensing a powerful premonition. "Claxton's not the kind of man to take his licks and walk off. I'll have to watch my back for the rest of my life."

"You darn *near* killed him." Carnahan's voice was filled with pride. "You were kicking the stuffing out of him before we pulled you off. Here, take this." Carnahan extended his hand. In it he held a red handkerchief.

John accepted it, but didn't smile. "Thanks, Pete."

The smile eventually left Pete Carnahan's face as they watched Claxton, still sitting immobile on the sand bar, fade farther and farther into the distance. "Yep," Carnahan finally agreed, frowning. "Maybe I should have let you kill him. Now you have an enemy for life."

Chapter 13

Tyler Fitch sat at the wooden desk in his office in Cape Girardeau. He glanced out the window. The *Andrew Jackson* and the *Andrew Jackson II* were tied up next to each other, riding low in the water like majestic floating palaces. His ownership of the towering white steamboats gave him a feeling of immense satisfaction. He adjusted his red bow tie absently as he closed the account books he'd been studying. Life was going well. The *Andrew Jackson II* was earning between six and ten thousand dollars per trip between St. Louis and New Orleans. The *Andrew Jackson* was making between four and seven thousand. He was fast becoming the richest man between St. Louis and Memphis.

He caught himself stroking the scarred tissue of his wounded ear and hurriedly removed his hand from the year-old injury. His temper had mellowed since the last duel. After six of them, his enthusiasm for that peculiar and violent method of resolving disputes had dimmed. Perhaps the change correlated with how close Austin Carmichael's shot had come to ending his life.

In addition to his business, his quest to establish himself in the social community was going well, too. He'd quit frequenting Samantha Peabody's brothel. He'd quit drinking in public. He'd taken an active part in community issues, strongly backing the *Western Eagle's* editorial calling for a ferryboat across the Mississippi at Cape Girardeau. Best of all, though, his courtship of Rosalind O'Malley was beginning to get results. He'd visited her whenever business allowed him to stop in Cape Girardeau. He'd even sent his boats on trips without him a time or two just to stay near her in Cape Girardeau. Last night, she'd finally permitted him to kiss her for the first time. After tasting her lips, Tyler

Fitch had decided that marrying her for her position and money might include certain unbusinesslike fringe benefits as well.

His thoughts were interrupted by the opening of the door to his office. Horace Claxton lumbered into the sparsely furnished room.

"May I help you?" Fitch asked coolly. Fitch was shocked by Claxton's appearance. The big man's nose was swollen three times its normal size, a grotesquely distorted mass of bulging purple bruises. His right eye was almost hidden by an ugly, swollen, balloon of bluish flesh.

"The question," rasped Claxton, "is how can I help you."

His interest piqued, Tyler Fitch invited him to sit. "Very well, Claxton. What are you talking about?"

Claxton collapsed onto a chair. "As you know, Fitch, I used to work for Patrick O'Malley. I was the mate on the *Lucky Molly*."

"I didn't know you'd quit."

"Didn't quit. I was fired. Fired by that brown-nosing jerkwater scum, John Carmichael."

John Carmichael! His rival for Lindy! This was getting more interesting by the minute. "How is it this young Carmichael had the authority to fire you?"

"O'Malley's building a new boat in Louisville. He made Carmichael acting captain of the *Lucky Molly*."

"I see," said Fitch, brushing lint from the sleeve of his white coat. "Look. Get to the point. What are you doing here? Are you looking for a job?"

"You might say that."

The big man leaned forward in his chair, swollen face close to Fitch's desk. "I'd like a job on one of your boats, yes. But I'm also here for something else. I've got information about Patrick O'Malley that might be useful to you."

Tyler Fitch kept his expression cool. He'd negotiated too many deals to let his interest show. "What makes you think I'm interested in anything you know about Patrick O'Malley?"

"Oh, let's see. O'Malley's your main competitor, for one thing. You're interested in his daughter, for another. What I know could help you in both areas."

"Who says I'm interested in O'Malley's daughter?"

"I got eyes. I got ears. When I was on the *Lucky Molly*, I often used my ears when others didn't know I was listening. I know my share of O'Malley's secrets."

"Did you get those bruises from listening to conversations you had no business hearing?"

Claxton's lips formed an ugly snarl. "I got surprised by Captain O'Malley's little pup. I had no idea he knew how to fight. Otherwise I'd have been more careful. Next time he won't walk away. I promise you that."

"John Carmichael did that to you?" Fitch was surprised. He recalled Carmichael as a skinny youth. Although, thinking back on it, the young man had been much bigger the last time he'd seen him.

"Carmichael won't live out the year," Claxton vowed.

Tyler Fitch felt the menace in Claxton's tone. "What is it you expect from me in return for this information you think I'll want?"

Claxton's bloodshot eyes didn't waver. "I want a job as a deck hand on one of your steamboats, with the understanding I'll become mate when you have a vacancy. Also, I want 500 dollars."

"The job is yours," said Fitch. "But I'll decide about the 500 *after* you've told me the information. It might not be worth anything to me. If not, I won't pay for it. On the other hand, if it's worth the money, I'll pay."

Claxton smiled grimly. "Fair enough. My information is that O'Malley is way over his head in debt. He gave a 100,000-dollar note to a Jackson banker named Jason Farley. Payable on demand. O'Malley doesn't have enough money now to pay the note if demand is made. He doesn't have enough equity to cover it, either, so nobody else would give him a loan. If you could somehow get possession of that demand note, you'd have O'Malley by the balls."

"Why would Farley give the note to me?" asked Fitch, thinking even as he spoke. He knew Farley. He had large accounts at the bank in Jackson. Perhaps he could persuade him.

"Farley's dead," rasped Claxton. "Killed this morning. His buggy overturned between Cape and Jackson. Horse must have been spooked by something. Farley's neck was broke. His widow's going to be needing money, you know. She might be willing to sell you that note if you talk to her about it real soon."

Fitch studied Claxton, invisible icy fingertips tickling his skin. Claxton had killed Farley. No question about it. He ought to report him. Yet, he had no proof. The fact of the matter was that Claxton was right—if Tyler Fitch could get O'Malley's note from Farley's widow, O'Malley would be at his mercy. Grimly, Tyler Fitch removed a key from his pocket and opened a drawer at the bottom of his desk. Glancing surreptitiously at Claxton, he lifted a small gun from the drawer and placed it in his lap, carefully keeping it out of sight. He probably wouldn't need it, but, considering Farley's fate, he couldn't be sure. He then removed 500 dollars and passed the money across the desk to Claxton. "Here's the 500. Your information was worth it. Buy yourself a bath and some clean clothes. See my clerk on the *Andrew Jackson II* about signing on as my new second mate."

"Yes, sir," Claxton grinned.

After Claxton left, Tyler Fitch began making preparations to pay his respects to Jason Farley's bereaved widow. Her husband's death was such a tragedy. Perhaps he could be of help.

Several days later, Tyler Fitch and Lindy O'Malley sat on a love seat in the parlor of her home. She'd invited him for dinner. It had been a success. Aunt Maude was in the kitchen putting away the dishes.

"Will you marry me, Rosalind?"

Shocked by the unforeseen question, Lindy stood abruptly. Obviously her flirtation had gone too far. "Tyler, this is so sudden!"

"No, it's not," he said, rising to his feet. "I've wanted to marry you for months. Say you will."

She looked into his dark brown eyes, then turned away.

"If you say yes," he continued, "we'll make the rest of the world green with envy. We'll have balls and parties every month. We'll build the grandest mansion in town. You'll be the most admired woman in Cape Girardeau."

Lindy heard his words and didn't doubt they could all be true. He was a handsome man, a self-made man. She was fond of him. But marriage? She hadn't pictured herself married to him. She had never imagined herself married to anyone but John Carmichael.

John! How she missed him! The last time the *Lucky Molly* had docked in Cape, he'd sent for her. She'd been insulted he hadn't bothered to come personally and had refused to go. Later she heard he'd been suffering from broken ribs and other injuries incurred during a fight with Horace Claxton. She felt terrible about not going to him.

"Rosalind, if you say yes, I'll be the happiest man in Cape Girardeau." Tyler Fitch, darkly handsome in white suit and red bow tie, was watching her expectantly, awaiting a reply.

As she stared at him, she confirmed in her heart that she didn't love him the way she loved John Carmichael. It was as simple as that. There was only one man she wanted to marry, and she hadn't spoken to him in months. It was stupid of her. "I'm sorry," she whispered. "I care for you a lot, honestly, but I can't marry you."

Tyler Fitch was unperturbed. "Isn't it important to you to see your father happy?"

"Of course it is." Thinking of her father, Lindy smiled faintly. She knew he'd be much happier if she married John Carmichael rather than Tyler Fitch. John was like a son to O'Malley.

"If you want to keep your father a happy man, you'll need to marry me."

She heard his words with surprise and confusion. "What do you mean?"

"What I mean," he said smoothly, "is that I always get what I want. Always." He took her hands in his. "You see, I hold a demand note on your father for 100,000 dollars. He doesn't have the money. If I demand it, he'll lose both his steamboats and his house. I'd hate to do that to him, but I *will* if you don't marry me."

She jerked her hands away. "I don't like being threatened."

"I'm not making threats. I'm simply telling you where we both stand so you can make an informed decision." He winked at her. "All's fair in love and war."

"Which is this?"

Tyler Fitch laughed easily. "I love your sense of humor."

Her mind was racing. Was he telling the truth? Did he really have the power to ruin Patrick O'Malley? Looking at his calm face she felt her stomach lurch. It was the truth! What was she to do?

"Tell you what," he said, taking a gold watch out of his pocket and checking the time. "Think about your answer. I'll come by at ten o'clock tomorrow morning to hear your decision. If your answer's no, I'll have my attorney contact your father next time he's in town."

After he left, Lindy sat numbly on a chair by the parlor fireplace, trying to decide what to do. She didn't realize Aunt Maude had entered the room until she heard her speak.

"Young lady, do I need to ring a steamboat bell to get your attention?"

"Sorry, Aunt Maude. What were you saying?"

"I asked where Mr. Fitch went."

"He left." Lindy felt tears welling in her eyes. "Aunt Maude, would it just kill Papa if he lost his steamboats?"

"Has there been an accident!"

"No," said Lindy, blowing her nose with a handkerchief. "I'm just wondering what it would do to Papa if he should lose his steamboats."

Maude O'Malley patted Lindy's leg. "There's no need to think about such sad things, Rosalind. Think happy thoughts."

"Alright. But first, tell me what it would do to Papa if he lost his steamboats."

"Your father's a strong man. But steamboating is his life. He wouldn't make a good retiree. I suspect when his working days are over he will simply shut off his engines and fade away. But what's this talk about losing his steamboats? He's a careful captain with careful pilots. Nothing's going to happen to him."

Lindy felt her insides convulsing. "Do you really think he'd die without his steamboats?"

Maude O'Malley frowned. "I've had absolutely enough of this conversation. Let's drop the subject and discuss more pleasant things."

Lindy put the handkerchief to her eyes and began sobbing. "Fine," she said, after a few minutes. "Here's a happy thought. I'm going to marry Tyler Fitch. He proposed tonight. I'm going to accept tomorrow."

Chapter 14

In late October, 1852, Patrick O'Malley picked up his new steamboat from the shipyard in Louisville. With O'Malley captaining the *Girardeau Rose* and John captaining the *Lucky Molly*, they steamed side by side, river-width permitting, all the way to Cape Girardeau. The *Girardeau Rose*, at 321 feet in length and 95 feet in width, was one of the most spectacular steamboats on the Mississippi. She was painted white, with red trim. Her towering red chimneys rose 75 feet above the hurricane deck. Her massive white paddle wheel housings measured 44 feet by 19 feet. The name GIRARDEAU ROSE and a bright red flower were painted on each.

After helping tie up the *Lucky Molly* at the Cape Girardeau levee, John walked resolutely down the gangplank bearing the present he'd bought Lindy. She'd barely spoken to him since her party, but he'd decided to try apologizing again, this time in person. The present he carried was a sturdy white metal strongbox, four feet long, two and a half feet wide, and three feet tall. On top of the chest was a brass plate with the steamboat's name engraved in bold letters: GIRARDEAU ROSE. He was sure she'd like it. The question was whether she would accept it from *him*.

When Lindy greeted him at the door of the O'Malley house, he read surprise and sorrow and perhaps even love in her eyes. She let him in and touched his cheek with her fingertips.

"John! What happened to your eye?" Her fingers gently traced the vivid pink scar that ran from eyebrow to temple.

"Horace Claxton and I had a serious disagreement. If I'd have known it would get you to talk to me again, I'd have had someone kick me in the face a long time ago."

Her fingers lingered on his face.

"I'm sorry for what I said on the night of your party," he said. "Like I told you in my note, I only lost my temper because I love you so much."

Her fingers froze on his face. "What note?"

"The one I wrote you the morning after our fight."

"You didn't write me any note."

"Yes, I did. I gave it to a roustabout to hand deliver."

"Well, I never got it." Her hands fell to her sides.

John thought of the months and months that had passed since they'd talked. All the silence. All the heartbreak. "I'll wring that scalawag's neck."

Lindy's face was turning a bright shade of pink. "What did your note say?"

He smiled. "Oh, I apologized, groveled, and begged for forgiveness. That sort of thing. It was shameless, really."

She smiled, too. "Did you tell me you loved me?"

"Repeatedly. And I'm telling you again. I love you." He took a step toward her, but she backed away, shaking her head, her face flushing more and more. Feeling awkward, he pointed to the chest. "I brought you a present. It's a strongbox to take with you when you ride with your father on the *Girardeau Rose*."

She was crying. He moved near her and put his hands on her small shoulders. "What's wrong? What have I done?"

"I'm so confused," she whispered. "I love you so much."

He encircled her with his arms and hugged her tightly. She was limp, almost lifeless. When her sobs faded, he put a hand under her chin and raised her face. He tried to kiss her but she pulled away.

"I can't kiss you. Not now. Not ever again. I'm going to marry Tyler Fitch. I told him so yesterday."

"What!"

"I'm going to marry Tyler Fitch."

"Fitch! The man who killed my father!" He backed away from her. "I don't understand! You just told me you love me. How can you marry him?"

"John," she stammered, sobs beginning anew. "Please don't hate me."

"Hate you? You're crazy! I came here willing to make a fool of myself. I guess I have!"

Tears streamed down Lindy's cheeks as John slammed the door.

John had no idea where he was going or what he was doing. Not since his father's death had he felt such anguish. Eventually he found himself on board the *Girardeau Rose*. Patrick O'Malley was in the captain's quarters, showing off the resplendent room to Maude O'Malley. Maude was chiding her brother for overspending on furniture when John barged into the room, interrupting them.

"Don't you knock, now that you're a captain?" Maude O'Malley asked curtly.

He ignored the question, looking past Maude O'Malley to her brother.

"Captain O'Malley, we need to talk. It's important."

"Would you excuse us, Maude?" said O'Malley.

"She doesn't need to leave, sir. She can hear everything I have to say."

O'Malley shrugged. "Very well. What is it? What's so all-fired important?"

"I'm quitting, Uncle Pat."

"Balls of fire!" O'Malley sputtered. "What on *earth* has got into you?"

"I'm quitting. Nothing more to say."

O'Malley rose to his full height. His face darkened. "I'll be hanged if there's nothing more to say. You're like a son to me. The good times we've had! Our plans! You owe me lots of words, John Carmichael. I'm entitled to know what the blazes is going on!"

"I'm quitting because I love Lindy. I always will."

O'Malley rolled his eyes.

"Well, hell's bells, John, that's no reason to quit. It's all the more reason to stay. You're not making any sense."

John glanced at Maude O'Malley. Her eyes were moist. She knew, he realized. She knew Lindy was going to marry Tyler Fitch. Evidently her brother did not.

"Uncle Pat, Lindy's engaged to Tyler Fitch. I couldn't stand working with you if Fitch were married to your daughter, to the girl I love. I'm leaving. It'll be best for everybody."

Patrick O'Malley's face registered his astonishment. "Lindy is what!?" The big captain swung to face his sister. "What do you know about this? Is it true?"

"That's what Rosalind says. I promised not to tell you. She wants to tell you herself."

"Oh, she does, does she!" O'Malley thundered. "You," he said, pointing to John, "stay right here until I get back. I'm not accepting your resignation just yet." O'Malley slammed the door as he left.

Lindy was sitting in a stupor on the loveseat in the parlor when she heard her father storm into the house. She was on her feet by the time he reached the parlor.

"What's this I hear about you marrying Tyler Fitch!" he yelled.

She saw the fury in his eyes and was frightened. "It's true," she whispered. She thought of her father being stripped of his steamboats, of his pride. The conviction that she was saving him gave her the strength to face him.

"Why am I the last person to hear of this?"

"I'm sorry I wasn't the one to tell you, Papa. I told Aunt Maude not to tell you. I was afraid she would."

"Your aunt didn't tell me. John Carmichael did. He just quit working for me."

Lindy began crying again.

Her father touched her shoulder gently. "My little Rose," he said, fondly. "I've seen your face light up around John Carmichael. I've listened to him mope around like a lovesick puppy over you. Your face never shines around Tyler Fitch. Never. I want to know why you've chosen to marry him. All I want is an explanation. I'll let you do whatever you want. It's your life."

She turned her face away from her father. He was so persuasive. She loved him so much. If she weren't careful, he'd soon have her blubbering out the whole story. "I have my reasons. I don't want to talk about it. I'm going to marry him and that's it."

"By thunder!" O'Malley shouted. "This is the second time today someone has refused to give me an explanation! I won't stand for it! I *demand* an explanation!"

Lindy ached to tell him. She wanted to let him make it better like he always did. She wanted to protect him, though. She closed her eyes and looked away from him.

He grabbed her by the arms and held her firmly. "Lindy, do you love me?" She opened her eyes.

"Oh, yes, Papa. More than anything."

"Then tell me what's going on here. You don't love Tyler Fitch, do you?" Lindy was silent.

"Do you?" he said louder.

"No," she said in a small voice.

"Why are you marrying him, then?"

She shook her head from side to side, noiselessly.

"Darling," he said, eyes narrowing. "What has Tyler Fitch done to you? Has he violated you? Are you pregnant?"

"No," she said indignantly. "I've only kissed him once. Really, Papa, how could you say such a thing?"

"Rosalind, do you love John Carmichael?"

Lindy looked at her father. He had more wrinkles in his forehead than she remembered. His eyes were deep with understanding.

"Yes," she whispered, almost inaudibly.

"You still haven't told me why you're marrying one man when you love another. Are you hungry for more money than I can give you? Is it greed?"

"No!" she answered, insulted.

"Rosalind," said her father, "we've always been honest with each other, you and I. If you don't level with me now, our relationship will never be the same. I'll ask you one more time. Why? Why did you tell Tyler Fitch you'd marry him?"

Lindy lost herself in her father's loving eyes. He'd always been there for her. Always. He was there for her now. She found her will breaking. She hugged him and he held her in his arms. As she cried she told him between gasps and sobs that Tyler Fitch possessed the $100,000 note, and of his threat to make demand for payment if she didn't marry him. She felt O'Malley stiffen as she poured out the real reason she'd accepted the proposal.

When she finished crying, she pulled away from her father. The captain's coat was wet from her hot tears. His eyes were cold pools of green ice. "Tyler Fitch has gone too far this time," whispered O'Malley slowly, his thick lips trembling with rage.

"Papa, don't you see? If I don't marry him, we'll lose everything."

"You're not marrying him, *now or ever*." O'Malley turned to leave.

She felt a rush of fear. "Papa, where are you going?"

He paused and looked back at his daughter. "I'm going to call on Tyler Fitch. After that, I expect we'll pay a visit to Cypress Island."

Lindy was horrified. "No, Papa, please don't. That won't solve anything!" He left abruptly, her useless protests echoing in the empty room.

John Carmichael and Maude O'Malley were both sitting silently at the table in the captain's quarters on the *Girardeau Rose* when Lindy burst through the door.

"John, you've got to help me!"

He started to tell her to go beg her fiancé for help, but held his tongue when he saw her grief-stricken face.

"What's wrong?" he asked, rising to his feet.

"I explained to Papa the real reason I told Tyler Fitch I'd marry him. I wasn't going to tell him, I really wasn't. I couldn't help it, though." She began sobbing.

"Well, enlighten us, too, child," said Maude O'Malley, peevishly. "What's the reason?"

"Tyler Fitch has a 100,000 dollar note that he can collect from Papa any time he wants. He told me he'd ruin Papa if I didn't marry him. Papa would lose his steamboats."

"Must be Jason Farley's note," mused John. "I wonder how Fitch got it."

"You've got to help me," she repeated.

"What do you want me to do?"

"Papa said he's going to Tyler Fitch's office right now, then to Cypress Island. He means to fight a duel with him. You know Papa's not good with pistols. Tyler's an expert. He'll kill him. Just like he killed your father. I'm so afraid. Please stop them."

John sprinted all the way to Tyler Fitch's office. When he rushed through the door, both men were glaring at each other. Tyler Fitch, cool and immaculate in his white suit, sat behind his wooden desk, only one hand visible. O'Malley paced in front of the desk, livid and sputtering.

"Captain O'Malley," said Tyler Fitch, smiling a deadly smile and fingering the lopped off ear. "I don't want to fight a duel with you, sir. I wouldn't want to kill the father of the woman I intend to marry. But if you insult me one more time, you'll have your duel." Fitch's smile thinned. "Perhaps young Mr. Carmichael could be your second, if a duel proves necessary."

Patrick O'Malley glowered at Fitch with hatred. "You slimy . . ."

"Hold it, Uncle Pat," John interrupted, grabbing O'Malley by the arm. O'Malley looked at him with surprise. "Captain O'Malley, Captain Fitch, I have an idea how this whole affair can be settled honorably, without a duel."

Both men were silent.

"The way I see it," continued John, "Tyler Fitch has Patrick O'Malley's note for 100,00 dollars. That means Patrick O'Malley owes Tyler Fitch the money. O'Malley is mad because Fitch tried to use that debt to force O'Malley's daughter to marry him. Now you're talking about having a duel, in which case one or both of you will be killed." John paused, looking at both men. They were listening. "My proposal, gentlemen, is for the matter to be resolved by a steamboat race, not by dueling pistols." Both men smiled grimly. He got the impression they liked the idea. "I'm sure Captain Fitch thinks the *Andrew Jackson II* is the fastest boat on the Mississippi. I know for a fact Captain O'Malley thinks the *Girardeau Rose* is the fastest. Let's have a race and find out."

"Does the winner get Rosalind?" asked Fitch, icily.

John suppressed his anger.

"No. The winner gets the *Girardeau Rose*, free and clear of the note. If O'Malley wins, Fitch tears up the note. If Fitch wins, O'Malley signs over all interest in the *Girardeau Rose*."

"An interesting idea," murmured Tyler Fitch, stroking his bow tie.

"Why should you go for it, Fitch?" said O'Malley. "You wouldn't have a chance of winning."

"Wouldn't I? You know, the idea has merit. We'd get lots of publicity out of a race like this. There'd be no need to drag Rosalind into it publicly, of course. We'd just say we were racing for title to the *Girardeau Rose*. The winner would certainly garner tremendous name recognition for his boats!" Tyler Fitch opened a drawer of his desk. He put something from his lap into the drawer. John couldn't see what it was, but heard a heavy thump. Fitch stood and walked out from behind the desk. "Captain O'Malley, I release your daughter from her promise to marry me. If she still wants to be my bride after our great steamboat race, I'll reconsider. For now, though, I'm inclined to settle the matter of the demand note in the manner suggested by young Mr. Carmichael. Deal?"

"Deal. We race from New Orleans to Cape Girardeau. Winner takes the *Girardeau Rose*, free and clear."

Horace Claxton worked by candlelight at the table in his small cabin on the *Andrew Jackson II*. In front of him were a dozen pieces of firewood, several newspapers, a sharp knife, a small saw, and a keg of black powder. He used the knife to cut a three-inch square notice from the advertisements section of the St. Louis newspaper, the *Missouri Republican*. The notice had been running for the past two weeks:

A CARD TO THE PUBLIC

Being satisfied that the steamer GIRARDEAU ROSE is the fastest steamboat currently oper-ating the St. Louis-New Orleans trade, I have agreed to race the steamer ANDREW JACKSON II, Tyler Fitch, Master, from New Orleans to Cape Girardeau; steamers to leave New Orleans at noon on November 11, 1852.

Freight will not be accepted for this trip. Passengers should understand that the GIRARDEAU ROSE will be traveling at speeds heretofore unseen on the river. Passengers make the trip at their own risk.

So confident of victory is the Master of the GIRARDEAU ROSE that the fine steamer herself has been wagered as the prize for the victor.

Patrick O' Malley,
Master, GIRARDEAU ROSE

Claxton also clipped out a similar notice placed by Tyler Fitch. As he set about his work, he thought again about the subject that had filled his mind for the past several weeks—John Carmichael. Temporarily put aside were Claxton's dreams of captaining his own steamboat. His sole goal of the moment was to avenge his humiliation at the hands of John Carmichael. Firing him had been bad enough, but beating him in a fight, something no man had done before or since, had been the ink on the death warrant of John Carmichael. He looked again at the materials on the table in front of him. He had a long way to go before he'd be finished. He needed to carve the insides out of each of the dozen pieces of firewood, fill them with deadly black gunpowder, and seal them so they'd look like normal pieces of wood. When he was finished, they'd be the means of blowing John Carmichael from one side of the river to the other.

Claxton laughed aloud. He caught himself and listened quietly for foot-steps. It wouldn't do for others to hear him laughing. He smiled silently. *Nobody messes with Horace J. Claxton and lives to brag about it. Nobody.*

Chapter 15

The race began at noon on November 11, 1852. A cannon sounded from the wharf in New Orleans, and both the *Girardeau Rose* and the *Andrew Jackson II* backed from their places at the levee. The *Andrew Jackson II* was docked four steamboats north of the *Girardeau Rose*, and thus took the lead as the two magnificent steamboats surged upriver.

John Carmichael stood with Patrick O'Malley and Lindy on the open promenade on the hurricane deck of the *Girardeau Rose*. A crowd of people packed the New Orleans waterfront, shoulder to shoulder, a sea of animated faces, shouting and waving from the stone-covered levee, from iron-grilled balconies, and from red-tiled rooftops. "Look at all the people!" Lindy murmured.

"It's the buildup this race received," said O'Malley. "Fitch is a salesman, that's for sure. He's been passing out handbills at every stop on the river the past three weeks. He's given interviews to every newspaper between here and St. Louis. Newspapers back east are even taking interest."

"If we lose, Papa, what happens?"

"We lose the *Girardeau Rose*. She'll be Fitch's. We'll still have the *Lucky Molly*, though. We'll still earn a living, and I won't have to worry about you marrying anybody unless it's for love."

Lindy glanced meaningfully at John.

The *Andrew Jackson II* was fifty yards ahead of them. Fitch's steamboat left a rough wake. The choppy water impeded the *Girardeau Rose* as she pursued her rival.

"I thought Fitch would let us pull alongside him in order to start the race right next to each other," complained John. "It isn't fair we're starting out behind him."

"No real rules in steamboat racing, John. The only certain rule is that the one who gets to Cape first wins. It was stupid of me to let him dock upriver of us. I should've known he'd pull a stunt like this."

As the two steamboats raced out of New Orleans, spectators on several excursion boats waved and yelled.

The *Girardeau Rose* had been stripped, to a certain degree, for the race. The heavy doors at each end of the large saloons had been taken out, cutting air resistance. All heavy furniture had been carted off and stored in New Orleans, leaving only a minimum number of chairs and beds. The heavy mirrors, ornate chandeliers, and stained glass windows had been removed. The splendid saloons were now nothing more than wind tunnels.

On this trip, the most important O'Malley had ever made, he carried no freight. Passengers had been accepted, but only those willing to go straight from New Orleans to Cape Girardeau, with stops only for wood. Scores of passengers jumped at the chance to participate in the greatest steamboat race yet to take place on the Mississippi. Several were newspaper reporters, and they scribbled their stories amid the thundering of the engines and the shuddering of the hull of the massive steamboat. The ride was not as smooth as usual. The engines roared full out, the pilots aiming for the shortest course. Passenger comfort played no part in the captain's considerations.

O'Malley had filled the entire steamboat with firewood. The fewer stops he was forced to make to refuel, the faster his time. The strong sweet smell of knotty pine engulfed the long cabin. The freshly cut wood oozed pitch and dripped turpentine. It would kindle quickly and burn hot. Country people called it "lightwood" because it burned so brightly it could substitute for candles.

"This stretch of river north of New Orleans is a natural place to pass him," said O'Malley. "The river's wide and straight here. I'll bet Abner Conrad will do his best to get around Fitch before we get to Carrollton."

As expected, the one-armed pilot brought the *Girardeau Rose* to the left of the *Andrew Jackson II*, trying to pull alongside her. The *Andrew Jackson II* moved farther and farther to the left, forcing O'Malley's boat closer to the shore. Unable to pass, Conrad cut the *Girardeau Rose* to the right and crossed the other steamboat's backwash. The rough water slowed the *Girardeau Rose* a fraction, and the *Andrew Jackson II* pulled another twenty yards ahead. Conrad tried to pass on the right, but again the broad stern of Fitch's boat remained barely in front of the *Girardeau Rose*, blocking her path and pushing her closer to the rocky bank.

The nip and tuck of Conrad's efforts to pass the *Andrew Jackson II* continued for miles and miles. On the banks, whoops of encouragement came from crowds thronging the private landings of the white-columned mansions in the heart of the Louisiana river plantation country. The cutting and blocking continued all the way to Carrollton. Their time to Carrollton of 27 minutes was a new record. As the dueling steamboats shot through the river near Carrollton, the 1,400 townspeople waved and cheered.

In a wide stretch of river just north of Carrollton, Abner Conrad finally managed to bring the *Girardeau Rose* parallel to the *Andrew Jackson II*. The pilot of Fitch's boat tried to force the *Girardeau Rose* into the riverbank, but Abner Conrad set his jaw and refused to budge. The wooden stern of the *Andrew Jackson II* smacked against the bow of O'Malley's steamboat. Paint scratched off both steamers, but the aboardage was slight and the wooden hulls were not damaged.

The steamboats were beside each other, only inches separating their paddle wheel housings. A man could have jumped from boat to boat.

Tyler Fitch, clad in white suit and red bow tie, stood in the pilothouse with his pilots. He bowed toward Lindy. She looked away and hugged close to her father's arm.

John felt a thrill of satisfaction as the *Girardeau Rose* gradually pulled ahead of the *Andrew Jackson II*.

"Let them eat our wake for a while!" shouted O'Malley jubilantly, as Abner Conrad guided the *Girardeau Rose* past Fitch's boat. The engines thundered and orange sparks speckled the dark smoke spewing from the tall chimneys of both steamboats.

"We *are* the faster boat!" John shouted to O'Malley, straining to make himself heard above the din of roaring engines, splashing paddle wheels and shouting passengers and crew.

"Oh, if Mike Fink could only see me now!" whooped O'Malley. John thought he saw tears in the captain's eyes.

After the *Girardeau Rose* took its position ahead of the *Andrew Jackson II*, John moved to the stern of O'Malley's boat and watched the receding opponent.

Horace Claxton stood at the front of the lower deck of the *Andrew Jackson II*. John felt a chill run down his back when their eyes met. Even from the distance separating them, John could see the malice in Horace Claxton's eyes.

By sunset, the *Girardeau Rose* had built a quarter-mile lead. John glanced up at the towering red stacks of O'Malley's pride and joy, marveling at the beauty of the crimson chimneys silhouetted against the pink sky. Behind the *Girardeau Rose*, the tall dark stacks of the *Andrew Jackson II* stood straight and tall beneath thick clouds of black smoke. As the rosy sunset turned to night, the dark stacks faded from view. Every time the yawning furnaces of the trailing steamboat opened to admit more fuel, they glowed like predatory wolf-eyes in the night.

People from the towns and plantations along the riverbank had built bonfires at the water's edge. Abner Conrad guided the *Girardeau Rose* easily down the corridor of yellow bonfires. The gleeful shouts of spectators floated dream-ily to the steamboat across water glittering orange in the firelight. The night was cloudless, and the sky was filled with stars. The November air was cool, but not yet cold.

It was a wonderful night.

They passed Baton Rouge at 8:30 on the same evening they'd left New Orleans. The crowd was wild and screaming. They passed Bayou Sara at 10:26 that night. At midnight John was standing alone on the hurricane deck at the stern of the *Girardeau Rose* when Lindy came to him.

"John," she said softly, "I've never really thanked you for stopping Papa from dueling Tyler Fitch."

He could see the sleek lines of her face in the starlight. "You don't owe me thanks. Your father's family to me. I did what I could to keep him from being killed by the same hand that killed my father."

"How did you know they'd go for the race idea?"

"I didn't." He felt her hands slip into his own.

"John, I never did love Tyler Fitch. I've always loved you. I swear it's true."

He heard the words and his soul soared. "You're the only girl I'll ever love." He knew he spoke the truth. They kissed as the *Girardeau Rose* glided smoothly past the mouth of the Red River.

At 5:12 in the morning, Patrick O'Malley ordered his steamboat to pull alongside the wharf in Natchez. Quickly, his men scurried down the landing stages and began running cord after cord of firewood onto the *Girardeau Rose*. It would take quite a while to refuel, but it was absolutely necessary. Fortu-nately, Fitch's boat would need to refuel eventually, too. As the *Girardeau Rose* loaded fresh firewood, the *Andrew Jackson II* steamed into view. As she neared Natchez, another steamboat pulled from the levee and soon raised a full head of steam. John saw with surprise that it was the *Andrew Jackson*, Fitch's other boat.

"What in tarnation?" he said aloud.

John left the deck hands loading firewood and joined O'Malley at the bow of the *Girardeau Rose*. They watched in silence as the *Andrew Jackson* pulled alongside the *Andrew Jackson II*. The crew of each steamboat hurled ropes to the other. Within seconds, they had lashed the boats together, never decreasing speed. They slid planks across the guardrails of the two steamboats, tying them quickly and securely, providing walkways. Deck hands from the *Andrew Jack-son* rushed firewood onto the larger steamboat, then returned to the smaller one via another plank, only to gather additional armfuls of wood. Working like a train of ants, they carried firewood onto the racing boat.

''I'll be darned!'' said O'Malley. "They aren't having to stop for firewood. They're refueling at full speed!"

By the time the *Girardeau Rose* stockpiled her fresh supply of knotty pine, the *Andrew Jackson II* had passed them and was far out of sight to the north. The *Girardeau Rose* pulled out of Natchez and tore after the *Andrew Jackson II*. They passed the *Andrew Jackson* just north of Natchez. It was on its way back to Natchez, fueling mission completed. The *Girardeau Rose* didn't catch up to the *Andrew Jackson II* until Cole's Creek, two hours later. Once again, the pilots played a high stakes games of chicken with each other, as Abner Conrad tried to pass Fitch's boat, and Fitch's pilot tried to block the way of the *Girardeau Rose*.

After several tense hours, the cords of his neck straining, Abner Conrad managed to slip the faster *Girardeau Rose* around her rival. Once again, O'Malley's steamboat had the lead. She would need to refuel again, though. Twice. At Helena and at Cairo.

At 11:30 in the morning on the second day of the race, the *Girardeau Rose* stopped to refuel at the small town of Helena on the Arkansas shore. Even in the middle of a business day, a large crowd waited on the levee for the approach of the racing steamboats. Newspaper reporters hurried ashore to relay their stories to their papers. O'Malley warned each person who left the boat that the *Girardeau Rose* would wait for no one after she refueled.

Once again, the *Andrew Jackson II* caught and passed the *Girardeau Rose*. She stormed past while O'Malley's steamboat was tied up at Helena. The *Andrew Jackson II* was once again lashed to another steamboat. The two steamboat shot by, connected to each other like huge mating water bugs.

Six hours out of Helena, the *Girardeau Rose* reached Memphis. By that time she'd caught up with the *Andrew Jackson II* and had been riding in her wake for over two hours.

Memphis in 1852 had a population of 9,000, every one of whom had turned out at the supper hour to watch the steamboats speed through their town. A huge crowd jostled each other on the wharf. Another group perched on the purplish bluff that towered 80 feet above the water, the highest point on the Mississippi between the mouth of the Ohio and Natchez. A newspaper reporter from the *Memphis Daily Appeal* commented to John that such a crowd had never been gathered in Memphis before. As they shot by the town without stopping, the bow of the *Girardeau Rose* nearly touching the stern of the *Andrew Jackson II*, the Memphis reporter tied his story to a billet and threw it to some colleagues who rowed into the channel to get it.

"Well, the race is two-thirds over, and your boat is behind," the reporter said to John.

"We'll win."

"Hope so. I bet 50 dollars on the *Girardeau Rose* myself."

Just above Memphis, the racing steamboats had to thread through a maze of little islands, Numbers 45, 44, 43, and 42, all bunched in a dangerous group called **Paddy's** Hen and Chickens. The *Girardeau Rose* followed the *Andrew Jackson II* through the path between these islands. It was impossible to pass at this point in the river. O'Malley paced the hurricane deck, cursing with frustration. **Abner** Conrad steered the steamboat between the rocks, aided by comments from other pilots gathered in the pilothouse.

Two hours later, the pilothouse of the *Girardeau Rose* buzzed with excitement. The steamboats were nearing the recent wreck of the steamboat *River Gypsy*. She lay 50 yards from the Tennessee shore. The water on either side of the wreckage was plenty deep to navigate at full speed, but the sunken boat herself was close enough to the surface to maul the bottom of any steamboat foolish enough to pass directly over her. It was twilight as the *Andrew Jackson II* approached the *River Gypsy*, the *Girardeau Rose* right on her tail. John and O'Malley stood in the pilothouse, watching silently as Abner Conrad handled the huge wheel, sweat soaking his clothing.

"This is one spot the *Andrew Jackson II* won't be able to butt us," Conrad said. "We'll head straight for the wreck of the *River Gypsy*. The *Andrew Jackson II* will be forced to veer one way or the other. Whichever side she takes, we'll slip around the other."

As the *Girardeau Rose* bore down on the wreck of the *River Gypsy*, the pilot of the *Andrew Jackson II* tried to stay in front of O'Malley's boat. As the deadly wreckage neared, the *Andrew Jackson II* cut sharply to the left, back into the main channel of the river. Conrad cut the wheel abruptly and the *Girardeau Rose* shot to the right of the deadly wreck. Within seconds, O'Malley's boat was running parallel to the *Andrew Jackson II*. The group of pilots in the cubicle on top of the *Girardeau Rose* roared their approval of Conrad's handling of the boat. Minutes later, the *Girardeau Rose*, asserting her superior speed, pulled ahead of the *Andrew Jackson II* again.

"If only we didn't have to refuel again," moaned John. The other men nodded.

During the long night, the *Girardeau Rose* opened up a lead of perhaps a mile. When she rounded the bend below New Madrid at 7:30 in the morning, the dark smoke of the *Andrew Jackson II* far behind, the people of the town greeted them noisily, shouting, cheering, and discharging guns. Most recognized O'Malley as he stood on the hurricane deck waving at them. Minutes later, as the *Girardeau Rose* passed Island Number 10, John heard New Madrid give an equally enthusiastic greeting to Tyler Fitch's boat.

The *Girardeau Rose* held a commanding lead by the time she reached Cairo at 1:00 that afternoon, three days and one hour after the race had begun. O'Malley and his men were worried, though, because they were desperately low on wood and needed to refuel at Cairo. If Fitch passed them, it would be difficult to regain the lead in the treacherous stretch of river between Cairo and Cape Girardeau.

Cairo was located at the triangular juncture of the Mississippi and Ohio rivers, approximately 1,060 miles from New Orleans, and approximately 40 miles by river from Cape Girardeau. Slightly more than 200 people inhabited this levee-surrounded town in 1852, and they packed the waterfront as the steamboat race arrived at their town.

The *Girardeau Rose* stopped to take on more firewood at Cairo. John worked furiously, helping load fresh wood onto O'Malley's steamboat. The *Andrew Jackson II* was coming back into sight even as they began loading the wood. Once again, the *Andrew Jackson II* lashed itself to another boat and took firewood on the move. This time, neither boat needed so large a quantity of firewood, since Cape Girardeau was not much farther upriver. The *Girardeau Rose* was not stopped as long as she had been before, and O'Malley's boat pulled into the river just as the *Andrew Jackson II* cut away from her supplier. As the racers left Cairo, the *Andrew Jackson II* was a mere twenty yards ahead of the *Girardeau Rose*.

"Here comes the worst part of the race," Abner Conrad said to John as they rode the backwash of the *Andrew Jackson II*.

The Mississippi River just past Cairo made a large "S" curve. A steamboatman found himself going north, then south, and then north again when maneuvering through this treacherous water. The *Andrew Jackson II* and the *Girardeau Rose* slowed as they navigated past Elk Island, and then wriggled past the Two Sisters, a pair of islands occupying the exact center of the channel at the apex of a tricky bend. Once past the Two Sisters, the racers carefully negotiated the maze of Dog Tooth Bend. Twice the *Andrew Jackson II* went aground. The river was so narrow at these points, though, that the *Girardeau Rose* was forced to wait and bide her time while the *Andrew Jackson II* backed off the sand bar and resumed her trip, still in the lead.

Patrick O'Malley was livid with frustration. "Damnation! We've got the faster boat! But it doesn't mean a blessed thing because we're stuck behind Fitch's wide tail!"

Twenty-two miles north of Cairo was another bad spot in the river known as Hackett's Bend. It had a plethora of islands strewn in places that gave pilots fits. It was at Hackett's Bend that disaster struck the *Girardeau Rose*.

John had been on the boiler deck when he heard an uproar below. Following the shouts and screams, he ran down the steps to the main deck, then shoved his way through deck hands to the engine room. When he reached the engine room, hot water soaked his boots and steamy air filled his lungs. Pete Carnahan lay writhing on the floor, hands over his face, hissing hot water spraying from a disjointed pipe.

"Get Pete out of here!" John ordered two nearby deck hands.

A pipe connecting the heater tanks to the boilers had broken. If not repaired quickly, the water already in the boilers would evaporate and the boilers would begin exploding, one after another, in a holocaust of destruction. He donned thick gloves and grabbed a wrench and several rolls of packing. He'd helped Pete Carnahan fix busted joints before, but never under such emergency circumstances. And never by himself. He was relieved when he was joined by the red-headed Second Engineer, Roscoe Pollack. Together, they made their way to the severed pipe. When close enough, they saw that a sleeve joint had jarred loose and apart.

John and the Second Engineer worked furiously. They forced the separated sections of pipe back together and crammed packing in and around the joint. As John worked, scalding water soaked through his gloves. He ignored the pain and kept wrapping the packing tighter and tighter. They closed the joint and quickly fastened a makeshift packing gland around it, tightening the gland's screws firmly. Water still oozed and trickled from the packed joint, but it was obvious that the danger of explosion was over. The repairs had been made while the *Girardeau Rose* was underway. They had been made in a matter of minutes, without stopping, without losing momentum.

The Second Engineer stayed in the engine room to watch for other problems. John left the steaming caldron, his scalded fingers tingling. Deck hands applauded as he walked by them. He reached the pilothouse as the *Girardeau Rose* followed the *Andrew Jackson II* into the treacherous stretch of river known as the Grand Chain.

The Grand Chain was a succession of sunken boulders, jagged and sharp, along the bottom of the river. The wrecked corpses of sunken steamboats lay strewn along the Grand Chain, increasing the danger. Abner Conrad was stiff as a marble statue as he handled the wheel through the deadly maze. The other pilots crowded around the veteran in the cramped pilothouse, offering whispered advice to the one-armed expert.

"Maybe we'll get lucky and the *Andrew Jackson II* will hit a rock," whispered John nervously.

"Hush, lad," said O'Malley. "Abner's got to give his full attention to the river."

John remained quiet as the pilot performed his difficult task. Abner Conrad breathed heavily as he worked, pausing only occasionally to wipe his perspiring forehead with his stump.

Soon, John spotted the small town of Thebes, Illinois, approaching on the right. Thebes was a welcome sight to all. It meant they had gotten through the Grand Chain. The cheering spectators at Thebes were quickly passed. After Thebes, the river became more navigable. The steamboats increased their speed. Just past Thebes was a stretch of river known as Steersman's Bend, so named because it was easily navigable year round, and virtually the only part of the river between Cairo and St. Louis where a cub pilot could take the wheel.

Abner Conrad tried again and again to pass the *Andrew Jackson II*. Fitch's pilot kept planting the stern of his boat directly in the path of the *Girardeau Rose*, and Conrad was unable to get past his opponent.

"Hang it!" said O'Malley. "You need to do something, Abner. We're only ten miles from Cape Girardeau. He's got us beat!"

The one-armed pilot raised his eyebrows. "You're forgetting something, Captain. Rock Island. River's deep enough to pass on either side. Fitch can't block both sides."

Rock Island soon loomed in the distance. It was a towering piece of whitish-gray rock rising out of the middle of the Mississippi River about two miles north of Thebes. The racing steamboats were going full throttle as Rock Island came into clear view. The *Girardeau Rose* bounced roughly in the wake of the *Andrew Jackson II*, darting to the left and right, trying to pass.

"Fitch is going to have to choose one side or the other of Rock Island," said Abner Conrad with satisfaction.

Not surprisingly, the *Andrew Jackson II* chose the deep channel on the larboard side. The *Girardeau Rose* veered right and the two steamboats were temporarily out of each other's sight as they circumvented Rock Island. The pilothouse erupted in bedlam when the *Andrew Jackson II* came back into sight. The Girardeau Rose had regained the lead.

Abner Conrad cut in front of the other steamboat and gave Fitch's pilot a taste of riding in another boat's wake. The *Andrew Jackson II* stuck doggedly to the flanks of the *Girardeau Rose* as the steamboats strained their engines, roaring full speed for Cape Girardeau.

John watched the smoke of the *Andrew Jackson II*. It turned from black to gray and finally to white. He knew Fitch was adding lard to his furnaces, playing his last trump card. He watched with dismay as the *Andrew Jackson II* began gaining on O'Malley's already straining steamboat. John hurried to the engine room. Water still sloshed back and forth on the floor from the earlier broken pipe.

"Do you think the boilers will hold if we weigh down the safety valves?" John asked the young Second Engineer.

Roscoe Pollack glanced with uncertainty at the pounding machinery. "Don't know. We're already taxing her to the limit."

"Fitch is catching us! Let's find out how tough these boilers are."

Together, they weighted down the safety valves, allowing even more pressure to build dangerously inside the straining boilers, turning the paddle wheels even faster than before.

John raced back to the deck and saw they were once again outstripping the *Andrew Jackson II*. Cape Girardeau loomed in the distance. The small red brick buildings on the waterfront became larger and larger. Soon, he could detect the crowds thronging the cobblestone levee. People packed into second story windows of the brick buildings. Others covered the rooftops. Someone in the cupola of the St. Charles Hotel was setting off fireworks. A band was playing. People were shouting and waving flags. Cape Girardeau was ready to see the finish of a grand steamboat race. For John, the finish of the race *was* grand. The *Girardeau Rose* shot past the finish line ten lengths ahead of the *Andrew Jackson II*.

As the *Girardeau Rose* sliced through the river in front of the Cape Girardeau waterfront, John rushed back to the engine room and unleashed the safety valves. The poppet valves clattered noisily as tremendous pressure escaped with a hiss of fiery hot steam. John and the second engineer backed away from the scalding steam and exchanged knowing looks. They could have killed everyone on board by their rash act.

Having stormed victoriously past the finish line, the *Girardeau Rose* turned gracefully in the water and pulled up to the levee in Cape Girardeau. She lowered her planks amid the frenzied applause and cheering from the crowd. The magnificent steamboat had made the 1,100 mile trip from New Orleans to Cape Girardeau in three days, four hours, and, ten minutes. It was a new record.

John found Pete Carnahan sitting quietly on a chair on the boiler deck. The engineer's face was dark red, covered with blisters and blotches of white. His eyes were watering and bloodshot. He sat with his elbows on his knees, a half-empty bottle of rum between his feet.

"How do you feel, Pete?"

"Like a boiled egg. A drunk boiled egg."

The odor of liquor was strong on his breath.

"They gave you a little something to ease the pain, huh?"

"Yeah. Medicinal purposes, you know."

"Are your eyes all right?"

The engineer nodded.

"I can see, anyway. That's the important thing."

The engineer winked one of his swollen eyes.

"Quit wasting your time jawing at me, boy. You and I can talk later. Go find your lady. You belong with her."

John found Lindy on the hurricane deck, and the hug they shared was spontaneous.

"Lindy," he said softly, his voice sounding hoarse. "I want to marry you."

Her brown eyes sparkled. She tossed her head, the dark curly hair moving in waves across her shoulders. "I thought you'd never ask!"

They kissed. Her mouth was warm and delicious.

"You know," she said, when their lips parted, "Papa would probably allow us to get married on board the *Lucky Molly* tonight, if you'd like." Her eyes spoke eloquently of her love.

Minutes later, Tyler Fitch removed the sign from the poles in front of his store and handed it to O'Malley. Grinning, O'Malley read the sign out loud: "*FASTEST STEAMBOAT OF CAPE GIRARDEAU.*" The large crowd surrounding them applauded.

"You won fair and square," Fitch said gallantly. "It's yours. Until I win it back."

"You mean it's mine for keeps, then."

Several people in the crowd laughed.

"Also," said Tyler Fitch, reaching into the pocket of his coat. "I believe I must return this little item to you." Fitch handed the $100,00 note to Patrick O'Malley. He had scrawled CANCELLED across its top.

The wedding was held in the grand saloon of the *Lucky Molly*. O'Malley had meant at first for it to be a small family affair, but as the victory celebration continued throughout the day, more and more invitations were extended and eventually the long room was packed, each person listening intently as O'Malley conducted the service.

After the exchange of vows, John and Lindy danced in the middle of the room amid other happy couples. It was lively and fun, but John saw only Lindy. She wore a glistening white dress with small mother-of-pearl buttons down the front of the slim bodice. She'd complained it was a summer dress, out of season for November, but it was her only pure white one, and she'd worn it anyway. Its whiteness accented her glowing complexion and her lustrous dark hair. As his hands held her tiny waist, he found himself thinking how lucky he was to have her as his wife. Lindy smiled with glee as they polkaed and reeled. Her knowing brown eyes seemed to read his mind.

After a few dances, O'Malley stopped the piano player and stepped up onto a chair near the piano. "I'd like to make a toast to my new son-in-law. When I first met him, just over a year ago, he was a gangly frail little pup. I had my doubts about his ability to make it as a steamboatman, but one person knew he had something special. That person was my daughter, Rosalind, now his wife. She told me from the beginning that he possessed that rare commodity so much a pleasure to run across—strength of character. I've discovered since then that she's right. John's a young man I'm proud to have as a friend, even prouder to have as an addition to my family." Several people began clapping.

"Hold your paddle wheels. I'm not done just yet." He raised his glass. "This toast is to John Carmichael. John, I ask you to always cherish my lovely little Rose, as I've cherished her since infancy. Make her the happiest woman between Memphis and St. Louis. Stand shoulder to shoulder with her and me, helping build our steamboat business into a fine line of boats, the pride of the Mississippi. And, both of you, give me grandchildren. Lots of them!" Several men hooted. "Finally, John," concluded O'Malley, smiling, "I request that you have your tail out of bed by 6:00 tomorrow morning, because we're leaving bright and early for St. Louis with both the *Lucky Molly* and the *Girardeau Rose*. Going to cash in on all the publicity we've had the last few days. You may bring the little wife along with you, of course."

The crowd laughed, tipping glasses to John and Lindy. The piano player hit the keys with a passion. The tinkling notes of Stephen Foster's "Suwanee River" was soon drowned out as guests resumed conversations. John had hoped to make a return toast to O'Malley, but the moment had passed.

The party lasted well into the night. Shortly after midnight, O'Malley took them aside, gave them a key to the captain's quarters on the *Girardeau Rose* moored nearby, and ushered them away to savor their wedding night alone. They walked to the boat under the gleaming stars in the cool November night. They passed the night watchman on duty on the *Girardeau Rose*. They were soon alone in the candlelight of the captain's quarters, cozy and secure behind locked doors.

When John lit the last candle in the room, he saw the white chest he'd given Lindy sitting next to the bed. Its brass plaque glistened in the light. He looked at Lindy with surprise.

"Had you forgotten you gave it to me, John? It's a hope chest now. I packed all kinds of things I'll be needing as your wife. Want to see them?"

He moved toward her, shaking his head. "I'll look at them in the morning."

In the flickering candlelight, he undressed her slowly, his eyes savoring the beauty of her smooth body. Timidly, she began untying his tie. When it was off, she moved to his shirt, unbuttoning him slowly, languidly. Minutes later, they were naked in the bed, mouths meshed hungrily, bodies pressing together, legs and hands and thighs and lips knowing each other so very intimately, bodies joining hard flesh to yielding flesh, fumbling at first, but moving within seconds to a wonderful natural rhythm that mounted and stretched into minutes and hours. Alternately sapped and gorged, John's spirit soared during a night in which he hardly slept, taking Lindy to the summit with him as often as possible, on sublime flights that left both of them shuddering and clinging.

Horace Claxton knew it was about an hour before dawn. Now was the time to plant the explosives. Six hollowed-out logs lay on the wooden table in his cabin on the *Andrew Jackson II*. He picked one up. He had done a good job of workmanship. Just from looking at it you couldn't tell it had been carved out and filled with gunpowder. The firemen on John Carmichael's steamboat would certainly not notice anything unusual when they tossed the lethal logs into the blazing furnaces.

"Good riddance, John Carmichael," he whispered aloud, as he gathered the half dozen logs in his powerful arms. His only regret was that Carmichael would have no idea that Horace J. Claxton had been the instrument behind his fiery death.

Claxton cracked open the door to his cabin and listened intently to the noises of the night. Water lapped at the sides of the boat, wooden planks and beams creaked, a distant steamboat bell rang somewhere downriver. When he was satisfied he wouldn't be seen, he slipped out of his cabin. He moved from shadow to shadow next to the brick buildings on the Cape Girardeau waterfront. His breath came in hoarse rasps as he neared the quiet resting shapes of O'Malley's two steamboats. The wedding party had long since ended on the *Lucky Molly*. The older boat rested quietly near the *Girardeau Rose*, muddy river waves slapping the hulls of the two dormant steamboats. Claxton lurked in the dark shadows near them and watched for several long minutes. Both were quiet. Sleeping giants, each with a night watchman stationed near lowered gangplanks. He began planning how to get on board.

He considered trying to swim to the boat, but he respected the power of the Mississippi too much for that. The current could easily drag him underneath one of the steamboats or pin him to its hull under the dark cold water. No, he wouldn't swim.

When Claxton made his decision, he placed the firewood on the ground and began creeping across the moonlit cobblestone levee toward the closest gangplank. As he crept, he removed his knife from his boot. Reaching the gangplank without being seen, he scaled it silently, wriggling on his chest. The night watchman was sitting on a crate near the top of the gangplank, chin nestled on his stomach. Claxton gripped his knife firmly in his hand and moved forward in the night. His heart was pounding, but his mind was keen, as it always was in life and death situations. He rose to a crouch and moved within four feet of his prey. The moonlight shone on Claxton's knife. He was preparing to lunge for the man when he realized the watchman was asleep, snoring lightly. He was a young man, probably the lowest in seniority on the boat.

"Lucky bastard," Claxton thought to himself, smiling grimly. "He's a poor excuse for a watchman, but it saved his life. Least until the bombs explode."

He turned and crept down the landing stage. Moments later, firewood in his arms, he slipped past the dozing guard. His large bulk moved silently toward the cords of wood stacked near the furnace doors. From years of experience, he knew which piles would go into the yawning mouths of the furnace first. He knew which stacks would be added as the steamboat moved upriver. He placed all six deadly logs into the same pile, one he knew would not be the first to go into the furnaces. He didn't want the boat to blow up while there was any chance John Carmichael might still be on land, helping with business matters.

Once the wood was in place, he again moved stealthily past the sleeping guard and down the landing stage. Crouching low, Claxton made sure the guard from O'Malley's other boat didn't see him as he glided across the cobblestones and back into the darkness. It was so easy, Claxton thought to himself. He probably could have placed the explosives on both steamboats, if he'd cared to, but he didn't want to destroy them both. He wanted O'Malley to live. Carmichael was the one who had to die. With Carmichael out of the way, O'Malley might even rehire Claxton as First Mate. Things might be like old times again.

Claxton's shirt was soaked with sweat. The damp cloth felt cold against his skin in the cool November night. Whether or not O'Malley took him back,

Claxton thought with satisfaction as he made his way cautiously through the dark night, one thing was certain—John Carmichael was going to die a very violent death. Soon.

Shortly after dawn, John was awakened by light streaming through the window of the captain's quarters on the *Girardeau Rose*. He opened his eyes groggily but came awake quickly when he saw Lindy propped on her elbow next to him, smiling.

"Your hair is so beautiful," she said. "Like finely-spun gold. You look like a little boy when you're asleep."

He reached out and pulled her close. "How long have you been up?"

"Since dawn."

"Why didn't you wake me?"

"I was having fun watching you sleep. You're so handsome. I could watch you for hours and hours."

Thirty minutes later they were dressed and talking with Patrick O'Malley on the hurricane deck. The crews of both the *Girardeau Rose* and the *Lucky Molly* were bustling about, loading freight onto the boats and feeding firewood into the furnaces.

"We'll take both boats to St. Louis, load up, then make a joint trip down to New Orleans," O'Malley was explaining. "And we won't be racing on this trip, John." O'Malley suddenly smiled broadly. "By the way, newlyweds, I have a wedding present for you."

"Oh, Papa," said Lindy. "You don't need to give us anything else. You gave us that wonderful party on the *Lucky Molly* last night."

O'Malley pulled some papers from his coat pocket. "Years ago Louis Lorimier gave me a piece of property on Lorimier Street that would be the perfect place in Cape Girardeau to build a house. It's close enough to the river so you have a good view of the Mississippi. It's on high ground, though, so you don't need to worry about floodwater." O'Malley handed the papers to John. "Here's the deed. Had it drawn up last night for you and Lindy. I want to build you a house, if you'll let me."

John accepted the papers. He was speechless.

"Let you?" he finally said. "It would be wonderful. But what about your financial situation? Can you afford to be so extravagant?"

"Now that I'm out from under that debt on the *Girardeau Rose*, I can. Besides, it's important to me that my daughter and her husband have a good place to live."

"Thank you, Papa," said Lindy, hugging her father.

"The house I have in mind," said O'Malley, "will be a home worth seeing. Had the plans drawn up years ago, but never built it. I picture a riverboat pilothouse set smack on top, complete with a wheel and a fantastic view of the Mississippi River, so even when you're home you can go upstairs and get the feel of the river. Gonna be a fantastic house." O'Malley smiled as he thought of it. "One other present for you, John, is that I'm going to let you captain the *Girardeau Rose* up to St. Louis on this trip. You and Lindy are already moved into the captain's quarters for now. We'll switch once we load up at St. Louis, then you can take the *Lucky Molly* down to New Orleans."

John liked the idea of captaining the *Girardeau Rose*. She would be basking in the glow of her victorious race with Fitch. It would be a fine time to be her captain, even on a short run like the trip from Cape Girardeau to St. Louis.

"You won't mind leaving your pride and joy for the trip to St. Louis?" John asked.

"I'll trust her to you, just like I'm trusting the real Cape Girardeau Rose to you. Besides, the *Lucky Molly* and I are old companions."

"Why, look!" said Lindy. "Here comes Aunt Maude. She's got a suitcase!"

"Your aunt's making this trip with us. First time she's been on a steamboat in years."

Maude O'Malley, carrying a small suitcase, joined them a few moments later on the levee in front of the *Girardeau Rose*.

"I want to thank you, Patrick, for leaving my suitcase for me to carry myself. I put it by the front door so you could carry it for me. I guess you wanted me to get some exercise." Maude O'Malley, forehead creased with dozens of deep wrinkles, glanced from the *Lucky Molly* to the *Girardeau Rose*. "Which contraption am I suffering upon?"

"Suffering!" said O'Malley. "Why, you've never ridden in such comfort. You'll ride from here to New Orleans on the *Lucky Molly* and make the homeward trip on the *Girardeau Rose*. Afterward, you can let me know what a good captain I am."

"Well, come on, Patrick. Show me to my room. Goodness, how I hate steamboats. They're so noisy. So dangerous."

"Keep your voice down, Maude. What do you think puts the food on your table, anyway? Besides, my boats aren't dangerous. I've built my reputation on it."

John felt a renewed twinge of guilt about fastening down the safety valve on the *Girardeau Rose* during the race. O'Malley still didn't know he'd done it. He decided he'd never mention it. He hoped Roscoe Pollack wouldn't, either. John stood with Lindy at the wheel in the pilothouse of the *Girardeau Rose* as the boat backed away from the Cape Girardeau levee. Several early morning spectators waved from the cobblestoned riverbank. He felt a surge of pride at being the captain of such a magnificent steamboat. Nearby, Horace Claxton stood at the stern of the *Andrew Jackson II*. John noticed a look of fright on his face. *Maybe my troubles with Claxton are over*, he thought, feeling pleased. Everything seemed to be going well.

The *Lucky Molly* pulled into the channel behind them. Patrick O'Malley and Abner Conrad were in the pilothouse. John waved, and O'Malley waved back.

"It's such a gorgeous morning," sighed Lindy. "Look how bright blue the sky is!"

He followed her gaze. The sky was a dazzling azure, almost devoid of clouds. The November sun shone on the brownish-blue water of the Mississippi. The leaves on the trees along the shoreline had turned yellow, red and orange. Most formed a multicolored blanket on the ground. Some still clung tenaciously to their branches. The colors were particularly bright on the trees covering the slopes leading up to Cape Rock. The steep mountain was ablaze with color. The white rock promontory looked like the head and crown of a huge monarch, with the colorful slopes below as his flowing robes.

John guided the *Girardeau Rose* through shallow water near Cape Rock, staying out of the deeper part of the channel since they were going upriver. After passing Cape Rock, John turned the wheel over to a pilot, and he and Lindy watched as the *Lucky Molly*, 500 yards behind them, steamed past the towering landmark. Black smoke poured from the *Molly's* chimneys. She was easily keeping up with the leisurely pace John had set.

"Look," said Lindy, smiling. "Aunt Maude is on the hurricane deck, talking to some passengers. I'm so glad she's not holed up in her cabin. You know how frightened she is of steamboats. I can't believe she's making the trip at all."

"Guess she's tired of staying home alone," said John.

"More likely she's wanting to go to the city to get us a wedding present," Lindy said.

Suddenly the cloudless sky was jarred by a tremendous thunderclap. The repercussion rattled the pilothouse of the *Girardeau Rose* and threw Lindy against John's shoulder. John knew the noise was not thunder. It was a boiler explosion. Before his eyes, the tall chimneys of the *Lucky Molly* shattered like breaking china.

A second deafening explosion followed a moment after the first, and the entire midsection of the *Lucky Molly* disappeared in a cloud of smoke and steam. Wood, metal, and bodies hurled 200 feet into the air, debris raining like a summer thunderstorm into the water surrounding the stricken steamboat. Some pieces were landing on the banks on both sides of the river.

"Oh, no!" Lindy shrieked in his ear.

''Turn around!" he ordered the pilot.

As the *Girardeau Rose* wheeled to move back downriver, John got a good look at the situation on the *Lucky Molly*. Where the pilothouse should have been, there was nothing. Along with the chimneys, it had been blown completely away. Patrick O'Malley had been standing in the pilothouse, John realized sickly. So had Abner Conrad. So had Artemus Primm. The entire midsection of the steamboat, about a third of its bulk, had been torn away, top to bottom, as if a huge animal had chomped a bite out of the middle of the boat. Orange fire raged on the front and back sections of the wooden *Lucky Molly*, spreading with unbelievable speed. One of the paddle wheels was nowhere to be seen. Helpless, the battered steamboat was drifting downstream, being dragged into the deepest part of the channel by the swift and merciless current.

"Oh, Papa! Papa!"

John winced at the sound of Lindy's horrified voice. He saw the remains of the *Lucky Molly* spin slow circles in the water like a one-legged duck. "Hurry!" he called. "We've got to help them!"

The wide bow of the *Girardeau Rose* cut through the water and in less than a minute she was at the place where the *Lucky Molly* had exploded, but the *Lucky Molly* was already 100 yards downriver. The *Girardeau Rose* slowed as she neared the floating debris in the water. Bodies littered the river, some floating lifelessly, others swimming. Cries and screams filled the air.

"Throw ropes to these people. Pull them in," John ordered from the pilot-house. The orders were unnecessary. The deck hands were already working feverishly to save the lives of the people in the water. The *Girardeau Rose* was forced to halt to avoid running over the wounded in the water in front of them. Looking again at the *Lucky Molly*, John gave a surprised yell.

"There's Uncle Pat!"

Lindy's tearful eyes followed his pointing finger. Patrick O'Malley was on the very front of the boiler deck of the sinking steamboat. The main deck was already underwater. The rest of the steamboat was a flaming inferno. O'Malley was handing boards to terrified passengers and was helping them leap off the boat and into the water.

O'Malley paused in front of one of the passengers, a woman dressed in dark clothing. It was Maude O'Malley. They argued. O'Malley finally took his sister's hands in his own. Whatever he said ended the argument. He led her to the edge of the boiler deck, gave her a board to hold onto, kissed her, and helped her jump.

"Hurry! We've got to save him!" John told the pilot.

"Can't go forward now. There's people all over the water in front of us."

John leaned forward and yelled at the deck hands below. "Hurry up down there! Get those people on board! Lower the yawl! Use it to gather them up!" He looked again at the *Lucky Molly*. O'Malley had cleared the passengers from the front boiler deck. He was moving toward the back of the steamboat, where two children were hugging each other and crying. He lurched and lunged like a dog hit by a stagecoach.

John realized O'Malley was hurt. He must have been blown into the air from his position in the pilothouse and must have landed on the boiler deck. No telling what bones were broken.

"Oh, Papa," Lindy was whispering. "Get off the boat. Get off, please!"

O'Malley slipped out of sight as he worked his way toward the rear of the flaming *Lucky Molly*. They watched impotently and waited for him to reappear. The *Girardeau Rose* still sat stationary in the river, deck hands working tirelessly to rescue conscious people from the sucking current of the river.

"Oh, there he is!" Lindy cried out. O'Malley had reached the stern of the *Lucky Molly*. He held the two children in his arms. "He's got them," Lindy cried.

Suddenly, another explosion wracked the burning wreckage of the *Lucky Molly*. Flaming embers shot in all directions. Fire engulfed the entire lifeless skeleton of the boat, including the area where O'Malley had stood with the children. With the hissing steaming anger of fire meeting water, the remains of the *Lucky Molly* sank quickly, carrying down with her the struggling people and bits of debris in her immediate vicinity. After a final reptilian hiss, the *Lucky Molly* was gone. Only three minutes had passed since the first explosion. Only widely strewn debris marked her final resting place in the deep muddy water.

For hours, the *Girardeau Rose* steamed slowly through the debris in the river, plucking survivors from the cold water. The scalded and maimed were laid on the lower deck, tended by two physicians who happened to be passengers on the *Girardeau Rose*. Many survivors were calling out for loved ones who'd also been on the *Lucky Molly*. Most cries went unanswered.

As John paced the lower deck of the *Girardeau Rose*, despair tugged at his heart. Of the 235 passengers and crew members of the *Lucky Molly*, only 58 were rescued by the *Girardeau Rose*. Some managed to swim to shore and save themselves, but in the year 1852, few people could swim at all, much less well enough to survive the deadly current of the Mississippi River. By anyone's estimation, the explosion of the *Lucky Molly* had been a major tragedy. The most tragic loss to John, though, was the one that hit closest to home—Patrick O'Malley was never found.

John was at the side of the boat when Maude O'Malley was pulled aboard, still gripping the piece of lumber O'Malley had forced into her hands. He knelt next to Maude as Lindy cradled the older woman's head. She looked like a drowned cat, all skin and bones and wet black cloth.

"Your Papa," Maude O'Malley gasped, "told me to tell you he loves you, Lindy. He loves his little Rose."

Lindy's eyes clamped tight. She held her aunt's head in her lap, rocking back and forth.

"I saw him blown up, child," Maude continued. "He's gone."

Tenderly, John put one hand on Lindy's heaving shoulder and grasped Maude's hand with his other. Maude O'Malley's clear blue eyes filled with tears. "I wanted him to get off the boat with me. I insisted I'd never make it without him. He wouldn't do it. Wouldn't leave the *Lucky Molly* until the last passenger was off."

Lindy pressed her face into the wet cloth of her aunt's bosom, and Maude patted the back of Lindy's head.

"I told your Papa I absolutely refused to leave without him. He said if I didn't leave voluntarily, he'd throw me off. Said he wanted to make sure I was around to help John take care of you." Maude O'Malley shuddered with violent sobs. "I'm sorry I couldn't save him, Rosalind. I'm so, so sorry."

Three days later Patrick O'Malley's funeral was conducted in Lorimier Cemetery in Cape Girardeau. O'Malley's body had not been found, so the service was conducted next to an empty grave beside his wife's headstone, upon a site commanding a fine view of the Mississippi River, not far from the grave of Louis Lorimier. Mr. Bercier from St. Vincent Marble Works Company worked overtime preparing O'Malley's tombstone. It bore a simple epitaph:

PATRICK O'MALLEY
1793–1852
A CAPTAIN'S CAPTAIN

A large crowd attended the funeral service, almost as large as the crowd that had gathered for the mass service for all victims held earlier at St. Vincent's Church next to the river. John and Lindy stood with Maude O'Malley near the white tombstone. A local minister, the same clergyman who'd said prayers over Austin Carmichael's grave after the duel, was praying aloud. Several hundred mourners surrounded the family, covering a large part of the cemetery. John didn't listen to the words of the minister. He simply heard the comforting tone of the voice and let his mind float with the gentleness of the sound. He reached out and took Lindy's hand and squeezed. He felt so sorry for her. Both of them were orphans now. Both her parents were dead. She was only sixteen years old. Maybe a married person wasn't considered an orphan when her parents died. Still, it is an awful feeling, a grim rite of passage, an empty abyss of pain, to have lost both parents. At least they had each other and Maude.

As the priest's voice sanded patiently upon the sharp edges of their grief, John thought of Patrick O'Malley, Abner Conrad, Artemus Primm, Roscoe Pollack, and the other crew members who had died.

"Before we leave," the minister said, "Captain John Carmichael has a few words he wants to share."

John, more nervous than he'd expected, looked at the crowd. He had asked the minister for the opportunity to say a brief eulogy for O'Malley. John's hands were cold as he began speaking.

"Lindy, Maude, and I want to thank each of you for coming here today to pay your final respects to Patrick O'Malley. It's comforting to his family to see that he had so many friends." He glanced at the individual faces forming the mosaic of the crowd. He saw merchants, steamboatmen, doctors, lawyers, politicians, farmers, and crew members, past and present. He saw scores of people he recognized, including Pete Carnahan, Tyler Fitch, Horace Claxton, and Samantha Peabody. "It's not surprising that Patrick O'Malley had so many friends. He was a man who made friends easily because there was so much to like about him, so much good in him. O'Malley once told me that once or twice a lifetime each of us meets someone who impacts our life tremendously. For me, Patrick O'Malley was such a person. I suspect he was such a person for many of you. He was a man who perhaps didn't read the Bible as much as he should have, but he truly lived the idea of doing unto others as you'd have them do unto you. He treated everyone fairly. He was honest in everything he did, to the smallest detail. He was a man's man in fights and quarrels, but carried endless compassion close to the surface of that thick skin of his.

"I never met a finer man than Patrick O'Malley. I'm proud and honored that I had the opportunity to work for him and that I had the brief opportunity of being a part of his family."

Maude O'Malley was holding Lindy's hand so tightly the older woman's knuckles were turning white.

"Death can come to each of us at any time," he continued. "An accident like this reminds us all of our tenuous grasp upon life. Today is a time of sadness, of course. But, of all the men I've known, Patrick O'Malley is one I feel would not have liked to grow sickly and feeble in old age. He was rugged. He was tough. He wore the red kerchief. He fought pirates. He built a steamboat business. He loved his life on the Mississippi. He died like he lived, refusing to save his life while others remained in danger. He was a man's man, a captain's captain, at rest now in the place he loved the most—the Mississippi River. He'll be a part of it forever. I have a hunch he would like that idea."

The funeral ended. Most of the crowd drifted away. Several paid their respects to Lindy.

John found himself staring at Horace Claxton as the big mate stood twenty yards away, dark head lowered. When Claxton raised his eyes, they were wet and glistening, framed with dark circles. When he caught John staring at him, he averted his eyes and hurried down the hill. John found Claxton's grief touching. If he was capable of feeling pain at O'Malley's death, maybe he wasn't so bad after all.

Pete Carnahan touched John's arm. "Nice speech, lad. O'Malley would've liked it. Hell, maybe he did hear it."

"Who knows?" John said, not seeking an answer.

Carnahan leaned close. "Could I have a word with you, private-like?" They moved a few steps away from the women. They faced the river as they spoke. "John, ninety-nine out of a hundred times, steamboat accidents are just that, accidents. Lots of steamboats have gone down due to boiler explosions. Happens a lot. Accidents."

"What are you saying, Pete?"

"I'm saying I checked out the boilers on the *Lucky Molly* just hours before that explosion. Them rascals was in perfect working order. Wasn't a weak spot in 'em. Not a bit of rust. No worn places. Roscoe Pollack, may he rest in peace, knew what he was doing around those boilers. I'm saying somebody blew up the *Lucky Molly*. Did it on purpose."

"Why would anybody want to blow up the *Lucky Molly*?"

"I don't know the answer. I just know it was no accident. Needs to be investigated. I'll be glad to help."

"I appreciate the offer, Pete, and I appreciate your telling me this." They shook hands and John returned to Lindy's side.

"John," she said, her brown eyes regarding him with affection, "walk me over to the river for a moment, would you?"

They held hands as they walked down the green hillside of Lorimier Cemetery. They stopped at the edge of the graveyard. A steep hillside covered with forest separated them from the muddy water of the Mississippi

"John," she said softly, "could Aunt Maude live with us for a while? She has nowhere to go, no place . . . "

"Of course. She can stay with us as long as you like."

Lindy hugged him, her face close to his. "Do you know what I realized while we were standing there at the funeral?"

"What?"

"I'll never again hear Papa call me his little Rose."

A painful lump punched at the insides of John's throat. "Lindy, maybe if we listen to the wind together some night when we're on the river on the *Girardeau Rose,* we'll hear him. The spirit of a human being like your father is too strong, too vital, to be snuffed out like a candle. Something in the human soul elevates us above the rocks, the birds, the animals. The life force of your father is alive and well somewhere. He might be swapping yarns right now with Mike Fink and Louis Lorimier. I'd like to think he might check in on us from time to time, to see how we're doing." He gestured toward the *Girardeau Rose*. The steamboat was tied at the levee. "I haven't forgotten the promise I made your father. I'm going to make you happy. I'm going to make the *Girardeau Rose* the best steamboat on the river. He'll be proud of us."

"I hope so, John. I do hope so."

Together, they gazed at the Mississippi River. The massive river, oblivious to their presence, lumbered slowly southward, its surface a murky brownish-gray, its depths and secrets impenetrable, its past and its future stretching out of sight like the long infinite body of the river itself.

PART III

The Call of the Confederacy

"Civil War military leaders recognized the importance of the Mississippi River in the conduct of the war and Cape Girardeau's strategic location on the first accessible high ground above the juncture with the Ohio River."

Felix E. Snider & Earl A. Collins
Cape Girardeau: Biography of a City, 1956

"CAPE GIRARDEAU"
April 26, 1863 - 6 p.m.

GENERAL:
I am attacked by 8,000 men under Marmaduke. I have repulsed them this after-noon. Expect to be stormed to-morrow. Can you send me two regiments of infantry and a field battery with supply of ammunition? Answer.

John McNeil
Brigadier-General, Commanding
*U. S. Army Official Records
of the War of Rebellion*, Series I, Volume XXII

"The enemy's forts and batteries [at Cape Girardeau] continued to play upon our battery for more than one hour without intermission, and now and then swept the woods with shell and shot, canister and grape, while the mineballs came hissing a treble to the music of the roar."

Gideon W. Thompson
Colonel, Commanding Brigade
Sixth Missouri Cavalry
(Confederate)
Official Report
May 15, 1863
U. S. Army Official Records of the War of Rebellion,
Series I, Volume XXII

Chapter 16

July 19, 1861
Cape Girardeau, Missouri

Rosalind O'Malley Carmichael was 25 years old. After enjoying a happy and enduring marriage to the love of her life, enhanced by the knowledge that her partnership with her husband, while producing no children, had helped make the *Girardeau Rose* the most successful steamboat on the Mississippi River, she now found herself virtually a prisoner in her own hometown. The Twentieth Illinois occupied Cape Girardeau for the North. Colonel C. C. Marsh had issued mysterious orders earlier in the week for the town's entire population to report to the fairgrounds at noon on Sunday.

Lindy and Maude were walking to the fairgrounds. They hadn't been out much since the occupation. Lindy was amazed by the changes in Cape Girardeau in the month since John had left to join the Missouri State Militia in Jefferson City. Union soldiers, brass buttons gleaming on dark blue coats, were everywhere. Their main encampment was on the fairgrounds in the south part of town, where hundreds of tents had popped up, a fire in front of each. Scores of others bivouacked throughout the city, tents scattered from the public square to fields near private homes. Ingram's Mill, a four-story brick building on the riverfront, had been converted into a barracks. The soldiers spent most of their time drilling and marching, although 300 were kept busy building the forts. Every day, the hot summer afternoons echoed with the thunder of musketry as the new soldiers practiced their marksmanship. Occasionally the big cannon on the forts overlooking the Mississippi rattled the riverfront with booming explosions as artillery men shot at snags in the river.

The Union solders constructed four forts in Cape Girardeau. Fort A was at the northeastern corner of town, on a high bluff overlooking the Mississippi River, with walls of earthworks and logs, dozens of intimidating pieces of artillery, and rifle pits dug into the side of the bluff. Fort B occupied a high point at the northwest corner of the city, its cannon and rifle pits easily covering any approach by way of Perryville or Jackson roads. Fort C guarded the southwest corner of town, its tall earthworks shaped like a sassafras leaf, surrounded by a moat, with 32-pound cannon stationed at each corner. Fort D was built at the southeast edge of Cape Girardeau on the bluffs overlooking the river, its menacing cannon and rifle pits facing both the river and the fields south of town.

Lindy's circle of friends had dwindled. Many families of Southern stock had left town, some selling their homes voluntarily, others forced out by the military. Most Cape Girardeau male folk of soldierly age had joined one side or the other and were long gone to encampments elsewhere. Some seventy families of Northern supporters had hustled to town from outlying areas, driven to the protection offered by the Union troops from marauding bands of rebels and bushwhackers. In spite of the flow of new people, Cape's population had shrunk in the past months from 6,000 to 4,000.

Steamboats still came and went at the levee, but they now carried only troops, weapons, and supplies. She'd seen the three impressive Union woodclad gunboats, *Conestoga*, *Lexington*, and *Tyler*, when they chugged up from Cairo one afternoon, cannons peering wickedly from gunports in oak bulwarks. She even saw the *Girardeau Rose* occasionally. Tyler Fitch, who had bought her from John just before the war, was providing transportation for the Northern forces. Lindy often wished John had kept the steamboat business instead of selling it to Fitch. At least Tyler Fitch made it to Cape every now and then. The gold buried in her basement meant nothing to Lindy without John to share it.

The headquarters for the Union Provost Marshall for the Cape Girardeau District was the large red brick courthouse on the commanding hill in the center of town. The dungeon beneath it was used as a jail for traitors and captured rebels. The Union forces had most definitely taken over the town. With all the changes, Cape Girardeau just wasn't the same. Except for her own house, built according to O'Malley's plans, Cape no longer seemed like home.

As they walked toward the fairgrounds, Lindy and Maude fell in step with Doc Wilson. Doc, thinning white hair glistening in the July sun, dabbed his wrinkled face with a handkerchief as they neared the crowded fairgrounds.

"Have you heard from David, Doc?" Lindy asked.

Doc's only son had joined the Union Army. He'd been stationed in St. Louis the last Lindy had heard.

"Got a letter yesterday. He's still excited about army life. Thinks he's going to win the war all by himself. What about you, Rosalind? Heard from John?"

She wondered how much she should tell anyone about the correspondence from her husband. She decided to tell only a part of the truth. "I had a couple letters the first week, but since the occupation I haven't heard a thing. Guess there's no way for mail to get through since all the Southerners have been run out of town and anyone carrying rebel mail is put in jail." She didn't mention the three letters mysteriously appearing in her foyer one morning. She didn't know how they got there, but they'd been from John and she'd read each one twenty times.

Doc's distinctive face, framed by a white handlebar moustache and wrinkled like an old hound dog, radiated kindness. "This war won't last forever, child. You'll see him again soon." He brightened. "Say, I've been assigned to the military hospital on Washington Street. We've got sick soldiers all over the place. Congress passed a new law permitting female nurses. Would you two be interested?"

Maude frowned. "Tending unclothed and wounded men? Washing them? Cleaning up their messes? Doesn't sound very ladylike, Doc."

"Maude, certain things are more important than being prim and proper. The hospitals are already filling up with sick men. We need help. We're talking life and death. We're so desperate for nurses, I'd even accept Lindy."

"Why, Doc Wilson, I thought you liked me!"

He smiled.

"Dorothea Dix, Superintendent of Female Nurses in Washington, has ordered that all female nurses must be past thirty, healthy, plain almost to repulsion in dress, and devoid of personal attractions. You're healthy, Lindy, but lack the other qualifications."

Maude harrumphed, removing her bonnet. "Doc," she challenged, a sparkle in her eye, "are you saying I fit all Dorothea Dix's standards?"

He glanced at her drab, brown dress. "Let's just say I wouldn't be reprimanded for hiring you. What do you say, Maude? Salary's forty cents a day plus one ration. May I hire you both?"

"We'll do it," Maude said. "Lindy needs something to take her mind off her loneliness, and who knows, maybe I'll find a husband. Any of those soldiers around sixty?" They all laughed.

At the fairgrounds a wooden platform dominated the landscape. Colonel Marsh was standing on it, motioning for the crowd of 5,000 to quiet down. Rows and rows of armed soldiers surrounded them. Colonel Marsh, his back ramrod straight, was clad in a dark blue frock coat with two rows of brass buttons down his breast. Once he began speaking, his booming voice was authoritative. "On behalf of the Twentieth Illinois Infantry and Cavalry, I thank the citizens of Cape Girardeau for your friendly welcome."

Lindy thought of the dozens of families whose homes had been commandeered by the Federals. Friendly, indeed! But, she had to admit, at least half Cape's population welcomed the Union occupation.

"We come," Colonel Marsh continued, "with a sword, not to slay, but to defend you. We are rejoiced to find you all sound on the Union and hope you will remain so until Gabriel blows his trumpet and summons you to Abraham's bosom.'"

Lindy and Maude shared a knowing look, both realizing Lindy's allegiance to the Union came second to her love for John. How could it be otherwise? Maude, on the other hand, was firmly committed in her support for the Federals. It was somewhat awkward living under the same roof, but aside from Maude's claim that she would never speak to John again, which Lindy didn't believe for a minute, they hadn't allowed politics to come between them.

"As you are all aware," Marsh said, "Cape Girardeau occupies an important position on the river, the most strategic location between Cairo and St. Louis. Holding Cape Girardeau—protecting you citizens—is important to the Federal government. We won't let Cape Girardeau fall to the Confederacy." The crowd murmured approval. "As you know," said the colonel, his voice rising, "we are building four strong forts. The guns of Cape Girardeau will not be silenced by rebels." Most of the crowd applauded. "I must warn the citizens of this lovely town, though, *especially* those with friends or relatives fighting for the South, that some of the guns at Fort A are aimed at downtown Cape Girardeau. If we are attacked by the Confederacy, and if the people of Cape Girardeau encourage the attack or otherwise help the rebels, we'll level the downtown area. If you have friends in the Confederacy, warn them to leave Cape Girardeau alone, for their sakes and yours."

The Union colonel ignored the stunned silence of the crowd and launched into a partisan speech designed to convert even the most avowed secessionist to the Federal cause.

Lindy found herself dreaming of John, remembering every line of his handsome face, the fine texture of his sun-bleached hair, the dancing blueness of his eyes, and the feel of his body pressed to hers.

She was brought back to the harsh present when a piece of paper was thrust into her hands. "We're handing out the Oath of Allegiance," Colonel Marsh was saying. "Each citizen of Cape Girardeau must take it. Divide yourselves into groups of fifty and come forward. Anyone refusing to take the oath will be considered disloyal and will be arrested on the spot as a traitor."

So this was why they'd been forced to come to the fairground! Lindy was shocked not only by the mandated oath, but also by the cheers that met the speech. Perhaps she had underestimated the fervor of the pro-Union segment of Cape Girardeau. Weren't they concerned by the colonel's threat to bombard the town if attacked? The man was prepared to destroy the very city he was protecting! She hastily read the lengthy document in her hands. As she read it, nausea built in the pit of her stomach.

OATH OF ALLEGIANCE
I, of the County of Cape Girardeau, State of Missouri, do solemnly swear that I will bear true faith and allegiance to the United States of America

and support and sustain the Constitution and laws thereof; that I will maintain the National Sovereignty paramount to all State, County, or Confederate powers; that I will discourage, discountenance, and forever oppose secession, rebellion, and disintegration of the Federal Union; that I disclaim and denounce all faith and fellowship with the so-called Confederate States and Confederate armies; that I will never knowingly give aid, comfort, or information to the enemies of the United States, whether domestic or foreign; that I will, to the best of my ability, protect the property and persons of all loyal citizens within my reach, by giving them timely notice of all approaching danger (known to me) either to themselves or property; that I will, if necessary, assist to defend them from any such attack to the utmost of my power; that I will, at all times, hold myself SACREDLY BOUND to give immediate information to the Commander of the nearest Military Post or detachment, of the approach and subsequent movements of any squads or organized bands of rebels within his jurisdiction or vicinity, that may come to my knowledge; that unless specially ordered by the competent United States authority, I will not go beyond the military limits of the United States forces; that I will neither keep nor carry arms, except by permission of the Commander of the Military Post in whose district I reside, to whom I will deliver all arms now in my possession; that I will, in no case, speak or write in favor of the Confederate Government, or its armies, or disrespectfully of the Government of the United States and the armies which defend it, and further; that I will well and faithfully perform all duties that may be required of me by the laws of the United States.

I take the oath freely and voluntarily, without any mental reservation or evasion whatsoever, honestly intending at all times to keep the same, in letter as well as spirit, with a full and clear understanding that DEATH or other PUNISHMENT by the judgment of a military commission, will be the penalty for the violation of this my solemn oath and obligation.

This I do solemnly swear, so help me God.

NAME_____

Lindy touched Maude's arm lightly, whispering in her ear, "I can't take this oath! They consider John an enemy. It says I'm promising never to give aid, comfort, or information to him. I *can*not keep this oath!"

"Rosalind, you must take it. They won't let you stay in Cape, otherwise. They'll put you in prison. Better to stay where John can find you when the war's over."

Lindy studied the oath again. Punishable by DEATH! Death for aiding and comforting John? For providing him information? Her husband!

Hours went by as group after group swore allegiance. Several refused. Each was immediately carried away to the dungeon under the Courthouse. Lindy and her group advanced to the platform. To make matters worse, Horace Claxton traded places with another bluecoat to be the one who read the oath to her. With great gusto, he read it line by line, leering at her as she repeated the detestable words. She glanced at Maude O'Malley nearby, but her aunt was concentrating on the young soldier who read the words to her.

Claxton was sweating heavily in the July heat. The odor of his perspiration was sickening—heavy and thick and permanent. The piece of paper looked tiny in his massive hands. She shuddered as he stared at her, lust in his blue eyes. Claxton was dangerous, she realized. Not just in general terms but to her personally.

"Sign it," he ordered.

She felt his eyes peering down her dress as she bent forward to sign.

"Now you are mine," he whispered.

She stepped back. "I ought to report you!"

"What for? All I did was ask how your husband's doing." Claxton elbowed the soldier next to him. "Ain't that all I did, Blight?"

The homely, big-nosed private nodded, his beady eyes resting on Lindy's bosom. "Whatever you say, Corporal Claxton."

In spite of the heat, Lindy pulled her shawl over her shoulders. "Wherever he is, I'm sure my husband's doing quite well, Mr. Claxton. Thank you for your concern." She hurried away from him, feeling soiled and violated.

Nearby, Samantha Peabody, wearing a low-cut red dress, entertained several admiring Federal soldiers. Her raven-black hair was pulled into a bun. The summer sun emphasized her high cheekbones and Indian blood. The prostitute waved and hurried over to Lindy. "Hello, stranger. How are you?"

"Been better. How about you?"

"Business is booming! All these soldiers, they keep my girls busy! You'd think these bluebellies never saw a woman before!" Tears gathered unsummoned in Lindy's eyes. Samantha Peabody winced. "I forgot! Your husband's off at war, too! I'm so sorry, Rosalind. The last thing you want to think about is the randiness of soldiers. Please accept my apologies."

"It's all right. You didn't offend me. I've got other problems, that's all."

Samantha Peabody fluffed her skirt, then spoke in a soft voice, inaudible to anyone else. "I saw you taking the oath. How in the world will you keep it with your husband fighting for the South? Way I read it, you can't even communicate with him. Your own husband!"

Lindy felt hot tears streaming down her cheeks. "I don't know what will happen to me. I love John. I wish I were with him now. I hate this war and everything about it!"

"Now, now. Don't cry. You and your husband will reunite soon. Surely you'll hear from each other. Maybe I can help."

Lindy covered her eyes with a handkerchief as she cried, dimly aware of Maude O'Malley exchanging cool but polite words with Samantha Peabody and leading her home by the elbow, the rousing music of the Twentieth Illinois Military band playing in the background. Mostly she felt profound emptiness, thinking of John, of the possibility of not seeing or hearing from him for weeks or months or years, if ever.

When she regained her composure the thought struck her. What had Samantha Peabody meant when she said she might be able to help? What could a brothel owner do to help Lindy keep in touch with John?

In the last week of July 1861, six weeks after the Missouri State Militia had been trounced in the embarrassing battle of Booneville, Lieutenant John Carmichael stood next to Major General Sterling Price on the dusty fields of Cowskin Prairie, a vast grassland in the extreme southwestern corner of Missouri, just a few miles from the Arkansas border. They were watching recruits perform drills. John's face was shaded by his wide-brimmed clay-colored felt hat. His calloused right hand rested on the butt of the Navy Colt revolver worn in the holster on his hip.

"The Butternut Boys are starting to look like real soldiers," Price said. The nickname was a natural for the State Guards. For most, the only uniform consisted of everyday homespun material, dyed light brown by butternut juice. They all wore hats like John's. Some officers, John included, wore gray wool uniforms. Others wore their rank in the form of colored patches on their shoulders.

John shot an affectionate look at the portly fifty-two year old General. Price was probably the most popular man in Missouri. A former Missouri Governor and former Brigadier General in the Mexican War, he had been named Commander of the State Militia by Missouri Governor Claiborne Jackson.

"The way you've been drilling them morning, noon, and night, sir, they'd have to be fools not to have learned something by now."

"They're not fools. They're brave men. Patriotic men."

The General squinted. "Impossible to overemphasize the importance of drilling a fighting unit. In the midst of battle, a man needs to be able to react unthinkingly to a command. Needs to follow familiar orders as naturally as he breathes. Our men are getting there."

John recalled how the numbers of recruits had swelled dramatically after the State Guard had retreated from Booneville to Cowskin Prairie, accompanied by Governor Jackson. The ranks had increased daily, men arriving by pairs, by dozens, by companies, including rich planters, well-to-do merchants, smalltown farmers, and log cabin cornhuskers, all spoiling for a fight with the Federals, and Price had promised one.

"We got 7,000 men now," Price said. "Not quite the 50,000 the governor called for, but it's a start."

"Sure, General, but of our 7,000, two thousand are unarmed."

Price's face grew stern. "The State Guard is as ready for combat as it ever will be. Cowskin Prairie has served its purpose. Even the unarmed men are ready. They'll follow the armed men into battle, ready to pick up and use weapons dropped by the dead and wounded of both sides." He smiled grimly. "It takes a special breed of courage to go into a battle unarmed, carrying only the optimism that you'll have a gun in your hand before finding yourself face to face with an enemy bayonet."

John nodded silently.

Drilling. Drilling. Drilling. Cowskin Prairie had been a grueling training experience. The weather had been terrible. When the sun was in the sky, the heat was unbearable and the dust ankle deep. When it rained, mud sucked at marching feet. But the men had learned the rudiments of soldiery. They knew how to take orders and use their equipment.

"Now," said Price, "if we can just talk McCulloch and Pearce into joining us, we'll be ready to attack Lyon at Springfield before he gets reinforcements. Now's the perfect time to hit him."

Brigadier General Nathaniel Lyon was in charge of the Union garrison in St. Louis. After seizing the State Militia's 700 men and weapons at Camp Jackson near St. Louis on May 10, 1861, just three weeks after Fort Sumpter fell, he'd beaten the Militia decisively at the Battle of Booneville on June 17, 1861. The red-haired Lyon was a West Point graduate, eleventh in his class, and a veteran of the Mexican War and several Indian campaigns. He was a formidable opponent.

Ben McCulloch was a Confederate Brigadier General from Texas who'd recently come to Cowskin Prairie to meet with Price. The Texan's nose visibly wrinkled at the sight and smell of the Missouri troops. While McCulloch's 2,700 regular cavalry men were professional soldiers, fully-equipped and immaculate in appearance, the Missourians were unwashed, unshaven, and ill-equipped. Many of the State Guard members were already noticeably thin, appetites decreased by a steady diet of cornmeal mush.

"Our fellows didn't make a good impression on General McCulloch, Pap," John said, using Price's nickname.

"McCulloch may not have liked their looks, Lieutenant, but wait until he sees them fight. They'll be hellcats, these Butternut Boys. Make us proud to be Missourians."

Price removed his hat from his ivory hair. "Draft an order for me to sign, John. We're striking camp tomorrow, heading for Cassville. When we get there, I'm going to persuade McCulloch to join us in an attack on Lyon. If he supports us, we'll have almost 12,000 men. Lyon only has 5,000. This is our chance for a decisive victory that could sweep Missouri into the Confederacy."

Excitement tingled throughout John's body. Missouri was in the bizarre position of having two governors. Claiborne Jackson, the governor when the war broke out, claimed Missouri had seceded and was fighting with the South. He'd responded to Lincoln's call for Union troops by answering: "Not one man will the State of Missouri furnish to carry on such an unholy crusade." On the other hand, a Constitutional Convention in St. Louis on July 30, 1861 had declared all state offices vacant and elected Hamilton Gamble, former Missouri Supreme Court Judge, as Governor. Gamble favored the North and declared Missouri officially neutral. If Price could win Missouri for the Confederacy, the war might end quickly, and John might see Lindy soon.

That same evening, in his tent, John drafted the next day's orders for General Price. Then, his mind alive with excitement, he wrote a long letter to Lindy. The words flowed from his heart to the paper. Writing had never been so easy, the sentences never so simple and pure. She'd love this letter, he realized as he wrote, a smile playing at the corners of his mouth. She'd always been thrilled when he got romantic. He was definitely romantic in this one.

Someone pulled the tent flap back. A man in shabby clothing stood just outside the entrance, three Army Colts jammed behind the belt of his pants.

"May I come in, Lieutenant Carmichael?"

John nodded, his hand near his gun.

"Don't recognize me do you?"

"Should I?"

"Maybe this will jog your memory."

The man held out an envelope. John recognized Lindy's handwriting. "I'm Stan Phelps, Confederate Mail Runner."

John accepted the letter with thanks. He remembered meeting the mail runner five weeks earlier. He ached to read Lindy's letter, but preferred to wait until he was alone. "You look different," John said.

Stan Phelps was twenty years old, with short black hair, green eyes, and a handsome boyish face. He had peculiar reddish fuzz on his chin and a protuberant Adam's apple that jerked up and down as if he had a jittery mouse under his skin. "Last time you saw me I had red hair. Had it blackened so I won't be recognized. Starting to get quite a name as a mail runner. Red Rover they call me."

John offered a seat. Phelps took it. "Tell me about your mail running, Red Rover."

"Be honored if you'd call me Stan." Phelps nodded to the unfinished letter lying on the order box. "I've carried enough of your letters I figure we're almost friends."

"You don't read them, do you?"

"No, sir! But I think about how happy I'm making people and I feel real good inside. Couple of yours have set the record for thickness. You're a wordy guy."

John chuckled. "Guess I *am* a little long-winded at times. Tell me, how does mail running work? I've often wondered whether my letters are getting through to Lindy."

"She's getting them. Thanks to Red Rover." He leaned back proudly, hands clasped behind his head. "We all got to serve our country our own ways. I chose mail running. I'm a natural. Know Eastern Missouri like the palm of my hand. Can swim and run and ride fast as any man you'll meet. Don't need much sleep and can be quiet as an Indian." Phelps smiled, teeth white and perfect. "There's a bunch of us mail runners. Officially, we're members of the State Guard. When we're caught, though, they usually call us spies since we're out of uniform behind enemy lines. Particularly like to hang us, though firing squads are popular, too." Phelps winked, his green eyes glistening. "Won't catch me, though. Never in one place long enough to get caught. Too careful."

"How do you get the mail delivered once you get to a place? Cape Girardeau, for instance?"

"Got a contact or two in each town. Sneak in at night. Drop off the mail. Light out. I leave it to the contact to deliver the letters."

"Who're your contacts in Cape? Maybe I know them."

Phelps put a finger to his lips. "I'd like to tell you, but like I said, I'm careful. Got to protect them. What if you accidently let it slip? Better you didn't know."

"I understand."

"Tell you something, though. Last time I was in Cape my contact pointed out your wife to me—beautiful woman. Probably the prettiest I ever seen. You're a lucky man."

John reached for the letter on the order box. "If you'll wait a second, I'll finish this one and you can take it with you."

He completed the letter, sealed it, pulled another three finished ones from his knapsack, and handed them to Stan Phelps. "I feel better having met you, Stan. Least now I realize the letters I'm writing my wife are actually getting to her. Thanks." He took five gold coins from his pocket. "Will you accept these?"

Phelps took them. "Sure will, but not for personal use. I'll spend 'em only for military purposes, I promise. In my line of work I often need to bribe someone or buy a horse or a steamboat ride on short notice."

John grinned. "If it keeps you alive and keeps my letters getting to Lindy and hers getting to me, it'll be the best investment I ever made."

Chapter 17

By early August, 1861, 3,000 Union troops occupied Cape Girardeau, a large percentage of them spending a great deal of time on sick call. Hundreds suffered from measles, mumps, malaria, typhoid, pneumonia,and smallpox. Dozens returned mangled and bleeding from daily excursions against roving rebel bands in Scott, Madison, St. Francois, Stoddard, Bollinger, and Cape Girardeau counties. Three army hospitals were established in Cape: the general hospital in the Johnson house, on the river; a smallpox hospital in the Moore house, conveniently close to Lorimier Cemetery; and another smallpox hospital at the corner of Lorimier and Harmony.

Lindy and Maude worked full time as nurses at the general hospital in the Johnson house. The work gave Lindy's life purpose, filling empty hours that otherwise would have been spent pining for John. Her time was occupied bandaging, giving medicine, washing, cooking, reading, singing, writing letters, praying, and wiping sweat from brows of sick and dying men, most merely boys. She'd grown accustomed to the sights of twisted flesh, burning fevers, rampant pus, and oozing raw stumps, but she knew she'd never be able to come to grips with the vile odors of the hospital—the rotting smell of gangrene, the continual stench of human excrement and urine, and the noxious effluvium of sickness and disease.

She was giving a typhoid patient his daily dose of quinine one hot August afternoon when a yell went up announcing the arrival of more wounded from another skirmish with Jeff Thompson. She hurried to the operating room, a large area crammed with a dozen tables made from doors, tubs underneath to catch blood, with pails of water, rags and sponges handy to swish away scarlet slime. The room had large open windows to provide plenty of light for surgeons.

Doc Wilson was already there, wearing his familiar bloodspattered apron. "Glad you're here, Rosalind. We've got a couple serious ones. I'll need your help." Four uniformed Federals lay on the tables. Two were unconscious. The other two were groaning. Doc Wilson worked on one of the groaners, a sandy-haired freckled boy whose right arm was shattered just above the elbow. The blood-streaked white bone was protruding from the torn skin. "He's taken a mineball in the arm. Broken the bone. Compound fracture."

"Will you amputate?" she asked, looking at the boy's grimacing face, wondering if he were fifteen or eighteen.

"Always amputate if there's a compound fracture. You know that. Prepare the anesthetic."

Lindy took the U.S. Army pharmacy bottle labeled "16" and sprinkled the chloroform onto a handkerchief. A male nurse held the boy down as she pressed it to the freckled face, holding it firmly over his nose and mouth until he went limp.

Lindy, who at first had not been able to watch the operations, kept her eyes on Doc Wilson's steady hands as he used a large knife to slice to the bone and the soft tissue just above the damaged area. Working quickly, he sawed through the humerus with a hacksaw, then clamped the severed arteries and tied them off with oiled silk. The operation only took minutes.

"You're good," she told the elderly doctor.

He harrumphed. "I guess I ought to be getting the hang of it. Three out of four operations at this hospital are amputations." Doc Wilson handed the freckled arm to the male nurse for disposal. Knife in bloody hand, without washing himself or his instruments, he and Lindy moved to the next table where he began working on a leg wound.

"Bone's not hit, so we won't amputate unless infection sets in. Let's just tie off this vein."

As Doc Wilson worked, Lindy glanced over to the next table, where Doctor Meade was operating on one of the unconscious men. It was a head wound. He was trephining the injured skull. Meade stopped his work abruptly. "He's gone. Let's move to the next one." Doctor Meade hurried to the next table, to the groaning man with a gut wound. "Nurse, bring the chloroform, please."

Lindy hurried to him, slipping on the slick blood covering the hardwood floor. After administering the chloroform, she watched the doctor examine the gunshot wound to the abdomen. The ball had torn completely through the soldier.

Meade finally sighed and poked the protruding intestines back into the wound. "Wish I could do more," he said. "Ninety percent of abdomen wounds are fatal. Just can't stop the fever. Thank God most men are hit in the arms or legs."

Lindy supervised as the orderlies carried the three living men to beds at the front of the hospital. The dead man was taken out the back door. She watched the calm sleeping face of the boy with the amputated arm as he was carried to a hospital bed. "May I give that boy something for his pain when he wakes up, Doc Wilson?"

He nodded. "Get him two opium pills."

"Bottle '42'?"

"Rosalind, you're getting to know the army's identification system better than I do." The doctor pulled at his handlebar moustache. "First I thought it was ridiculous, having no markings on the bottles except identification numbers. Now I see it's a good idea. Keeps people from wanting to steal medicine, they don't know whether they're getting morphine or iodine."

She got the opium pills and sat next to the boy. After a few minutes, he began stirring.

"Water," he whispered hoarsely. She put a cup to his lips. He drank eagerly.

Leaning his head back onto the pillow, he looked at Lindy. As always, she felt tremendous tenderness for a wounded soldier. She knew, too, the horror he would experience when he realized his arm was gone. She'd been through it before.

"Where am I?" he asked.

"In Cape Girardeau, in a hospital."

"What happened to me?"

"I don't know. Don't you remember?"

The boy closed his eyes. "Yeah, I remember. We got bushwhacked. Jeff Thompson's men. The Swamp Fox. I never even seen them. Suddenly we was getting shot at. My whole arm was on fire." He twitched and opened his eyes. "My arm! It hurts so bad. Am I all right?"

She watched, fighting back tears, as he looked down. His lips quivered when he saw the stump. She clasped his remaining hand between her own.

"You'll be all right. You will."

Eyes glazed with tears, the boy sank back into the pillow. "Oh, God. How will I ever be a farmer now?" His eyes were wide and bulging. "My fingers hurt, ma'am. They hurt. But they ain't even there. How can that be? Where's my arm? What have you done with it?"

She thought of the bloodstained wagon behind the hospital, where amputated limbs were tossed.

"Here, take these pills," she told him. "You'll feel better, I promise."

Later that afternoon, Lindy stood at the front door of the hospital, gratefully inhaling gulps of fresh air, when Pete Carnahan approached her. The former engineer of the *Girardeau Rose* was wearing the dark blue uniform of the Cape Girardeau Guards, a lieutenant's epaulet on each shoulder. He was as wiry and tough as ever, but his eyes were friendly.

"Heard from John?" he asked.

She was wary. Pete Carnahan was an old friend, but he was, after all, a Federal. No need for him to know about the letters that kept appearing mysteriously in her foyer. "No. Wish I had. I don't know if he's even alive."

"Too bad. John's the most decent man I ever met. Fair. Honest. Turned out to be just as good a steamboat captain as your Papa. Really built up the company. I was disappointed when he sold it to Fitch, though I can see it was a good move. John was smart, always reading. Saw the war coming before the rest of us." He gestured toward the river. "Say, I'm on my way to the riverfront. They say General Fremont will be arriving with his fleet of steamboats any minute. Want to walk down with me?"

After securing Doc Wilson's permission, Lindy accompanied Pete Carnahan to the levee and watched as a fleet of eight steamboats rounded the bend by Cape Rock and steamed past Cape Girardeau.

The *Girardeau Rose*, by far the most splendid, led the procession. Tyler Fitch was in the pilothouse. Other steamboats included the *City of Alton*, the *Empress*, the *War Eagle*, the *Jenny Dean*, the *Louisiana*, the *Warsaw*, and the *G. W. Graham*.

"Fremont's on the hurricane deck," Carnahan said, pointing to a tall, bearded man wearing a dark General's coat. Two rows of brass buttons gleamed in the summer sun.

Lindy found herself staring at John C. Fremont, a legend in the flesh. The "Great Pathfinders" who had led countless expeditions to the West before the war, had just been appointed Major General in charge of the Western Department, which consisted of Illinois and the States and Territories west of the Mississippi and east of the Rocky Mountains, including New Mexico. He was a former candidate for President and the husband of Jesse Benton, beautiful daughter of Missouri's Senator Thomas Hart Benton. Lindy had heard that after only a month in his position, Fremont was already ruffling feathers in St. Louis. His first act as Major General had been to establish his St. Louis headquarters in the Chouteau Avenue Brant mansion, at a rent to the government of $6,000 per month. Three hundred personal bodyguards patrolled the streets, and high walls surrounded his palatial estate.

"Fremont is a hated man in many places," said Carnahan. "He really inflamed the local secesh when he issued his Martial Law Proclamation saying the Federal lines of occupation extend from Leavenworth, Kansas to Cape Girardeau, Missouri, and that rebels found with arms in their hands within those areas would be court-martialed and shot."

"I remember it well," said Lindy. "It also says anyone who corresponds with the enemy is giving aid to the insurgents."

Carnahan glanced at her knowingly, then reached into his pocket.

"Ever see the handbill Jeff Thompson printed and circulated after Fremont's proclamation?"

"No."

He unfolded a wrinkled piece of paper and read aloud: "'To Whom it May Concern: For every member of the Missouri State Guard or soldier of our allies who shall be put to death in pursuance of said order of General Fremont, I will hang, draw, and quarter a minion of said Abraham Lincoln.'"

"No wonder the soldiers around here hate Jeff Thompson so much," Lindy said. "Good thing for him he has the knack of disappearing into the Mingo Swamps, or he'd have been hanged by now."

Carnahan nodded and looked toward the river. "The General has 4,000 men on those steamers," he said. "He heard that Confederate General Pillow in Tennessee is thinking of invading Cairo, Bird's Point, and Cape Girardeau. He's come down here to prevent it. Doesn't want to lose control of the Mississippi River."

"It's a magnificent sight," said Lindy. "I wish John could see the *Girardeau Rose* now, as a General's flagship. Those red chimneys look more impressive than ever."

"It's a pretty parade," Carnahan said. "Only problem is that General Lyon, the best general the North has, is stranded down in Springfield and needs reinforcements. Fremont is letting him fend for himself while he takes this excursion down the Mississippi looking for Pillow. Just hope Lyon can handle the rebs without help." He winced with sudden embarrassment. "Sorry, Lindy. Forgot John is with the State Guard. He might be down there fighting Lyon, I guess."

She tried to look calm. From John's last letter she knew quite well he was with Sterling Price near Springfield. He expected to fight Lyon any day. "I just hope he's safe," she said softly.

A large crowd gathered on the levee, murmuring disappointment when it became clear that Fremont was not going to stop in Cape Girardeau on this trip. Horace Claxton was at the other end of the levee, standing with a pregnant woman.

Lindy nudged Pete Carnahan. "Pete, who's that woman with Horace Claxton?"

"His wife. Used to be one of Samantha Peabody's prostitutes. Claxton married her when the war broke out. Surprised the hell out of me. Can't see what any woman would want with him."

Horace Claxton stared at Lindy, grinning. He said something to his wife and left her side, swaggering toward Lindy and Carnahan.

"Please, Pete. Claxton's coming this way. Take me home? I can't stand the thought of talking to him. He's so awful."

"Listen," Carnahan said as they hurried up the cobblestone levee, "if Claxton gives you trouble, you call on me. I was a friend of your Papa's, and I'm a friend to you and your husband. I can handle Claxton if he bothers you."

"Thank you, Pete. I'll remember it."

That evening, just past dark, Lindy and Maude were in the dining room having dinner when a light knock sounded at the front door. "I'll get it," Lindy said.

She considered getting John's extra Navy Colt out of hiding, but decided not to, in case it was a Federal. Possession of a gun was a violation of martial law. Punishable by death. When she opened the door, she was surprised to find Samantha Peabody waiting for her.

"May I come in?"

Lindy glanced over her shoulder. Aunt Maude was standing in the doorway to the dining room, watching. "Certainly," said Lindy, opening the door wider. Aunt Maude shook her head and disappeared into the kitchen.

Samantha Peabody wore a black velvet basque over a dark-green hooped skirt , her petticoats bustling noisily with each movement. She craned her smooth neck as she removed her shawl and surveyed Lindy's foyer.

"Are we alone?"

"Yes."

"Then I have this for you." The prostitute handed her four envelopes bearing John's unmistakable scrawl.

"Oh! So you're the one! You're how these letters keep appearing out of nowhere!"

"That's right. The Confederate Mail Runner brings them to me—just one more man paying a visit to a brothel. I then distribute them around town."

"Thank you so much!" Lindy said, taking Samantha Peabody's hand. "You don't know how much they mean to me."

"I think I do." She smoothed her hooped skirt with her hands. "Rosalind Carmichael, I have a question for you."

Lindy felt a touch of dread.

"Will you help me deliver letters from local boys to their families? It's getting hard for me to be inconspicuous. People will wonder why the harlot keeps going to the nice folks' homes. I need someone who has an impeccable background herself. Like you."

Lindy shivered, remembering the oath she'd taken. What would the Federals do if they caught her? "Miss Peabody, I don't know!"

Samantha Peabody's eyes hardened. "In other words, it's nice enough to get your husband's letters when the local harlot risks her neck for the cause, but you aren't willing to help deliver letters to other women like yourself?"

Lindy felt herself blushing. "I feel ashamed, truly I do. Please let me think about it first. I don't know what to do. My aunt would disapprove. My husband, too."

Samantha Peabody snorted. "Your husband, who is risking his life for Missouri, would disapprove if you helped deliver letters from his friends to their families? I hardly think so, Mrs. Carmichael. Besides, I know for a fact that you've never let your aunt's disapproval control your life. I seem to remember a coach ride when we first met."

Lindy thought of the thrill she felt with each letter from John. She had the chance to give other families that same feeling. Yet, there were serious consequences if caught. "May I have a bit more time to think it over?"

The prostitute nodded. Her expression was understanding.

"I'm sure you'll decide to help us. It's a small price to pay for the letters you get from your husband. And when you do start working with us, call me Sam. All my friends do."

Even in the worst steamboat disasters, John had never seen death and destruction on the scale he witnessed at Wilson's Creek. Wilson's Creek, as a waterway, meandered about fifteen miles, beginning in a field five miles southwest of Springfield, Missouri, and ending with a merger with the James River. The terrain in the area consisted of tall wooded hills, sliced here and there by ravines. Thorny thickets and stunted oaks called blackjack contributed to dense foliage, thick and tangled. In 1861, Springfield was a bustling boom town of 2,000 people. Lyon and his force of 5,400 men had occupied it since his movement south from Booneville.

State Militia General Sterling Price was determined to attack General Nathaniel Lyon before the Federal officer got reinforcements from Fremont. Price and his 7,000 men joined forces with Confederate Generals Ben McCulloch (2,700 men) and Nicholas Pearce (2,300 men). McCulloch was reluctant to join Price, obviously distrusting the training and quality of the Missouri troops. There was also a disagreement whether State Militia Major General Sterling Price outranked Confederate Brigadier General Ben McCulloch. But Price talked him into it, agreeing to subordinate himself to McCulloch, even though Price had been a brigadier general in the Mexican War when McCulloch was just a captain. They had been advancing toward Springfield, planning to attack the Union forces. They outnumbered Lyon's men two to one.

On August 9, 1861, when the Confederates reached the area of Wilson's Creek, a light rain began falling and the darkening skies foretold heavier rain to come. Price and McCulloch realized the rain was potentially disastrous, because most militiamen did not have leather cartridge belts like the Federals, but carried their ammunition in pockets or cotton sacks. If the paper cartridges got wet, they'd be useless. The generals conferred and ordered the men to set up camp, cautioning them to remain prepared to march on short notice.

Much to everyone's shock, Lyon and his outnumbered men attacked the Confederate camp at dawn. It was a complete surprise. John was having breakfast in Price's tent with McCulloch, Price, and other staff officers when the first gunfire erupted. Soggy cornbread, tough beef, and weak coffee were forgotten as the shout arose that large numbers of Federals were attacking. Quickly, McCulloch dashed off to deal with the attack coming from the south of camp. Price was left to organize his men to meet the onslaught coming at them from the tall hill above camp.

Sterling Price, bare-headed and in shirtsleeves, buttoning his suspenders and carrying his coat, ran to his horse and swung his huge frame into the saddle.

"Come on, Lieutenant, let's rally the men!" They galloped toward the thick of the firing, meeting a crowd of frenzied Missourians running toward them.

"Squad, halt!" Price thundered. The Butternut Boys, falling over each other, stumbled to a stop in front of the general. "You got guns in your hands!" he yelled. "You came here for a fight! So fight! Show 'em what Missourians can do!"

Price pointed to a nearby knoll, covered with thick brush. Explosions from Federal cannon were coming from the top of the eminence. "You men take positions on Oak Hill. We gotta take it. I'll send you reinforcements quick. I'll be near you, and I'll take care of you. Don't yield an inch!"

John was amazed at the sudden change in the militiamen. Panic gone, they followed orders and charged up Oak Hill, yipping and yelling. John and Price galloped onward and found several hundred Missouri troops bolting in confusion. Price calmed them and sent them to support those he'd stationed on Oak Hill. Again and again, the process was repeated, wildly panicking men calmed by the composed commander. John was at the general's side as Price ordered most of his brigades to hasten to the front. Soon, he'd placed 3,000 men and four cannons in line.

The fighting centered mainly on Oak Hill. The ground was covered with trees and underbrush so thick the enemy couldn't be seen until just a few score yards apart. Thick clouds of powder smoke hovered amid the foliage, marking spots where fighting was the fiercest. Explosions, flying debris, and barking gunfire filled the air. Screams of pain and cries for help punctuated the sounds of destruction. Most men were on foot, since horses were almost useless in the thick underbrush. Again and again the Federals advanced, sometimes within fifty yards of the Missourians, but the heavy and hot fire of the longrifles, squirrel guns, shotguns, and pistols drove them back.

While the battle raged, John rode at Price's side as the general's horse picked its way around fallen bodies littering the ground. Price rode up and down the line, encouraging his men, sending fresh troops to bolster weak points, craning his neck during lulls in the firing to check for signs of enemy movement. John heard the hissing of minéballs as they scorched the air near his head. Several times his clothing was ripped and tugged by bullets. Men on horseback made attractive targets, he realized as he rode next to the portly general. But Price was determined to lead his men personally. It was John's duty to stay by his side. He marveled at the serene confidence Price exuded. The Missourians were noticeably inspired by his calm, dignified presence, though many were alarmed by his reckless self-exposure.

"Get back, General," privates yelled repeatedly, when Price moved to the front lines to check the enemy. "We don't want nothing to happen to you! We ain't gonna run! Ain't no need for you to be up here with us!"

Slowly, the tide of battle shifted. Price's men became the aggressors as the Federals were beaten further and further back. Steadily, the Missourians stormed up Oak Hill, throwing themselves repeatedly into the Federal lines. Standing, kneeling, prone on the ground, they fired, reloaded, and fired their guns. Time and again, they came within 40 yards of the Federals, only to be checked by the enfilading fire of Union regulars.

During these charges John first heard what became known as the "Rebel Yell." Not simply a shout, nor a cheer, nor a typical battle cry, it was one long sustained howl of hate and triumphant malice, cruel and cold as death itself. John was relieved the yells were coming from men on his side. John, riding with Price, held his reins in one hand and his revolver in the other. Price frequently sent him on short dashes to deliver orders to other officers. Each time he returned safely to the white-haired general.

The battle had been raging for two hours when John heard Price grunt in pain. Price grimaced and gripped his portly side.

"I've been nicked."

They both examined the bloody spot on the ample gray cloth of the general's jacket.

"Isn't fair," he said, winking at John. "The fellow who hit me would have missed completely were I as skinny as Lyon."

John encouraged him to fall back for treatment of the wound, but Price gruffly refused.

As morning progressed, overcast skies gave way to sunlight, but clouds of smoke kept visibility poor. Heat, humidity, and powder smoke made the air so thick you could almost chew it. Price's face, usually bright pink under his white hair, was now dark burgundy, sweat and powder streaking his cheeks. Still, he rode up and down the lines, exhorting his men, John with him every dangerous moment.

Soon McCulloch joined them, having beaten off the Federals to the south. The secessionist leaders now merged forces and the combined might of their armies concentrated on the main body of Lyon's men, who were still manning the treacherous cannon at the top of Oak Hill, spewing deadly canister and grape at the advancing rebels. The cannon was capable of firing a variety of other projectiles, including solid balls or exploding conical missiles with percussion fuses. As the Federal cannon raked his men, Price stared at the heaps of bodies surrounding them.

"Oak Hill's not the right word for this place. We'll call it Bloody Hill from now on."

By 10:00 in the morning, both sides still occupied ground they had taken four hours before. The lines were within shotgun range of each other. Intense firing continued for another half hour, followed by a lull lasting 30 minutes. During the lull, Price wiped his brow and pointed to his right. "Get to Dockery's Fifth Arkansas and tell them to advance. I caught a glimpse of Lyon earlier. Bet he's stationed just in front of Dockery. Get the Fifth Arkansas up that hill if you have to drag them yourself."

John rode his horse as far as possible, then dismounted and worked his way through blood-splattered brush and bodies to Colonel Dockery's Arkansas Infantry.

"General Price says to advance immediately," John told the colonel. "Says Lyon is just in front of you."

The weary officer turned to his men. "We'll be in a hot spot, boys, but keep cool."

Dockery's line moved forward. John, sensing the importance of the maneuver, accompanied them, Navy Colt in hand. The Federals in front of Dockery had pulled back, leaving the gray line unopposed as it made its way to a clearing. From the thick underbrush, fragrant with the heavy smell of honeysuckle, they suddenly spotted a mass of Federals reorganizing on the plateau at the top of Bloody Hill, only a few rods away. Bluecoated officers sat on horses amid the infantrymen. John immediately recognized the linen duster, straw hat and red beard of Brigadier General Nathaniel Lyon. He was barking orders to the men around him.

"That's Lyon!" John yelled.

The Federals turned toward them. Dockery's men wore gray uniforms, similar to those worn by Union Colonel Sigel's troops. "Sigel?" called out one of the Federal officers. "Who are you?" yelled another. "Friend or foe?" Lyon pointed his saber at them. The general seemed to be looking directly at John.

"Shoot them! Shoot them!" ordered Lyon, obviously the first to recognize them as enemy. Dockery's men fired instantly, before the Federals could raise their weapons. Lyon was knocked from his horse. The men around him also fell. The Federals scattered as volley after volley blasted from the thicket.

An orderly knelt next to the fallen general. "He's dead!" the orderly yelled. "General Lyon's dead!"

The Federal lines began retreating quickly. The rebels yelled victoriously and charged from the woods. John ran with them, pistol in hand. He stopped when he reached the body of Nathaniel Lyon. The blue eyes of the general stared sightlessly at the sky, his mouth open in a noiseless gasp. His torso and legs were soaked with blood. He had a bullet hole in his coat, just over his heart, and another in his thigh. John could also see crusty blood in the red hair on the side of his head, where he'd evidently been creased with a shot earlier in the day. Solemnly, John knelt and closed the general's eyes.

"Look out! Here they come again!"

He leaped up at the words from the man next to him. More Federals were pouring from the woods across the field, charging toward them at full speed, bayonets fixed.

"Hold your positions!" Colonel Dockery yelled. "Fire at will!"

The rebels fired and reloaded as fast as they could, but still the Federals stormed closer and closer.

Forty yards away, the Federals stopped abruptly, raised their weapons, aimed, and fired. The deadly round tore into the men around John with lethal accuracy. The man immediately next to him caught a ball in the throat and fell to the ground, gagging and choking.

Within seconds, the bluecoats were charging again, clearly within range of John's revolver. He held his fire as long as possible, surprised at the coolness he felt as the line of soldiers advanced toward him. He was certain he would die, but he was determined to die bravely, taking as many as possible with him.

They were close enough for John to see their faces, these charging enemy, young men, practically boys. He knew he would get six shots. He wouldn't have time to reload before they'd be on him with their bayonets. Still he held his fire, wanting to make his six shots count.

When the charging Federals were only fifteen yards away John fired three shots, each shot drilling a clean hole in a different face behind a bayonet. Three men fell hard.

Elsewhere, the lines clashed, troops locked in mortal hand-to-hand combat. Organization was gone. It was now a fight for survival. The Federals thrust at the Arkansans with deadly Union bayonets. The Confederates countered with close range pistol fire and wicked jabs from razor sharp double-edged Bowie knives.

John emptied his pistol into the chest of a Yankee who had pinned a rebel to the ground with a bayonet. He shoved his empty gun into its holster and yanked the bluecoat's bayonet from the impaled and dying rebel. He pointed its bloody tip at another charging Federal.

John realized the ringing Rebel yell was coming from his own lips as he and the Yank charged each other, bayonets brandished waist high.

Chapter 18

Lindy was in the hospital, sitting at the bedside of the sandy-haired freckled boy whose arm had been amputated two weeks earlier. She'd grown fond of him. His name was Elijah Pitts. He was sixteen years old, from Assumption, Illinois, a bugler for Colonel Marsh's regiment. As she had every day for the last week, she read to Elijah from the novel *David Copperfield*. Usually, she loved brightening his spirits by reading to him. Today, though, her mind was on Wilson's Creek, on the rumors circulating Cape Girardeau.

She'd heard that Wilson's Creek had been the fiercest and bloodiest battle of the Civil War to date, the biggest Confederate victory since Bull Run, but also the most costly. The Union suffered 1,300 casualties, one-fourth its force; the South, even more. Lyon had been killed, and she had seen fear and anger in the eyes of the local Federal soldiers. When a leader like Lyon falls, every man from general to private has a heart-to-heart talk with his own mortality. Worst of all, she'd heard nothing from John since the battle. It had been almost three weeks. She had no way of knowing if he was dead or wounded, healthy or maimed.

"What's the matter, Mrs. Carmichael?"

The page had become blurry. She heard the high voice of Elijah Pitts even though she couldn't make out his face through her tears. Lindy fought to regain control of her emotions. *Attention to morale is medically sound*, Doc Wilson always said. *Keep cheerful. It will save lives.*

"Nothing," she said, closing the book. "Don't pay any attention to me. I'm fine."

"You're crying," the boy said, accusingly, leaning toward her. "Please let me help. I'd be dead weren't for you."

She smiled, wiping her eyes with a handkerchief. "Don't be silly, Elijah. The doctor's the one who operated on you. All I've done is read to you and write letters for your folks."

"No, ma'am, I mean it. You saved my life. The things you told me about Abner Conrad, that one-armed man who was such a great riverboat pilot, and your father, who lost his fingers but didn't let it slow him down. You've helped me see I can still do something with my life."

Lindy felt the misery retreating into the depths of her mind, but she knew it would return later, sneaking up on her at a weak moment. She managed a smile. "Elijah, if I've helped you feel better, I'm as happy as I can be. You're a wonderful boy."

His freckled face was serious. "You're not happy, Mrs. Carmichael. Not today. Can't fool me. Tell me what's the matter."

She debated whether to confide in him. He was just a boy, a Yankee soldier to boot. But he truly wanted to try to help. For his sake, she spoke.

"My husband was at Wilson's Creek. I don't know if he's dead or alive."

They sat silently for a while.

"If he's lucky," said the boy, "he's only wounded, like me, and has a nurse as wonderful as you."

Lindy thought of John. She pictured him in a hospital, an arm sawed off, a leg sawed off, a hole in a gut or lung. She pictured him crying out for her, a voice she could not hear, 400 miles away. *Please, God, let me see him again*, she prayed silently. *Please let him be alive.*

"I know your husband's fine," Elijah Pitts was saying. "You're too good a person. God wouldn't let something bad happen to you."

She sighed. "God works in peculiar ways sometimes, Elijah. Men on both sides of this war pray to the same God. Everyone's prayers can't possibly be answered. I'm afraid I don't know how one goes about getting priority."

"Maybe by helping soldiers like me." The boy held up his bandaged stump. "My arm's healing real well. Infection's almost gone. People like me, you, and your husband—we'll whip those stinking Rebs and we'll come home alive to brag about it."

Lindy bit her lip. Again she had to decide how much to tell him. "My husband's in the Missouri Militia, Elijah. He's fighting for the South."

The boy's mouth gaped. "The South! You mean, I've been nursed back to life by the wife of a Reb!"

She nodded.

"How do you like them apples! *Mr.* Carmichael's off trying to kill Union soldiers while *Mrs.* Carmichael's trying to keep us alive. It don't figure!"

"Elijah, would you rather not have me tend to you? I can have one of the other nurses take care of you. Maybe you don't trust me anymore."

"Mrs. Carmichael, figure if you was wanting to kill me off, you'd have done it long ago. Besides, those other nurses are all about 90 years old. I'll keep you, I reckon."

The sound of a marching band caught their attention. "A parade!" someone yelled. "General Grant's in Cape, and they're having a parade for him."

Lindy felt another wave of sadness. She'd promised Aunt Maude she'd accompany her tonight to the ball in General Grant's honor. She definitely didn't feel like going to a ball. She certainly didn't feel like dancing.

When Lindy first saw Ulysses S. Grant at the ball given in his honor, she was surprised. He didn't look like a man just commissioned Brigadier General in command of Southeast Missouri and Southern Illinois. He wasn't even wearing a uniform. He wore civilian clothes, a drab dark suit. His grizzled beard needed a considerable amount of trimming. Grant had arrived in Cape Girardeau that afternoon. He'd set up temporary headquarters in the St. Charles Hotel, his steamboat docked nearby. As he stood in his wrinkled suit surrounded by soldiers and local citizens in the ballroom of the St. Charles Hotel, he looked uncomfortable. Yet he kept up a cordial conversation with the dozens of people near him.

Maude had been anxious to meet the general, and maneuvered herself and Lindy close to Grant. She had primed a Union captain to make the introductions, but before he could open his mouth, Grant's eyes met Lindy's.

"How do you do, Mrs. Carmichael? Nice to see you again."

Lindy was flabbergasted. She'd never seen the general in her life, she was sure.

He grinned. "Don't remember me?"

She wracked her memory. She wanted to remember. She felt her neck growing hot and was glad she was wearing a high-necked dress. Surely she would recall meeting a general! "I'm sorry, General. I don't."

"Ulysses Grant. Had a firewood business in St. Louis shortly before the war. Had the pleasure of meeting you several years ago, when your father was alive, and again four years ago, when your husband did me a great favor by buying my entire stock of wood for use on the *Girardeau Rose*." He bowed slightly. "Who could forget the lovely Rose for whom the *Girardeau Rose* was named? You're as pretty as ever."

Lindy was embarrassed. She sensed hundreds of eyes upon her, whether they were or not. She groped for something to say. "Thank you, General. I'm impressed by your memory."

He smiled. "I'm glad you're impressed by something about me. I know I don't look like much right now. Been in the same suit for days. They haven't sent me my general's uniform yet. Guess I'll get it pretty soon."

The military band launched into another song. General Grant nodded toward the dance floor. "May I have this dance, Mrs. Carmichael?"

Lindy didn't want to dance, especially with a Federal general. Yet, he seemed like a nice man; he wasn't the ogre she'd pictured. She had the urge, though, to turn him down curtly and walk off. Instead, she met his eyes with her own.

"Of course, General."

She smelled a trace of alcohol on his breath when they were on the dance floor, but he was definitely sober, a good dancer, and a complete gentleman. "How is your husband?"

She hesitated. The painful uncertainty of John's health again stabbed her like a dagger. It would do no good to lie, though.

"John's in the Missouri State Guard, General. He's with Sterling Price. I'm afraid he was at Wilson's Creek." She watched Grant's face for a reaction. His ruddy features were inscrutable.

"Lots of good men killed there," he said. "If your husband's fighting for the South, why are you still in a Union stronghold like Cape Girardeau?"

"This is our home. I have no place else to go."

He smiled faintly. "Julia and I have been married thirteen years. We were apart from 1852 to 1854 when I was stationed on the West Coast. It was agony to be separated so long. We swore never again to be apart more than a few weeks. I know the pain you must be feeling."

Lindy could see he was telling the truth. "Where's your wife now, General?"

"Home in Galena. I'll bring her to me soon as I establish headquarters in Cairo. In fact, I'll probably leave for Cairo tomorrow."

"Cape won't be your permanent headquarters, then?"

"No. Cairo, at the juncture of the great rivers, is the natural place. Closer to the action."

For an instant Lindy glimpsed frightening strength and determination in Grant's square face. In a moment, though, he was again animated and friendly.

"The borderland's a strange place in this war of rebellion," he said. "We've got the unusual situation of Union forces defending and playing nursemaid to scores of wives and womenfolk of Confederate soldiers off fighting us elsewhere. Peculiar."

"I wish it were over," she said simply.

"Will be. Eventually. Once the politicians in Washington realize you have to fight a war in order to win it."

He escorted her back to Maude when the music ended.

"I hope your husband makes it home to you, ma'am. He's a good man. I'll never forget the kindness he did me. I was down and out when he bought my wood."

Lindy and Maude moved to another side of the room as others monopolized Grant's attention. Now and then he returned to the dance floor. Over the course of the evening, he danced with several belles of Cape Girardeau.

Lindy was surprised when Tyler Fitch, dressed in white suit and bright red bow tie, approached her. "May I have this dance?"

She felt no hesitation this time. "No, thank you, Mr. Fitch."

His fingers played with the hair covering his mangled ear. "I understand your feelings, Rosalind. I did your family a great wrong that time long ago. I want to apologize to you. I'm sorry. Honestly."

She looked at him coolly. She would have spit on him if she could have thought of a ladylike way to do it.

"I can't help but remember, Mr. Fitch, that you would have put my father out of business had you won the race against the *Girardeau Rose*. Frankly, I'm surprised you have the nerve to ask me to dance. Particularly since you didn't have the nerve to join the service, *either* service."

He was still unperturbed. "I don't care who wins this war, so why should I risk my neck? I'm taking advantage of the situation. Making good money transporting troops and supplies for the government. If John were smart, he'd have done the same."

"John said the steamboat companies would be destroyed by the war. That's why he sold ours."

Fitch was looking at her shrewdly. "By the way, Rosalind. What did John do with all the money I paid him for the business? It's not in the local banks. I've checked."

She felt her heart rising in her chest, climbing toward her throat. "He took it South. It's none of your business what he did with it down there."

He shrugged. "You're absolutely right." He bowed gracefully. "I'm at your service, Mrs. Carmichael, if you ever need me for anything. As I said before, I'm truly sorry for any wrongs I've done you in the past. I'd like the chance to make up for them."

After Fitch left, Lindy tried to convince Maude that it was time to go home, but Maude wasn't ready. Reluctantly, Lindy stayed at the ball. She found herself thinking constantly of John. She felt guilty wearing a bright dress and attending a dance when he might be lying killed or wounded at Wilson's Creek. She'd heard that many of the wounded hadn't been removed from the battlefield for more than a week. How would she ever find out what happened to him if he were buried in an unmarked grave on a battlefield on the other side of the state?

She stood at the edge of the dance floor, impatiently waiting for Maude to finish talking to Doc Wilson on the other side of the room. Suddenly, hands gripped her waist from behind and pushed her onto the crowded dance floor, her feet barely touching it. When she was dropped to the floor, she whirled in outrage to face the person behind her. It was Horace Claxton. He was in full dress uniform: dark blue frock coat with a single row of buttons up the middle, sky-blue trousers with a half inch stripe of dark blue down the outer seam, sky-blue corporal's chevrons on his sleeves. He grinned at her lewdly, his eyes bright and nasty.

"Always wanted to dance with you, little Rosie," he said, pulling her to him. "Ever since you were a tiny girl."

"Let go of me! I swear I'll scream."

"Perhaps you're right," he said. "We shouldn't embrace on a dance floor in front of all these people. We'll save our dances for private places."

She raised an arm to slap him, but he easily caught her by the wrist. His eyes gleamed as he looked at her.

"Excuse me, Corporal, but I'd like to cut in." A young lieutenant tapped Claxton on the shoulder. "One of the privileges of rank, Corporal," he said, shrugging.

Claxton stood mute for a moment, as if unable to decide what to do. Finally he muttered something and whirled away.

"Thanks," Lindy said to the young officer. He was about twenty years old, clean-shaven, with dark hair and fair skin. His Adam's apple was very noticeable.

"What's your name?" he asked.

Lindy didn't feel like talking to him or anyone else. She hoped he didn't expect anything other than the one word of thanks for getting rid of Claxton. She just wanted to go home.

"That's all right," he said, "no need to tell me. You're Rosalind Carmichael, aren't you?"

She studied him closely. It seemed everyone had the advantage of her. "Do I know you, sir?"

"I'm a friend of your husband, actually. Just saw him four days ago, matter of fact. Thought you might like to know he survived Wilson's Creek. He was something of a hero. Helped lead the charge that killed General Lyon."

She stared at the man with shock. She could see from the sincerity in his boyish face that he was telling the truth. She felt weak, lightheaded. John was alive! Unsummoned tears of happiness filled her eyes.

The lieutenant's arms were holding her up.

"Name's Stan Phelps, Confederate Mail Runner. One of the best, if I say so myself."

She glanced about worriedly. The dance floor was crowded, Union soldiers all over the room. "What are you doing here? Where'd you get the Yankee uniform?"

He grinned slyly. "They call me Red Rover. I have my ways. I promised John I'd deliver his latest batch of letters to you. Decided I wanted to see you in person. Heard about this dance. Ran into a rather naive Federal lieutenant. Here I am."

"My God!" Lindy exclaimed. "This is so dangerous for you!"

"I like danger. Spices up life."

She again felt a flood of happiness swamping her senses. "You are *sure* John's alive?"

"Healthy as you or I."

She closed her eyes, happier than she'd been in a long time.

"Mrs. Carmichael," he whispered, "I have letters for you from John. Got some for lots of other women in Cape Girardeau from their loved ones. Samantha

Peabody asked you before, but never got an answer. Won't you help us deliver them?"

Lindy, floating as if on a cloud, knew there could be only one answer. "I'll do it."

As she and Stan Phelps finished the dance, her gaze landed on Horace Claxton, who was glaring at her from the other side of the room. She felt tendrils of dread encircle her heart when she saw his malignant expression.

By late October 1861, Lindy and Maude had become excellent nurses. They worked long hours at the army hospital. Both, especially Lindy, had become very popular with the wounded soldiers.

Lindy still found time to visit local families regularly. Without Maude's knowledge, she was delivering letters she received from Stan Phelps and Samantha Peabody to kinfolk of Confederate soldiers in Cape Girardeau. It was scary work, but she loved seeing the happiness in the eyes of those who received the letters.

The Federal soldiers in Cape Girardeau had become an accustomed sight. They were everywhere, tents scattered throughout the city. Some soldiers stationed at Forts A and D, both located upon the bluffs overlooking the river, dug caves into the sides of the bluffs, preparing for the approaching winter months. Evenings were often filled with the laughing and cheering of soldiers at Fort D, who took up the sport of bowling. They'd built a wooden planked bowling alley in the center of the terreplein of the rampart. They used 32-pound cannon shells for bowling balls and round chunks of wood as pins.

Lindy savored each of the many letters she received from John, but never showed them to Maude. She knew her aunt wouldn't report her for corresponding with him, but it was better not to place her in an uncomfortable position. She found a special place to hide the letters. Even Aunt Maude didn't know about it.

Lindy was at the hospital on October 23, 1861, when the wounded were brought in from the battle of Fredericktown, fought two days before. One of the wounded was Pete Carnahan. She was horrified when he staggered into the hospital, profanely refusing to be carried. His blue coat was saturated with blood, his face pale under the dark stubble of whiskers. She stayed at his bedside long after Doc Wilson treated the arm wound. She was greatly relieved when she realized it wasn't serious. His only danger would be from infection, or from the measles outbreak making the rounds among the soldiers.

"You're lucky," she said. "The bullet didn't hit the bone. You ought to heal up just fine. Sure bled a lot, though."

Carnahan regarded the bandaged arm with distaste. "It's embarrassing to come to the hospital for something like this. Hell, it's just a flesh wound. I been hurt worse in the boiler room." His expression turned thoughtful. "Rosalind, I've heard tell that the doctors have a big supply of whiskey for killing pain. Any truth to that?"

"We have whiskey."

"Why don't you give a stab at rounding some up? This wing's killing me. Guess I've earned a shot or two. Medicinal purposes, you know."

Moments later, a glass of whiskey was clasped in his hand. She wiped perspiration from his brow with a damp towel. "Was the fighting bad at Fredericktown?"

"We darn near caught the Swamp Fox. Jeff Thompson and his men ambushed us, but we outnumbered them. Bullets flew all over the place for about three hours. He got away, though. Like always. He's a slippery devil." He added a few profanities to his description of Jeff Thompson, then made a face. "Excuse my language, Rosalind."

"That's all right. I was raised on a riverboat, remember?"

They both smiled.

"What's Jeff Thompson's background?" Lindy asked. "Seems like the soldiers in Cape are always talking about him. I never heard of him before the war. Now his name comes up every day."

Carnahan raised his glass. "To M. Jeff Thompson. May he catch one in the gut."

Lindy frowned. He apologized again.

"I'll tell you everything I know about Jeff Thompson, and I'll try not to cuss. He's about thirty-five, tall, and skinny. Once won a jackknife for being the ugliest man at the Buchanan County fair. Wears a white hat with a plume and carries a white-handled Bowie knife stuck in his belt. He rides a spotted stallion called Sardauapalus and has an Indian orderly named Ajax. He was mayor of St. Joseph, Missouri before the war. For some reason he ended up in the Bloomfield area when the State Guard was being divided into military districts, and when old Nathaniel Watkins of Cape Girardeau resigned as Brigadier General of the State Guard from this area, Thompson took his place." Carnahan sipped his drink. "Thompson is colorful, crafty, and knows every inch of the swamps in Southeast Missouri. He and his men will attack a patrol of Federals like a swarm of flies on manure, then vanish into the woods before you can say Jack Diddley. We never know how many men he's got because he purposely circulates lies and exaggerations. He causes just enough trouble that the government is forced to keep thousands of soldiers stationed here in Cape to ride out every now and then looking for him. I'd like to be the fellow who catches him!"

Carnahan drained his glass. "No doubt in my mind," he continued, "that Thompson would love to capture Cape Girardeau and would have done so by now if we hadn't built the forts."

As Lindy listened to Carnahan, Maude O'Malley hurried toward them. Maude glanced with silent disapproval at the glass in Carnahan's hand, but then placed her fingertips softly on Lindy's shoulder.

"Rosalind, it's Elijah Pitts. His fever's gone up. He's calling for you."

Lindy hurried to the next room, where Elijah lay in a bed by a window. He'd been recovering nicely from his amputation, but then came down with measles. She was shocked when she saw him. He looked so much worse than the day before. His face was horribly pocked and sweaty, his breathing hard and loud.

"Elijah," she said. "Oh, Elijah!"

He opened his eyes. They were glassy. "Mrs. Carmichael. I'm feeling real poorly."

She knelt next to him and bathed his face with a towel. "Lots of soldiers are getting measles," she said. "You can pull through." She did her best to sound optimistic. Actually, she knew measles had killed a large number of soldiers in the hospital. Their defenses already weakened by wounds, they often did not survive.

"Know what's funny?" Elijah asked her.

"No. What?"

"I'm sixteen years old. Been through two battles. Been shot at by cannon and gun. Had an arm amputated. And I'm gonna die of measles. Measles!" He was crying. "My sister had measles when she was three. Didn't kill her. Here I am a soldier. And I'm dying. I know it. Measles!"

Lindy was crying, too.

"If I was gonna die," he said, "why couldn't it be on a battlefield? Why couldn't it be in glory? If I die of measles I've got nothing to show for my life. Here lies Elijah Pitts, soldier. Died of measles!"

She gripped his hand and held it as spasms shook his thin body.

"Mrs. Carmichael?" he whispered, staring at her with unseeing eyes. "Write another letter for me, please?"

"Of course I will, Elijah."

"Write my momma. Tell her I love her. Tell her I died in battle, that I was shot off a horse as I was sounding my trumpet. Tell her the Colonel himself took me in his arms and told me how brave I was."

"You are brave. You're the bravest soldier I know."

His body convulsed. He was dead when the shaking stopped.

She sat by his bed a long time, crying until there were no more tears left, and held his hand until it became cold. She thought of Elijah Pitts' mother. Somewhere in Assumption, Illinois, the woman was tending to her daily affairs, unaware that her son had just died, an endearment for her on his lips.

"Well, well, look at them crocodile tears."

Lindy looked up. Horace Claxton stood at the foot of Elijah Pitts' bed, staring at her. His hand was bandaged.

"Makes a nice scene, Rosalind Carmichael, you crying for a poor Yankee boy." Claxton spit on the floor at her feet. "Your little act don't fool me none, Rosie girl. You're a Rebel lover. Married to one. They shouldn't let you work in this hospital. Hell, you probably killed this boy yourself, you little secesh wench!"

Doc Wilson grabbed Claxton by the arm. "Get out of here, Corporal! Your wound's been tended to."

Claxton yanked his arm free. "I want to know why you've got this Rebel-loving traitor in your hospital, killing good Union men!" He shoved the doctor, who stumbled and sat heavily on the edge of Elijah Pitts' bed. The corpse bounced and rolled toward him.

"Get out of here now, or I'll have you prosecuted for assault!" Doc Wilson yelled, leaping to his feet, his face vivid pink behind the white handlebar moustache.

Claxton leaned close to Lindy, speaking in a harsh whisper. "I'll be back to see you, little Rosie. I'll come to your home when you least expect me. I figure with your husband gone over four months now, you're needing a man. I'll be around, you can count on it."

Chapter 19

The first week of April 1862 was a tense time in Cape Girardeau. Confederate General Pillow had advanced to New Madrid, planning to move north to capture Cape Girardeau and St. Louis. General Halleck, who'd replaced Fremont as head of the Western Department, responded by hurling thousands of Federals south to meet the advance. The forces clashed at Island Number 10 near New Madrid. The Rebels had been driven back. Lindy heard that Grant had taken the offensive in Tennessee and that a terrible battle was being fought near Pittsburg Landing at a place called Shiloh Chapel. All things considered, she was relieved that John was in Northern Arkansas with Sterling Price.

She was in the parlor, a whale-oil lamp burning, rereading the dozens of letters received from John over the ten months he'd been away, when a soft knock sounded at her door. She hid the letters and hurried to the foyer.

"Who is it?"

"Red Rover."

Lindy smiled and unlocked the door. Stan Phelps slipped in noiselessly.

"Is your aunt home?"

"She's asleep."

He handed her a heavy canvas sack. "Here's the latest batch."

"It's been so long," she said. "What did you do? Take a vacation?"

He took off his hat and ran a hand through his hair. He wore a beard that hid the Adam's apple she recalled so vividly. He looked better with the beard.

"I got caught in St. Louis. Was in jail for a while, but escaped."

"I heard there was a reward out for you, Stan. I didn't know they'd caught you."

"The jail hasn't been built could hold Red Rover."

She dumped the letters onto a table and separated John's from the others.

"You don't know how happy this makes me, Stan. Getting John's letters is the most important thing in my life right now."

"You should see his face when he gets yours." His expression turned serious. "I wish you'd let me tell him about the service you're performing for the Confederacy. He'd be proud of you."

"He'd worry about me."

"Maybe, but if I had a wife risking her life to deliver mail for good soldiers, I'd want to know."

"I'd rather he didn't know. I want him concentrating on staying alive, not worrying about me. Please promise you won't tell him what I'm doing."

He shrugged. "All right, I won't tell. You can count on me to keep a secret. When I was in the Yankee prison they tried to get me to tell them a thing or two, but I have a high tolerance for pain." Phelps was a gangly young man, much like a red colt. But his tremendous inner strength and courage were obvious.

"Was it hard in the Yankee jail?"

"Wasn't a picnic, but could've been worse."

She handed him dozens of letters she'd collected from relatives of local Confederate soldiers, plus several of her own to John. Stan Phelps bowed slightly as he accepted the mail. "Lindy, thanks again for helping us. There's no way Samantha Peabody and I could keep the mail moving without you."

Moments later, he snuck out the back door, crossing the yard silently, bathed in moonlight. When he disappeared into the night, she closed the door, locked it, and hurried to the parlor where she eagerly opened John's latest letter. She read it by dim lamplight, holding her wedding ring to her lips. She was thrilled by his words of love and amused by anecdotes of camp life. She was horrified, though, to read that he had joined Brigadier General John Sappington Marmaduke in Tennessee as his adjutant in mid-March. Shiloh was being fought there now. Bloody Shiloh!

Horace Claxton and Rufus Blight lurked in the shadows in the alley behind Lindy's home. They had seen the man come to the front door of her house, carrying a sack. They had seen him leave by the back door ten minutes later. Claxton smiled grimly. He liked the way things were shaping up.

"Should we go tell the Colonel?" Blight asked, his voice sounding hopeful.

"No," Claxton said, watching the window where a light burned behind a white curtain. "I think it's still a little too early to go to the Colonel about Mrs. Carmichael. I'm sure she's violating Order 13, but we need more proof." Claxton found it impossible to keep from smiling. Rosalind O'Malley Carmichael was corresponding with her husband. Better yet, she might even be helping the Confederate mail runner distribute the mail. Things were certainly working out well.

Claxton had managed to become a deputy provost marshal, and he loved the work. He enjoyed catching people violating martial law, and the position could be quite lucrative at times, if one wasn't adverse to employing a little extortion.

Union military leaders in Missouri had convinced President Lincoln to suspend the writ of habeas corpus in Missouri and to authorize them to exercise martial law in the Western Department. They established and utilized a system of local provost marshals to act as policemen, empowered to apprehend and arrest those guilty of violating martial law. The provost marshal general stationed in St. Louis was the primary police officer of the state. He stationed district provost marshals with numerous deputies throughout Missouri. In Cape Girardeau, as elsewhere, the local provost marshals had unlimited powers of arrest and imprisonment.

As deputy provost marshal, Claxton carried Order 13 in his pocket. It read:

> VI. All persons found in disguise as pretended loyal citizens, or under other false pretenses, within our lines, giving information to, or communicating with the enemy, will be arrested, tried, condemned and shot as spies. It should be remembered that in this respect the laws of war make no distinction of sex; all are liable to the same penalty.

"Shouldn't we be following the man who just left her house?" Blight asked.

"I was planning to keep following him," Claxton said, "but that was before I saw that Miss Lindy was involved. She's the one I'm after now. Wait until you see what I got in store for her, Blight. She'll wish she'd been nicer to Horace Claxton."

"I still think we should report her tonight," Blight said.

Claxton glared at him. "Private Blight, when we have enough evidence against her, we'll do much worse than report her to the Colonel, believe me. Much worse."

Blight cocked his head. "What could be worse than a firing squad?"

The next morning, Lindy set about delivering the letters to local families of secessionists. She sewed several pockets into her petticoats, slipping each letter into a pocket. It was Sunday, her day off, so it was easy to take a stroll around town, enjoying afternoon visits with several families. As always, Union soldiers permeated the streets. Each time one looked at her, goose bumps rose on her arm.

The deliveries went smoothly, though. Half of the letters were in the hands of family members within an hour. It was then she began to suspect she was being followed.

At first, she noticed nothing unusual, but as the day wore on she sensed someone watching her. She began looking over her shoulder frequently. Soon she noticed that Horace Claxton and Rufus Blight seemed to be a block behind her everywhere she went. They never looked directly at her, but were always there, ominous dark blue shadows.

Lindy didn't realize it, but John hadn't made it to Tennessee soon enough to participate in the battle of Shiloh. He arrived only in time to witness the aftermath of the bloody fight. He came to Tennessee to join the staff of Brigadier General John Sappington Marmaduke, a twenty-nine year old West Point graduate, son of former Missouri Governor M. M. Marmaduke. General Marmaduke had joined the Missouri State Guard at the outset of the war and befriended John, but after the State Guard was beaten by Lyon at Booneville, Marmaduke resigned and traveled to Richmond, Virginia, where he was appointed Colonel and assigned to Bowling Green, Kentucky. When he made Brigadier General, he sent for John, getting approval for John's commission as a captain in the C.S.A.

Finding Marmaduke, however, proved difficult. The Confederates had retreated from Shiloh, most ending up at Corinth. Several soldiers told John they'd seen Marmaduke during the battle, fighting valiantly, personally leading several charges, having at least three horses shot out from under him, but each had no idea where he was now. Finally, a lieutenant on General Hardee's staff confirmed that Marmaduke was in a hospital in Corinth. John found Marmaduke in the hospital, lying on a bed, chest bare, arm bandaged in a sling. He was deep in thought.

"General Marmaduke?" John said softly.

"Carmichael!" Marmaduke bounded out of bed and shook hands enthusiastically.

"Your wound?" John said, touching the bandages.

"Nothing. Just a flesh wound and a bunch of bruises."

As they talked of things that had happened to them since they were last together, John realized he'd forgotten just how much he liked and admired John Sappington Marmaduke. Sterling Price was a gallant man and an adequate general, but he was not a handsome and dashing young cavalry officer with a brilliant military mind. John Marmaduke was that rare sort of leader and friend whose life you valued more than your own. John felt guilty for not having been at Marmaduke's side at Shiloh.

"Sorry I missed the battle. Got here as quickly as I could."

"I know you did. As it turned out, you missed a grand opportunity to be killed. Shiloh was a slaughterhouse. Never seen so much blood. I walked on a field strewn with so many bodies you could literally walk from one side of the field to the other, stepping from body to body, with your feet never touching the ground." Marmaduke shook his head sadly. "We missed a chance for a great

victory. Instead, we've been handed an embarrassing loss. I'm told we're scheduled to pull out of Corinth soon. That Grant! You can count on most Union
Generals to be cautious, to fall back and wait for reinforcements every chance
they get. Not him. He'll throw everything he's got at you and keep coming until
the fields are red with blood. They say U.S. Grant's initials stand for Uncondi-
tional Surrender. Those were his terms at Fort Donelson."

Marmaduke paused, then brightened. "Got some good news for you,
Carmichael. Plans are in the works to transfer me to Arkansas, where I'll be
one of several Confederate generals organizing an invasion of Missouri. We
may even be in the vicinity of your old hometown."

"I hope so," said John. "The closer we get to Cape Girardeau, the better my
chances are of seeing my wife again."

John saw another familiar face in Corinth later that day when Stan Phelps
rode into town carrying saddlebags full of mail. Soldiers ran to the russet-bearded
youth like children sprinting to Santa Claus. A shout circulated the camp, and
soon the laughing and joking mail runner was surrounded by hundreds of ragged
soldiers. John joined other excited men crowding around the smiling Phelps.
As he handed John a packet of letters from Lindy, Phelps whispered that he
wanted to talk to him later.

John waited nearby until the mail had been distributed, then accompanied
Phelps to the military corral. He stood next to him as Phelps worked his horse's
coat with a curry comb.

"Love the smell of a sweating horse," Phelps said, working the comb vigorously.

John laughed. "Can't say I share the feeling, Stan. To me a sweating horse
conjures up memories of long days in the saddle, tremendous thirst, and a sore
backside. Give me a steamboat pilothouse any day."

Phelps chuckled. "Where's your sense of adventure?"

John thought of Lindy. "Lost it somewhere after the first six months. Now
I'm just doing my duty to my country, hoping I live long enough to see my wife
again. Hoping that if I must die, I'll do so bravely."

They fell silent until Phelps revived the conversation.

"Had the pleasure of meeting your wife."

"When? How was she?"

"Fine, far as I can tell. I talked with her a bit. She misses you. You got a
thoroughbred when you picked her. Prettiest woman I ever seen."

"I always thought so. Is she safe, do you think?"

Phelps frowned as he stroked lather off the horse. "I suppose she's as safe
as the wife of a Confederate officer can be in a town that's become a Union
fortress. That's all I can tell you."

Somehow, John got the impression Phelps was hiding something from him. Quickly dismissing the thought, he invited Phelps to share his campfire for supper.

By July 1862, the Union forces held an iron grip on Cape Girardeau and the surrounding area. On the same home front, the Union controlled the political situation. The Missouri legislature, under Provisional Governor Hamilton Gamble, a Union sympathizer, had passed a law requiring all public officers, even at the local level, to take oaths of loyalty to the United States. Those who refused were replaced by Unionists. As a result, the provisional government soon had a set of loyal civil officials in each county throughout the state.

In Cape Girardeau, Colonel Edward Daniels assembled every person over sixteen years of age on the Fourth of July, forcing them again to either take an oath of loyalty or be arrested. The local newspaper, once owned by Matthew Moore, now a Confederate colonel, had been seized by the army and was being published under the name *Cape Girardeau Eagle, Union Series*. The paper served as both a source of local news and as a mouthpiece for the views of Colonel Daniels. Most stores and homes now flew Union flags provided by the Federals. The few who declined were watched closely. The District Provost Marshal actively enforced martial law, announcing that if any Union man were robbed, he would levy ten times the amount of the loss on those who were not actively loyal. The criminal process under martial law was a speedy system. Any Rebel suspected of disloyalty was arrested, the evidence against him put into writing and verified under oath, and the originals or certified copies thereof filed with the Provost Marshal. Commissioners were then summoned from headquarters for trials so perfunctory there were often as many as 30 in one day.

Lindy and Maude continued to hold their jobs as nurses at the hospital. For each of them, the job gave some purpose to life. Lindy was concerned about Maude's health, though. The elderly woman was working long, hard hours at the hospital. She refused to slow down, even at the urging of Doc Wilson. She had clearly become the most efficient and knowledgeable nurse on the staff. Lindy, like the others, admired her for it.

Lindy and Maude were on their way to the hospital one bright July morning, walking on the wooden sidewalk, when they paused to watch a procession of soldiers riding into town. It was one of Colonel Daniels' squads of cavalry, returning from an expedition. They had Rebel prisoners with them. A band played a jaunty march, and the uniformed soldiers surrounded the prisoners, whose horses were tied together in the middle. The Federal soldiers looked grim and satisfied, the prisoners exhausted and despondent.

Pete Carnahan rode at the end of the procession, his uniform caked with dust. He tipped his hat to Lindy as he rode by.

"Look, Rosalind, isn't that the Rodney boy?"

Lindy studied the ragged prisoners and recognized at least four young men from Cape Girardeau.

"Sure is," she said. "I see some other Cape boys, too."

A crowd was gathering on the walk near Maude and Lindy. The people pointed and whispered as the parade made its way to the courthouse.

"They've captured Colonel Phelens and his men," said a voice near Lindy. It was Samantha Peabody. The prostitute nodded her dark head politely at Lindy. "Several Cape boys were riding with Phelens," said Samantha Peabody. "He was part of Jeffers' group. Looks like the war is over for that bunch of fellows."

"What will happen to them?" Lindy asked, as the prisoners were taken to the courthouse.

Samantha Peabody toyed with a closed parasol. "If they consider them soldiers and prisoners of war, they'll be shipped off to a military prison, probably Graitot Street Prison in St. Louis or the federal prison in Alton, Illinois, or Johnson's Island in Sandusky, Ohio. If they think they're spies, they'll be shot or hanged."

The crowd began dispersing after the procession passed. Maude was busily talking with an old friend from the Daughters of Temperance. Lindy found herself standing alone with Samantha Peabody.

"Rosalind, I want to thank you again for helping distribute the mail. I could never do it without you."

Lindy glanced around nervously. She wished Samantha wouldn't talk about it in public. "No need to thank me," she whispered. "I'm just doing my duty." She glanced toward Maude O'Malley. "Aunt Maude doesn't know anything about it, so I'd rather not talk about it here."

Samantha Peabody nodded. "Bet your aunt would pop a corset if she suspected you and I were associated in any sort of endeavor."

"You're probably right." As she spoke she noticed a tall pregnant woman walking toward them. The woman had dark, stringy hair. She was looking directly at Lindy. She looked familiar, but Lindy couldn't place her.

"Who's that pregnant woman?" she asked Samantha Peabody.

"Eula Claxton, Horace Claxton's wife. She used to work for me."

"She looks angry about something."

"She's always angry about something. One of the most unpleasant girls I ever had in the house."

Lindy realized with discomfort that Claxton's wife was coming directly toward her. She steeled herself for an unpleasant encounter. When close enough to speak, Eula Claxton pointed an accusing finger at Lindy.

"Rosalind Carmichael, I'm warning you—stay away from my husband or you'll be sorry!"

Lindy was speechless.

"Oh, don't play dumb with me, sister. Horace told me you've been throwing yourself at him like a cat in heat. He's my man, not yours. Better remember that or you're liable to get hurt!"

Samantha Peabody stepped between them. "Eula, quit making a fool of yourself. Rosalind Carmichael isn't after your husband. If she were, she'd have him."

"You should hear what Horace says about her!" the pregnant woman screamed.

"Listen to me," Samantha Peabody said, eyes flashing. "If you harm a hair on her head, you'll find out how ruthless I can be."

Eula Claxton looked at her with surprise. "What do you care about her, Sam?"

"Save your questions for your husband, Eula. I don't know why he fabricated stories about Mrs. Carmichael. Maybe it's to get even with you for something. But I assure you Rosalind Carmichael has no interest whatsoever in Horace Claxton."

"Amen," muttered Lindy.

Confusion twisted Eula Claxton's face. "Just the same," she said to Lindy. "Stay away from my man." She walked away, chin held high.

"Thank you, Sam," Lindy whispered. "Where in the world did she get the idea I was after Horace Claxton, of all people!"

"Her deck's missing a few cards," said Samantha Peabody. "She used to work for me, but I caught her stealing from the other girls. Gave her one week's notice to get out. Within the week she married Claxton. Since then, her face has been black and blue once a fortnight. Must suffer a hellacious home life."

Later at the hospital, Lindy encountered her second surprise of the day. Tyler Fitch was a patient. He had come in during the night, brought upriver by steamboat. Fitch was in bad shape. From the way the sheet lay over his body, it was obvious both legs had been amputated just above the knee. His usual white suit and red bow tie were gone. His bed reeked of urine and sweat. His eyes were open, and he watched Lindy cross the room and look down at him. She felt sorry for him, even after what he'd done to her family in the past.

"Hello, Tyler."

Contortions in his face told her he was in considerable pain. He groaned. "I guess you heard about the *Girardeau Rose?*" he said.

"No."

"Sunk. North of Vicksburg. I was carrying some Union troops, protected by two gunboats. A Rebel ironclad called the *Arkansas* came out of Vicksburg and blew the hell out of the gunboats, then came for the *Girardeau Rose* and sunk us. I was in the pilothouse when a cannonball tore through it. Broke both my legs and killed the pilot next to me. Other shots tore holes all over that beautiful boat. Both big red chimneys shot to pieces. She sunk in the deepest part of the channel. More than half the soldiers drowned."

Lindy was quiet, recalling the glorious steamboat that her father had built and her husband had captained for so many years. It was hard to believe that the splendid, magnificent creation, so much a part of her life, was gone forever. Such beauty, destroyed intentionally!

"Papa would be sick."

"Yeah," agreed Fitch. "O'Malley's grand steamer, fastest boat on the river, couldn't outrun a cannonball." Fitch shuddered. He looked miserably at Lindy. "Can't you do something for the pain?"

She found Doc Wilson. At his direction she got some morphine powder, undressed Fitch's wounds, and applied it directly to his bloody stumps. When she finished, she again sat in the chair next to him.

"I appreciate your kindness," he said softly. "I know you don't like me."

"I've forgiven you for what you did."

He closed his eyes for a few seconds, then reopened them. "Ironic, isn't it?" he said. "Last time we talked you told me I was a coward for not joining either side. Your words cut me to the quick. Because they were true. I *am* afraid of dying. I don't care *who* wins the war. Still can't see risking my life for something I don't care about." He coughed. "But I care about money," he added. "I was getting paid good money to transport those troops. I put my life on the line for money. Didn't join either side but got killed anyway."

Lindy grabbed his hand. "Don't talk like that, Tyler Fitch! You're not dead yet."

"I am," he said sadly. "I'm killed. I know it."

"You've got to have determination," she urged. "Don't give up too soon."

"Ah, Lindy, you would have made such a fine wife."

She looked at him but thought of John. Tyler Fitch couldn't hold a candle to John. How could she ever have even momentarily thought otherwise?

Doc Wilson called for her to assist him in the operating room.

"I've got to go now," she said.

Fitch nodded. She'd already turned to leave when he called her name.

"In case I don't see you again," he said, face deathly pale, "I want to warn you about Horace Claxton. He hates you and your husband. I've listened to him rant. He blames John Carmichael for everything that's gone wrong with his life. Be careful of him. He's a dangerous man."

Doc Wilson yelled a second time for Lindy. She hurried to the operating room.

When she returned, Tyler Fitch was dead.

Chapter 20

It was late October in 1862. Lindy was in bed just after midnight when she was awakened by pebbles striking her window. Within minutes, Stan Phelps was in the parlor, giving her the latest batch of letters.

"There were too many uniformed soldiers near Samantha Peabody's house tonight. My face is becoming too recognizable. Thought I'd come directly to your place again." He removed his hat, running a hand through his coarse, red hair. "It's getting tougher and tougher getting through the lines," he said, almost apologetically. "The Yankees have telegraphs now, and each Union post knows what's going on all over the state."

"Stan, I don't mind having you come to my house. We don't always need Samantha Peabody as the middleman. I like visiting with you, anyway. Makes me feel a little closer to John, seeing someone who's been talking with him."

The mail runner glanced down at his hat. "You know, Mrs. Carmichael, I told Captain Carmichael you were the prettiest lady I'd ever seen. Meant it, too."

Lindy saw color coming into the young man's cheeks. She was touched. "Why, thank you, Stan. What did John say when you told him that?"

"Said he'd always thought so, too."

Lindy recalled the last night she'd been with John. It seemed so long ago. "How is my husband?"

"Doing just fine, far as I can tell. Hasn't got sick like so many of the soldiers. Must be used to all the miasmas and such, being from Swampeast Missouri."

She knew from her nursing experience that seven soldiers were killed by disease for every one who died of a battle wound. She was relieved to hear he was healthy.

"How does he look?"

"Not near as pretty as you, Mrs. Carmichael." He chuckled, spinning his battered felt hat on a finger. "He's tan as a mulatto, with hair as yellow as straw. Got himself a regular double-breasted C.S.A. cavalry coat now, with captain's collar badges, and a pair of butternut trousers. He packs a cavalry saber on one side and his Colt in a holster on the other. Wears a floppy white wide-brimmed hat these days, but half the time it's dangling on a string down his back."

"I mean his face. How does his face look?"

"Well, like I said, he's real tan. Makes those eyes of his look blue as the sky. You should see his face light up when I'm telling him about you. Yes, ma'am. That man loves you."

She smiled and sat quietly, thinking of John.

"Got me a girl now, too," he said proudly. "Her name's Clarissa. She's from St. Louis. Her Papa's a colonel, fighting down in Mississippi. Met her just like I met you. She and her mother help deliver letters to families in St. Louis."

"Is she pretty?"

He beamed. "Oh, yeah. I told Captain Carmichael she's almost as pretty as you."

Lindy smiled. "When the war is over, maybe you'll be with her more often."

"Most definitely. We're going to get married. Got to win this war first, though." He pulled gently at his red beard. "The Federals are starting to get downright nasty. Did you know 'The Butcher' is being transferred to Cape Girardeau?"

"Who?" she asked.

"Brigadier General John McNeil, Union Army. He's earned himself the nickname 'The Butcher' for what he did in Palmyra, Missouri, earlier this month." Phelps grew angry as he spoke. "A Union sympathizer named Andrew Allsman disappeared, supposedly caught by Porter's Rebel band. McNeil issued an order saying unless Allsman was returned unharmed within ten days, he'd execute ten of Porter's men held as prisoners. Ten days passed. Allsman wasn't returned. Sure enough, McNeil marched out ten Rebels, all native Missourians, lined them up sitting on the ends of wooden coffins, and shot 'em so each fell back into his own pine box."

Lindy put a hand to her forehead. What was the world coming to?

"Like I said, 'The Butcher' is taking over in Cape Girardeau."

She felt goose bumps rising on her arms. "When is this nightmare going to stop, Stan?"

Phelps shrugged. "Now that Marmaduke has been transferred to the TransMississippi, maybe he and Sterling Price will be able to win Missouri back for the South. Maybe that will end the war."

Lindy realized she was crying, and she fumbled for a handkerchief.

Stan Phelps had been gone over twenty minutes before Lindy felt calm enough to read John's latest letters. Reading them was like drinking a miraculous tonic. Shortly, her spirits were restored. Not only did his letters touch her heart with their words of love, they made her marvel at his writing ability. He'd always been a good writer, but his prose was getting better and better. Reading them, she felt transported to the war zone. She was there at his side, seeing the things he saw, hearing the things he heard, feeling the things he felt.

She read with mixed emotions his letter relaying information about their friend, Sam Clemens. John and Lindy had become close friends with Clemens during the years preceding the war. After short stints as a printer and newspaperman in New York, Philadelphia, and Keokuk, he had persuaded a veteran steamboat pilot, Horace Bixby, to accept him as a cub pilot on the *Paul Jones* in 1857. On April 5, 1859, he received his pilot's license. A careful and competent pilot, he had no trouble finding work on numerous steamboats, including the *Edward J. Gay*, the *City of Memphis*, the *Arago* and the *Alonzo Child*. Clemens had taken the wheel of the *Girardeau Rose* several times, often urging Lindy to read Shakespeare to him during long afternoons on the river, and frequently commandeering the piano in the grand saloon for long renditions of his favorite song about the old horse named Methusalem.

In May of 1861, one month after Fort Sumpter fell, Clemens was in the pilothouse of the *Nebraska*, one of the last steamboats to reach St. Louis from New Orleans before the river was closed by the Union blockade above Memphis. Clemens had mysteriously vanished, and they had not heard from him since. John's letter explained the disappearance of their friend:

Dear Lindy,

A talkative fellow in my company is from Hannibal and turns out to be an old acquaintance of Sam Clemens. It seems that when the war broke out, Sam's family was as fractured in sympathies as was our own. His brother-inlaw, Will Moffett, the St. Louis businessman, was strongly Southern, but chose to go to jail rather than fight. Sam's brother, Orion, became a Republican and campaigned vigorously for Lincoln. Sam, it seems, was extremely fearful of being impressed by the federal government to pilot their steamboats. First he went into hiding with some cousins in St. Louis, then traveled home to Hannibal, where he joined fifteen to twenty boyhood friends as volunteers planning to attach themselves to the Missouri Militia under General Sterling Price. They called themselves the "Marion County Rangers." The name had great militaristic potential, even if the boys didn't. Imagine! If he had stuck with them, he and I would have been reunited at Wilson's Creek.

The Hannibal boy reports that Lincoln appointed Sam's brother, Orion, to be Secretary of the newly created Territory of Nevada. It seems Sam's brief stint in the Marion County Rangers did not prevent him from hiring on as Orion's Assistant Secretary in July of 1861. Thus, Sam seems to have managed to render service to both sides in this war. I'd love to hear him tell the story.

At least Nevada will be a safe place for a fun-loving vagabond disenchanted with real soldiering to sit out the war.

As much as I detest deserters and cowards and malingerers, I find that I bear no ill feelings toward Sam. If someone of his remarkable intelligence and wit can't fire himself up to shoot people to whom he hasn't been properly introduced, perhaps the rest of us, blue and gray alike, answered the siren's call a bit too quickly.

At any rate, it seems that Sam, safe in the West, enjoys a greater life expectancy than the rest of us. Perhaps he will be the only one of our group of friends who lives to a ripe old age. How I would love to hear him sing that song about Methusalem again!

I miss you more than words can tell.

Love,
John

Lindy wished she could share John's letters with someone. They were so beautiful, so poetic. She wished she could show them to Aunt Maude, but her aunt had made it clear she didn't want to hear from John, and Lindy felt it better not to put Maude in the position of knowing her niece was violating martial law. Maude was sickeningly careful about obeying martial law. She'd even surrendered to Union authorities the gun John left her. Lindy had kept hers, and it had caused a bitter quarrel between them.

After reading each letter once, Lindy started at the top of the pile and read through them a second time. It was a long while before she went back upstairs.

The next day was a Sunday, and Lindy had the day off from work. Shortly after noon, she calmed her nerves by playing Chopin nocturnes on the piano, then carefully placed the letters she needed to distribute into the pockets of her petticoat and set out to make deliveries.

She was walking past a blacksmith's shop on Main Street when an arm shot out and dragged her roughly into the wooden building. A hand covered her mouth and muffled her startled scream. The big wooden door closed swiftly.

Horace Claxton stood in front of her, grinning broadly, orange light from the roaring furnace bathing his face in an eerie glow. Rufus Blight held her from behind. The hand pressed to her face was dirty and smelled of campfires. She wanted to bite it, but controlled the urge.

"If you'll promise not to scream, I'll have Private Blight remove his hand," Claxton said, moving closer. His eyes narrowed. "Better keep your hand over her mouth real tight, Rufus. I don't like what I'm seeing in her eyes. She's scared. Real scared. But she's still uppity."

Claxton was directly in front of her now. A nauseating fog of body odor enveloped her face as he shoved his sandpaper chin close to her own. "Maybe you didn't hear what happened last night, Miss Lindy?"

She wanted to pull her face away, but Blight was holding her tightly, cutting off the circulation in her arms.

Claxton smiled, obviously enjoying himself. "Let's see. It was shortly after midnight. A visitor you'd just entertained got himself caught. Stan Phelps? Red Rover?"

Lindy felt weak and helpless. The hand over her mouth seemed to be suffocating her.

"Now, I wonder what he was doing at your house?" mused Claxton.

Lindy watched helplessly as Claxton lifted her skirt and groped at her petticoats. He would find the letters. It was inevitable.

"Well, what have we here? Rufus, look at this." With a ripping sound, Claxton yanked off a large section of her petticoat. He held it under her nose, precious letters visible in secret pockets, and shook his head reproachfully. "Rosalind Carmichael, shame on you! Carrying mail for Confederate soldiers. Helping Red Rover. Thought you were smarter than that." Claxton nodded to Rufus Blight. "Cut her loose. She can howl her way to the gallows, if she wants to make any noise."

The hand left her face. She gulped a deep breath. The torn white material in Claxton's hand was a frilly death warrant.

"What's going to happen now?" she asked. Her voice was unnaturally soft. She was surprised she could speak at all.

Claxton removed a thick envelope from the petticoat and studied the return address diffidently. "Well, the affidavits are already sworn out against the Red Rover. Already filed with the Provost Marshal. The Commissioners will come from Headquarters as soon as it's convenient. Stan Phelps will get his trial. After that, he'll be hanged or shot, I imagine."

Lindy shuddered.

"Well now," said Claxton, "don't get sick on us yet. We haven't even got to the best part. We need to talk about what's going to happen to *you*."

Her legs felt weak. She sat on a bale of straw.

Claxton stood over her, triumphantly. "I can't remember, Rufus," Claxton said, glancing at the private. "Did we mention Miss Lindy's name in our affidavits?"

In the dim light of the blacksmith shop, Rufus Blight looked like a rat. His big nose quivered and his eyes glittered in the shadows. "Don't believe we used her name, sir. Must have forgot. We could always swear out another affidavit, though."

Claxton grinned. "We could at that." He knelt in front of Lindy, his big thighs straining the light blue material of his Union issue pants. "On the other hand, we could keep quiet about what we know. The only way Miss Lindy would get caught would be if they torture her name out of Red Rover. What do you think, Miss Lindy? What are me and Rufus to do?"

She glared silently at Claxton, who shrugged and stood up.

"Cat's got her tongue, Rufus. Or maybe she didn't hear me."

"I could loosen her tongue," Blight said. Lindy glimpsed a knife in his hand.

"No need to get rough with her, Rufus. Wouldn't want to mess up that pretty face."

Lindy rose slowly to her feet, brushing pieces of straw off her dress. "What do you want from me, Claxton?"

He laughed. "I thought you'd come around." He pointed to her skirts. "First, I want the rest of them letters you're carrying."

Silently, she removed the mail from what was left of her torn petticoat. As she tossed each envelope to the floor, Blight retrieved it. When she finished, she glared at Claxton.

"Now," he said, "I want you to write out a nice little confession on this here piece of paper."

He handed her paper and pencil. When she didn't use it immediately, he sighed. "Ah, Rosie. It's your choice. Either admit in writing that you were helping Red Rover deliver mail or we'll march right down to the Provost Marshal and tell him all about it." Claxton examined black dirt under his fingernails. "You may have heard of General McNeil. Rebs call him 'The Butcher.' He'll be in Cape soon. Bet he'd like to get his hands on you. You'd make a fine example of what happens to a spy who delivers mail for the Rebs. McNeil is big on examples."

Feeling the weight of defeat, Lindy wrote a few short sentences of confession.

"That's my girl," he said, watching.

When she finished, he snatched the paper away from her, folded it, and slipped it into a pocket of his dark blue infantry coat. "Now," he said, "for the last thing."

She stared at him coldly.

"If it's money you want, I don't have any. John took it all to Memphis before the war."

Claxton laughed loudly. "She thinks I want money!"

Blight was laughing, too, a sniffling wispy noise.

"No, Miss Lindy," he said, the smile leaving his face. "I don't want money. I want what you carry between your legs."

Lindy felt nausea building in her throat. "Never. I'd die first."

Claxton grinned evilly. "You just might." He moved to the door and swung it open. The dirt floor of the big room was suddenly bathed in sunlight. "No need to make a snap decision, Mrs. Carmichael. I'll come calling on you real soon. You can let me know your answer then."

Dazed, Lindy stumbled out of the smithy.

The next two weeks passed in a blur for Lindy. Brigadier General John McNeil took command in Cape Girardeau. Stan Phelps was tried and convicted at the headquarters of the provost marshal in the Common Pleas Courthouse. The *Cape Girardeau Eagle, Union Series* screamed happily about the hanging scheduled for noon on a day in late October, 1862.

On the morning of Red Rover's date with the noose, Lindy secured an appointment with John McNeil at his headquarters. When they met in his office, she was surprised by his appearance. "The Butcher" didn't have evil eyes or cleft feet. Instead, he was a rather handsome man with short brown hair and beard. He wore the clean and simple navy-blue coat of a Union brigadier general, a double row of brass buttons on his chest and a single star on each epaulet. He looked overworked and harried, but otherwise quite human. Lindy's spirits rose when she saw him. She might have a chance.

"General, thank you for taking the time to see me."

John McNeil waved his hand in dismissal. "It's nothing, Mrs. Carmichael. I'm always interested in talking to a local citizen, particularly one so pretty." The General glanced at his aide, a lieutenant standing nearby. "Lieutenant Owenby informs me you wouldn't tell him your business, that it was secret. Do you have any objection if he stays while we talk?"

"I'd rather he leave, if you'd permit it."

"Very well, have a seat."

General McNeil ordered the aide out of the room and seated himself behind the desk. Lindy sat in front of it, on an uncomfortable wooden chair.

"I've come to beg you to spare the life of Stan Phelps," she said, watching him closely. His face lost its good humor. He had obviously been in similar situations before.

"So that's it," he sighed. "I'm sorry, Mrs. Carmichael, but you're wasting time, both yours and mine. He's set to hang at noon. There's nothing I can do."

"That's not true, General. Each commander has the authority to review the actions of his Provost Marshal."

McNeil didn't flinch. "I never reverse a decision of my Provost Marshal."

"Please, General!"

"No."

He looked at her coolly, yet Lindy could see pain deep within his eyes.

"My job isn't an easy one, Mrs. Carmichael. Life and death decisions must be made nearly every day. The lives of thousands of men depend upon me. The fate of our country rests upon officers like me." He coughed. "The hardest part of my job is refusing pleas such as yours. Almost every condemned man has family or friends, someone who cares. But I must do the right thing, not just for that one man, but for the army and for the country. A prolific mail runner like Stan Phelps must be hanged when caught, as a deterrent to others like him." McNeil stared silently at Lindy, hands motionless on his desk.

She considered trying to bribe him with the gold in her basement. She could tell it would be useless.

"There's nothing you can do to help Stan Phelps," said McNeil softly. "Absolutely nothing. I suggest you go home."

At noon, Lindy pressed against Maude O'Malley in the huge crowd of people gathered at the intersection of Themis and Lorimier streets. A freshly built scaffold stood like a carnival ride in the grassy field next to the red brick courthouse. The noose at the end of the hangman's rope waved gently in the autumn breeze. Glassy eyed, Lindy scanned the crowd. Soldiers in smart blue uniforms constituted a large part of the throng of thousands, but scores of local citizens also pushed forward for a view of the spectacle. She spotted several worried faces of women to whom she'd delivered letters carried by Red Rover. When eyes met, fearful looks were exchanged.

Samantha Peabody sat nearby on a carriage with several female employees, all showing off bright dresses and coats, chattering excitedly, as if at a horse race. Yet, when Samantha's eyes met hers, pain shimmered underneath the glitter, laced with hurt and fear. No one knew what Stan Phelps might have told the authorities. Lindy, for one, was positive his secrets would die with him. He was young, but brave and tough. Her concern came from another source.

On the scaffold, Horace Claxton sat joking with other deputy provost marshals, lounging on the edge of the tall platform, legs dangling over the side. Occasionally his raspy chuckle rose distinctively above the din of the crowd. It made Lindy's skin crawl. Near the scaffold, Claxton's wife, that peculiar dark-haired woman, stood with an infant in her arms. The Claxton family had all turned out to watch the hanging, Lindy noted with disgust.

Pete Carnahan stood with a squad of bluecoats on the other side of the street. His jaw was firmly set. He, for one, was not smiling.

"Rosalind," said Aunt Maude, touching her arm gently. "Maybe we should go home. You don't look well at all. I don't know why you wanted to come here in the first place. This is dreadful, standing here like a bunch of vultures. It isn't like we even know the man. Come on, let's leave."

"No, Aunt Maude. I must stay." She caught the quizzical expression on Maude's face.

Moments later, the sound of a drumbeat cut through the noise of the crowd. All eyes turned to the west. At first, Lindy could see nothing. People in front of her blocked her view. Presently, though, the object of attention became visible, and she felt a sob catch in her throat. Stan Phelps was riding to his hanging astride his own coffin. He sat on top of the closed pine box, in the middle, riding it as if it were an ox, a long leg hanging down each side, ankles chained together underneath. His hands were tied behind his back, shoulders slumped. Beard shaved, he once again was the gangly boy Lindy had first met. His red hair shone in the sun, the most beautiful red hair she had ever seen. A grim-faced drummer marched in front of the casket, keeping steady time. At least 200 armed guards surrounded the coffin, marching stiffly. Her heart sank as she realized escape was utterly out of the question.

As they approached, Lindy had the urge to run forward and proclaim her part in the crime. At least then Stan Phelps would not die alone. The urge passed as she glanced again at the hangman's noose. It was agony, watching the slow processional. As they passed her position, Stan Phelps turned his head toward Lindy. His green eyes brightened, his back straightened perceptibly and a reckless grin crept onto his face. *I'm a soldier to the end*, his expression boasted. Her heart went out to him, this twenty year old boy who was dying like a man, taking her secrets, and those of so many others, with him to a cold, dark grave. Lindy wished she'd asked Stan the full name of the girl Clarissa. She wanted so much to visit her some day, to tell her how much Stan had cared for her. But, of course, the girl undoubtedly knew all that. And she'd hear soon enough of Stan Phelps' death, of the fact they'd never be married. The editor of the *Cape Girardeau Eagle* would see to it the event was well-publicized. The hanging of Red Rover was big news.

Lindy watched silently, her body numb, as Stan Phelps was dragged off the coffin. Large soldiers on each side of him gripped the boy by the shoulders and carried him up the steps of the scaffold, the toes of his boots barely touching the wood. Somehow, Lindy wasn't surprised when it became obvious that Horace Claxton was the executioner.

Stan Phelps proudly declined the proffered black hood. Standing tall, arms behind his back, the coltish boy faced the crowd. He tilted his head slightly to make it easier for Claxton to apply the noose. Claxton read woodenly from a small card.

"Stan Phelps, condemned to death for violating martial law, have you any last words?"

"I do."

Surprised, Claxton moved to the side, near the wooden lever controlling the hatch beneath the prisoner's feet.

Stan Phelps, utterly alone in a crowd of thousands, glanced up at the rope above him and spoke in a loud high-pitched voice.

"I admit I've violated martial law, but do each of you know my crime? I've been convicted of delivering mail from soldiers to their families. A husband's loving letters to his wife; a son's notes to his cherished mother; a brother's teasing message to his sister. I delivered mail, but it shouldn't be a crime. These soldiers are men just like each man in blue gathered here today. They ought to be able to communicate with loved ones even if our nation is at war with itself."

Lindy felt tears unleashed down her face. The skinny boy's Adam's apple, always so noticeable, worked ferociously under the thick hemp rope encircling his neck.

"I'm proud I brought happiness into the lives of so many people. I thank everyone who has helped me and assure you that your names never left my lips. My only regret is that . . . ."

The words ended as a gurgle in his throat as Horace Claxton hit the lever controlling the hatch and the trapdoor sprang open, suddenly dropping the prisoner four feet.

"We've heard enough," Claxton proclaimed loudly.

The jolt was sharp, but the mail runner's neck did not break. He swung from the rope, lurching wildly, eyes protruding bug-like from a purple and swollen face, tongue stretched like a contorted snake from his silently screaming mouth, feet kicking and gouging at the air as he strangled to death. The rope dug so far into his neck it disappeared into the darkening flesh. Spreading patches on the seat and legs of his pants proclaimed to all who cared to look that he'd lost control of his bladder and bowels.

Sobbing, Lindy buried her face in Aunt Maude's shoulder.

"Honestly," she heard her aunt saying. "I don't know why you wouldn't leave when I suggested. This is sickening!"

Later that afternoon, Lindy went to Samantha Peabody's brothel, drawn as if by magnet. She felt an urgent need to talk to someone else who'd known Stan Phelps.

She knocked on the back door, hoping she hadn't been seen. A surprised negro cook hurried off to get the madame. In moments, Lindy was alone with Samantha Peabody in an ornate bedroom, decorated in pink and blue, with an oversized canopy bed in the center of the room. They sat on a love seat near the window.

"He was such a good young man," Lindy said.

Samantha Peabody nodded. "He was, but he's gone now, and we need to carry on. I'm sure the Confederacy will have someone take his place. I just hope it's soon."

Lindy bit her lip. "Sam, I've got some bad news."

"What, Lindy?"

"Horace Claxton caught me delivering letters, the day after they caught Stan." She felt her voice break. "I've been waiting for the sky to fall every day since, but nothing has happened. I think he's waiting to see if I'll give him what he wants to keep quiet."

Samantha Peabody smoothed her skirts, glancing nervously toward the window. "Did anyone see you come here?"

"I don't think so. I tried to make sure I wasn't being followed."

The prostitute exhaled sharply. "We need to be sure you aren't connected with me. As far as I know, Stan kept quiet about my involvement. I hope you'll do the same."

Lindy was hurt. "Of course I will. I wouldn't tell a soul about you."

"Do you promise?"

"Promise."

Samantha Peabody looked relieved. "What is it Claxton wants? Money? I can get you some."

"No," Lindy said, feeling her face reddening.

"Well, what is it then?"

"He wants my body."

"What?"

"My body. Sexual intercourse."

"Is that all!" Samantha Peabody put her hands on her hips. "Well, give it to him for Christ's sake."

Lindy couldn't believe her ears. "You must be joking!"

"Joking? I'm dead serious. Around here a bit of flesh isn't such a precious commodity. We sell it every day. What my girls peddle for ten dollars, he's offering you your very life for. I wouldn't think twice about it, dear."

"I won't do it. I'm married."

"All the better. It will be painless."

Lindy rose to leave. "I can see I'm wasting my time talking to you. You don't understand at all." She started for the door, but then turned back. "I'm trapped, Sam, don't you see? He can have me hanged at any time just by telling the Provost Marshal what he knows. I can't go to the authorities for help no matter what he does to me because I could never tell them I'm a spy."

Samantha Peabody hugged her sympathetically. Lindy smelled the heavy rose perfume.

"I don't know what to tell you, Lindy. If I were in your shoes, I'd give him what he wants. Sometimes that's the only thing a woman can do. Besides, the female anatomy can be a powerful weapon. I've used it many a time."

That night Lindy sat despondently in front of the fire in the parlor, long after Maude had gone to bed. The fire was popping gently when she heard her aunt's soft steps coming down the stairs. Shortly, the white-haired woman was seated next to her, compassion etched amid wrinkles.

"Rosalind, what's wrong?"

Lindy stared at the fire.

"It has something to do with the boy who was hanged today, doesn't it?"

Lindy didn't blink. The room was silent except for the crackling of the fire until Maude spoke again.

"I suspect it has something to do with the letters you've been delivering to the families of Confederate soldiers."

Lindy looked at Maude with shock.

"Oh, yes," said Maude, "I know about it. Several women in town have thanked me profusely for letting you smuggle their sons' letters to them. They had no idea, obviously, that you'd do such a thing without telling your aunt. They just assumed I knew." The elderly woman put a gentle hand on Lindy's leg. The blue veins protruded like railroad tracks under the tissue paper thin skin. "I suppose that fellow who died today was a friend of yours?"

Lindy felt the roaring approach of a torrent of grief. "He was such a good boy, Aunt Maude."

"And you're a good girl, Lindy. Always have been. Ever since you were a child. Your father would be so proud of the way you've turned out, if he were alive."

Lindy fell into the arms of her aunt, finally abandoning herself to the crying and the comforting she'd needed for so long.

When she could speak again, between sobs and gasps, she told Maude O'Malley every detail of her participation in the mail running, including her apprehension by Claxton and Blight. She blushed when she described the ransom demand and the advice she'd received from Sam Peabody.

"What do you expect from her!" said Maude O'Malley, angrily. "She couldn't possibly have the vaguest notion of the importance a lady places on the privacy of her body, she's sold hers so many times."

Lindy wiped her nose with the back of her hand.

"No, Lindy," said Maude. "There must be a better answer. Let me think about it awhile. I'll find a way to handle Horace Claxton. He was no match for your Papa, and no match for your husband. He'll not fare so well against your Aunt Maude, either."

Lindy felt better than she had for weeks.

"Aunt Maude, I was so afraid to come to you."

Maude's piercing eyes looked directly at her. "Don't ever be afraid to come to your family first. I'm not sure what we can do, but I'll think of something."

Lindy felt that somehow the ninety-pound woman would prove a match for Horace Claxton.

After the Confederate retreat from Shiloh and Corinth, Major General Thomas C. Hindman was assigned command of all Confederate forces in northwest Arkansas, southwest Missouri, and the Indian Territory. His command also included southeast Missouri, but there were no official Confederate forces in the region at the time—only Jeff Thompson and other State Militia and rebel bands. Marmaduke was assigned to duty under Hindman. The Major General invited Marmaduke and his men to report to Little Rock to make preparations for an invasion of Missouri.

At the same time, Federal forces west of the Mississippi conducted a full-scale invasion of Confederate Arkansas. An army led by General Samuel R. Curtis and General Frederick Steele moved down the White River in eastern Arkansas, capturing everything from Batesville to Helena. A second force commanded by James G. Blunt drove into northwestern Arkansas, shoving Confederate forces back across the Boston Mountains to Van Buren.

When Marmaduke arrived in Little Rock, General Hindman was engaged in building defenses against these Federal invasions. Marmaduke was quickly assigned the command of a cavalry division and was ordered to get into position to intercept General Blunt's invasion of northwestern Arkansas.

As Marmaduke's adjutant, Captain John Carmichael was a member of the General's seven-man staff. In late November and early December 1862, he was at Marmaduke's side in northern Arkansas as the Confederates met Blunt's Federal forces at Cane Hill and Prairie Grove. The Confederate plan called for Marmaduke's cavalry to divert the attention of the Federals at Cane Hill, while General Hindman marched his main forces to Blunt's rear, cutting him off and crushing him before he could receive reinforcements. Blunt, however, had not been fooled. He moved two of his three brigades to Cane Hill, where he intended to scatter Marmaduke's men and smash Hindman's infantry when they tried to catch him from behind.

The fighting at Cane Hill was desperate and deadly. The battle lasted over nine hours and extended over fifteen miles of ridges, heavy timber, brush, mountains, and valleys. Marmaduke's force of 2,000 finally found it necessary to retreat from the 5,000 Federals. Blunt then regrouped his forces and attacked Hindman at Prairie Grove a few days later. The valley echoed with artillery fire as the 8,000 Federals met the 10,000 Confederates. The armies fought from dawn to dusk, ending in a stalemate.

At 6:00 A.M. on December 8, 1862, Hindman and his generals held a council of war inside the Prairie Grove Church. He was undecided whether to resume the fighting or to retreat. The officers reported that the men didn't have enough ammunition to fight another day; battery animals were dying of starvation; the men were destitute of food; and the Confederate supply wagons, thirty miles to the rear, could not be brought forward without danger of losing them. Furthermore, the Union forces expected 7,000 reinforcements within hours. The decision was made to retreat. The main force of Confederates retreated to Van Buren, and from there to Little Rock, to wait out the approaching winter. Marmaduke's cavalry went into camp at Lewisburg, on the Arkansas River.

Although each side suffered comparable casualties at Prairie Grove,

Marmaduke and his staff realized that the battle had been a significant loss. The Confederates had not been able to check the Federal advance into Arkansas.

Lightning and thunder shook the old frame hospital building. Lindy ran from window to window, closing them hastily, trying to keep the heavy rain from drenching the wounded men as they lay in their beds. The wind whipped at the curtains and a wet spray stung her cheeks. From the corner of her eye, she could see Aunt Maude doing the same for the other side of the big room. Maude moved quickly for her age.

"Nurse," a wounded soldier called as Lindy hurried by his bed. "I need some water. Please."

"I'll be with you in a minute," she said, rushing past him.

Even though it was midafternoon, other nurses were lighting the candles in the candelabras. The storm had kidnapped the sun; the room was dark as night. A sharp crack of thunder made Lindy jump, and a terrifying scream from a nearby bed unnerved her even more.

Maude hurried to the screaming man. He was delirious and blind, a bandage over his eyes. He thought he was back on the battlefield, mistaking thunder for cannonading. He was yelling and screaming, trying to burrow deeper into the bed. The elderly woman struggled with him until he relaxed, his head pressed against her flat chest. She stroked his temple and cooed in his ear.

Lindy marveled at her aunt's ability to calm other people. The soldiers always responded to Maude's caring touch. Lindy, too, had felt better these last two days, since Maude's vow to think of a way to deal with Horace Claxton. Lindy didn't know what could be done, since Claxton and Blight were eyewitnesses to her violation of martial law, and actually had possession of her multi-pocketed petticoat and written confession. Still, since she'd unburdened herself to Aunt Maude, she'd felt vaguely optimistic. Maude O'Malley would think of something. She was the sort of person you could count on.

Eerily, the room was illuminated by another burst of lightening. Seconds later, the inevitable clap of thunder rattled the building to its bowels. Lindy carried a glass of water to the man who'd called for it. She was helping the grateful soldier sip from the glass when she noticed Maude O'Malley swoon.

"Aunt Maude!" she cried, as the tiny woman slipped to the floor.

Two male nurses, convalescent soldiers, rushed to Maude O'Malley and moved her to an unoccupied bed. Lindy was right behind them. Maude was unconscious, her face pale.

"Aunt Maude!" Lindy whispered.

Doc Wilson was at her side in a matter of minutes. He examined Maude tenderly and told Lindy she'd had a stroke. He stayed with her for a while, but then left to tend other patients.

Many thoughts jammed Lindy's mind as she sat next to her unconscious aunt, holding the feeble hand. She remembered the constant battle of wits Maude had enjoyed so much with Patrick O'Malley. She remembered the stern affection she'd always received from her father's only sister. Most of all, she wondered what would happen to her if Maude should die. Lindy would be absolutely and utterly alone. Maude would not be around to protect her from Horace Claxton.

"Please, Aunt Maude, don't leave me now. I need you."

She sat at her aunt's bedside for hours. Maude died shortly after the storm passed.

When Lindy awoke, she was at the hospital, in a bed in a private room. Doc Wilson was sitting next to her.

"What am I doing here?" she asked.

Doc smiled gently. "After your aunt died, you fainted. I decided it best to let you sleep. You were here all night. Feeling better?"

Aunt Maude was dead. Now she remembered.

"At least your aunt died painlessly," Doc Wilson said. "She probably never knew what happened. Knowing her, she appreciated dying on her feet, right in the midst of helping other people."

Lindy put a hand to her forehead. "I feel awful."

"You'll feel better after you eat something," Doc Wilson said. "I'll see that you get some soup." He stood up. "Oh, I almost forgot. While you were sleeping, a soldier brought this letter for you."

Listlessly, Lindy accepted the envelope. It had no return address, merely her name and the address of the hospital. As she opened it, she harbored a vague hope it was from John. Yet, she knew that would be impossible. It wasn't his handwriting. He wouldn't know how to deliver it here, anyway.

Doc Wilson disappeared down the aisle as she opened it.

The note was written in a messy, careless scrawl. When she read it, her hands began trembling.

Miss Rosie,

Sorry to hear about your aunt. What a shame! You have my deepest sympathy. I hear you are alone in that big house. I'll be paying my respects soon.

H C

Lindy felt a weird anger at Maude for leaving her before helping solve her problem with Horace Claxton. Now that Maude was gone, she felt helpless.

She thought of Samantha Peabody. Maybe Sam would come live with her. But how would that look? Taking a prostitute into her home? It was out of the question.

She considered leaving town, but again the inescapable fact remained—she had no place to go.

She remembered Pete Carnahan's offer of friendship. But he was a Union soldier. How could she admit to him she was a mail runner and expect him to help? What would happen to him if he tried to help her?

Lindy wadded the note from Claxton into a tight ball and clenched it in her hand. She stared with frustration at her small fist, so much smaller than Horace Claxton's.

Lindy spent New Year's Eve at the hospital, tending wounded soldiers. She went home just as the sun was setting.

She felt uneasy as she ate supper alone in the big house on Lorimier. The Union soldiers, normally so well-mannered, had seemed restless and rowdy all day. Many had broken regulations by discharging weapons in town. Several had galloped horses up and down Main Street. Lindy was nervous.

As midnight approached, bringing with it the year 1863, Lindy sat alone in her bedroom, burrowed comfortably underneath the covers of her bed, a fire crackling softly in the fireplace, candles burning brightly in the brass candelabra nearby. She was reading a medical text Maude had borrowed from Doc Wilson. Maude had always been studying, trying to become a better nurse. Lindy planned to do the same, but she was having trouble keeping her attention on the book.

She was reading about the comparative advantages of chloroform versus ether as an anesthetic when she heard glass break.

She froze. She listened carefully.

It sounded like it came from downstairs. Someone may have broken one of the windows. Perhaps someone was breaking into the house. She kept listening. The big house was silent as a tomb.

Perhaps she had imagined the noise. There was certainly no sound now. She closed the book softly. If only she weren't alone. If only John were here. If only Aunt Maude were still alive.

The Navy Colt John had left her was in a drawer at the bottom of the armoire next to the bed. Perhaps she should get it out.

Yet, it was probably nothing.

Still, what if someone had broken in?

Lindy got out of bed. The hardwood floor was cold, her feet bare. Something, some unheard sound or sense, made her look toward the bedroom door. The doorknob was turning.

She wanted to stoop, open the drawer and grab the gun. Instead, mesmerized, she stood transfixed as the doorknob continued turning. The door opened slowly and silently. Finally, a face peered around the wooden door. Horace Claxton!

"Get out of my house!" Lindy shouted, aware that her voice betrayed the fear that was twisting her entrails into knots.

Claxton glanced around cautiously, smiled smugly, and closed the door behind him. He had always been a big man. Abnormally big. Alone with her in her bedroom he looked bigger than ever. He wore a lopsided grin on his face. The flickering candlelight darkened the shadows of his stubble.

"Come to wish you a happy new year, Rosie."

His eyes flicked up and down, rudely appraising her figure. Lindy, wearing only a nightgown, pulled a blanket from the bed and wrapped herself in it.

"I told you to get out of here, Mr. Claxton. I mean it."

"Mister now, is it? Finally showing me a bit of respect, aren't you? What's the matter? A little scared?"

The armoire containing the Navy Colt was directly behind her. To get the gun she'd need to bend over, open the drawer, and pull it out. She realized with despair that he could easily grab her before she'd be able to get the drawer open. If only she had gotten the gun out when she'd first thought of it.

He moved toward her slowly. "Yeah, you *are* a little scared, aren't you?"

She didn't answer.

He sneered. "Captain O'Malley's daughter was always just a bit too good for Horace Claxton, wasn't she? She'd flirt around with John Carmichael and Tyler Fitch, but good old Horace Claxton was beneath her sweet notice, wasn't he?"

"Please! You must leave." Her voice sounded feeble, even to herself.

"Not until I get what I came for, and I think you know what I mean."

Lindy took a step back, but then realized it had placed her closer to the bed. She stopped abruptly. Claxton was between her and the door, blocking any escape. She remembered that he was married. "Think of your wife," she said. "She wouldn't want you here. For her sake, please leave."

Claxton's eyes narrowed. "Leave my wife out of this, you little secesh slut. You mention her again and I'll kill you."

Lindy, all hope gone, turned to try to get the gun out of the drawer. His beefy arms clamped around her waist in an instant, easily lifting her from her feet and slamming her onto the bed. One of the bed slats clattered to the floor. Lying on her back, she looked up at him.

"I'll pay you," she said. "Please leave. Please don't do this. I'll pay you to leave me alone."

"I don't want your money, Rosie! I want by all rights what I should've had years ago. I want what you've always been too high and mighty to give me." He was unbuttoning his pants as he spoke. "Hell," he said, an ugly grin suddenly stretching over his face, "after you've sampled Horace Claxton, you'll be offering me money to do it again."

Lindy rolled quickly to her left, trying to get off the bed. Claxton was fast. Instantly he was on top of her, pinning her roughly to the bed, his weight bearing down on her. He gripped both her wrists in one beefy hand. In his other was a knife he'd pulled from somewhere. Its point pressed her neck.

"In case you're thinking of screaming," he said, brushing the sharp blade against her pliant skin, "keep in mind I'd just as soon cut your throat as rape you."

His face was directly above hers, his beady eyes glaring at her. The body order from his flesh and dirty woolen uniform filled her nose. She closed her eyes. "For my father's sake, please don't do this. He was good to you. He paid you well."

She heard him spit and felt the spittle slap against her right cheek, just under her eye.

"I don't give a rat's whisker about your father. And your stinking husband's the one who fired me, don't forget. The fact you're his wife is going to make this doubly enjoyable."

Lindy clenched her eyes shut. She could feel the point of knife against her throat. Her hands tingled numbly, his grip on her wrists was so tight.

Suddenly the knife was gone from her neck. She felt a moment of hopefulness, replaced by overpowering revulsion when she felt his hand groping between her legs, prying her thighs apart. She tried to press her knees together, but he gripped her thigh in a vice-like hold and twisted the muscle until she screamed in pain. He yanked her leg viciously. Before she knew it he had locked his right arm behind the knee of her left leg and had pulled her thighs apart.

His tremendous weight was on top of her, bearing down upon her, suffocating her. She screamed, as loud as she could.

Suddenly the hand he'd been using to hold her wrists clenched on her windpipe throttling her scream in her throat. She choked and gagged as she struggled for air. Her face and neck swelled to the brink of bursting. Her lungs clamored for breath. She beat feebly at his face and head with her fists. She became lightheaded, everything cloudy.

When he finally released the choke hold, she retched and gasped. As she sucked in needed air, she felt him violate her to her core, literally pinning her to the bed, his beefy thighs pressed to hers, his massive hands and arms crushing her efforts at resistance. She began crying.

"Yes, I like that! Keep crying!" His bristly chin raked her neck.

She sobbed uncontrollably, helpless underneath him as he mashed her body with his. It seemed it would never end, his endless attack. The bed shook under his heavy thrusts. The mattress lurched awkwardly as another slat fell noisily to the floor. She closed her eyes and prayed for it to end. It did, finally. She shuddered with revulsion when he arched his back, groaning loudly.

When he was finished, he stood up, wiped himself on her pillow, buttoned his pants, and adjusted his dark blue frock coat. Lindy lay away from him, knees pulled to her chin. She heard him chuckling. "That was worth the wait!" She ignored him.

"Nice thing is, you can't tell the Provost Marshal about it. Not when you face hanging as a spy if Blight and I tell him what we know about you." He snorted. "I imagine you'll tell your husband. Fact is, I hope you do."

Lindy stared at the wall.

"Yes, I'd like for you to tell your husband. Because I plan to kill him, first chance I get. He'll give me the opportunity pronto if you tell him about our little get-together."

She kept still.

Claxton laughed. It was a horrible raspy sound. "Guess I might as well tell you, Rosie. There's nothing you can do about it now. I tried to kill your husband once before. Let's see, about ten years ago it was. I put some explosives on the *Lucky Molly*. Thought he'd be on it. Turned out I blew up old Captain O'Malley instead."

Lindy whirled and sat up in the bed. "You killed my father!"

Claxton shrugged. "It was an accident. I was trying for your husband. I felt bad about it for a while, before I decided your father owed me at least one life and deserved what he got."

"You pig!"

Claxton slapped her face, knocking her backward on the wrecked bed. She tasted blood in her mouth.

"Now look what you did," he said savagely. "I wasn't wanting to leave any marks on you."

Lindy heard him walk around the bed. He grabbed her by the hair and pulled her to a window. He opened a shutter and yanked her head so she had no choice but to look out.

"See that man on the corner across the street? That's Rufus Blight. Don't forget he and I have your written confession. If you so much as hiccup a word of my being here to a soul, we'll submit the evidence we have on you. Besides that, Blight's my alibi for tonight. He and I are out celebrating New Year's Eve someplace else. It'll be both our words against yours. Two deputy provost marshals against one little secessionist spy. Your neck will be the one that stretches if you tell on me—either about tonight or about your father." He flicked the shutters closed and shoved Lindy onto the bed.

She pressed her face to the covers, refusing to look at him as he walked heavily across the room.

"I'm leaving, but I'll be back. Mark my words, Rosie. I haven't had the last of your body, nor you the last of mine."

After he was gone, Lindy lay motionless on the bed. She felt his juices leaking out of her, like wet leeches crawling on her legs.

Later, she stumbled to the chamber pot and cleaned herself. An inverted US was branded to her abdomen, where Claxton's belt buckle had pressed into her during the rape. She stared at it a long time, wanting it to fade quickly.

She moved to the desk near the fireplace, the one where she'd written John letter after letter filled with happy stories and declarations of love. Crying, she wrote him again, pouring out what had happened, tears puddling the ink as she wrote. She urged him to come home, to help her, to avenge both her and her father, to hold her and convince her that life was not as ugly and meaningless as Horace Claxton wanted it to be. When the letter was completed, she clasped her face in her hands and cried like a child alone in the world.

After she finished crying, she decided she couldn't send the letter to John. He'd be devastated. He'd desert the service, or go crazy thinking about it. Still sniffling, Lindy wrote him another letter, one that sounded happy, one that failed to mention a word about Horace Claxton. The second one finished, a pack of lies by omission, Lindy sat quietly at the desk. The numbness had left her mind. She could think clearly, but the thinking provided no answers.

Claxton said he would return. What could she do to prevent another rape? As Claxton knew, she couldn't go to the authorities. She would hang as a spy.

She thought of Pete Carnahan. Although a Union soldier now, he had been a friend of her father's. He'd been fiercely proud of the *Lucky Molly's* engines and had never believed the explosion to be accidental. He'd told her to call on him if she had trouble with Claxton. Did she have the right to involve Pete Carnahan in her problem with Claxton? To explain to him why she couldn't report the rape, she'd have to confess to him her mail running activities. Was it fair to make him an accessory to her crime? She couldn't decide.

Finally, she crossed the room and lifted the heavy gun from the drawer. Never again, she promised herself, would she be caught without it. That much she knew.

It was March 1863, when Lindy realized with certainty that she was pregnant by Horace Claxton. She was horrified. There was no doubt as to the identity of the father. She hadn't seen her husband in nineteen months, much less made love to him. The only man during the last nine months had been Horace Claxton. That one awful time.

A child of rape.

The winter wind whipped at Lindy's face as she hurried to the hospital. She needed Doc Wilson's help. She simply couldn't bear to have this baby.

A child of rape.

The phrase kept ringing in her head. She'd read it somewhere once.

A child of rape.

She just couldn't be the mother of Horace Claxton's child. She'd do anything to prevent it. Anything. It was so unfair, this pregnancy. She and John had tried for years to conceive. They'd tried often and passionately, longing for a child. But they'd been unsuccessful. Claxton had impregnated her with one act of rape. It made her sick, sick, sick. The cold air caused her eyes to tear. Or was it despair?

She found Doc Wilson in the operating room at the hospital. He was amputating a soldier's frostbitten toes. She waited outside the operating room door. The sight of blood was making her queasy.

As he came through the heavy wooden door, she asked to see him in private. They went into the tiny room that served as his office. Doc Wilson's cheeks were speckled with flecks of blood obviously acquired during some operation earlier in the day. Unaware of the morbid badges of his profession, he twisted the ends of his white handlebar moustache. His eyes were kind. Easy to talk to.

Or at least they always had been. This time, she found it hard to speak.

"If I tell you something," she said, "will you absolutely promise not to tell another person?"

He looked surprised. "You ought to know I respect confidences. What's the matter, dear?"

"You've got to promise not to tell a soul."

"All right. I promise.

She took a deep breath, and let it out slowly. "I was raped."

His brow furrowed. "Who did it?" he said angrily.

She looked at her hands. "Does it matter, Doc?"

"It most certainly does! We'll report the scoundrel to the Provost Marshal. He'll get a ten-cent trial and a neckstretching."

She shook her head sadly. "I can't report him. He's got evidence that he could use against me that would get me in terrible trouble."

Doc Wilson frowned, puzzled. "You? Trouble? What have you done?"

Lindy covered her eyes with a hand. "It doesn't matter. None of it matters except one thing—he got me pregnant. With one rape, he got me pregnant."

"I see."

They sat silently for a full minute.

"I can't have this baby, Doc. I just can't have it. The man is a horrible beast. I can't carry his child."

He clasped his hands in front of him, thin delicate surgeon's hands. "Rosalind, you're talking about abortion. I can't help you with that. I don't believe in abortion. The child inside you is a human life. Blameless. You shouldn't destroy innocent life."

"Innocent!" Lindy shrieked. "It's a child of rape! The seed of an evil man! I won't carry it! I simply won't!" She felt herself losing self-control. She buried her face in her arms.

"Rosalind," Doc Wilson said softly, "no matter how bad the man who did this to you, the life inside your womb has done nothing to deserve your hatred." Tears shone in his eyes. "I understand how you must feel, my dear, but abortion is against the law in Missouri. It has been since 1828. I've been affiliated with the American Medical Association since it was founded in 1847. One of our specific policies is to oppose abortions. You're asking me to do something I've been opposed to all my professional life."

Lindy's vision was blurred by tears. "Doc, I thought I could count on you, of all people, to help me. Obviously, I was wrong!" She lurched to her feet and stumbled to the door, where she paused. "I won't be back for a while, Doc. I hope the job will still be here for me when I return."

Crying, she left the hospital.

That night, shortly after sunset, Lindy heard a knock at her front door. Horace Claxton. She knew it. She grabbed the loaded Colt and crept to the door. She threw it open and pointed the gun at his face.

Except it wasn't Horace Claxton. It was Samantha Peabody. "Good gracious, Lindy! Don't shoot me!"

Lindy stared at the frightened face on the other side of the gun barrel. With a sigh, she lowered the weapon.

"Lady!" Samantha Peabody brushed past Lindy and closed the door behind her. "You scared the hell out of me!"

"Sorry."

"I expect a nicer welcome, Rosalind, when I'm bringing you letters from your husband."

"From John?" Lindy dropped the gun onto the table.

"That's right. We got a new mail runner. He brought me a batch of letters last night. Here's a slew for you."

Lindy accepted the letters and pressed them to her bosom. She closed her eyes and thought of him. If only he were here!

Samantha Peabody was watching her closely. "You look awful. What's happened to you?"

Lindy told her the problem, and Doc Wilson's reaction.

"So that old fart won't give you an abortion. He's not the only show in town."

Lindy felt a spark of hope. "What do you mean?"

"I've performed an abortion or two in my time, Lindy. Once on myself."

"Oh! Could you? Would you?"

"We'll do it at my place. Tonight."

Lindy lay on her back on a table in a second-floor room of the brothel, legs spread and raised in the air. Dozens of candles flickered and glowed, providing Samantha Peabody with adequate light for her work. Several of Samantha's girls gathered around the table. Some held Lindy's legs up, keeping them apart and out of the way. Others rested fingers gently upon her arms, making sure she made no sudden movements.

Lindy found her gaze moving from face to face in the circle of harlots hovering over her like angels. Most bore expressions of concern and sympathy; one seemed disinterested, as if she'd seen it all before. Lindy couldn't see what was happening, but she'd watched carefully when the tool Samantha Peabody was using had been carried into the room—a long piece of whalebone, sharp at one end. She wasn't allowed an anesthetic because she needed to be able to tell Samantha if she felt herself being poked in the wrong place. So far it had been smooth. She could barely tell anything was inside her.

She was surprised by the warmth of the room. Perspiration crept over her eyebrows and temples and sweat rolled into her left eye. It burned. Suddenly she felt a sharp pain deep in her abdomen. She cried out and the pain stopped.

"Sorry," said Samantha Peabody, "Went a little too far to one side, I think."

The whalebone had now penetrated deep enough that Lindy could feel each probe. It was decidedly uncomfortable. *Damn, you Horace Claxton*, she thought silently. *Damn you. Damn you.*

"That'll do it," Samantha Peabody said, finally.

Lindy was aware of the whalebone being removed. "Is it over?" There hadn't been enough pain. The baby hadn't come out. She sat up. Samantha Peabody was cleaning off the whalebone.

"I believe I was able to rupture the sack carrying the baby. You'll probably start dripping fluid soon. You'll drip for two or three days, with the discharge rapidly increasing until your body expels the fetus."

Lindy took a deep breath. "I don't feel any pain. Are you sure you got it?"

Samantha Peabody shrugged. "If I didn't we'll try again. In the meantime, walk up and down your steps vigorously, carrying something heavy; bathe in water as hot as you can tolerate, using this mixture of linseed, mallow and wormwood; and jump up and down several times a day."

Lindy wondered if Samantha Peabody knew what she was talking about.

The prostitute's method worked. Three days later the abortion occurred, with more than enough pain and blood to convince Lindy it was for real. In spite of a slight fever, Lindy went back to work a few days later. Doc Wilson let her have her job back. She found it impossible, though, to look him in the eye.

Chapter 21

Batesville, Arkansas was a small city about 80 miles north and a bit east of Little Rock, nestled on the north bank of the White River. In 1863, it had a population of about 2,000. Marmaduke's men had been exhausted and ragged when they'd set up camp near Batesville on January 25, 1863. They were returning from an expedition into Missouri that included battles at Springfield, Sand Spring, Marshfield, and Hartville. The retreat had been one of tremendous suffering. A raging snowstorm lasted ten hours, leaving two feet of snow on the ground and ice dangling from the hats and saddles of the weary men. Two hundred horses were abandoned on the roadside to die, their riders marching on foot during the remainder of the trip. Many of the wounded men, unable to endure the grueling march, dropped off, one by one, sitting silently at the side of the road, waiting for friend or foe to come along with aid or death.

At Batesville, the citizens of the small community came to General Marmaduke's assistance. They willingly provided food to the hungry soldiers and took the sick into their homes, nursing them back to health, and returning them to camp cured and comfortably clad. The months of February and March gave the troops a temporary respite from the horrors of fighting. The Batesville girls lost no time in meeting the eligible bachelors, and when the soldiers weren't drilling or repairing equipment, they were attending balls, dinners, lint-pickings, and other social engagements. There were even two quick weddings.

For those who didn't fit in with the teasing innocence of the local girls, a group of prostitutes from Missouri had rented a house and established a temporary shop advertising by word of mouth. There was also a bar in town, and Marmaduke lifted the usual ban on alcohol and allowed the men to visit it in the evenings.

Marmaduke and his staff set up headquarters in the Main Street office of Thomas Cox, a local man away on active duty as a quartermaster in the Confederate Army. Marmaduke had even been affected by the pleasant surroundings. Several times he quoted poetry in his general orders, and Colonel Joseph O. Shelby's brigade gave him a beautiful horse as a present, to his obvious delight.

John was one of the few who failed to join the happy mood of the Batesville interlude. He hadn't heard from Lindy since Stan Phelps had been caught and hanged. He had no idea whether the scores of letters he'd sent with the new mail runner were getting through; he simply knew he hadn't received a word from his wife since November. Watching the other officers on the staff laugh and joke with the pretty local girls made John's heart ache even more. He desperately wanted to hear from Lindy. He *needed* to hear from her. The silence was excruciating.

In late March, Marmaduke traveled to Little Rock to meet with Major General E. Kirby Smith, who had replaced Hindman as commander of the Trans-Mississippi.

Marmaduke was beaming when he returned. "I have tremendous news for you." John tore his thoughts away from Lindy long enough to listen. "We're going to Cape Girardeau!"

John was stunned. "What?"

"You heard me. We're going to Cape Girardeau. Blunt's moving south toward Little Rock again, and Vicksburg's still under siege. I proposed to Kirby Smith that he let me make another cavalry invasion of Missouri, this time to Cape Girardeau. Hopefully, Blunt will pull back from Little Rock, and some of the pressure on Vicksburg will be relieved."

John jumped up. "Cape Girardeau! It's been almost two years since I've been home, nearly two years since I've seen Lindy."

"You just may get the opportunity to visit her," said Marmaduke. "Our plan is to sweep through the Iron Mountain area, destroying telegraphs, bridges, and forts as we go, and then swing east and capture the forts and supplies at Cape Girardeau. We also hope to pick up a large number of recruits as we go through Missouri."

John sobered. "If Cape Girardeau becomes a battleground, Lindy might be hurt."

"For all you know, she's hurt already. At least this gives you a chance to find out if she's alive. I know how long it's been since you heard from her." Marmaduke tossed John his hat. "Come on," he said. "Jeff Thompson of the Missouri State Militia has arrived from Missouri. He's going to accompany us on the raid. Let's go talk to the 'Swamp Fox' about conditions around Cape. I hear he's sitting in the bar right now."

John was anxious to make the acquaintance of Jeff Thompson. He'd heard much about him. He wasn't adequately prepared, though, for the man he met when they found Thompson at the rowdy bar. Thompson was about 35, a tall, lanky, wiry man, with a long sharp face, a prominent nose, blue eyes, and a mane of yellow-brown hair combed back behind his ears. He sported a mous-tache, but no beard, and wore a white hat with a feather. His boots were unusu-ally tall. He carried a white-handled knife on his belt in the middle of his back. He was sitting at a table in the noisy bar next to one of his colonels, a handsome young man in his early twenties, with wavy black shoulder-length hair and a smooth, impudent face. The colonel was obviously drunk, though Thompson appeared sober.

After exchanging formalities and introductions, John and Marmaduke joined the two men at their table. John noticed the colonel looking at him with a pecu-liar expression. He nodded politely to him and listened to the conversation between Marmaduke and Thompson.

"What can you tell me about the situation in Cape Girardeau?" Marmaduke asked.

Thompson took off his hat and adjusted the feather. "The second American Revolution is burning brightly in the Cape Girardeau area, General. The invad-ing horde has gripped Cape by its entrails these last two years, bullying and intimidating good Southern men and women into taking oaths that compromise their souls. With my command of brave Missourians, though, living in the swamps of southeast Missouri, surrounded by a powerful and vindictive en-emy, I've managed to wage moderately successful guerrilla warfare."

"I'm aware of your success," Marmaduke said. "I'm sure they don't call you the Swamp Fox for nothing. Tell me, what are the fortifications at Cape Girardeau like?"

"Like the River Styx. They've got four forts on some pretty impressive hills, with another garrison at Bloomfield, about 45 miles to the southwest. They usually have anywhere from 2,000 to 6,000 men in the area. Cape would be a pretty tough place to take."

"We're going to give it a shot," Marmaduke said. "Are you game?"

"Does the rooster crow?" Thompson grinned. "My biggest problem will be getting Lothario, here, away from the harlots."

The colonel hiccuped and grinned. He wore the lazy air of a boastful lover like an invisible crown. "Jeff, these fine girls, working women all, have come down to this remote wilderness of Arkansas, clear from St. Louis and Cape Girardeau, just to bring us a bit of pleasure. The least I can do is pay my re-spects to every one of them, giving each a little something for her trouble."

The colonel glanced at Marmaduke and John, apparently gauging their re-actions. He obviously didn't care whether or not they approved of his conduct. John wondered if it was due to the liquor, or whether the State Guard colonel always displayed such a lack of restraint in front of superior officers. Marmaduke's face was a mask of indifference.

Jeff Thompson shook his head, carefully phrasing his words as though he'd said them before. "You're a married man, Colonel Worley. What would your wife say?"

"She'll never know. Hell, a man's got to kick up his heels now and then."

John frowned and looked into a fire burning in a nearby fireplace. He thought of Lindy. He didn't understand how a married man who truly loved his wife could disgrace her by consorting with prostitutes. When his gaze left the fire, Colonel Worley was staring at him.

"What's the matter, Captain Carmichael? Don't you approve of my conduct?"

John didn't like the smug expression on Worley's face, but the last thing he wanted was trouble with a drunk. "It's not my place to approve or disapprove of your actions, Colonel."

Worley continued to stare. "I thought I detected a bit of distaste on your face. Perhaps I was mistaken."

Thompson and Marmaduke were looking angrily at Worley. John chose his words carefully. "The fact you're committing adultery behind your wife's back is none of my business, no matter how distasteful I might find it."

"Adultery!" said Worley in a voice loud with whiskey. "You're saying I'm an adulterer?"

John wanted the whole conversation to end, but saw no way to end it gracefully. "I don't know you, Worley. Don't know what you may or may not have done. But the definition of adultery is well known. You know whether the shoe fits. Personally, I don't care what you do."

"Come on, Colonel, let's leave." Thompson took Worley by the arm. "Sorry, gentlemen. Never seen him this drunk. If he's not careful, he'll sober up a private."

Worley jerked his arm free and leaned toward John. "I don't like your holier-than-thou attitude, Carmichael."

"How unfortunate."

"I could wipe that smug look right off your face right quick, if I wanted to," challenged Worley.

"I'm sure you could."

Worley laughed. "I could do it without raising a finger."

"That would be interesting, but unlikely."

Worley leaned forward, conspiratorially. "Your wife, Rosalind Carmichael, is cheating on you."

John felt his mouth drop open.

"Yes!" Worley laughed. "Told you! Without raising a finger!"

John grabbed Worley by the collar of his uniform. "What do you mean?"

"Let go of me!" Worley slurred.

John backed him up and slammed him against a wall. "I asked you what you meant, talking about my wife!"

"I mean she's been sleeping around. She even had an abortion. One of the sluts I was with told me about it last night. She was there. Saw the abortion. We were talking about it because she knew you were on Marmaduke's staff." Worley glared drunkenly at John. "So don't act holier-than-thou with me. Tend to your own house first."

John cocked his arm to punch Worley.

"Whoa, Carmichael. Don't hit me. It's the truth. Get that girl. Ask her. She'll tell you."

Within an hour, John had confirmed it. In the most humiliating 60 minutes of his life, he located the prostitute and listened to her description of the abortion at Samantha Peabody's brothel. Devastated, he sat on the riverfront in Batesville, staring at nothing. The pieces were fitting into place in a way John didn't want to believe. Lindy hadn't written him in four months. She'd had an abortion within the past few weeks. She'd been unfaithful to him. Of all the tragedies the world had to offer, John had not expected this one. The love they'd shared had always been so strong, so powerful. It was hard to believe she'd taken a lover. Yet, on the other hand, he'd been away for almost two years, and Cape Girardeau was full of soldiers, some undoubtedly attractive.

John knew he had to see Lindy in person, confront her, talk to her. He was glad Marmaduke's division was heading that direction because he would have deserted if necessary to get to Cape Girardeau quickly. Once he got to Cape Girardeau, he'd get some answers from Lindy. Or die trying.

It was late April 1863, four weeks since the abortion. Lindy had a slight fever that wouldn't leave, and she'd been losing weight. What worried her most, though, was the vaginal bleeding and the tenderness she felt in her belly. Sam Peabody told her it wasn't normal.

Lindy lay on the bed in her bedroom, a blood-spotted handkerchief clutched in her hand. It was after ten o'clock at night, and she was worried. Perhaps she should talk to Doc Wilson about it tomorrow. Even though he didn't approve of abortions, he might at least check to verify she was healing properly. She felt her face reddening just at the thought of talking to Doc Wilson. How could she approach him for help when he'd told her so plainly that he considered abortion immoral? Maybe he was right, she thought with a wave of guilt. Maybe she had been wrong to abort the life of the baby.

Lindy dismissed the thought quickly. She'd made her decision. No sense second-guessing herself now. Horace Claxton had murdered her father and raped her. No way she would carry his child. Wrong or not, abortion had been her only choice.

Suddenly and unmistakably, Lindy heard the sound of breaking glass. *Oh, no, not again!* She leaped to her feet and retrieved the Navy Colt from the drawer, then hurried to the window and peered out. Blight was standing across the street.

Claxton's lookout! So he *had* returned.

She sat on the edge of the bed, gripping the gun in her right hand behind her back, staring at the closed door of her bedroom. As she listened for the sound of footsteps, she wondered if she could really kill a man, even Horace Claxton. *Thou shalt not kill. Turn the other cheek.* It went against everything she'd ever been taught. Could she actually shoot someone? She'd heard of people freezing, unable to pull the trigger, unable to take the life of another human being. Then, too, there was the question of whether she was physically capable of stopping a man as powerful as Claxton. And the matter of accuracy. John was an excellent shot. He'd practiced often. Lindy had never been much interested in guns, though. She now wished she'd worked at it a little bit harder. What would happen if she were to shoot and miss? The gun had six shots. How many could she get off? What would Claxton do to her if she missed?

She watched with a detached sense of inevitability as the door knob turned. She wasn't surprised in the least when Horace Claxton stepped into the room. He stood by the door, smirking. The brass buttons on his dark blue Union frock coat glistened in the candlelight. He removed his fatigue cap and tossed it to a nearby chair. "I've come for another payment, Miss Rosie." He licked his lips. "Been thinking about you a lot since last time. You're the best roll in the hay I ever had."

Lindy's fingers tightened on the gun behind her back. She could feel the sweat on her hand. The trigger felt slippery. Claxton was still on the other side of the room. *What if she would shoot and miss?*

Claxton's eyes narrowed. "How come you're just sitting there?"

Her heart skipped a beat. Did he suspect she had the gun?

He rubbed his massive hands together. "Don't just sit," he said, his voice husky, "take off your clothes. This time I want to see that pretty body of yours. I was in too much of a hurry last time." He grinned. "This time I'm going to stay here all night. You'll be amazed at the things a man and woman can do when they've got the time and inclination."

"Please, Claxton. Get out of here. Just leave me alone."

"Claxton, is it? Last time you called me mister. Am I gonna have to beat a little respect into you?"

He still stood by the door. Lindy wasn't at all sure she could hit a target so far away. Yet, if he got closer, he'd see the gun. She was surprised he hadn't noticed that her one arm was behind her back.

Suddenly, she had a premonition that discovery was inevitable. He would notice the hand behind her back. She would shoot and miss. He'd make her suffer like she'd never suffered before.

A woman's anatomy can be a powerful weapon. Samantha Peabody's words came to her unsummoned.

"Well, if you won't leave, Claxton, let's get this over with."

Lindy lay back gracefully on the bed, her legs still dangling off the edge. Her right hand, holding the gun, was underneath the small of her back. With her left she pulled her nightgown slowly up her legs. Claxton's eyes fixed on her nightgown as it traveled up her thighs. She watched his face closely as she pulled on the soft flannel. He was staring and grinning. She shifted her buttocks as she hitched the nightgown almost to her waist. She wore nothing underneath. She slowly spread her legs.

Claxton was moving heavily toward her, hastily fumbling with his belt. She was breathing fast, wondering how quickly she could pull the gun and how soon she should try. His gaze never left her open thighs. Lindy watched as he came to the edge of the bed and unclasped his belt.

"You're about to be ridden by a riverboat man who's a ripsnorter, a screaming eagle, who can out-fight, out-drink and out-cuss any man or beast ever born or yet to be born," he bragged, struggling with the buttons of his pants.

She pulled the gun from behind her back. He glanced up at the sudden movement. His eyes widened and a big hand shot out for her arm. She pointed the Colt at his face and squeezed the trigger as his arm moved in a blur toward her.

"You slut!" His words were drowned out by a tremendous explosion. As the gun recoiled, his arm knocked it from her hand. The gun spun in the air as it sailed across the room, and Lindy felt a sinking moment of despair; but within a fraction of time she saw Claxton falling, falling, falling, his mouth twisted and open, his angry eyes unfocused, a black and bloody hole in his forehead, his head surrounded by a spray of blood-red raindrops, cascading with his body toward the floor, where he landed with a heavy thud on the hardwood next to her bed.

Lindy staggered to her feet and grabbed the gun. She pointed it at Claxton's still form, circling him warily. He wasn't moving. He wasn't breathing.

She thought of Blight, waiting outside. Carefully, she crossed the room, never ceasing to watch the man on the floor. When she reached the window, she glanced out. Blight was running down the street, not looking back. She looked down at Claxton. His eyes stared sightlessly at whatever awaited him in the next world. She sank to her knees and cried.

After a time, Lindy was calm.

If Claxton's body were found in her house, she'd hang as a spy. *Wife of Confederate Officer Shoots and Kills Yankee Soldier.* What would the *Eagle* and "The Butcher" make of that? Particularly if Blight came forward with her written confession to smuggling Rebel mail?

Her only hope was to hide Claxton's body and pray that Blight would keep quiet. Maybe she could convince Blight that Claxton had left town. Or maybe she could bribe him. At any rate, she'd deal with Blight later. For now, she had Claxton's corpse lying on the bedroom floor. She couldn't take him outside; someone might see. The only answer was the basement.

Lindy stared at the dead body. A pool of blood under the head was growing larger by the minute. She wrapped a pillowcase around it to soak up the blood and hide the face. Straining every muscle in her body, she grabbed him by the legs and pulled. His sky-blue pants were soaked at the crotch. The intense smell of his evacuated bladder and bowels made her gag over and over again. He was incredibly heavy, but she managed to drag him across the room, leaving a snail-like trail of blood. She dragged him through the hall to the top of the steps. Holding a leg under each arm, she backed down them. His skull knocked loudly on each step as she dragged him down the staircase.

She left him for a while at the foot of the stairs on the first floor as she lit candles and placed a candelabra in the basement. She then returned for the corpse. He slid somewhat more easily on the shiny first-floor hallway. When she got to the rough wooden steps leading to the basement, she again backed down them, his head thudding a one-note funeral march as they descended.

It was hard work dragging him across the rough dirt floor of the basement, constantly stooping to avoid bumping her head on the low ceiling, fighting the resistance of the dirt, but she finally got him to the place where the chest was buried. The pillowcase had pulled off his head as she crossed the basement, revealing a messy mottled mass of coagulating blood and dirt.

With John's spade, she began digging. She dug for hours in the cold, dark basement. When the grave was finished, she was so tired she could hardly lift the shovel out of the hole where she stood, blistered hands stinging and aching. From her vantage point in the open grave, the uniformed body of Horace Claxton was only a few feet from her face, dead blue eyes sightlessly watching the final preparations for his basement entombment.

Weakly she pulled herself out of the dank abyss. Her nightgown was torn, caked with dirt and soaked with perspiration, even though the room was cold as death. It took every ounce of her energy to roll Horace Claxton into the hole. She cried as she shoveled load after load of dirt onto the lifeless body.

Her face burning with fever, belly aching, upper thighs sticky with blood, she kept shoveling as if her life depended upon it, because she was certain it did. It was dawn when she finally went back upstairs to clean up the rest of the blood.

Chapter 22

On April 19, 1863, Marmaduke's division set out on the Cape Girardeau raid, riding north from Batesville at an easy gait. It would be 180 miles to Rolla.

The division was made up of four brigades, totaling 5,086 men, with eight pieces of artillery, two of them Parrot guns. Each of the four brigades was led by an experienced and competent commander: Colonel George W. Carter led his brigade from Texas; Colonel John Q. Burbridge commanded a Missouri Brigade, many of whom were from Cape Girardeau County; Colonel Colton Green led Emmett MacDonald's Missouri Brigade (MacDonald had been killed at Hartville); and Colonel Joseph O. Shelby, Marmaduke's most capable and reliable cavalry leader, led the Missouri fighters who had forged the nickname "Iron Brigade" through the hot fires of countless battles.

John rode with Marmaduke at the head of a long column. The weather was beautiful as the expedition got underway. Springtime in northeast Arkansas and southeast Missouri always brought a symphony of color to the lush woods. April of 1863 was no exception.

"General, are you sure it's a good idea to bring along the unarmed men?" John asked, speaking in a soft voice. He was referring to the 1,200 weaponless men who made up over twenty percent of the force. "If we have a pitched battle, those men will be defenseless."

Marmaduke nodded. John was raising points he'd obviously already considered.

"And what about our two-legged cavalry?" John continued. "They'll have trouble keeping up if we need to move quickly."

Marmaduke glanced over his shoulder at the long line of men behind them. Most were armed with shotguns, Enfield rifles, or Mississippi rifles, although some carried only small caliber squirrel guns. Yet, they were smiling and happy, well rested from the stay at Batesville. The great majority were Missouri boys returning to their home state after a long exile. The mood of the army was definitely one of excitement and optimism, in stark contrast to the gloom that had followed Prairie Grove.

"I brought the unarmed and dismounted for two reasons," answered Marmaduke. "First, I hope to arm and mount them from our spoils of victory. Second, I know how anxious they are to return to Missouri. If I left any Missouri boys behind in Arkansas, they'd desert." Marmaduke's cool blue eyes turned north. "We're going to head first for Rolla," he said, outlining the plan John already knew. "Hopefully the Federals will fall for our feint and think Rolla is our objective. Then we'll swing east and smash Cape Girardeau. 'The Butcher' is the commander there now. I'd love to capture him. Perhaps give him a taste of his own medicine."

John's thoughts drifted away from military strategy and returned again to the subject that had been torturing him night and day for a week, causing dark circles under his eyes that even two years of warfare had never produced: Lindy's abortion. He'd considered every possible reason she might have gotten it and all feasible explanations why her letters had quit coming. The most obvious answer—she'd found another man. He was being cuckolded.

He couldn't talk about it with anyone. The subject was too embarrassing and too painful, eating at his soul like a monstrous tapeworm. He no longer enjoyed anything in life, not even the simple things, previously sources of so much pleasure; the smell of pine burning in a campfire, the taste of freshly shot squirrel cooked on a spit, a carefully crafted and well written report to the Chief of Staff, and especially the tattered and dog-eared letters from Lindy carried in his saddlebags.

He still read the letters of love sent to him months earlier, but without the uplifting joy of confident fidelity. Yet, reading them gave him hope. It was incomprehensible that the woman who'd written those beautiful declarations of enduring love not so long ago had already given her heart to someone else.

One thought kept him guardedly hopeful—if she truly loved another man, why had she gotten the abortion? For appearances? Lindy wasn't the sort to care so much what others thought. Maybe she'd made just one transgression and was sorry about it. If so, would he forgive her? He honestly didn't know. He wouldn't be able to answer the question until he talked to her. In person. One way or another, he swore to himself, he'd find a way to see her when they got to Cape Girardeau. No matter what risk. No matter what danger.

His feelings about the impending attack upon his hometown were jumbled and mixed, and he sorted through them during the long hours on horseback. On the one hand, he was determined to find Lindy, somehow, and to talk to her. For that reason alone, he was grateful for the raid on Cape Girardeau. He was also excited about the chance of driving the Federals out of his hometown, even if only temporarily. Fighting for home soil would provide a special urgency that other battles had lacked. On the other hand, he worried about the safety of Lindy, Maude, and countless other friends in Cape. Flying shells and canister never distinguished soldier from civilian. Anyone in town would be in danger. Furthermore, Lindy had mentioned in a letter that some Union jackass had threatened to destroy the downtown area if attacked by Confederates. It hurt to think of the destruction of their beautiful home on Lorimier Street, built on property O'Malley himself had chosen. And finally, many friends like Pete Carnahan were members of the Home Guard, and would very likely fight to the bitter end to defend Cape. The battle would truly be friend against friend, since many of Marmaduke's command were also from the area. In Colonel William L. Jeffers' regiment, the Eighth Missouri Cavalry, six of the eight companies were Cape County boys. Colonel Solomon G. Kitchen's regiment was composed of men from neighboring Stoddard, Dunklin, and New Madrid counties.

Yet, all things considered, John was glad they were going to Cape Girardeau. The sooner they got there, the better.

As they neared Missouri, Marmaduke's scouts returned with the news that the Federal garrison at Patterson was lightly defended by only 600 men, and that McNeil himself headed about 2,000 men at the post at Bloomfield. A Federal courier had been captured, providing Marmaduke with information that McNeil had received orders directing him to Pilot Knob in the event of attack. To reach Pilot Knob, he would need to go through Ironton and Fredericktown. Marmaduke quickly formed a plan of operation, dividing his forces into two columns. Shelby's and Burbridge's brigades would continue toward Rolla via Van Buren, creating the illusion of a Confederate attack on Rolla, hopefully drawing the enemy out of northern Arkansas and throwing the garrisons at Patterson, Ironton, and Bloomfield off guard. Meanwhile, Carter's and Green's brigades would take a shorter, less traveled route via Doniphan, and strike at Patterson. The two columns would unite near Ironton, where they would crush McNeil as he traveled from Bloomfield to Pilot Knob.

The first stage of the plan worked well. John and Marmaduke rode with Carter's brigade to Patterson. At dawn on April 20, they encountered the Federal pickets twelve miles outside the post. They fought a short stand up battle, and easily defeated them, taking 24 prisoners. The sound of the skirmish, though, alerted the Union troops at Patterson, and they set fire to their Quartermaster's stores and galloped for Bloomfield. The Confederates pursued them for seven miles, but then gave up, rendezvousing with Shelby's column at Patterson, Shelby's men having completed their demonstrations near Rolla.

Marmaduke divided his brigades again on April 21, sending Carter's forces to Bloomfield to attack McNeil and taking Shelby's men to Fredericktown, where they would wait for McNeil to come their way. The plan looked good. If

McNeil chose to fight Carter at Bloomfield, Carter would beat him. If he fled, as ordered, to Pilot Knob, Marmaduke would intercept him and smash him. The chances for a significant victory looked bright.

Marmaduke's column arrived at Fredericktown on April 22, after fording the treacherous St. Francis River. They captured a small Federal force, destroyed a bridge over Big Creek, and wrecked a long stretch of the St. Louis railroad. Still having heard nothing from Carter's column, they began moving toward Bloomfield, hoping to encounter McNeil along the way.

Scouts and couriers soon arrived with alarming news. McNeil had not followed the orders they'd intercepted. Instead, he had fled from Carter, burning his supplies at Bloomfield. Carter's wagons and cannon were bogged down in the Mingo Swamp, southwest of Bloomfield, and McNeil had successfully retreated into Cape Girardeau. Carter had followed him and was only four miles from Cape, but was in real danger of being cut off from Marmaduke.

To make matters worse, scouts had spotted a large force of 5,000 Federals coming east from Camp Totten near Rolla. They rode under the battle flag of the First Iowa, which was under General William Vandever. Apparently the feint near Rolla had drawn the bees out of the hive.

With Vandever coming from the west and McNeil safely inside the fortifications of Cape Girardeau to the east, Marmaduke hurried his men through the darkness and rain to reinforce Carter. They reunited at Jackson just before dawn on April 26, 1863. Cape Girardeau lay only a few miles away, its lights flickering in the distance.

Rain came in torrents. Water stood inches deep on the road to Cape Girardeau. John and Marmaduke huddled under a hastily erected tarp.

"Did I show you the demand for surrender Carter sent into Cape Girardeau before we got here?" Marmaduke asked, handing John a copy of the document.

John read it with interest.

HEADQUARTERS FOURTH DIVISION
Near Cape Girardeau, Mo.
April 25, 1863

Officer Commanding U. S. Forces in and around Cape Girardeau:
    SIR: By order of Gen. John S. Marmaduke, commanding, I formally demand of you the immediate surrender, unconditionally, of the troops in Cape Girardeau and the adjoining forts, together with all the ammunition, stores, and other property belonging to the United States in the same. If the surrender is made, I pledge myself to treat the troops as prisoners of war, and to parole and exchange them as soon as practicable. I shall scrupulously protect private property. No difference will be made in this particular be-

tween parties, whether Union or Southern sentiment. One-half hour is allowed for your decision.

Colonel Watson, commanding Second Texas Cavalry Brigade, who bears the flag of truce, will present this demand and wait for your reply.

I am, sir, very respectfully, your obedient servant,

> G. W. Carter
> Comdg. Fourth Div.
> First Army Corps
> Trans-Mississippi Dept.

John returned it to Marmaduke. "Sounds a bit too optimistic under the circumstances, but wouldn't it have been something if they'd surrendered without a fight?"

"Yes, but they didn't. We'll attack Cape Girardeau when the rain stops. They have a strong natural position, with hills and forts, but we'll test their defenses a bit."

John slipped from underneath the tarp and stared toward the river town, water pouring from the brim of his hat. He remembered the first time he'd seen Cape Girardeau when he'd arrived with Austin Carmichael that sad day so many years before. He recalled the happy years spent steamboating on the Mississippi, with Cape as home port and base of operations. He savored memories of the peaceful life shared with Lindy in the house on Lorimier Street. It all seemed so long ago. Faded memories, still sweet to touch. He wondered what Lindy was doing this moment.

On Sunday, April 26, 1863, at 10:00 in the morning, Private Rufus Blight marched in double-quick time with other reinforcements as they hurried from the riverfront toward Fort B at the northwest edge of Cape Girardeau. The sound of heavy gunfire coming from that end of town filled the air. Every few seconds the ground literally shook in response to the thunderous cannon.

"What's going on, sergeant?" Blight called out to the blue back of the man in front of him.

"Marmaduke and 8,000 men! Attacking Cape Girardeau!"

Blight felt cold fear in the pit of his stomach.

The sergeant was in an unusually talkative mood as they hurried toward the sound of the gunfire. He ignored the usual ban on conversation.

"Talked to Colonel Baumer a minute ago. He says we'll meet the enemy outside our fortifications, drive them back if we can. If they overpower us, we'll fall back to Fort B. If they overrun us at Fort B, we fall back to Fort A. The devil himself couldn't take us at Fort A."

Blight gripped his rifle tightly, listening as the noncom continued. "General McNeil and 2,000 men barely made it back from Bloomfield day before yesterday by the skins of their teeth. Marmaduke's 8,000 were right behind them and almost caught them. Don't you know the Rebs would love to get their hands on 'The Butcher.' We're getting more and more reinforcements by water. McNeil says we'll fight to the last man. We'll never surrender Cape to the Rebs!"

As he hurried up Main Street, Blight saw soldiers piling commissary and quartermaster supplies of all kinds into stacks in the streets. As standard procedure, these supplies would be soaked with turpentine and set on fire should it appear the Confederates would take the town. Some of the more excited commissary boys were already slinging turpentine.

As they ran past the hospital, Blight gaped with surprise at a slender woman making her way slowly up the steps of the building. It was Rosalind Carmichael. He couldn't believe it. As he ran by, he kept staring over his shoulder.

She was alive?

As Blight jogged toward the battle in progress, his thoughts were on the woman he'd just seen. He had been in the street outside her house on Lorimier one week before, standing a quiet watch while Horace Claxton paid her a visit. He'd heard the gunshot, and he'd run. He'd assumed Claxton killed her. He knew Claxton was capable of murder. He knew Claxton hated the Carmichael woman, hated her whole family. He'd figured Claxton had murdered her and vanished. Claxton had been gone seven days. Blight had decided he'd either run to avoid prosecution, or was off somewhere disposing of the body. But he'd seen Rosalind Carmichael alive just now.

Then where was Horace Claxton?

It had simply never occurred to him that the slender little woman could kill a brute like Claxton. But she must have. It was the only explanation.

As hundreds of soldiers' feet pounded toward the scene of the fight, Rufus Blight thought of Rosalind Carmichael. She was the most beautiful woman he'd ever seen. Her face was the sort you saw only in paintings, her body the type few men ever touched. He'd thought she was dead. Yet, she was alive and alone. Claxton had told him she was a delectable wench. How had Claxton gotten his sample? By extortion. By threatening to expose her mail running to the authorities. Blight had the same information. He could blackmail her, too. Sample that body. Maybe make some money.

One thing Rufus Blight knew for sure. He'd be more careful than Horace Claxton. He wouldn't underestimate her. As soon as this battle was over, as soon as he could get away, he would pay her a little visit. For now, he realized as they neared the embattled First Nebraska, he needed to concentrate on staying alive in this fight. Rosalind Carmichael would come later.

The Rebels were making their attack in the area between Perryville and Bloomfield roads, their forces centered on the ground northwest of Jackson

Road. They charged the Union positions, running fullspeed, whooping and firing. Most were on foot, but many rode horses.

The First Nebraska had moved Welfley's battery, consisting of six pieces,
to a hill between Bloomfield and Jackson roads. The hastily set-up cannon,
surrounded by five companies of Federal soldiers, kept a steady stream of shot
and shell whistling toward the Confederates. To the left, the guns of Fort B
roared and thundered, placing the Rebels under a deadly crossfire.

Rufus Blight joined other bluecoats in rifle pits dug into the hillside. He
added the fire of his own musket to the mass of explosions. The Rebels retreated to the edge of the woods, which they used for cover, and began a constant fire upon Blight's position. Within minutes, shells blasted nearby, and
Blight felt terror for the first time. Confederate artillery! Aimed his way! Mouth
dry, Blight peered from the earthworks as the artillery duel commenced.

Lindy leaned against the wall after entering the hospital. Her face was burning hot, and the sharp pain in her belly implored her to curl into a ball. This was
the first time she'd left the house since Claxton's last visit. She'd been too sick.
Fever burning hotter and hotter day by day, pains in her abdomen increasing in
intensity, and frightening blood flowing from her vagina had brought her to
Doc Wilson's doorstep. Dizzy and light-headed, she stumbled past soldiers in
beds, feeling the familiar urge to care for them, but forcing her rambling mind
to concentrate on her mission of finding Doc Wilson. She was relieved when
one of the male nurses took her by the arm.

"Mrs. Carmichael, what's wrong?"

"I'm sick. Real sick. Need to see Doc Wilson."

His face was a blur, his voice kind. "He's in the operating room now, but
you can wait in a chair near the door and see him when he comes out."

Lindy let herself be guided to the chair.

"He's going to be busy all morning," the nurse said, "what with
Marmaduke's attack."

Lindy was so ill she didn't catch the significance of his words. She groaned
and held her stomach.

"You're in pretty bad shape," said the nurse. "Wait a minute. I'll get you
something."

Lindy was aware only of the sharp pain in her gut. She drifted in and out of
consciousness. Soon she sensed the male nurse wiping her forehead with a cool
moist towel. It felt good.

"Your forehead's burning hot," he said. "You've got a bad fever. Hope Doc
Wilson can see you soon."

Lindy heard thunder in the distance.

"The battle's been going on almost an hour. Wish I knew how it's going,"
the nurse said nervously.

Lindy's eyes seemed to be swimming in the heat of her face. Her mouth was parched. "May I have some water, please?" she whispered, thinking only of how good it would feel in her cottondry mouth.

"I don't know. Wish I were the doctor. Some patients can't have water. You know that."

Lindy's mouth tasted like dust. "Please?" It seemed as if only a second passed before he put a cup to her lips. She drank. It was cool. Her head quit spinning, but the pain still throbbed in her abdomen.

"Even if Marmaduke does take Cape," the nurse was saying, "I don't guess he'll do anything to the hospitals."

"Marmaduke?"

The nurse looked at her as if she were a fool. "Where've you been, Mrs. Carmichael? General Marmaduke and 8,000 Rebs are attacking Cape Girardeau right this minute!"

An explosion shook the hospital. The fog in Lindy's mind seemed to clear. Marmaduke was attacking Cape! John was with Marmaduke! John was nearby! He might come looking for her!

"I've got to get home," she said, staggering to her feet.

"What about Doc Wilson?"

"I'll see him later."

Outside, Lindy paused on the steps of the hospital to rest a moment before going home. She was having difficulty breathing.

On the riverfront, Union soldiers, rifles in hand, were hurrying down ramps of arriving steamboats. Frantic townspeople were crowding onto departing boats, arms filled with baskets, bundles, and other moveable belongings. The boats carried some to Cypress Island and others to the Illinois bank. Two Union ironclads were steaming up the river from Cairo, preparing to add the support of their cannon to the defense of the city. To the northwest, a cloud of gunpowder hovered in the air, gunfire, and explosions roaring like thunder.

Lindy made her way down the steps, moving gingerly to avoid sharp jabs of belly pain. At the bottom of the steps she found herself face to face with Eula Claxton. The woman was wild-eyed.

"Where's my husband!"

Lindy could not meet her eyes. "I don't know."

"I don't believe you!"

Lindy staggered past the woman. When she glanced back, she was gone. Slowly, Lindy made her way to the house on Lorimier Street. Her home. The place where she'd last seen John. The place he would come looking for her if he possibly could.

John was at Marmaduke's right hand during most of the attack upon Cape Girardeau. They stood under a tree, behind their lines on an elevation that provided an excellent view of the battlefield. The rain clouds had blown across the river to Illinois. In the bright daylight under the pale gray sky, Marmaduke got a good look at the impressive strength of Cape Girardeau's fortifications.

"A full-scale attack on those forts would be wanton butchery and slaughter," Marmaduke said, his voice tired.

He sent John forward with a message to Shelby: Make a demonstration, take a fort if you can do so with light casualties, but don't mount a major attack. After John relayed Marmaduke's message, Shelby muttered, "How does the bull pull out gracefully after the thrusting's already begun?"

John stayed with Shelby's men throughout midmorning as the "demonstration" on Cape Girardeau became a hot and deadly assault. The Federal pickets were driven in by Major Shanks and his men in the advance, and the Confederates pushed their way to the base of the chain of hills at the foot of town. After the Federal pickets dashed wildly back behind their main lines, the Federal cannon opened fire upon the Rebels with shot and shell from the commanding heights of Fort B.

Once the pickets were driven in, Shelby, gunfire bursting overhead, formed his command into a long battle-line extending from the woods left of Jackson Road nearly half a mile to Bloomfield Road. The roar of artillery was constant, the heavy guns of Fort B hurling heavy shot and screaming shell furiously at the Confederate battery. Still, the Rebel artillery kept up its own fire, exploding shells blowing clouds of earthworks skyward with each well-placed shot.

John joined the Confederate charge that met the Yankees midway across the field, the two forces crashing into each other at full speed, colliding like trains on the same track. The Rebel cavalrymen were on foot, their horses being held behind their lines by unarmed soldiers. Like the other charging men, John had dismounted.

The earth shook with artillery fire. John, his pistol blazing, fought hand-to-hand with the Federal infantry. As always, everything was forgotten except staying alive in the cut and slash of close-quarter killing.

The deadly skirmish was brief, lasting only minutes. A Federal officer soon ordered retreat, and the shrill sound of the bugle could be heard over the thunder of the weapons. Bluecoats pulled back across the open field in wild disorder, Rebels chasing them, yelling and yipping. John drew a bead on the chest of a Union captain desperately trying to preserve order among his men.

John froze, finger immobile on the trigger. The officer was Pete Carnahan. Their eyes met. John's finger tightened on the trigger, but in spite of the frenzied anger of combat, something kept him from squeezing it further. It seemed their eyes held for hours, though it couldn't have been more than a fraction of a second, recognition flashing between them, knowledge of his peril registering on Pete's face, John looking down the gun barrel at the blue-covered heart of the man who'd first taught him how to fight, recalling visions of homemade barbells, a hot engine room, and the smell of sweat and whiskey.

Suddenly he was knocked from his feet by the concussion of a nearby explosion. The Federal batteries had shifted their fire from Collins' position to the charging Rebels, raining heavy balls, exploding shells, canister, and grape upon them. Numb from the shock of the blast, yet with his gun still clutched in his hand, John crawled on palms and knees back toward the Rebel lines, minéballs and shrapnel shrieked past him. When he reached the comfort of the woods, he took a deep breath and reloaded.

His hat had come off his head and was dangling down his back, held in place by the cord around his neck. John examined it. There were three holes through its crown.

From somewhere, Shelby was suddenly kneeling next to him. "Go check with Marmaduke. Find out what he wants me to do."

Seconds later, John was back on his horse, galloping for Marmaduke's position.

The artillery battle continued past noon; the firing, constant and terrific. Marmaduke, seeing that Shelby's demonstration had amounted to an attack, brought Carter's column up to support him. The two combined Confederate forces continued the assault throughout the early afternoon. Marmaduke ordered a retreat about 3:00 PM, leaving 40 Rebel dead and wounded scattered over the field.

The Confederate forces bivouacked for the night in Jackson, eight miles northwest of Cape Girardeau. Marmaduke sent a Confederate surgeon to Cape, with a written request that he be allowed to attend the Rebel casualties.

As soon as the moment presented itself, John spoke with Marmaduke alone. "I want to ask a favor."

Marmaduke nodded, eyes knowing. "I've been expecting this."

"May I go behind enemy lines, sir, into Cape Girardeau?"

Their eyes met. Months of friendship were confirmed by the articulate silent gaze.

"I suppose it would be useful to have you go behind enemy lines, check upon the actions of the foe, and eventually report back to me. So ordered." Marmaduke frowned. "John, how will you find her? Cape Girardeau is teeming with Federals. How will you even get into town?"

"I know a place upriver from Cape. I can slip into the Mississippi there. I'm a strong swimmer. I'll get into Cape by water and make my way home. If Lindy's in Cape, that's where she'll be. I'm certain of it."

Marmaduke looked fondly at John. "Once you're finished in Cape, try to make your way back to me. We'll be crossing the St. Francis River at Chalk Bluffs. I've already sent Jeff Thompson and Bob Smith there to make us a bridge. Then we'll go to Jacksonport, Arkansas." Marmaduke smiled. Although he'd just turned thirty in March, he looked much older. "Try to get back to me within a month, John. I need you to help me write my reports. You're the best there is at report-writing."

As Marmaduke spoke, John felt a strong premonition he'd never see his friend again. He'd heard before of soldiers' accurate premonitions of impending death, but always dismissed such talk as silly superstition. He was sensing very definite warnings about his own grasp on life, though, and he wasn't sure the feelings should be ignored.

"If I don't see you again, Marmaduke, I want you to know I think you're the best officer in the army."

"If I don't see you again, Carmichael, I'll court-martial *you* in *absentia*. Now, get yourself to Cape and back in one piece."

They shook hands and John rode off into the night.

John unsaddled his horse in the woods north of Cape Girardeau and tethered her where she could feed on nearby grass. He found a large dead tree and dragged it to the edge of the river. He debated which clothing he should shed. He finally decided to wear his cavalry jacket, pants, gun belt and boots. He'd rather wear them sopping wet than leave them behind. He hid his hat, overcoat, and other gear in the brush.

Putting the cool metal barrel of his Navy Colt between his teeth, he pushed the log into the fast current of the Mississippi River and slipped into the water next to it, careful to keep the gun out of the muddy water. Noiselessly he floated downstream, pulled by the powerful current, his head hidden from view behind the floating tree.

Shortly after nightfall, Rufus Blight made his way to Lindy Carmichael's house. He wore his uniform and carried his rifle. Word was the Rebels had retreated to Jackson. It wasn't certain whether they'd be attacking or fleeing in the morning. Part of McNeil's command had ridden out into the night to find and attack them. Blight's company had been assigned the defense of the city and had been allowed to return to their tents for the night. He'd slipped away to pay a visit to Rosalind Carmichael.

He tried the door and found it locked. He kicked it hard, until it finally swung open. He held his rifle ready to fire as he came in. The wench wouldn't catch him by surprise.

The house was dark, except for an upstairs light. Cautiously, Blight worked his way up the steps. One second-floor door had light coming from underneath it. He moved quietly to the door and turned the knob. Slowly, he pushed the door open. She was in a nightgown, lying on top of the bed, looking at him as he entered the room. He pointed the muzzle of his rifle at her face and cocked it.

"Hello, Mrs. Carmichael," he said. "Remember me?"

Her face was flushed and perspiring. The room emitted a sickly smell. Her voice sounded soft and weak.

"Of course I remember you, Private Blight."

He let his eyes wander over her body. Even a flannel nightgown couldn't hide her exquisite shape. He felt himself growing excited as he stared at her legs, bare below the knee. He never let his rifle waver, though. He kept it pointed at her face. Claxton came into this house and never came out. He wasn't going to make the same mistake.

"If you're through looking, would you leave now?"

Her words surprised him. "Is that any way to talk to a guest?"

"You're not a guest; you're a trespasser."

Blight didn't like the way the conversation was going. She wasn't quaking the way a woman should when a gun is pointed at her. He wasn't in complete control of her. Not yet.

"Actually, Mrs. Carmichael, I'm looking for a friend, Horace Claxton. Remember him?"

She gave him no reaction. She was a stubborn woman.

"Last time I saw him was Friday night, coming into your house. He never came out. What'd you do, kill him?"

She was silent.

"I heard the gunshot," he said. "I know you shot him." He noticed for the first time that she was lying with one hand out of sight.

"I didn't shoot him," she said. "I shot at him, one time. He ran off like a rabbit. That's your brave Horace Claxton, Private. I have no idea where he went after leaving here. If you'd stayed around, maybe you'd have seen him come out the door."

Blight kept watching for sudden movement as he inched closer to her, keeping his rifle trained on her face. He particularly watched the place where her right hand disappeared out of sight.

"Maybe you killed him, maybe you didn't," he said. "I know what Claxton was here for, and I want some of the same."

Circles of perspiration drenched her armpits. It occurred to him she had a fever.

"I could have you hanged," he said. "If not for the murder of Horace Claxton, then for your violations of martial law. I know where Claxton stashed your confession. I know where all the letters are. If you don't give me what I want, I'll see you hang." He was only five feet from her now, the rifle barrel close to her nose.

"What do you want from me?"

"Whatever money you've got in this house, and your body. Claxton recommends it highly."

She pulled her arm out from under her back. A gun was in her hand. He swung his rifle barrel down sharply on her forearm. She cried out as the Navy Colt dropped harmlessly to the bed. With a laugh of triumph he grabbed it.

"I thought so! I'll bet that's how you got Claxton." He tossed the gun onto a chair next to the door. "Let's just see if you've got any other hidden fangs."

Keeping the rifle trained on her, he searched the area near the bed. He found nothing.

"Now, let's talk terms," he said. He felt much better. He was in control now. He could tell from the hopeless expression on her face. She huddled on the bed like a frightened kitten. He felt strong and powerful. He liked the feeling. "If I report you to the authorities, you'll be arrested. Your house will be searched." He grinned. "I just wonder what they'd find if they searched your house tonight. Perhaps evidence of a murder?"

He walked casually back to the chair where he'd put her gun and leaned his rifle against it. "On the other hand, Mrs. Carmichael, I find you to be an extremely desirable woman, even though you don't seem to be in the best of health." He took off his heavy wool coat and draped it over the back of the chair. "Like I said, I want whatever money you have in the house. I also want your body, as often as I feel like it. I believe I'll take the first installment now." He came toward the bed, looking hungrily at her fever-wracked body.

John Carmichael, his clothing still soaked with river water, slipped from building to building, making his way stealthily through Cape Girardeau, an invader in his own hometown. The Navy Colt he'd carried in his teeth as he floated down the Mississippi was now in his hand. He'd managed to keep it dry. He had six shots to fire if necessary, no more, no less.

It seemed to take forever to reach the familiar porch of the beautiful house on Lorimier, although probably only fifteen minutes had passed since he'd emerged from the river. John thought of Lindy inside the house. She would be surprised to see him. There had to be an explanation for her infidelity, he told himself over and over as he walked up the familiar steps. This was his house, his home, with his wife inside. They loved each other. He was certain of it. She would never betray his love by willingly taking another man into their bed. He stopped abruptly at the front door. It was ajar, the lock broken.

Gripping the pistol tightly, John nudged the door open slowly with the toe of a mud-caked boot. It swung open silently. Darkness inside. His pistol poised in front of him, John moved quickly through the doorway, darting instantly to his right into empty blackness. He waited for something to happen. Nothing did.

He stood silently for almost a full minute, listening to the silence of the big house. The entire first floor was shrouded with complete darkness. Eventually, he heard voices drifting down from upstairs. They were coming from the bedroom. The voices were too faint to distinguish words, but one of the voices sounded male. The other was Lindy's.

John moved through the hallway to the foot of the staircase, his wet boots stepping noiselessly across the hardwood floor. He moved quietly up the staircase, his gun held ready. One of the steps creaked. He caught his breath, finger on trigger. The voices continued, though, and he resumed his climb up the steps. Reaching the top step, he could see the doorway to the bedroom, *Lindy's* bedroom, *his* bedroom, *their* bedroom. The door was closed, but a strip of light crept from underneath it. John slipped to the door and stood next to it, listening, close enough now to distinctly hear the voices, even through the door. Lindy and a man were talking. In her bedroom.

So it was true! She had taken a lover. He felt a sickening sensation in his gut. His grip on his gun loosened. His mind flashed a phantasmagoria of the times he and Lindy had shared: John riding behind her on a pony rushing breakneck to Cape Rock to watch the duel, Lindy gently holding his head comforting him after his father died, the sound of her laughter watching O'Malley teach him to swim, the studious look on her face as she set up the steamboat library, the straightness of her back as she played Chopin on the piano, the stolen kisses on nightrunning steamboats, the fiery passion of their wedding night, and that last bittersweet kiss when he'd left for war. Now another man had taken his place.

John clenched his eyes shut. With effort, he forced himself to listen to what was being said in the bedroom.

"Please don't," he heard Lindy say. Her voice sounded weak, faint.

The male voice laughed harshly. It sounded unfamiliar. "You thought you were pretty clever hiding that gun, didn't you? You'll wish you never tried to get smart with me. Take off your clothes!"

"No!"

"You'll do as I say!"

John heard cloth tearing. He'd heard enough. What was going on in Lindy's bedroom wasn't consensual. His heart pumping wildly, John kicked the door open and lunged into the bedroom. The room was bathed in candlelight. Lindy was lying on the bed, her nightgown torn to her waist. A wild-eyed man was straddling her, sitting on her thighs, his knees at her sides. He gripped her hands in his, pressing them onto the bed at each side of her head. The man's face jerked toward John as the splintered pieces of door swung on broken hinges and bounced against the wall.

With a roar, John leaped across the room. Rufus Blight let go of Lindy's hands and struggled to get to his feet. John caught him by the shirt collar and yanked savagely, pulling him off the bed and throwing him to the floor. Blight landed hard on his knees. John jerked upward, gripping the bunched cloth under Blight's chin. Blight's hands were like claws. He scratched and tore at John's arm. With his right hand, John struck downward with his Navy Colt. The barrel of the gun ripped across Blight's face. Rufus Blight screamed in pain. John hit him again and again, holding him up with his left hand and pistol-whipping his face with his right. Blood splattered from Blight's mouth and nose onto the white sheets of Lindy's bed.

In moments it was over. Blight was limp, held up only by the strength of John's anger. John heaved the unconscious man across the room. The body landed heavily near the door. He turned his attention to Lindy. She was sitting up in the bed, holding a sheet to her chin. Her eyes were wide and slightly swollen. They seemed dull, emotionless. Her face was covered with a sheen of perspiration, and her hair was damp, clinging to her neck. Her face was drawn and thin, cheeks hollowed.

"John!" Her eyes suddenly radiated bright unmistakable happiness. She dropped the sheet and held out her delicate hands.

He was with her in a second, holding her in his arms, smothering her hot face with wildly aimed kisses. For a long time they said nothing. They didn't need to. They held and clung to each other, her happy sobs ringing in his ears.

"I love you," she whispered. "I love you so much."

As he listened to the words, he knew with certainty that the things he'd heard about her weren't true. She had been faithful. He had no doubt.

"Lindy," he said. "I had to see you. I heard the most terrible rumors. Someone said you'd had an affair. An abortion, even."

He watched her eyes as he said it, and was surprised by the flash of guilt he saw in them. She closed her eyes, and when she opened them he saw the most profound sadness he'd ever seen.

"Claxton raped me. One time. I became pregnant from it. I had an abortion at Samantha Peabody's. Claxton came back a second time to rape me again. I killed him and buried him in the basement next to the gold."

She shuddered. "Claxton told me he killed Papa. He planted explosives and blew up the *Lucky Molly*. It wasn't an accident. I wrote you a letter telling you all about it, but I just couldn't mail it. I just couldn't bear to tell you."

Frustration swelled in John's heart. Horace Claxton raped his wife! He should've killed the bastard the time he kicked him off the steamboat. If only he had. He had failed to protect her.

And she looked so ill! "Lindy, you look awful sick! What's wrong?"

Her eyes were glassy, but filled with love as she looked at him. "I've had a fever ever since the abortion. Past few days my stomach's been hurting real bad. Must have poked a hole in my insides. I think I'm dying, I really do."

"No!" He pulled her to him, clasping her to his chest. "You can't leave me now, Lindy. Not after I've finally made it home to you. Not after all we've been through!"

They held each other tightly, both crying softly. It was the first time John had cried since the death of his father.

Rufus Blight, still lying on the floor near the door, inched slowly toward the gun he'd left on the chair ten feet away. He kept his eyes fixed on John Carmichael's back, especially on the handle of the revolver in the holster at Carmichael's side. Through the pain of his wrecked and swelling face, Blight had heard the talk. He knew the secesh wench had killed Claxton. He also knew Claxton was buried next to the gold. There was gold to be found if Blight played his cards right. The first thing he had to do was get to the gun on the chair before either of them noticed. Silently, he continued crawling, ever so slowly.

John dabbed at his own tears with the sleeve of his jacket and held Lindy's hands in his own. "Lindy, you've got to get well. I'll stay with you. Or better yet, we'll both leave. We'll take the gold and make a new start somewhere else."

She was pale as marble. He had never felt so helpless. She wasn't exaggerating. She was dying!

"I feel so bad, John. I'm so tired. So weak."

"Please, Lindy. Don't die!"

She smiled faintly. "I don't want to die. Believe me. I want to live. To be with you. To have your children." She broke off, lips trembling.

"Lindy, you won't die. Believe me. Please." He felt a sinking helplessness constricting the air from his own lungs as her breathing became labored and stentorious.

"The war's been terrible, darling. But someone has to live through it. Let it be us!" He grasped her hands, trying by sheer willpower and love to shoot his life force into her weakened body. "I'll take the oath, Lindy. I'll stay right here in Cape with you. I'll never leave you again, ever."

She sighed. "What a wonderful thought, John. Together always." Her face brightened, even in the candlelight. "When I die, John, don't stay here. Run. Get away. Don't let them kill you. Make a new life."

His throat ached as though he were being choked. "Don't talk like that. If anything happened to you I don't know what I'd do. I can't live without you. Don't die, Lindy. Please don't die."

Her voice was softer than a whisper. "I love you."

They were her last words. Stunned, he realized she was dead.

He sat on the edge of the bed for a long time. He marveled at the beauty of her face. She was, he knew, the most beautiful woman he'd ever seen, the most effervescent, the most full of life. She had loved him, of all men. No one could ever take that away from him. She had chosen him. She had loved him. His Rosalind. His Lindy. His Girardeau Rose.

John was still sitting at her side, motionless, not having moved even an inch, when he heard the click of the gun.

Blight was standing by the door, pointing a pistol at him, grinning through a blood-splashed face. John ignored him and turned his attention back to Lindy.

"Look at me, Reb!"

He glanced again at Blight, and then back at his beloved wife. He simply wasn't sure he cared to live. If Blight would shoot him he might join Lindy, wherever she was. He decided to keep ignoring Blight.

"The little slut is dead, ain't she?" Blight snorted. "Damn rude of her to knock off before I could get me a piece."

John's mind focused sharply as if clouds were suddenly being blown away. Blight had been trying to rape Lindy, trying to hurt her. John had failed in protecting her from Claxton, for avenging what Claxton had done, but Blight was here. Right now. He had purpose in life again. He had to live long enough to kill Blight.

"Now, you just stand up real slow," Blight said, keeping the gun pointed directly at John.

John rose slowly. His gun was in its holster on his leg. He was fast at drawing it, but no one was fast enough to outdraw a gun already trained on his chest.

"Now, Carmichael, why don't you lift your hands up nice and high?"

He raised his hands to shoulder level, watching Blight, studying Lindy's Navy Colt, barrel aimed directly at his heart. Blight was grinning. "What was your wife saying about gold, Carmichael? Seems you've got some buried next to Claxton? Now how about you and me going to find that gold right now?"

John wondered what it would feel like to be shot. Would he still have time to shoot Blight, even if shot first? With his hands up in the air, his right hand was three feet from his gun. He knew he was going to go for it. He just wasn't sure when. He wanted to stall for more time.

"All right," John said. "I'll show you where the gold is. But what's in it for me? I have the impression you'll kill me, anyway."

Blight chuckled. "Smart fellow, aren't you?" He touched his lacerated cheek with his free hand. "I ought to kill you for what you done to my face, you bastard."

"You kill me, you'll probably never find the gold."

Blight's gun never wavered its aim. "How much gold we talking about?"

John intentionally looked away from the gun, glancing toward the ceiling. "Oh, must be close to 50,000 dollars."

Blight licked his lips. "Tell you what. I promise I'll let you live if you show me where it is. Word of honor."

John almost snorted. The word of honor of a rapist! He felt like spitting. But he kept his face emotionless.

"All right. I'll take you to it."

Blight grinned. "Thought you'd see things my way. First, though, I need your piece. Just stand there still as a statue while I take it off you. Move even an inch, you're dead."

Blight started toward him. At his second step, John dropped his hand to the holster and pulled the Colt.

Shock registered on Blight's face. His gun spat fire. The noise of the gunshot thundered and reverberated in the small bedroom. John felt the impact of the slug in his abdomen, but the searing pain was overpowered by the exhilaration of seeing his own gun in his hand pointing toward Blight.

Blight's gun fired a second time and plaster chips rained on John's head at the same instant John began firing. Blight's slender body twisted and spun like a puppet in a windstorm as John fired all six shots of his Navy Colt, each slug tearing a hole in Blight as the frantic predator-turned-prey tried to escape the relentless fusillade by hurling himself toward the doorway. John kept firing until the gun was empty. When it was over, Blight lay sprawled by the shattered door and John was slumped against the wall, his left hand gripping his gut.

John pulled his hand away from his belly and looked down. Blood was squirting from his torn clothing. His coat and pants were already soaked and heavy. An artery was certainly hit.

John tested his legs and found they still worked, more or less. Dragging his left leg, he struggled to the bed and sat next to Lindy.

His gun dropped to the floor with a thud as he took her white hands in his bloody ones.

"I love you," he said.

He felt incredibly dizzy. He was dying, he knew.

Is this what Lindy felt as she died? This weakness? This calmness? This resignation? What would he find when he died? Lindy?

He heard her voice calling his name. Or was it his mind playing tricks on him? "John," she was saying, "it will be all right. I am with you. I love you."

"Lindy," he whispered.

PART IV

Treasure Trove

"[T]he trial by jury has been, and I trust ever will be, looked upon as the glory of the English law."

Sir William Blackstone
3 Blackstone Commentaries 378, 1768

"[Jurors] . . . are hopelessly incompetent as fact-finders. It is possible, by training, to improve the ability of our judges to pass upon facts more objectively. But no one can be fatuous enough to believe that the entire community can be so educated that a crowd of twelve men chosen at random can do, even moderately well, what painstaking judges now find it difficult to do. . . . The jury makes the orderly administration of justice virtually impossible."

Jerome N. Frank
*Law and the Modern Mind ,*1930

" . . . Twelve men of the average of the community, comprising men of education and men of little education, men of learning and men whose learning consists only in what they have themselves seen and heard, the merchant, the mechanic, the farmer, the laborer; these sit together, consult, apply their separate experience of the affairs of life to the facts proven, and draw a unanimous conclusion. This average judgment thus given it is the great effort of the law to obtain. It is assumed that twelve men know more of the common affairs of life than does one man; that they can draw wiser and safer conclusions from admitted facts thus occurring, than can a single judge."

Ward Hunt, Justice, United States Supreme Court,
writing in *Sioux City & Pacific Railroad Co. v. Stout,*
84 U.S. (17 Wall) 657 (1873)

"The jury trial is at best the apotheosis of the amateur. Why should anyone think that twelve persons brought in from the street, selected in various ways, for their lack of general ability, should have any special capacity for deciding controversies between persons?"

Dean Griswold
Harvard Law School Dean's Report (1962-63)

Chapter 23

More than 50 spectators packed the courtroom of the Common Pleas Courthouse. Every inch of seating on the hard wooden benches was filled, and a hundred more waited in the hallway, hoping to get a glimpse of Steve Armstrong, Claxton Flint, or the chest of gold.

Every time Cory Blaze stepped into the hallway to film an update, the spectators crowded around the flashy reporter, both to hear his synopsis of the latest testimony and to seize the opportunity of being a face in the background on the 10:00 news. He was in the hallway now, his back to the wall, camera rolling, crowd packing around him.

The trial of the century in Cape Girardeau is half over. Dwight Pemberton, lead counsel for Claxton Flint, says he will rest his case within an hour. Judge Sterns has said he will make every effort to finish this trial today.

Although the lawyers refuse to predict what will happen, one courtroom observer who has heard all the testimony called it the biggest mismatch since David and Goliath.

Too early to say for sure how this multi-million dollar case will turn out, but it's clear that, so far, things have gone quite well for Claxton Flint.

Allison Culbertson will soon have the chance to present Steve Armstrong's side to the jury. Maybe she'll display a golden touch.

I'm Cory Blaze. In Cape Girardeau. More later.

In the courtroom, Allison Culbertson was remembering a case Dwight Pemberton used as an example when speaking to her trial practice class about the effect the litigation skills of a lawyer could have upon a trial. It happened in Texas. Two little boys were playing inside a cardboard box in the middle of the road. A truck driver in a big tractor-trailer rig came along, obeying the speed limit. He saw the box in his lane of traffic and had plenty of opportunity to avoid it, but thought it was empty and drove right over it, killing both children. Because of jurisdictional issues, the wrongful death suits filed against the driver on behalf of each child went to trial in separate cases in front of separate juries, with different lawyers involved in each case. One jury found him negligent; the other found him not negligent. Same exact facts. Same exact issue. The difference had been the persuasive abilities of the lawyers.

The skill of a lawyer *can* make a difference, and that's what worried Allison Culbertson as she watched Malcolm Flint standing in front of the court clerk, right hand raised, swearing to tell the truth. She dabbed her lips with her handkerchief, pulling it away quickly when she smelled the odor of vomit on the white cotton. She quickly stuffed it into the side pocket of her suit coat and glanced at Steve Armstrong, who sat with his elbows on the counsel table, hands clasped tightly together, long face looking as tired as she felt.

Malcolm Flint settled into the witness chair, eyes darting around the courtroom, finally coming to rest on Dwight Pemberton, who stood ramrod straight at the end of the jury box.

"State your name for the jury," boomed Pemberton's deep voice.

"Malcolm Flint."

"Speak up, so the jury can hear you."

"Malcolm Flint."

"How old are you?"

"Twenty-nine."

"What's your occupation?"

"I work for my father."

"Claxton Flint?"

"That's right."

Dwight Pemberton, immaculate suit as crisp and clean as if the trial had just begun, crossed the courtroom floor and held up the Bible for Malcolm Flint.

"Do you recognize this object?"

"Yes. Our family Bible."

"When you say 'our family Bible,' whose do you mean?"

"The Flint family's."

Pemberton stroked his powerful chin. "When was the first time you saw this Bible, son?"

Malcolm Flint sighed and looked at the ceiling. "Can't remember for sure. It's been around the house all my life."

Something seemed wrong to Allison about the way Malcolm Flint wasn't meeting anyone's eyes. He had not looked at Pemberton, his father, Steve, nor the jury. His tie was loose underneath the buttoned-down collar of his Oxford shirt. The top button was undone. She was surprised that Dwight Pemberton, who had lectured about properly preparing witnesses for court, would not have done a better job on Malcolm Flint's appearance.

Pemberton pointed to the Bible he'd placed on the bar of the witness box, directly in front of Malcolm Flint. "I'd like you to open the Bible to the first couple of pages, if you would."

Malcolm Flint flipped it open.

"Do you see the entry on the second page signed by Horace J. Claxton, mentioning that the Confederate army is nearing Cape Girardeau?"

"Yes."

"When did you first see that entry?"

"Can't say exactly. Like I said, it's been this way all my life."

Pemberton reached out and turned hundreds of pages until Malcolm Flint was looking at the family tree entries made at the back of the Bible. "What about these notations concerning your ancestors? Have you personally observed any of them being made?"

"No, sir. As you can see, I'm the last entry. Except for mine, they were all made before I was born, I guess."

Pemberton closed the book, letting his hand rest on top of the old brown leather. "Is anything in this Bible a forgery, Malcolm?"

"No."

"Your witness."

Allison Culbertson studied Dwight Pemberton as he returned to his seat. The experienced trial lawyer couldn't possibly be thrilled with Malcolm Flint's demeanor as a witness, but the veteran litigator's face was inscrutable as he lowered himself into the chair next to his client.

Looking again at Malcolm Flint, she stood up. She was certain he was lying. She thought she had a chance of shaking him.

"Tell me, Malcolm, have you ever been in Steve Armstrong's house on Lorimier Street?"

His eyes didn't waiver. "Never."

"Isn't it true, Malcolm, that you or someone you know burglarized Steve Armstrong's house on Lorimier Street and stole the key your father used to open the chest?"

"Objection!" thundered Dwight Pemberton. "There is no basis in fact for this question."

"I'll permit the witness to answer it," said Judge Sterns.

"You're fantasizing, Miss Culbertson. Nobody burglarized Steve's house. That key belongs to my father."

She put her hands on her hips and took a step toward Malcolm Flint. He met her gaze for several seconds, then looked down at the brown carpet. His left hand moved almost imperceptibly toward the pack of cigarettes barely visible in his shirt pocket, but stopped abruptly, before dropping to his lap.

"Mr. Flint," she said, in a voice barely above a whisper, "did you or anyone else forge that entry in the Bible supposedly made by Horace J. Claxton?"

"No."

Allison wanted to kick something. Frustration boiled in her veins. She sensed he was on the verge of telling the truth, but she lacked the skills to get it out of him.

"No further cross." She asked for a five-minute recess.

She found Malcolm Flint in the hallway outside the men's room, smoking a cigarette. He turned his back as she approached him.

"Malcolm, I've got something for you."

He turned, his face pale. She handed him a subpoena.

"Here's an invitation to stick around for the rest of the party. Don't run off. I'm not through with you yet."

Dwight Pemberton touched his fingertips to his coal-black hair as he donned a pair of horn-rimmed glasses. Allison Culbertson's face was impassive, but she was inwardly amused. She knew the glasses were not prescription lenses; they were plain glass.

Pemberton had mentioned to her at the podium after his lecture on trial technique: *I have a pair of horn-rimmed glasses I occasionally put on when I want to impress the jury with the scholarly achievements of the witness I'm questioning. It adds a bit more weight to my witness's academic background if I need to wear spectacles to keep up with his tremendous brainpower.*

Pemberton reminded Allison of Clark Kent, Superman's alter ego, as he studied the multiple-page *curriculum vitae* of his last witness.

"Your name, sir?" he asked, glancing up from the papers.

"Howard E. Hardesty."

Hardesty was a small man, not much taller than five feet. He was slim. His tweed sport coat seemed too big on his slight frame. He wore dark slacks and a striped red tie. His eyes blinked frequently behind wire-rimmed glasses. His hairline had receded to the point of borderline baldness.

"What's your profession?"

"I am an examiner of questioned documents." His voice was a high-pitched tenor, each word precisely enunciated.

"Would you tell the court and the jury just what course of studies you pursued to prepare yourself for your profession?" Pemberton was again examining the lengthy *curriculum vitae*.

"I have a bachelor's degree in Chemistry from Northwestern University and a Master's degree in Physics from the University of Chicago. I worked as an assistant for four years to Abraham Herzog in the Ink Analysis and Ink

Dating Program of the Bureau of Alcohol, Tobacco and Firearms as an examiner of questioned documents. For the past ten years I've operated Hardesty
and Associates. Our business is the examination of questioned documents for
clients. I've analyzed tens of thousands of questioned documents."

"Are you a member of any technical or professional societies?"

"Yes. I'm a member of the American Society of Questioned Document
Examiners and the American Academy of Forensic Scientists."

Pemberton, still wearing the glasses, handed the Bible to Hardesty. "Mr.
Hardesty, have you had occasion to examine this Bible?"

"I have."

"What can you tell the jury with regard to the age of the Bible and the age
of the entries made in it?"

Hardesty thumbed through the book as he spoke. "In my opinion, the Bible
was published, as the cover page indicates, in 1850. The entries made in the
family tree section were made on or about the dates indicated. The letter in the
front on the second page purportedly signed by a Horace J. Claxton is also
quite old."

Pemberton removed his glasses and began cleaning them with a handkerchief. "On what do you base your opinions?"

"Examinations and tests of the paper and ink." Hardesty held the Bible up
for the jury to see. "The physical appearance of the paper indicates that it is
very old. It's yellow and discolored. My chemical tests indicate the paper has
not been artificially colored." He turned to the family tree notations. "The ink
used to write these notations, as well as the Horace Claxton letter, was very old.
Iron-nutgall ink, which this is, goes through various changes in color as it ages,
finally reaching a permanent yellowish-brown color. The ink used in all notations in this Bible has reached that state."

"Did you find any signs that the pages of the Bible had been deliberately
soiled, torn or creased to give an artificially aged appearance?"

"No indications of that."

"Any indications whatsoever that any of these entries were forged?"

"No. Determinations of the precise age of ink are not easy to make, and are
very seldom positive, but in my opinion all of the entries are quite old. I found
nothing to make me think they were forged."

"No further questions."

Allison felt bats flying in her stomach again. Experienced lawyers seldom
successfully cross-examine expert witnesses. In spite of her hours of prepara-
tion, she had no reason to expect to do well.

"Mr. Hardesty, you said the ink used to write the Horace Claxton letter was
old. Just because the ink was old doesn't necessarily mean it was put on the
page one hundred years ago, does it?"

"No."

"It could have been placed on the page within the past year, couldn't it?"

"I wouldn't think so."

"Why not?"

"I examined all notations microscopically and they appeared to be dried, cracked and old."

"Are you positive?"

"One can never be absolutely positive, but I am staking my reputation on it."

Allison glanced at Claxton Flint. He was smiling broadly.

As Howard Hardesty left the courtroom, Dwight Pemberton, a grave expression on his handsome face, made a solemn announcement to the court. "The plaintiff rests."

Out in the hallway, Allison Culbertson paused to watch Cory Blaze film his latest update on the trial.

The anticipation is building here at the Common Pleas Courthouse in Cape Girardeau. Claxton Flint rested his case moments ago. Allison Culbertson, the lawyer for Steve Armstrong, is expected to call only two witnesses. The judge plans to have a verdict by midnight.

Attorneys for both sides refuse to speculate publicly on what the verdict will be in this eleven million dollar case, but if audience reaction means anything, Claxton Flint may be about to strike gold.

I'm Cory Blaze. In Cape Girardeau. More at 10:00.

As Cory Blaze talked with his cameraman, an idea took shape in Allison's mind. First a tiny flash, then a glimmer of remote possibility, it grew with the incomparable speed of the human brain into a workable plan, a useful trial technique. If only she could get Cory Blaze to cooperate.

"Cory," she said, working her way through the crowd surrounding him, brushing her hair away from her temples. "May I have a moment of your time?"

The courtroom was quiet, as portly Albert Spence Bigelow lumbered to the witness stand. His jowly face was clean shaven, the top of his head bald. A gold watch chain draped across the expansive girth of his three-piece brown wool suit. When he settled himself into the small witness box, he looked like a bear riding a tricycle.

Allison Culbertson questioned her witness. "Your name, please?"

"Albert Spence Bigelow."

"Occupation?"

"Examiner of questioned documents."

"What educational background do you have, sir?"

"I have a bachelor's degree in Chemistry from Southeast Missouri State

University. In acquiring that degree, I took courses in chemistry, physics, mathematics, criminology, photography, and drafting, among others."

"Is that the extent of your formal education?"

"I've been involved in more than 1,500 cases dealing with questioned documents. Also, during the past twenty years I have attended more than 25 seminars concerning questioned document analysis."

"Are you a member of any professional organizations?"

"Yes. I belong to the American Society of Questioned Document Examiners, the American Academy of Forensic Scientists, and the American Society of Criminology."

Allison Culbertson handed him the Bible.

"Now, Mr. Bigelow, have you examined this exhibit?"

"Yes, I have."

"Have you examined it with particular reference to its age and the age of the entries made therein?"

"Yes."

"From your examination, and based on your study and experience as an examiner of questioned documents, and to a reasonable certainty, do you have an opinion as to whether any of the entries in the Bible are of recent origin?"

"I do."

"What is that opinion?"

"While the Bible was indeed published in 1850, and while the entries made in the family tree section were made many years ago, my opinion is that the letter in the front of the Bible allegedly signed by a Horace J. Claxton was written within the past year."

The spectators in the back row of the courtroom buzzed with excitement. Allison glanced at Cory Blaze. He raised his eyebrows.

"On what do you base those opinions, Mr. Bigelow?"

"On examinations and tests made of the paper, ink and other standard analysis."

"What were the results of your examination of the ink used in the entries in the Bible?"

"Ordinarily it is not possible to determine with precision the age of a document from an examination of the ink. However, it can often be ascertained whether the ink was recently applied. I examined the handwriting under a microscope. The handwriting in the family tree section of the Bible showed indications of great age. Lines made with pen and ink develop certain characteristics over the years that are not easily imitated. They develop little hairline gaps, and in certain places the ink pigment stands out in ridges from the paper, which can be seen from a photograph taken under a microscope. These developments are caused by variations in heat and temperature through the years, and from very slow disintegration and shrinking of the paper. They are difficult, if not impossible, to imitate. The handwriting in the family tree section of the Bible has all these characteristics. On the other hand, I did not find the hairline gaps in the Horace J. Claxton letter on the second page of the Bible. In my opinion the ink was applied to that page within the past year. The ink, by the way, is quite old, as evidenced by its yellowish-brown color. The ink used in the Horace J. Claxton letter had reached that stage, too, but it could easily have reached that stage in a bottle before being applied to the paper."

Allison Culbertson glanced at the jury. They were listening intently, but she couldn't read their faces. "No more questions, Your Honor."

Dwight Pemberton eased out of his chair, studying a handful of papers. He looked at them carefully as he approached the witness. His glasses were off.

"Mr. Bigelow, you've stated your opinion that the ink used in the Horace J. Claxton letter was very old, right?"

"Yes."

"That ink could well have been around during the Civil War, couldn't it?"

"Yes. It was quite old."

"You didn't find any signs that the pages of the Bible had been deliberately soiled, torn, or creased to make it look older, did you?"

"No. "

"As I understand it, the only thing you found that indicated to you that Horace J. Claxton's letter was a forgery was the fact you did not find any of those little *hairline gaps* that you were talking about?"

"Right."

"*Tiny* hairline gaps."

"Right."

Pemberton grunted. He stood silent for several seconds. "Are you aware, Mr. Bigelow, that Howard Hardesty, another document examiner, also studied the entries in this Bible?"

"So I've heard."

"Are you aware that Mr. Hardesty testified to this jury under oath that in his opinion the Horace J. Claxton letter was in fact very old and authentic?"

"Yes."

"Does it disturb you that he reached a completely different conclusion than you reached?"

Bigelow knitted his brow. "As a professional, it does disturb me. Professional document examiners should reach the same conclusions in a situation where the ink has not developed the hairline gaps I discussed. I stand by my opinion, though, and have no doubt I am correct."

Pemberton frowned. "No further questions."

During the break between witnesses, Allison Culbertson used the telephone.

"That's right, Rita, a blank one. Bring it to the courtroom and hand it to him when I put my hands on my hips."

Allison Culbertson stood at the far end of the jury box as she conducted the direct examination of her client.

"You were previously called as a witness for the plaintiff, but would you please restate your name for the record?"

"Steve Armstrong."

"Now, you've already testified about finding the chest of gold, the buttons, the belt buckle, and the skeleton. We won't rehash all that." She handed him a bundle of papers with a Manila cover. "I'm showing you a legal document marked Defendant's Exhibit A. Would you identify it, please?"

"It's the abstract of title to my house on Lorimier Street in Cape Girardeau, Missouri."

"Does the abstract show who owned the property from 1858 through 1868?"

"Yes. A man named Patrick O'Malley received it directly from Louis Lorimier in 1812, and he owned it until 1852, when he deeded it to a John Carmichael and Rosalind Carmichael. Afterward, it escheated to the state when the Carmichaels died without heirs in 1863. The state sold it to a Marcus Presley in 1870."

"Do the names Horace Claxton or Claxton Flint appear any where in this abstract?"

"No."

"Other than this trial, has anything else out of the ordinary happened to you at your home on Lorimier Street since you found the gold, the skeleton and the other items?"

"Yes. The television people showed up at my house the day I found the gold, just after we filed the notice with the Court. Shortly later, I was burglarized twice."

"Tell the jury about the burglaries."

"Well, the first one happened the same night I'd been on TV. It was two young men. I caught them in my basement, looking at the hole, but they got away."

"Did they take anything?"

"No. I'd already moved the gold to a bank."

"What about the second burglary?"

"Objection," said Dwight Pemberton. "Irrelevant."

"Overruled."

"The second one happened on June 27th, while I was meeting with Claxton Flint at your office."

"Was anything taken during that one?"

"I didn't notice anything missing, but the whole house was messed up inside. Looked like a tornado hit it."

"Had you been on television discussing the gold you'd found before your meeting with Claxton Flint on June 27th?"

"Yes."

"So someone watching television could have heard you say that you hadn't found a key to the chest?"

Dwight Pemberton jumped to his feet. "Objection! That calls for speculation and conclusion. It's also leading."

"Sustained."

Allison Culbertson sat down.

Dwight Pemberton clasped his large hands and took a step toward Steve. "Mr. Armstrong, there has been all this talk about burglaries. Those two men you caught in your basement during the first burglary had absolutely no connection to Claxton Flint, did they?"

"Not that I know of."

"And you didn't even get a glimpse of the person or persons who broke into your house the second time, did you?"

"No. "

"That's all I have, Judge."

Chapter 24

The air in the courtroom was electrified. The crowd packing the spectator benches knew the trial was nearing its end and that the lawyers would soon be making their closing arguments. The newsmen still held their positions in the front row. Cory Blaze sat between a reporter for the *Southeast Missourian* and a reporter from the Associated Press. Malcolm Flint perched in a back row, alone, his eyes staring at the back of the bench in front of him.

"Does the defense wish to present any other evidence, Miss Culbertson?" Judge Samuel Sterns was thumbing through the *Missouri Approved Jury Instructions* book as he asked the question.

Allison glanced at Steve Armstrong. Should she take the risk? He was the client. It was his money. But this was a question of strategy. A matter the lawyer should decide. She whispered in his ear. "I've thought of a way we might win this case by knockout, but it's risky. I could end up with egg all over my face. You could end up with nothing. But I'm afraid we're going to lose for sure if I don't try something."

He frowned, then glanced over at Dwight Pemberton, who was watching them coolly. He reached over and scribbled a note on the legal pad in front of her: *GO FOR IT!*

Allison stood, her knees shaking, but her voice clear and precise. "The defense recalls Malcolm Flint to the stand, as a hostile witness."

Malcolm Flint gave a start, then slowly he rose to his feet and walked forward. His eyes never left the courtroom carpet until he reached the witness box. He glanced furtively at the judge, then at Allison Culbertson.

Allison dropped her gaze from Malcolm Flint and studied her notes one last time. For this witness, for this line of questioning, carrying the notepad would be impossible. She would need to be focusing her entire attention on Malcolm Flint.

As he was being reminded of his oath, Allison glanced toward the double doors at the side of the courtroom. Through the opaque windows at the top of the doors she saw the shadow of a bouffant hairdo. Rita was on time.

Allison walked slowly to the center of the courtroom, the jury box to her right, Malcolm Flint directly in front of her, his eyes fifteen feet from her own. As long as he was looking at her, he would not be able to see his father seated at the counsel table with Pemberton. She watched him closely as she asked the questions.

"Do you recall the testimony you previously gave this jury, Mr. Flint?"

He nodded. "Of course." His eyes met hers. He wasn't flinching. She felt despair.

"You testified that the entry in your family Bible allegedly signed by Horace J. Claxton has been in the Bible for as long as you can remember, is that correct?"

"That's right."

"And that's the truth?"

"It is."

"And nothing in this Bible is a forgery to your knowledge?"

"Right."

She put her hands on her hips, turned, and walked a few steps away from the witness. The door to the courtroom opened and Rita came in quietly, apologizing profusely to the deputy at the door. Allison paused and watched as Rita quickly made her way around the edge of the courtroom and stopped in front of Cory Blaze. She handed him a video tape, whispered a few brief words to him, then hurried out of the room.

The jury had seen it. More importantly, Malcolm Flint had seen it. Allison turned and faced him again. "Malcolm Flint, tell the truth. Isn't it true that the entry in the Bible is a forgery?"

"No."

"Isn't it true that you're lying when you say you've never been in Steve Armstrong's house? Isn't it true that you broke into the house and stole the key your father used to open the chest?"

"Objection, Your Honor!" Dwight Pemberton jumped to his feet. "There's absolutely no basis in fact for this question!"

Judge Sterns regarded Pemberton thoughtfully. "I'll permit the witness to answer the question."

"No. That's not true," insisted Malcolm Flint.

Allison made her voice sound as cold as possible. "Mr. Flint, are you aware that the penalty for perjury in the State of Missouri is up to seven years in prison?"

He shrugged. "I am now."

"Isn't it true, sir, that you were watching television on the night Steve Armstrong found the gold; you heard him say on television he'd found the gold and a belt buckle inscribed with the name Horace Claxton?"

He glanced at his father. "Sure. I saw him on TV."

"You also heard Steve Armstrong say on television in that same interview that he had *not* found the key to the chest, didn't you?"

"Yeah. So what?"

Allison moved closer to the jury. It would be even harder for Malcolm to look at his father. "Where were you on June 27th between 2:00 and 4:00 in the afternoon, the day your father and his lawyers first met with Steve Armstrong at my office?"

"I was home sick. Had the flu."

"Was anyone home with you?"

"No."

"Where were you the next day?"

"I don't know. Been a long time."

"Where were you the day before?"

"Again, it's been a long time. How would I know?"

"But you distinctly remember that you were home sick on the day your father met Steve Armstrong at my office?"

"Yes. The day sticks in my mind because I wanted to go along, but I was too sick."

A fleeting glimmer of frenzy sparked in Malcolm Flint's eyes. Allison was sure the jurors couldn't have seen it, but she was certain he was lying. She was certain he was terrified. Now was the time to spring the trap. If it worked, the truth might come out. If it failed, her credibility would be shot with the jury.

Her better sense cried out for her not to try it. Yet, there was that look in his eyes, the vulnerability, the weakness. He was the rabbit; she, the wolf. She smelled blood.

"You were aware, you already said, that KFVS television had taken pictures of Steve the day he found the gold?"

"Yes. I told you. I saw the news."

"You haven't seen all of the tape KFVS shot of Steve and his house, have you, Malcolm?"

"How would I know?"

"You haven't seen the extra tapes that were shot, the ones that never ran on television, have you?"

"I guess not."

Allison paused, then asked in a voice hardly louder than a whisper, "Would you be surprised, Malcolm, to learn that a week after the gold was found, at exactly the same time your father was meeting with Steve Armstrong at my office, KFVS-TV happened to have a camera crew taking an aerial shot of Steve's house to use on a story they are still putting together?"

He opened his mouth to answer but stopped. He looked toward Claxton Flint. "Don't look at your father for help. Look at me. Answer the question."

Confusion crossed Malcolm Flint's face. "I don't understand the question."

Allison Culbertson marched across the courtroom and stood in front of the spectator pews. Cory Blaze sat directly behind her. The video tape was in his hand, resting on the wooden railing in front of him.

"Would it surprise you, Mr. Flint, to know that the television camera, with its telescopic lens, photographed a man leaving Steve Armstrong's house when it was burglarized?"

Malcolm Flint's face was ashen.

"I object!" shouted Dwight Pemberton, rising to his feet. "This question is totally irrelevant!"

Judge Sterns leaned forward with interest. "Counselor, where is the relevance here?"

Allison was stricken with panic. If the judge cut off her questioning now, Malcolm would slither away. He was on the verge of breaking. She knew it.

"Your Honor, this is absolutely relevant." She plucked the tape from Cory Blaze's hands. "I intend to prove that Malcolm Flint broke into Steve Armstrong's home while his father was meeting with Steve at my office. I intend to prove beyond any doubt that Malcolm Flint stole the key."

There was a loud murmur from the crowd. Cory Blaze looked rather uncomfortable.

Judge Sterns, leaning back, took off his glasses. "If proven, that would most certainly be relevant. Objection overruled. Proceed, Miss Culbertson."

Allison held the video tape up for Malcolm Flint to see.

"Were you aware, Mr. Flint . . . "

"Objection!" yelled Dwight Pemberton. "I object to counsel's waving that tape around! It has not been introduced into evidence! It's not marked as an exhibit! Its contents have never been disclosed in discovery!"

Allison handed the tape back to Cory Blaze.

"He's correct, Your Honor. It's not in evidence. Not yet, anyway. I'll be glad to stop 'waving it around.'"

She moved two steps away from Cory Blaze, but kept him in Malcolm Flint's line of vision.

"May I continue now, Judge?"

"Please do."

Allison walked slowly toward Malcolm Flint. He was licking dry lips. She could tell he ached to look at his father, but that he knew she was ready to call him down if he did.

"Mr. Flint, you've already been advised of the penalty for perjury. I now want to notify you that if a witness admits his perjury while still on the stand, if he recants and tells the truth, it is a complete defense to the crime."

He bit his lip. "What did you say again?"

"If you tell the whole truth now, Malcolm, you can't be charged with perjury for what you said earlier. Admit it. You broke into Steve's house and stole the key, didn't you?"

The courtroom was absolutely silent. Malcolm Flint's eyes flicked to the tape in Cory Blaze's hands, then back to Allison Culbertson. His lower lip quivered.

"Yes," he said softly. "It's true."

For several long seconds the silence was complete.

"You idiot!" screamed Claxton Flint, breaking the stillness. He leaped to his feet and stood staring at his son with disbelief.

Malcolm Flint wept, his voice quivering as he continued to speak. "I did it for my Dad. He's almost bankrupt. He wanted the gold so much."

"You blathering idiot!"

The crowd uttered a collective gasp. Judge Sterns slammed his gavel so hard it shattered, the top bouncing off the paneled wall behind him.

"Order in the court!"

Malcolm Flint, tears covering his cheeks, continued talking to the jury. "I was with my Dad the night he saw Steve on television. We really did have the family Bible. It had all the entries except the one. He recognized the name Horace Claxton. When he heard . . . "

"You stupid imbecile!"

" . . . that Steve hadn't found a key to the chest, he figured there had to be one hidden somewhere in the house. He bought a sophisticated metal detector . . . "

"Shut up, you fool!"

" . . . and had me break into Steve's house to look for the key while he met with Steve at your office. I found the . . . "

"Malcolm, shut the hell up!"

" . . . key hidden behind a brick in the fireplace. I also found . . . "

Claxton Flint's lawyers were struggling with him, forcibly restraining him from attacking his son.

" . . . a bunch of letters stashed with the key behind the brick." Malcolm Flint reached into his coat and withdrew a thick packet of yellowed letters. He held them up, tears streaming down his face. "They're from John Carmichael to his wife, plus a couple from her to him."

Claxton Flint yanked his arms free from his attorneys and glared ominously at his son. Malcolm let the packet of letters fall to the floor. "Horace Claxton wasn't a war hero. He was a rapist. I'm sorry, Dad. I'm sorry."

The spectators began applauding, tentatively at first, then with a rousing ovation. It sounded more like a theater than a courtroom.

"Order in the court!" Judge Sterns said loudly. "Recess! I'm calling a recess! Get that jury back into the jury room!"

Moments later Dwight Pemberton asked to meet alone with Allison Culbertson in the conference chamber at the back of the courtroom. When they were alone in the tiny room, he shrugged.

"I don't suppose you'd care to settle?"

"Not on your life."

"Didn't think so. As a lawyer, an officer of the court, I abhor perjury, Miss Culbertson. Don't forgive it. Won't be a party to it. Won't condone it in my clients. You did a nice job out there, a very nice job."

"Thank you."

"I'm just curious—there wasn't really anything on that tape Cory Blaze was holding, was there?"

"No."

"Sort of a cheap trick, wasn't it?"

"If you consider eleven million dollars cheap."

He chuckled. "I had a suspicion when you came up to me after my lecture to your law school class that you'd make a good trial lawyer."

"You remembered me?"

"From the minute I saw you. Thought I was going to take advantage of a fledgling lawyer still wet behind the ears. Guess I taught you too much that day I spoke."

"My notes reflect that you gave us an example of a trial lawyer named Abraham Lincoln using an almanac to force a witness into admitting the moon had not been overhead as he had previously testified, and thus it had been too dark for him to have seen the assault he had earlier claimed to have witnessed."

"*People versus Duff Armstrong*," Pemberton said. "Tried in 1858 in Cass County, Illinois."

He picked up his leather briefcase.

"It should come as no surprise to you that I've talked to Claxton Flint. We're dismissing the suit, costs to plaintiff."

"I had the feeling you might."

"Soon as the dismissal's filed, I'll be resigning as his lawyer." He paused. "If you ever need a job in St. Louis, look me up. "

"Your firm already has one hundred lawyers. You don't need one more."

"On the contrary, Miss Culbertson. We can always use another good trial lawyer."

Allison felt a warm glow shoot from fingertips to toes. "Thanks for the offer. But I sort of like Cape Girardeau."

Chapter 25

A month later Allison Culbertson stood at the window of her office, gazing out at the Mississippi River, wondering what Steve Armstrong had up his sleeve.

"All right," he said. "You can turn around now."

On her desk were two documents, each beautifully matted and framed.

"For your office walls," he said.

"They're wonderful! What a surprise!"

One was the front page of the *Southeast Missourian* newspaper from the day after the trial, its bold headline proclaiming: FINDERS KEEPERS—ARMSTRONG WINS!

"It's hard to believe now," Steve chuckled, "but for a while I was actually wondering if I'd picked the right lawyer. I can see now you were in complete control the whole time."

Allison smiled, but didn't answer. *A good trial lawyer should have a poker face.*

She caught her breath when she identified the second framed document.

"Oh, Steve! Is this the original?"

"All yours. I could tell it was your favorite."

It was a two-page letter from John Carmichael to his wife, handwriting bold and clearly legible. Allison Culbertson read it for perhaps the one hundredth time.

March 12, 1863
Dear Lindy,

I sit at a campfire on a night the stars are out in battalion strength. We're in Arkansas now. As I look at the North Star I know that somewhere it shines above you, pale in comparison to your beauty.

You have been in my thoughts since the moment I left you standing in the doorway of our home. I can't believe it has been nearly two years. A bullet or bayonet may stop my body from making it home, darling, but my love for you will live forever.

When a soldier dies, his friends bury him, time permitting. Sometimes a eulogy is said, a hymn sung or a verse written on a homemade marker. My favorite was written on the joint grave of several young soldiers at Shiloh:

Soon forgotten here they rest,
Warriors for their land,
And what to show for bloody death?
Mere footprints on life's sand.

This war, my love, has drilled into my heart the shortness and uncertainty of life on earth. I thank God every night for the beautiful years we had together, grateful we lived our lives to the fullest. I'm glad I had the chance to make my footprints next to yours.

When and if I return to you alive, Lindy, I swear I'll never let a day go by without caressing you or an hour pass without a smile. Life is such a tenuous gift and love so precious and rare that man and woman must cherish both whenever lucky enough to find them.

I miss you. I love you more than words can express.

Your loving husband,
John

Allison Culbertson hugged the framed letter.

"Thanks, Steve. I'll treasure it always." She laid it carefully on her desk. "I've got good news for you, too. The prosecutor says he's filing perjury and forgery charges tomorrow against Claxton Flint. The sly dog's not going to get away with what he tried to do."

"What about Malcolm?"

"The prosecutor's going to let him plead to trespass and misdemeanor stealing if he'll testify against his father."

"I can't see Malcolm doing that."

"Can you see him going to prison for seven years for burglary? That's his choice." Her smile got even bigger. "And I have even better news!"

"What?"

"The New York literary agent who read John Carmichael's letters says he's lined up a history professor at Mizzou to annotate them. Says he sees nonfiction best-seller written all over John Carmichael's Civil War Letters."

"That brings an ache to my throat," Steve said.

"Mine, too. Maybe there is justice in the world after all. John Carmichael will actually accomplish the dream he mentioned over and over in his letters to Lindy. He's written a history book that will be read and enjoyed by lots of people. Ironically, he wrote it over one hundred years before its publication, not realizing it was history or even a book when he put pen to paper."

They left her office together. When they reached the sidewalk, Allison glanced up the steep hill crowned by the Common Pleas Courthouse. The red brick building, white columns glistening, stood proudly on the tall hill, high above Main Street, towering over downtown Cape Girardeau.

It seemed majestic. It seemed powerful. It seemed it would last forever.

Afterword

I think of a good historical novel as sugar-coated history—the reader learns interesting historical facts while being entertained with a good story. That was my goal in writing this book.

Researching an historical novel is a humbling experience. After reading more than 20,000 pages of Southeast Missouri history over the past decade, I came to realize how little most of us know about the history of our region. There is so much to read and so little time.

For those interested in reading more about the history of Cape Girardeau and Southeast Missouri I highly recommend *Cape Girardeau: Biography of a City* by Felix Eugene Snider and Earl Augustus Collins (1956); Goodspeed's *History of Southeast Missouri* (1912); *Old Cape Girardeau* by George and Fred Naeter (1946); Jess E. Thilenius's *Biography of Historic Cape Girardeau County, A Project of the Bicentennial Commission* (1975); and *A History of Missouri* (1908), *The Spanish Regime in Missouri* (1909), and *Memorial Sketches of Pioneers and Early Residents of Southeast Missouri* (1915), all written by Louis Houck.

A writer of historical fiction owes it to the reader to separate fact from fiction and to distinguish historical figures from fictional characters.

John Carmichael's references to the mound builders are based upon archeological fact. The rivers of the North American continent are lined with earthen mounds built by the mound builders in prehistoric times. Once thought to have been a highly civilized vanished race flourishing before the arrival of the Indians, modern archaeologists now believe the mound builders were American Indians, ancestors of the later Creeks, Cherokees, Natchez, and others who first greeted the white man. Cahokia was America's first metropolis north of the Rio Grande. The community reached its zenith between 900 and 1300 AD, its population reaching as high as 40,000. The huge man-made mound is one of the world's largest earthworks. With a height of 104 feet and a base covering 14 acres, it is the largest earthwork in the Western Hemisphere. Experts speculate that the mound builders practiced human sacrifice, evidenced by the burial mound unearthed at Cahokia, where more than 50 young women between the ages of 18 and 23 were buried side by side at the same time. Scientific digs in Cape Girardeau verify that some mound builders lived in a village at Cape Girardeau centuries ago.

The references to Hernando De Soto, while sounding fictional, are based upon accounts written by survivors of his expedition. The journals of these survivors claim that De Soto, a married man, was given the Indian girls Molchila and Maconoche as presents by Capaha, an Indian Chief probably located in Southeast Missouri. Historians disagree whether De Soto's expedition made it as far north as Cape Girardeau. Some put Capaha's village directly at Cape Girardeau; others place it further south. The tale of De Soto's bizarre burial and reburial in the Mississippi is taken directly from the accounts of the survivors. Many historical texts discuss the adventures of De Soto. One of the most helpful is Edward Gaylord Bourne's *Narratives of the Career of Hernando De Soto in the Conquest of Florida*, reprinted in 1973. This excellent book contains the complete text of the three most authoritative eyewitness accounts of the exploits of De Soto in North America: The Gentleman of Elvas account, written by a participant and first published in 1557; the official report of the expedition drawn up by the King's factor, Hernandez de Biedma in 1544; and the account of the conquest provided by De Soto's private secretary Rodrigo Ranjel, as edited by the Spanish historian Oviedo in 1557. Another entertaining source was *The Florida of the Inca, A History of the Adelantado, Hernando De Soto, Governor and Captain General of the Kingdom of Florida, and of Other Heroic Spanish and Indian Cavaliers, Written by the Inca, Garcilaso de la Vaqa, an Officer of His Maiesty, and a Native of the Great City of Cuzco, Capital of the Realms and Provinces of Peru*, edited by John G. and Jeannette J. Varner (1951). This book was first published in 1605 at Lisbon. The Inca who wrote it was the son of a Spanish soldier and an Indian girl in Peru and claimed to have obtained his information directly from men who had accompanied De Soto.

The references to Jean Baptiste Girardot are as accurate as possible. Girardot did in fact set up a trading post at Cape Rock. Little is known about the real man. Historical documents show that in 1722 in Kaskaskia he married Celeste Therese Nepveu, whose parents had been killed by Indians earlier that year. The same records show he had a son named Pierre, born in 1723, and that his widow remarried, having a child by her second husband in 1733. Thus, Girardot must have died before then. Several books have been written about the French and Indians in America. Natalia Maree Belting's *Kaskaskia Under the French*

Regime (1948) contains references to several old records pertaining to Jean Baptiste Girardot and his family. John H. Schlarman's *From Quebec to New Orleans, The Story of the French in America, Fort De Chartres* (1929) was very good.

Louis Lorimier and Mike Fink were real people. Lorimier was the founder of Cape Girardeau. The notorious Fink was a legend in his own time. They surely knew each other, although no records have been found to prove it. Lorimier undoubtedly would have achieved a more prominent place in Missouri's history books had he been able to read and write, thus leaving us with a written record of his remarkable life. Meriwether Lewis (of Lewis & Clark fame) spent five pages describing his meeting with him in *The Journals of Captain Meriwether Lewis and Sergeant John Ordway*. Lorimier is also mentioned briefly in *Undaunted Courage*, Stephen E. Ambrose's excellent book about the Lewis and Clark expedition. Patrick O'Malley is fictitious, but is modeled after numerous riverboat captains. The pirates O'Malley fought are based on real pirates like Samuel Mason and John Murrell, who robbed and murdered travelers on the Mississippi River in the years before 1830. In fact, Crow's Nest Island really existed, and an eyewitness reported that a band of pirates was wiped out when the New Madrid earthquake sank the island in 1811. The description of the New Madrid earthquake was based on reports of survivors. *The New Madrid Earthquakes* by James L. Penick, Jr., published in 1981, is a wonderful book about the earthquakes. Otto A. Rothert's *The Outlaws of Cave-In-Rock, Historical Accounts of the Famous Highwaymen and River Pirates Who Operated In Pioneer Days Upon the Ohio and Mississippi Rivers and Over the Old Natchez Trace* (1924) is as entertaining as its title. Henry Marie Brackenridge's *Views of Louisiana, Together With a Journal of a Voyage Up the Missouri River In 1811*, contains a description of Cape Girardeau in that year. Jane Cooper Stacy's *Louis Lorimier (1978)*, a children's book, was helpful. *Half Horse Half Alligator, The Growth of the Mike Fink Legend* by Walter Blair and Franklin J. Meine (1956) is definitely worth reading.

"Son of a Riverboat Gambler" contains several historical figures. John Carmichael, Lindy O'Malley, Maude O'Malley, Tyler Fitch, and Horace Claxton are all fictitious, but the details of Mississippi steamboating in the 1850s were extensively researched. Cannon's *Louisiana* did explode in New Orleans, causing the destruction depicted. The race between the *Girardeau Rose* and the *Andrew Jackson II* is based on the great steamboat race between the *Natchez* and the *Robert E. Lee*, won by the *Lee* in 1870. Duels were really fought on Cypress Island, which long ago disappeared into the Mississippi. Of the many books written about Mississippi steamboating, my favorites were Mark Twain's *Life On the Mississippi*, published in 1896; John Brunner's novel *The Great Steamboat Race* (1983); E. W. Gould's *Fifty Years On the Mississippi*, written by a veteran steamboatman (1889); Louis C. Hunter's *Steamboats On the Western*

Rivers, an Economic and Technological History (1949); Manley Wade Wellman's *Fastest On the River, The Great Race Between the "Natchez" and the "Robert E. Lee"* (1957); and William Robert (Bob) White's *Mississippi Steamboating* (1980). For details of gambling on the Mississippi steamboats, nothing compares to George H. Devol's *Forty Years a Gambler on the Mississippi*. This colorful autobiography (1887) was the source of John Carmichael's lessons on head-butting. The *Illustrated History of Paddle Steamers* by G. W. Hilton, R. Plummer, and J. Jobe (1976) contains plans and drawings of the third of the three steamboats that bore the name *Cape Girardeau*. *Steamboat Gothic* by Francis Parkinson Keyes (1952) and *Fevre Dream* by George R. R. Martin, (1982) are two novels in which Mississippi steamboating plays an important role. Samuel Langhorn Clemens, of course, really existed and eventually took the pen-name Mark Twain, gaining literary immortality for the masterpieces *The Adventures of Tom Sawyer* and *The Adventures of Huckleberry Finn*. The scenes involving Sam Clemens are based upon his well-documented and fascinating life. Three excellent books about his younger years are *Mark Twain: The Bachelor Years* by Margaret Sanborn, *Young Sam Clemens* by Cyril Clemens, and *The Making of Mark Twain* by John Lauber.

"The Call of the Confederacy" contains a great deal of historical detail. John Sappington Marmaduke looms large in Missouri history. The son of former Missouri Governor M. M. Marmaduke, he was later elected governor himself after the Civil War. A West Point graduate and brigadier general at the age of 29, he led the attack on Cape Girardeau on April 26, 1863. Sterling Price, Claiborne Jackson, Nathaniel Lyon, Ulysses Grant, John "The Butcher" McNeil, and Jeff "The Swamp Fox" Thompson were real Civil War participants. Each battle shown in the novel actually occurred. Details of the Battle of Cape Girardeau were gleaned from the reports of the officers involved. The "Jackson Road" of those days is now called Broadway. The Confederate battle line ran roughly from St. Vincent's Cemetery near Capaha Park, across the general area of Clark Street near Central High School, all the way to Bloomfield Road. Although no one named Carmichael appeared on the casualty reports, Marmaduke stated in his official report that his loss from the Cape Girardeau expedition (which included several other skirmishes in Southeast Missouri) was "some 30 killed, 60 wounded, and 120 missing." Confederate Colonel Gideon W. Thompson reported that his regiment alone suffered three men killed and 35 wounded on the field at Cape Girardeau. Confederate Colonel John Burbridge reported 13 men killed, wounded, or missing at Cape Girardeau. The Battle of Cape Girardeau was certainly not a Shiloh or a Gettysburg in military significance, but the purpose of Marmaduke's raid into Missouri was to force the Federal army to temporarily dismiss offensive movements in Arkansas as the Confederates spread terror and destruction behind enemy lines. Had Marmaduke not chosen to retreat, the battle could have had significant results indeed, since each general had more than 5,000 men under his command.

Although books on the Civil War are too numerous to list, several deserve mention because of their applicability to Cape Girardeau. *War of the Rebellion, Official Records of the Union and Confederate Armies,* is a 128-volume set published by the government between 1880 and 1901. Volume 22 of Series I contains the actual reports of the officers of both sides who fought in the Battle of Cape Girardeau. This was truly a "treasure trove" for me. Stephen B. Oates' *Confederate Cavalry West of the River* (1961) was extremely well-written and contained a detailed description of the Battle of Cape Girardeau. *Shelby and His Men; or, The War in the West* (1867) was written by one of Shelby's officers who participated in and describes the Battle of Cape Girardeau. *Tennessee Cavalier in the Missouri Cavalry, Major Henry Ewing, C.S.A., of the St. Louis Times* (1978) by William J. Crowley is a biography of Marmaduke's adjutant and includes a wealth of information about Marmaduke and a description of the Cape Girardeau expedition. Richard S. Brownlee's *Gray Ghosts of the Confederacy* (1958) is a wonderful source about the Civil War in Missouri, particularly martial law and guerrilla warfare. John C. Moore's *Missouri,* part of the 12-volume *Confederate Military History* set edited by Clement A. Evans and published in 1899, was written by a member of Marmaduke's staff. Leo E. Huff's "The Last Duel in Arkansas: The Marmaduke-Walker Duel," published in the *Arkansas Historical Quarterly* in 1964, contains the details of Marmaduke's duel with another general. *The Crisis* by Winston Churchill (not the British statesman, but an American novelist who lived from 1871 to 1947) was a best-selling novel half a century ago. It depicts conditions in St. Louis during the Civil War. M. M. Quaife's *Absolom Grimes: Confederate Mail Runner* (1926) and *Reminiscences of General Basil W. Duke, C.S.A.* (1911), an autobiography, were both highly readable and valuable sources of information. I shamelessly borrowed anecdotes from both. William Culp Darrah's *Powell of the Colorado* (1951) contains a description of Cape Girardeau during the Civil War. Bennett H. Young's *Confederate Wizards of the Saddle: Being Reminiscences and Observations of One Who Rode With Morgan* (1914) contains a chapter on the Battle of Cape Girardeau. Jay Monaghan's *Swamp Fox of the Confederacy: The Life and Military Services of M. Jeff Thompson* (1956) makes several references to Cape Girardeau. Jeff Thompson's autobiography, *This is the Story of the War Experiences of Brig. Gen. M. Jeff Thompson Written By Himself and Edited By His Youngest Daughter, Marcie A. Bailey,* is a typescript located at the State Historical Society of Missouri in Columbia, Missouri, and has many references to Cape Girardeau. Lindsay W. Murdoch's *Narrative of the Service of Lindsay W. Murdoch in the War of the Rebellion 1861 to 1865 and in Government Services in the Interest of Honesty in Operation of the United States Government,* is a typescript located at Southeast Missouri State University. Murdoch was stationed in Cape Girardeau during most of the Civil War. James E. McGhee's master's thesis "The State Guard in Southeast Missouri 1861-1862" is also on file at Southeast Missouri State University and was very helpful. Also useful were John F. Lee's "John Sappington Marmaduke," *Missouri Historical Society Collections*, Vol. II, No. 6 (1906); Paul M. Robinett's "Marmaduke's Expedition Into Missouri: The Battles of Springfield and Hartville, January 1863," *Missouri Historical Review*, Vol. 55, No. 2 (1976); and Karen J. Grace's *Let the Eagle Scream, A History of the Cape Girardeau Eagle* (1983).

The landmark Cape Rock, which plays such an important part in Cape Girardeau's history, still exists for the most part, although the massive portion extending into the river was dynamited in the late 1800s to make way for the Frisco Railroad tracks next to the Mississippi River.

All characters in "Treasure Trove" and the case itself are completely fictitious. Any resemblance to actual persons is entirely coincidental. The Common Pleas Courthouse, built in 1854 and located on a tall hill above the Mississippi River, has been and continues to be the scene of many exciting trials.

Morley Swingle
Cape Girardeau, Missouri

About the Author

Morley Swingle is the prosecuting attorney of Cape Girardeau County, Missouri, currently serving his fourth four-year term. He has prosecuted thousands of cases, from misdemeanors to death penalty murder trials. He has tried over 100 jury trials and published more than twenty articles and book chapters on criminal law in various legal periodicals. He has taught at the Missouri Highway Patrol Academy, the Missouri Prosecuting Attorney's Association, the Kansas District Attorneys' Association, the Iowa District Attorneys' Association, the Missouri Judicial College, and other legal education seminars. He was born in Cape Girardeau, Missouri, and earned an A.B. in creative writing from the University of Missouri-Columbia in 1977, and a J.D. from the same school in 1980. While in law school, Swingle was a member of the *Missouri Law Review*, a member of the Order of Barristers, and chairman of the Board of Advocates. As a law student, he served three months as an intern for Judge Robert T. Donnelly of the Supreme Court of Missouri. In 1992 he was selected by the FBI as one of 50 prosecutors in the country to attend the Advanced Course for Prosecutors at the FBI Academy in Quantico, Virginia.

About the Cover

Jake Wells painted the picture of the steamboat *Girardeau Rose* reproduced on the cover.

Jacob Kenneth "Jake" Wells (1918-1999) was a well-known artist and art instructor in Southeast Missouri. Born in Marble Hill, Missouri, he was educated at Southeast Missouri State University in Cape Girardeau; the George Peabody School for Teachers in Nashville, Tennessee (now a part of Vanderbilt University); and the University of Missouri at Columbia. He enlisted in the U.S. Army in 1942 and served in the Aleutian Islands during World War II.

He resided in Cape Girardeau County most of his lifetime. He taught fourteen years in the Jackson School District before joining the art department at Southeast Missouri State University in 1960. He served as chairman of the department from 1972 to 1976. He retired in 1980.

Wells has been called a "visual historian" because his works often depict historically relevant scenes from Southeast Missouri. He was best known for his historical mural at Kent Library on the campus of Southeast Missouri State University. The mural, completed in 1973, covers an area more than 38 feet long and 20 feet high. He was also renowned for "Missouri Mills," a collection of watercolors of water mills in Missouri, completed in 1977 and displayed at the University Museum. These paintings were featured in the book *Water Mills of the Missouri Ozarks*, written in collaboration with George Suggs in 1990. His 1992 Bicentennial mural located high atop a building at 405 Broadway in Cape Girardeau depicts the founding of Cape Girardeau and measures 40 feet by 27 feet.

Wells painted the watercolor of the *Girardeau Rose* in 1985, after reading excerpts of Swingle's manuscript and discussing with him the details of the steamboat's construction. The original watercolor is owned by Swingle.

Other works of Jake Wells can be found throughout the Southeast Missouri region. He was a prolific artist who often donated his works to local charities.

Southeast Missouri State University Press
MS 2650, English Department
Cape Girardeau, Missouri 63701